TRIPLE
IDENTITY

TRIPLE IDENTITY

a novel

HAGGAI CARMON

Zoland Books

AN IMPRINT OF

Steerforth Press

Hanover, New Hampshire

The Library of Congress has cataloged hardcover edition of
this book as follows:

Carmon, Haggai.
Triple identity : a novel / Haggai Carmon. — 1st ed.
p. cm.
ISBN 1-58642-090-9 (alk. paper) (hardcover)
I. Title.
PS3603.A7557T74 2005
813'.6--dc22

2004030178

ISBN-10: 1-58195-218-X (paperback)
ISBN-13: 978-1-58195-6 (paperback)

FIRST PAPERBACK EDITION

To My Family

FOREWORD

Intelligence gathering seems so glamorous. Hollywood movies contribute to the appeal; the general public's vision of an intelligence operative is of a sleek man in a three-piece suit moodily stirring his drink at a swank club.

There are no glitzy stories about missions that faced a dead end or about the long and cold nights spent outside in freezing temperatures waiting for a contact to show up, because routine is never headline news or the basis for a movie thriller. In reality, the villain is never as romantic or mysterious as its representation. It is rarely a gorgeous blond who tries to seduce you — most likely it's a man who could snap and behave like a truck driver with violent propensities.

In real life, however, clandestine operations sometimes overshadow even the most innovative thriller-writer's imagination. After nearly three decades in the Mossad, Israel's foreign-intelligence service, retiring as a member of the organization's top management, I thought I'd seen and heard it all. Haggai has managed to surprise even my skeptical mind with his seamless weaving of fact and fiction that has left me wondering which is which. Haggai found the gentle balance between the dull, plodding reality and the peaks of ingenuity, which makes this story so riveting.

Foreign gathering of intelligence is always problematic because governments do not appreciate foreign agents violating their sovereignty. Therefore confidentiality is a must, not only as a precautionary measure against the opposition but also against the wrath of the unsuspecting, uninvolved foreign country's government. Comprehensive planning, training, the element of surprise, and technical aides assist the agent, but a conniving mind is something you possess, not learn. Haggai's illustration of Dan Gordon's maneuvering tactics, self-motivation, and deceitful manners fit the profile of a successful undercover agent. "For by deception thou shalt make thy war," said King Solomon in Proverbs 24:6.* The Mossad adopted this verse as its motto because it engages in the war of minds, not weapons. Dan Gordon is a perfect example of how that philosophy is applied. Is there a real-life Dan Gordon? I'm sure my former colleagues would love to take him back.

ANONYMOUS

---

* The Hebrew word "tachbulot" (תַחְבֻּלוֹת) is often mistranslated as "wisdom." The correct meaning is somewhere between "trick" and "deception." — *Trans.*

PREFACE

One afternoon in 1993, in a windowless conference room in Washington, D.C., a tall visitor opened a powerful laptop and turned it to face a closed session of an interagency committee of senior investigative agents and lawyers from a dozen government offices.

Everyone sitting in that room investigated major multinational crimes or managed other substantial international cases on behalf of the United States. All of us were concerned with recovering profits of crime or to win redress for victims of civil wrongs.

Our successes, whether generally unknown or splashed across the media, were matters of public record. We of course relied for them on an array of law enforcement investigative tools and governmental mechanisms for international cooperation. But as he clicked on screen after screen Haggai Carmon, an international lawyer in private practice, surprised those of us meeting him for the first time with true tales of how, as a consultant to the U.S. government, his independent approaches had ferreted out millions in U.S. crime profits that perpetrators had cached abroad. In this work Haggai had also gathered legal intelligence in more than thirty countries that proved to be at least significant and sometimes crucial to civil and criminal cases, money laundering cases in particular, involving the U.S. government.

The methods Haggai outlined were original, effective, and unusually swift. Some made creative use of that slim computer of his. All were perfectly legal. Whether retained to work in tandem with government investigators or operating independently for the government, Haggai had in numerous major cases been responsible not only for tracking down ill-gotten assets abroad but for facilitating their return to the United States.

Nearly a decade later, Haggai surprised me again. By then I'd retired from my Department of Justice job as general counsel for the INTERPOL-

U.S. National Central Bureau, slipping gratefully off to a quieter life. But Haggai had another true tale, and he tracked me down to tell it.

During sleepless, jet-lagged nights in remote hotels, he'd pounded out an international legal/spy thriller based on his years as a money hunter in more than thirty countries. Would I look at *Triple Identity*'s discussions of INTERPOL to see that they were authentic?

I agreed to check relevant sections. When the bulky manuscript arrived, however, I glanced at its first page, the first sentence — and read straight through to the very last word.

Parts of the book sprang, it was obvious, from pure imagination. *Triple Identity*'s David Stone, mythical head of a nonexistent U.S. Department of Justice office, has "an ample budget." This does not happen. Given their heavy and ever-increasing caseloads, no government international office I've known, regardless of country, has had a budget that its agents or lawyers would call "ample." Nice thought! But it's fiction.

Nor would any government lawyer resort to a certain few of the ploys used by unbureaucratic Dan Gordon, the book's dual-nationality Department of Justice lawyer and a veteran of the Mossad. No government lawyer who tried them could keep job, law license, or, in the worst case, liberty. You'll spot these certain ploys. They're clever. They're highly entertaining. They're even plausible. In real life, though, they don't happen.

But what about that twisting plot, those interlaced subplots, incident after curious incident? What about much more than ninety million dollars spirited from a California bank? What about the fugitive banker, real identity as elusive as he, who spirited these millions away? What of that multinational cast of bad, good, and in-between guys crisscrossing Europe and the Middle East, double-crossing one another, intent on seizing the money, stalking the man, securing materials to manufacture weapons of mass destruction? Did these spring from Haggai's cases? From cases that others handled? From Haggai's innovative and inventive mind?

Haggai says that they're fiction. He certainly should know. So, fiction they are. But as far as my experience goes, they nonetheless ring true. I'd say that they could have happened.

SARAH McKEE

TRIPLE IDENTITY

1

Munich, Germany: October 1990

The white, masklike face wore an inquisitive expression, as if, when final darkness came, Raymond DeLouise had asked, "What happened?" then, "Who are you?" and finally, "I should have . . ." The entry wound on his forehead was barely noticeable but for the round gunpowder-burn marks from a close-range shot.

I identified him by comparing the passport picture I held of Raymond DeLouise with the corpse's face. I'd found the man I was looking for.

"That's what killed him," said the man in the white gown and clear plastic gloves, pointing at the tiny wound. I wanted to leave. The metallic click of refrigerated drawers and the cold glare of fluorescent lights sent chills down my spine. I was also uncomfortable with the harsh-sounding German words that, though attempting to be courteous, sounded almost sadistically gleeful. Duty or not, feeling sick to my stomach was not in my job description.

It wasn't the corpse. I had seen many before, including the poor souls I personally sent to their just rewards. But back then it was during battle, when it's your life or theirs, or — during discretionary warfare, sometimes also called "black operations," in which there are no rules, no records, no attribution — when it was only their lives.

What nauseated me was the smell of formaldehyde mixed with cleansing detergents: the stench of death. The odor seeps under doors, along hallways; it sticks to your clothes, infiltrates your nostrils, convulses your stomach.

This was my first visit to a morgue, and its deep-chill atmosphere put death in a different perspective. DeLouise was not my enemy, only my target, and we were not at war. At least I thought so then.

═══

In a hurry I left the morgue, located in the Munich City Hospital on Ismaninger Street, trying to mask my revulsion, and stepped out into the crisp October day. There were some leaves on the tall trees; autumn was still very much in the air. I looked at the clear sky, at the passing faceless people, at the cars, and took a deep breath. This case was certainly different from all the other cases I had investigated for the U.S. Department of Justice. This time an asset-recovery case involved more than money; it involved blood. Someone had killed DeLouise, execution style. It wasn't an accident. "He didn't die of measles," as they say in the intelligence community. You just don't walk the streets of Munich and get shot in the head. It wasn't a stray bullet that killed him either; DeLouise was the target. Raymond DeLouise, or rather his assets, were also my target, and now he was dead. New rules had been written.

I went to the parking lot outside the morgue and headed for my car. It was a shiny blue BMW, rented for me by Helga from the legal attaché's temporary office at the U.S. Consulate in Munich. I paused just as I was about to insert the key in the lock. I felt a sudden rush of adrenaline. I began to sweat even though the air was chilly. I needed to pull myself back to reality.

I stood for a moment, took a deep, long breath, and got into the car. I was being ridiculous. As a trained professional I knew that it took more than the twenty minutes I had spent in the morgue to booby trap a car parked in an open lot, in full view, without arousing suspicion. Besides, the assassin had to be a professional hitman, not a serial killer randomly selecting his next victim. The only people who knew about my pursuit of Raymond DeLouise and my efforts to seize his assets were the U.S. Department of Justice and the Mossad, Israel's foreign-intelligence service — my current and former employers, respectively. And neither eliminated people in the dirty-money business that way; they simply made the wrongdoers read their service and procedures manuals. That was ample punishment.

I tentatively turned the key in the ignition. No surprises. The engine roared to life and I drove off.

Though still on high alert I calmed down somewhat, scanning the streets as I drove. As I pulled up at a stoplight, I took a brief but thorough look at a couple of types in a blue Mercedes parked across the street. They were staring at me. Something about their appearance made me suspect they were not a natural part of the landscape. Military-type men, somber looking — are they on assignment? A scene from a black-and-white Hollywood movie ran fast-forward before my eyes. Soon one dark-skinned guy sitting in the car would jump out in front of me with a gun, shout something in an indistinct language, and start spraying the area with bullets. I'd run for cover, pull out the .22-caliber Beretta, aim with both hands (true to my Mossad training), and unload the entire clip into his head, watching as he collapsed in slow motion.

I smiled at the thought, culled from the many detective stories I'd read in my teenage years in Israel. These men were probably Turkish or Albanian *gastarbeiter*, guest workers, waiting for a friend to return from a visit to the nearby hospital. Besides, I was not armed.

The light turned green. I sped away.

Fantasy intrigues many people, because a mere glimpse into the world beyond the horizon changes everything, taking one into a wild twilight zone. As for myself, I need reality. It makes me strong and confident.

I was beginning to like the new challenge of this case. It would be a refreshing change from the routine of tracing crooks through endless reviews of paper trails, bank statements, and the smell of spilled coffee on documents and files retrieved through subterfuge and deception. Even the "social engineering," the current politically correct phrase for befriending a target to elicit information, would have to happen on a different level. This time the action was in the present tense. In all my other Department of Justice cases during my ten-year service as an investigative attorney, I was called in after the fact, after the crook had taken off with the money, after the money had been laundered, after the best lawyers and accountants money can buy had buried the money so deep in a warren of offshore trusts and shell companies that it would take an expert miner to dig it out. I was one of those expert miners, not a homicide detective. My target's sudden murder put my asset-recovery investigation into a whole new league. I wasn't complaining, though. I had to report my findings to David Stone, my boss at the U.S. Department of Justice, and thought it would be best to do it from the American Consulate through a secure phone. Clearly, murder made the case far more than a hunt for money.

But first I drove back to my hotel. I needed a shower to wash off the smell of the morgue. I also wanted to get some sense of whether the homicide was relevant to my assignment before getting a taste of the bureaucracy at the consulate.

Half an hour later, feeling a lot cleaner and wearing a standard soft hotel bathrobe, I opened my room safe and put in the documents Stone had given me two weeks ago. There was the usual stuff, all of which fell under the category of "Unclassified, but Sensitive" documents: the fact sheet on DeLouise containing his photo, bio, and vital statistics; a copy of his California driver's license, and the FDIC, the Federal Deposit Insurance Corporation, report. Nothing classified for national security purposes, but documents that could still damage our case if they fell into the wrong hands.

I dressed and started to leave my room but changed my mind. I felt as if I'd walked in on the middle of an action movie. Events were taking place quickly, and I was trying to catch up. In such a case, caution was never a bad policy.

I took an airline magazine from the coffee table and found an article describing the art treasures of the Orient. I highlighted several paragraphs at random with a yellow marker, took the DeLouise file from the safe, and locked up the magazine instead. I snapped a hair from my head, wet my finger with my saliva, and placed the hair carefully over the wooden door hiding the safe. When I returned, I would be able to tell immediately whether someone had tried to open the safe. Even if the safe were opened, the highlighted article in the magazine would be a puzzle for anyone trying to check out my papers. Alex, my Mossad Academy team instructor, had taught me that "Not only must you maintain combat-zone security during operations but also leave 'land mines' behind." The highlighted portion of the magazine would lead any snooper to wonder what was so important in a magazine article that it had to be locked behind a steel door.

Hotel-room safes are simple to open. Many guests forget the pass code or check out leaving the safe empty but locked, so hotel managements have had to devise ways to open them. All hotel security officers have a small wrench with which they remove the front panel of the electronic lock. You can do it in a minute if you know how. Obviously, such a wrench is readily obtained. With Alex's warning permanently imprinted in my mind, I never deposited anything valuable in a hotel-room safe. A hotel vault is much more reliable, because two separate keys are required: the guest keeps one, the hotel the other. Nevertheless, we were instructed in the Mossad to use a hotel central safe only for documents deemed to be at a "limited" confidentiality level, two grades of confidentiality below "Secret." Combatants, the term used for Mossad officers working outside Israel, store all other documents at the local Israeli Embassy's vaults.

I no longer worked for the Mossad, but old habits are hard to break. Apparently, this sort of thing becomes second nature after a while.

Alex had repeatedly indicated that we must adhere to safety and security procedures at all times. "In the field," his favorite term, meaning anywhere beyond our desks, "always look around you, physically and mentally. If you're not working alone, keep eye contact with your team; either hang together or be hanged together. You never know where the blow will come from. It's the guy you don't see who'll shoot you down."

Seeing DeLouise's body stretched out on a morgue slab had sharpened my senses. If I found that the strand of hair had been moved, I'd go into combat-level security for everything.

I took my file folder, went to the lobby, and deposited the folder in the hotel safe.

I drove through the bustling traffic of Munich to the American Consulate. Security around the building was very tight. Saddam Hussein had invaded Kuwait several weeks earlier and the world was tense. The United States had increased security around all its embassies and consulates, no matter how friendly the host country. Concrete barriers blocked one lane of the street to keep traffic from getting too close to the building. The terrible U.S. Embassy suicide car bombing in Beirut in 1983 that killed sixty-three people — seventeen of whom were Americans and eight of whom worked for the CIA — was still a vivid memory.

German policemen wearing bulletproof vests and holding German shepherds on short leashes were everywhere. I waited patiently at the end of the long line to enter the consulate. I passed through a metal detector and went to the reception booth. A Marine was sitting behind one-inch-thick bulletproof glass.

"I'm here to see the legat," I said showing him my Justice Department ID.

"Hold on, sir," he said, and picked up the phone. He handed me a visitor's badge and buzzed the heavy glass door separating the entry hall from the lobby.

"Mr. Lovejoy's office is on the third floor, sir, and the elevator is just past the lobby."

"Thanks," I said, and went inside.

A tall, rosy-cheeked blond woman in her midtwenties met me as I exited the elevator on the third floor. She wore an American Consulate photo ID around her neck.

"Hello, I'm Helga, Mr. Lovejoy's secretary," she said in a friendly voice, with a trace of a German accent.

"I know that."

"How do you know?" She was puzzled. "We've never met, have we?"

"No," I said, smiling, "I just read it on your badge."

She laughed as I followed her down the hall.

"Mr. Lovejoy is out of his office at the moment," said Helga as we walked, "but he is in the building and I expect him back soon."

"Good," I said. "Is there an office I could use until Mr. Lovejoy returns?"

Helga showed me into a small conference room with a round table in the center and five chairs. A single telephone was on the table.

"How do you get an outside line?" I asked as I sat down.

"Simply dial 9, but if you want to call the United States, you'll have to call me first to punch in the code. Here, let me do it for you now." She leaned over my shoulder, brushing her full breasts against me, punched a few numbers, and left the room. A subtle, flowery scent remained in the air.

I called Stone at his Justice Department office in D.C.

I liked working for David. He looked like the classic absentminded professor, but the mind was right there and it was shrewd. Always clad in outdated suits and loose ties, David was a Justice Department veteran. During his thirty years of service he had gained a reputation as a clever lawyer with outstanding integrity and professionalism. After ten years as the head of foreign litigation for the United States, he'd been promoted to director of the Office of International Asset Recovery and Money Laundering. There he had an ample budget, fifteen staff lawyers, and a free hand to recover internationally located funds, fruits of money laundering or bank and insurance fraud. In most of David's cases, the amount to be recovered exceeded ten million dollars. In at least six or eight cases a year, it topped one hundred million. DeLouise's case deserved special attention; the amount I was expected to retrieve for the U.S government was significant and DeLouise had brought about the collapse of a bank.

The phone clicked at the other end. "I found Raymond DeLouise."

"Great," said David. "Where is he?"

"In Munich." Before David could comment, I added, "In the city morgue. He's been on a cold slab for several days."

There was a pause. I could almost hear David's mind at work, analyzing the facts.

"How did he die?"

"A bullet to the head is detrimental to anyone's health," I said dryly.

"How did you find him?" he asked.

"It's complicated. Triple identity," I said. "It seems that there was more to DeLouise than met the eye."

"Why was he left in the morgue for so long?" he asked.

"Well, from what I could understand from the city morgue office, DeLouise wasn't carrying any ID. The German police traced him through a hotel key they found on his body, and they've just notified the hotel of his death. But it took them a while because the key didn't have the hotel name on it. They had to have a detective visit every Munich area hotel to compare keys. The police are waiting for instructions from the Israeli Consulate about DeLouise's relatives and what to do with the body."

"You mean the American Consulate," David corrected.

"No. The Israeli Consulate. He also had Israeli citizenship, and he registered at the hotel under his Israeli name. That's identity number two."

"Are you sure the body in the morgue is indeed our man?"

"Pretty sure; I went over the inventory list of personal belongings the police found in his room. There were some legal papers concerning his collapsed bank in California and a newspaper clipping describing his sudden disappearance from the United States. I think it's him all right. Besides, he looked just like his photograph only a lot paler. However, final identification will have to be made by the family. You can call the FBI directly because I'm not sure the Munich police realize that they should also notify U.S. authorities through INTERPOL."

"Why?"

"The question is how likely is it that Munich police will check INTERPOL 'wanted' info about this guy. They would only be likely to notify U.S. law enforcement through INTERPOL if they'd checked and found that we were looking for a man with that name and ID and this is not the case here."

"I see."

"You may want to spread the word and score some points for your office," I suggested.

David ducked the curve ball.

"I see you've already talked to the German police. Do you know who else might have been after him?

"No, I haven't talked to the police directly yet," I said. "But the office of the morgue showed me the police report that came with the body for autopsy. There was testimony from a bystander who said that he saw DeLouise standing near a newspaper stand when a man dressed in black leather overalls and a black helmet rode up on a motorcycle. He stopped next to the guy, got off his cycle, pulled a gun, shot him once in the head from a distance of approximately four or five feet, and rode away."

I let that sink in. "It seems like a professional hit. Not a robbery or anything else," I added.

"The German morgue let you see the police report?" he asked in surprise.

"Well, the technician needed some encouraging. He settled for a green picture of Ben Franklin."

David paused, as if to allow himself some deniability at a later stage. Federal employees are not supposed to break foreign countries' rules. I could live with that as long as the government could live with the few minor infractions I had to make, just to make major progress. Maybe I shouldn't have told David, but I trusted him, and more importantly, he trusted me. He knew and I knew that if the shit ever hit the fan, I'd be on my own. That was fine with me.

"Wasn't the report in German? How could you read it?"

"I'll tell you more when I get back home."

I didn't want to tell him, at least not yet, that I also managed to make a Xerox copy of the report and translated it word by word by combining my average command of German with a good dictionary.

"Sounds as if you're on the right track," he finally said. "Let me have your written report as quickly and completely as you can. I'll forward a copy to the Criminal Division, for information only. If I hear anything relevant to your investigation, I'll send you a memo through the consulate."

I left the small conference room and stopped at Helga's workstation. Lovejoy hadn't returned yet. I had more urgent things to do, so I thanked her and left the building.

I suddenly realized how much I missed the sheer excitement of my earlier days at the Mossad. Of course I hadn't thought so then. Those had been three long, challenging years.

"Those of you who survive this course will be the best of the lot," Alex had repeatedly said in his American-accented Hebrew. In fact Alex was born in Canada, but to us cadets, anyone with an accent like that must be American.

They'd recruited me at Tel Aviv University, which I attended after thirty months of active service in the Israeli military, a responsibility all young Israelis must fulfill. I was set to graduate that July of 1966 with a degree in international relations, a degree that offered few job opportunities outside academia or the government. I'd been easy prey.

"We want to talk to you," a stocky fellow said when he approached me in the university's hallway. A man in his late forties, he had a receding hairline and hair that had once been blond but was now a poor gray. He used the word *we* but he was by himself. Who the hell is "we"? I remembered thinking, while looking at him with an amused curiosity.

"What about?" I finally asked, trying to figure out if he was somehow connected to the girl I'd met a week earlier who'd refused to tell me where she lived because her parents didn't approve of her dating "older men." I was twenty-two and she was sixteen, and it was the sixties in Tel Aviv, a city that doesn't stop even at hours when Londoners in swinging Carnaby Street are already fast asleep.

His tone of voice became friendly. "I'm Michael from the prime minister's office, and I'm wondering if we can talk for a few minutes."

I followed Michael into the cafeteria on the lower level of a three-story faculty building just completed at the quickly expanding campus in Ramat Aviv, Tel Aviv's northern neighborhood. The place was notorious for its stale coffee and sticky Formica tables, which were never stable. The cafeteria was deserted, but we sat in a far corner anyway. I looked at Michael, waiting for him to start.

He was brief. In a barely audible voice he said, "We at the prime minister's office have reviewed your background and believe that you may be suitable for the screening process which, if successful, will lead to your being invited to join us." There were too many preconditions to this statement, I thought; it sounded like a preamble to a contract. I had to lean forward to hear the rest. He smelled of tobacco and Aqua Velva, the popular aftershave lotion one could buy at the army canteen.

I looked at his face, then at the small and wobbly table between us and said, as if I didn't know what he was talking about, "The prime minister's office? I'm still in school. Why would the prime minister's office be interested in a guy like me?" I played dumb, of course. I knew very well that the "prime minister's office" was the code name for the Central Institute for Intelligence, Israel's equivalent of the CIA. (In Hebrew, the word *mossad* roughly translates into "institute.")

"You're going to graduate in a few months," Michael said, "and your major is international relations. Your language skills and other traits as well as your Special Forces military background make you appealing to us. I can't tell you anything more at this time, but if you're interested, call me."

"What do you know about my background?" I asked in surprise.

"Everything there is to know," he said.

I didn't like the answer. I wanted to hear what he meant. I wanted to know how deep their inquiry went. The deeper the research, the more serious their offer.

"Tell me what you know about my parents," I suggested.

Michael gave me a long look and finally said, "Your father, Harry, came to Palestine from Eastern Europe in the 1920s. In Russia he was active in Zionist movements and emigrated to Palestine as a pioneer motivated by ideology. Here he first worked as a laborer in citrus groves and paving roads until he saved up enough money to go to London to study law. After graduating he returned to Tel Aviv and joined two other lawyers and established one of Tel Aviv's first law firms. Your mother is a librarian at the law school. Your only sister is six years older than you, married with two children. She is a homemaker and her husband a medical doctor. Do I need to continue?"

"Yes. That information is hardly a secret. Anything specific?"

"Last year you were arrested after you knocked down two guys in the Carmel fruit market."

I smiled. "I was released immediately. Those guys snatched the purse of an elderly lady right next to me."

"But was there a need to send them to the hospital?" he said, smiling.

"I had no choice. They used an old trick, shouting that I was the thief and they were trying to help the woman."

"Then a month ago you answered an ad in the newspaper seeking volunteers to go to Africa to teach English for one year."

"So it was you!"

He smiled. "Need I continue?"

"No. That's enough." They'd done their homework.

I realized with surprise that Michael had also read my university file. I didn't know whether to be proud that someone had bothered or ashamed that my so-so academic achievements were revealed. What did he mean by my "other traits"? I hoped that my ability to charm the faculty secretaries and the female lecturers to obtain academic and other more personal favors was still undiscovered. It didn't occur to me then that that quality — or drawback, depending on whom you're asking — was an important factor in the selection process. But I immediately thought of a James Bond movie I'd seen a week earlier. Fast cars and easy women. I liked that. "Please tell me more," I asked.

"I can't tell you anything further at this time, but if you're interested, call me at this number." He gave me a piece of paper with a Tel Aviv phone number scribbled on it.

I called Michael two days later. I didn't want to look too eager. The phone rang once and a woman answered. "Yes?" No hello, no announcement, no identification. Just an impersonal "yes." I asked for Michael. The phone went silent. No "hold on" or "please wait" — just silence. I thought it was stupid. With these responses they had assumed a face of mystery: "We are secretive. But you're not supposed to know."

Another female voice came on. "Michael is not available, but I can handle this for him. What is your answer?"

"Yes," I said in a choked, excited voice. "It's yes," I said again, clearing my throat, "I'd like to be considered." She took my name and number, told me I would be contacted, and hung up. I slowly lowered the receiver into its cradle. The conversation had left me puzzled. They couldn't be that obvious, could they? Where was the glory? I'd expected them to be more subtle, not like a regional office of the DMV.

Days went by — the tense waiting for a phone call slowly being replaced by a creeping feeling that they weren't interested in me after all. I became less and less enthusiastic about the whole thing. I found myself thinking that I didn't really care any more if the Mossad recruited me. I began to make plans to go to law school.

Then the brief letter came in a small, plain, government-like yellow envelope. No letterhead, just a typewritten message telling me that I should report the following week for evaluation at a psychologist's home in northern Tel Aviv.

The doctor was a fat woman in her forties with two chins going on three. Her face had seen better days. Or maybe not. The downward curve of her upper lip made her look as if she perpetually smelled something unpleasant. Maybe she'd decided that as long as other people had problems psychologists wouldn't have any. I walked into her office and sat down across the desk from the good lady. There were tacky landscape oil paintings of swans and rainbows on the wall and another wall full of professional books, many of which looked as if they hadn't been removed from the shelves in years.

Without any ado she put me on the spot in an obvious effort to make me feel uncomfortable and shake my contemptuous half-smile. She started with embarrassing personal questions about my family and my sexual habits: the works. Did she really need to know how I masturbated or was it her personal kinky curiosity? Then she showed me ink spots on paper and asked me to explain what I saw. For some reason it didn't seem to be a genuine psychological screening, like the ones I had been through during my military service. I began to think that this was their way of evaluating my conduct under pressure and embarrassment.

Three hours later I was back on the street relieved it was over. I thought of the psychologist as the kind of person you don't want to remember but nevertheless can't forget. The medical checkup came next; a variety of other aptitude and psychometric tests and interviews followed. The process went on for months.

The initial novelty surrounding my recruiting process and the interviews was fading fast. I was being stripped psychologically and intellectually bare. Facing up to that without any sense of accompanying challenge or reward became increasingly difficult.

After two weeks with no contact, a telephone message left at my parents' home, where I was still living, instructed me to appear for a personal interview. I looked at the address. It was on a side street in the southern end of Hakirya, a government center in eastern Tel Aviv. Strangely, most of the government and military offices occupied turn-of-the-century farm buildings built by German missionaries. Sarona, they called the neighborhood then. The buildings each had one or two floors with a red shingle roof covered by hyssop, with citrus trees in the backyards. In the 1950s, when I was six or seven years old, my dad sometimes took me for long walks into the same neighborhood to see the citrus trees in blossom. In later years, when it became a government center, the charm evaporated.

I went to the interview on schedule. A high limestone wall covered with ivy surrounded the inconspicuous building, but that wasn't unusual. Other government buildings in the area looked the same. I rang the bell on a wrought-iron gate. Again, a woman's voice, this time from a hidden speaker: "Yes?"

"I'm Dan Gordon. I'm here for an interview."

She said nothing, but a minute later the gate opened and a bald, short man in his early fifties asked me to follow him. We went through several narrow, mazelike corridors, then through a back door to an inner backyard with three lemon trees, then through another door into yet another building. I followed him into a small office.

There he turned to me and said, "I'm Mr. Shani. Please wait." I sat down as he left the room.

I looked around, but there was nothing to see. The only window faced the backyard and the three lemon trees. Although we must have passed offices, the view from the corridor had been blocked. I didn't see people, or desks, or anything other than the darkness of the corridor itself. Aside from my own chair, there were only a simple wooden desk and three more chairs in the room. A photo of Levi Eshkol, Israel's then-prime minister, hung on the wall. The door opened and three people, Mr. Shani among them, walked in. I stood.

"Sit down." The speaker was a tall man in his early sixties with white hair and a tanned face. I sat. The third person was a woman dressed like my high school biology teacher, in a business suit with shoulder pads that probably hadn't been fashionable since before I was born and a cut that killed any sign of femininity. If you have never met my biology teacher, then think of a female commissar in an early Soviet film.

Shani began. "Good morning, Dan. You're here today to allow us to get a firsthand impression. Thus far we've seen only the reports."

He saw the question in my eyes. "They're all positive," he added in response. "Tell us why you want to join us." He said "us," not "the Mossad." In fact, nobody used that word throughout the entire screening process. I wondered why.

Obviously, a simple answer would have been to retort, "*I* was approached by *you*, remember?" but it wasn't the place or the time to play cute. "I like the international nature of the work," I said. "I have a curious mind. I never take things at their face value. My military service has helped me realize that I have other character traits that I'm sure stand out loud and clear from my file and from the various tests I've undertaken. I may not be proud of some of them, but they're part of me."

The man with the white hair nodded as he went through some papers he brought into the room with him.

"Dan," the woman said, "tell us what your worst personal quality is."

"I have no patience for idiots," I said immediately.

"Is that all?" she insisted.

"No. I also tend to prefer working independently rather than in a team, and I find it difficult to follow stupid instructions without questioning them first, at least in my mind."

"So you're the judge of what is and what is not a stupid instruction?" There was a negative tone to the question.

"No," I replied quickly trying to control the damage, "I'm certainly not an expert on anything. But I have some common sense and principles, and if my instincts or my brain tell me that something is wrong, I ask. I'm sure you've seen my military file. I was never court-martialed for disobedience, and I was involved in many sensitive incursions across the Syrian border that demanded strict adherence to orders. But if you're looking for someone to follow any orders, with no questions asked, then I'm the wrong person. On the other hand, if original thinking and an inquisitive mind are traits that fit the job, then I'm your man."

The white-haired old man sitting in the center of the panel seemed to like my answer. He smiled.

"Let me hear your views about politics."

We talked local politics for an hour. I didn't think he wanted to hear my opinion; he simply wanted to be assured that I wasn't a radical on either end of the political spectrum. Then it was over.

"You'll hear from us," Shani said as he escorted me out.

Weeks went by with no word. Then one afternoon there was a knock on the door of my parents' home. I answered the door. Michael walked in and, without any prefatory comment, asked me to join him for a meeting elsewhere. I didn't ask any questions and went along to his car. Ten minutes later, we arrived at the Mossad headquarters. I followed Michael through the corridors and was asked to wait in an empty conference room. After what was for me an agonizing interval, Michael entered with Shani, who shook my hand and said with a broad smile, "Congratulations! You're in."

I was so unprepared that I didn't know whether I should be happy or sorry. Despite the long wait, it all seemed very sudden.

Michael handed me a stack of documents. "This is an oath of confidentiality," he said, pulling out two stapled pages. "Read it carefully, because it will remain valid all your life, even when you are no longer in the service."

I looked at the statement. "As a member of the Central Intelligence Institute, I understand that I will have access to confidential and top-secret information which concerns Israel's national security. By signing this statement, I am indicating my understanding of my responsibilities to maintain confidentiality and agree to the following." There followed a list of penalties for breach, of which prison seemed the lightest.

I signed.

In those few minutes, though I didn't realize it then, I had just begun the most fascinating time of my life.

It was only May, but Tel Aviv was already hot and humid. My acceptance came right on time; graduation from university was only two months away. I broke the news to my parents at the dinner table that evening.

"What about your plans to go to law school and then join my firm?" my father asked, looking at me and then my mother.

"It'll have to wait for a while," I responded. I don't think they liked the answer but they said nothing to discourage me. I didn't realize then that "a while" meant years.

On my first day on the job I was assigned to the archive. Thousands upon thousands of files, reeking of mildew, welcomed me. "Don't worry," consoled Michael when he saw my gloomy face, "this is how everyone starts." It took me two months to get the picture, reading endless files. I saw how many so-called accidents that had befallen terrorists had their roots in those files, in that stale room.

I was assigned to field training six months later, the first of its kind at the Mossad.

I packed a few things and took a bus to the Mossad training camp, twenty miles northeast of Tel Aviv, for what was called an "operations course." The camp was located in an agricultural area, on an old military base that was surrounded by citrus orchards and small red-roofed houses. It included an airstrip that had been built and used by British forces until 1948, when Jewish resistance made them give up their mandate over Palestine, leading to the establishment of Israel. Several elite forces of the Israeli armed forces had taken over the base. Behind a seven-foot gated metal fence topped by razor wire stood a few one-story buildings. The smell of cow dung hung in the air. There was no sign on the fence.

I showed the guard in the small concrete booth my invitation letter. He asked me for my government-issued photo ID, compared it with my face, and picked up his telephone and said something. With a nod, he hung up and opened the electric gate, which screeched as it slowly rolled on its rails. I walked inside the camp.

Manhattan, New York City, September 1990

The office secretary, Lan, knocked on my door, walked in unceremoniously, and handed me a file folder.

"This just came in," she said. "It looked like something you'd want to see right away." I reached across my desk, took the folder, and began to read a cover memo.

U.S. Department of Justice

Office of International Asset Recovery and Money Laundering
Washington DC 20530

Memorandum
To: Dan Gordon, Investigative Attorney
From: David Stone, Director
Date: September 15, 1990
Re: U.S. v. Raymond DeLouise

I'm assigning you this matter.
The subject Raymond DeLouise, born in Bucharest, Romania.
DOB: July 15, 1927.
Whereabouts: Last known address: 44–21 Glendale Boulevard, Los Angeles, CA 90021. Current address: unknown.

The subject absconded from the United States soon after federal regulators discovered a $90 million shortfall at First Federal Bank of Westwood, California, where he was chairman and chief executive officer as well as principal shareholder. The FDIC took over after the bank's collapse and paid back the depositors as required, up to $100,000 per account. The FDIC has referred the matter to this office to attempt retrieval of the missing funds. They found sufficient evidence showing that the shortfall was not an accounting error or an accrued loss but was rather a result of possible defalcation, probably by Raymond DeLouise. Remarkably, there are no suspicious international wire transfers in large amounts or other evidence of the whereabouts of the missing funds.

The criminal aspects of this matter were referred to the U.S. Attorney's Office for the Central District of California, which instructed the FBI to investigate. A grand jury is considering indicting him on multiple charges, including bank fraud and money laundering. Since the FBI believes that DeLouise has left the country, INTERPOL will be put on notice if he is indicted.

My office has been asked to locate DeLouise and recover the lost money that we suspect was laundered through foreign entities. Neither the FDIC nor the Department of Justice has a clue where Raymond DeLouise might be. I enclose the FDIC report together with its attachments. Please report your findings to this office.

David

I went through the twenty-page FDIC report and a brief FBI report. They looked very thorough but lacked a bottom line: If DeLouise or his money were outside the United States, they expected me to find both — and fast.

The government's working assumption was that he'd left the country — they all do. But where did he go? Was he sunbathing in the Bahamas? gambling in Monte Carlo? skiing in St. Moritz? Certainly with ninety million dollars in his pockets he didn't escape to a one-star hotel where, for an additional buck, they give you a mousetrap for your room. This guy probably wanted to keep his money in the dark and himself in the sun. The problem was that there were dozens of these sorts of places around the world. The FBI report indicated that his wife and adult son, who still lived in California, didn't know his whereabouts — or at least they claimed not to know.

I prepared a note to Lan.

I'm attaching David Stone's memo with the new file. Please call your contact at the INS and ask for Raymond DeLouise's file. His social security number is in the new file. The subject was born in Romania and lived in the United States; therefore he must have an INS file. Ask your friend if it would be possible to get the file before the end of the millennium.

Dan

The last time I'd asked the INS for assistance in retrieving an immigration file, it had taken six months. "It's a black hole out there," a Justice Department veteran had once told me. "Unless you know someone in the particular office you need, you're nonexistent. They're so overworked and underbudgeted that they look through you as if you were air. Their telephone extension numbers are kept secret even from other government agencies. If you call for telephone directory assistance, you get an 800 number with nothing but long recorded messages. You can punch all the selections, but you'll never talk to a live body."

Lan walked into my office. "I gave the INS the social security number you gave me for DeLouise, but they say another name came up."

"Ask them to send a copy of that file anyway, we'll figure it out."

The guy Lan knew at the INS must have owed her big-time, because I had the file on my desk within two days. I opened an old manila folder and read through it.

Bruno Popescu was born in Bucharest, Romania, on July 15, 1927. He first entered the United States on a tourist visa in 1957. He then sought political asylum and permanent residence, alleging that his life would be in peril if he ever returned to Romania. According to some documents in the file, Popescu claimed that he was suspected by the Romanian secret police as being "a provocateur in service of the decadent West." There was no indication in his asylum application, or in any of the other documents, that he in fact was politically active in Romania. The file contained no evidence corroborating his claim of fear of persecution. Asylum was granted.

Was Popescu DeLouise? I read the INS file again and compared it with the documents Stone had given me. There were several similarities: same date and place of birth, identical social security number and entry date to the United States. It was possible therefore that Popescu had changed his name to DeLouise after he had been naturalized. I made a note to revisit that issue.

The whole thing was unusual, though; DeLouise or not, how had Popescu obtained a tourist visa to enter the United States before he filed for asylum? The year 1957 was a time of great tension between the West and the Soviet-dominated Eastern Bloc countries. The Cold War was at its peak. In tandem with France and the United Kingdom, Israel had just invaded Soviet-sponsored Egypt's Sinai Peninsula and faced down Soviet and U.S. threats demanding its withdrawal. Polish students and workers were up in arms. Hungary had simmered politically until the rebellion finally erupted — the Soviets had sent in tanks in 1956 to quell it.

As a consequence the United States was substantially limiting entry of visitors from the Eastern Bloc countries, fearing that spies and saboteurs would arrive disguised as tourists. In that political climate, then, there must have been a good reason for an American Consulate to grant Popescu a U.S. tourist visa. But his asylum application wasn't convincing or supported by any evidence. So how had Popescu managed it?

I turned the yellowed pages and found a summary document, handwritten by the INS examiner of Popescu's asylum application. Among the routine bio data, I almost missed some information at the bottom of a folded page:

Passport: Romanian, issued in Bucharest, Romania, on February 21, 1947, valid for five years. U.S. visitor's visa issued by the American Consulate in Tel Aviv on November 23, 1957. Date of arrival to Idlewild Airport, New York, December 14, 1957.

"I'll be damned," I whistled in surprise. If this was the DeLouise file, what did he have to do with Israel? Nothing in the other documents showed any reference to his ethnic origin or how he might have ended up in Israel. This was really strange, I thought. If this person's Romanian passport had been issued for five years in 1947, it had expired in 1952. There was no indication that the passport had been renewed. Why did the American consul in Tel Aviv stamp a visa in 1957 when the passport had expired in 1952? That couldn't have occurred. Something else must have happened, something that was not reflected in this slender file. The passport could not just have been renewed. A whole slew of other possibilities quickly passed through my mind. Photocopy machines were rare in 1957, however, and there was no copy of the passport in the file. My seeds of suspicions would have to wait for further information in order to germinate and bear fruits of success. The INS file showed that DeLouise was issued asylee status pending the review of his political asylum application. The asylum application was approved on March 8, 1958, and subsequently a green card was issued, giving him permanent-resident status. Five years later, on July 4, 1963, Popescu was naturalized and became a U.S. citizen. There were no further records in the file.

I smelled a rat, but I didn't know where it was buried. Not yet.

I put the file aside, leaned back, and closed my eyes, shutting out the intense light in my office. If Popescu and DeLouise were the same person, he had been in Israel of all places! At the beginning of my career at the Justice Department I'd worked mostly on Israeli legal matters, but the scope of my work had gradually broadened to include international asset-recovery cases, some with an Israeli flavor. Eventually the asset-recovery cases I'd received had no known Israeli connection. This case was the first I'd seen to connect what seemed to be a non-Israeli matter with Israel, although the connection was hair thin.

I called my friend Benny's home number in Israel.

"*Shalom,*" said a man's voice.

"Hi, Benny," I said, and went on without waiting for a response. "It's Dan."

"Hold on," said the man on the other end, "It's not Benny, I'll get him for you." I heard him shouting, "Dad, it's for you."

"Dad"? A grown man was calling Ben "Dad"? When I last saw Lior, Ben's son, he was ten years old. But that, I realized, had been ten years ago.

"*Erev tov*, good evening," said the voice on the other end.

"Hi, Benny," I answered. "It's Dan Gordon. How are you?"

"Still pulling," he said.

"And your family?"

"Being schlepped."

"And how's Batya?" I'd always liked his wife.

"Well, on one of these days I'm going to catch pneumonia because of her."

"Why?"

"Because each time she sings in the shower, I have to go out to the balcony so that the neighbors won't think I'm beating her up," he said, and I realized that he hadn't changed.

"I need help."

"I'm here," he said.

"Well," I said, sounding a bit apologetic, "this time it's ancient history. Could you please see what you have on Bruno Popescu, born in Romania, a July 15 birth date? He could be a person I'm looking for, a man named Raymond DeLouise. I suspect he was in Israel in November 1957."

"What did he do?" Benny asked curiously. "Steal something?"

"Yeah," I said, "ninety million dollars."

"Is that all? Fax me what you have and I'll see what I can do."

"Thanks, Benny," I said, "and if this works out, I'll owe you lunch."

Benny mumbled his thanks. He knew he would not be making a sacrifice. As an observant Jew, he ate only kosher food, and there are few restaurants in Tel Aviv that are both kosher and good.

"Give me a little time," said Benny. "I'll call you right away if I find something."

Benjamin Friedman had been the odd man out in the Mossad's cadet course. The other eleven of us had been secular Israelis, like a substantial majority of the country's population. Benny was the son of Holocaust survivors who had owned a grocery store in central Tel Aviv. I used to stop by their store with Benny during our training years. His mother worked behind a tall display refrigerator that doubled as a counter. She wore the typical clothes of an Orthodox woman: head covering and long sleeves even in the height of summer.

I noticed that Benny was embarrassed each time we stopped by his family's store. His mother would approach him, asking, "Have you eaten yet? Come have a piece of cake, you look too pale." It hadn't mattered that Ben was a grown man of robust appearance. To his mother, he was still a child in need of her care.

The store was cramped and smelled of the matjes herring and pickles in brine kept in open wooden casks. The smell always made me hungry.

But I'd always restrained my urge to pluck a pickle while her own son was sidestepping her attempts to feed him. Benny never made an issue of his self-imposed dietary restrictions and unwillingness to work on Saturdays and other Jewish holidays. He had come to the cadet course from AMAN, the military intelligence division, where the words were not an oxymoron. AMAN was by far the largest intelligence agency in Israel. It was responsible for gathering all military intelligence concerning the surrounding Arab states and for submitting the periodic intelligence overview to the prime minister. All Benny had told us was that he'd served as a captain in what is now known as 8200, AMAN's secret communication and computer unit. Basically it did what the U.S. National Security Agency (NSA) did: intercept radio, telephone, fax, computer, and other communications; decipher their content; and draw intelligence conclusions.

I could still hear Meir Amit, then-head of the Mossad, lecturing us on the opening day of our course. "An intelligence service is expected to gather information concerning the enemy's intentions and capabilities — period," Amit said. "Governments that extend the scope of these duties are likely to lose control, because secret organizations have dynamics of their own."

Years later I grew to appreciate how right he was. Amit had been in the middle of his term as head of the Mossad, but his earlier bitter struggle with Isser Harel, his predecessor who mixed internal politics with his official capacity, must have given him that wisdom.

Two days later Benny called back.

"I think I have what you want," he told me, without much ado. "This person has a very interesting history. Write this down. Israeli records show that a Bruno Popescu left Israel with a Romanian passport on December 13, 1957. But we couldn't find a date of entry to Israel. The records from this period were handwritten and there is no information about what country's passport he used. Other records may have answered this question. A person named Bruno Popescu, with the same vital statistics as your Raymond DeLouise, entered Israel sometime between May and June 1948. These were the very first days of the state of Israel and there were no real records, as you very well know," he said, as if I could forget my background. "We rely on the immigration records of the Jewish Agency, which acted as an interim government from just before the British left to the time the state of Israel was created. Their records show that Popescu came by ship to Haifa and was sent to Shaar Ha'Aliya, a new immigrants' camp nearby. They received new immigrant ID cards. After about two years the family changed their name to an Israeli-sounding one, like most immigrants. Bruno received an Israeli ID card bearing his new name, Dov Peled." Benny paused. "Do you know what this means?"

"Yes," I said anxiously. "Go on, it's getting interesting. But how can you be sure that Peled-Popescu is indeed the same person as DeLouise?"

"I'm certain," said Benny. "In 1976 he entered Israel using his U.S. passport. Our computer matched his date and place of birth and other vital statistics with Dov Peled's. We compared your faxed photo with Peled's. DeLouise looks older, but it's the same guy."

"Fascinating," I said. "That explains why we couldn't find him. He simply has three legal identities: as a U.S. citizen named Raymond DeLouise, as a Romanian citizen named Bruno Popescu, and as an Israeli citizen named Dov Peled. Triple identity," I repeated in disbelief.

"But wait," he said, "it gets better. Why don't you come over to Israel and I'll show you something even more intriguing."

After finishing up with Benny, I called David Stone's office. Stone himself answered. It was not unusual for him to take his own calls. He was never formal.

"David," I said, "I need to go to Israel."

"Family?" he asked.

"No, this time it's pure business."

"What do you mean?"

"I think I found DeLouise's old tracks in Israel. I need to go deeper. I don't know much yet. I have footprints leading to Israel, so I hope to find out more while I'm there."

"Okay," said David briefly, "you know the rules. The U.S. Embassy in Israel and the state of Israel must approve your visit."

"I know that. This red tape is totally unreasonable; I'm also an Israeli citizen."

David was serious. "Well, it has some reason. You're not going to Israel on a family trip. You're going on official United States government business. Official visits must meet the approval of the host country — that's common courtesy. Besides not stepping on Israel's toes, under the Federal Chief of Mission statute federal government employees are allowed in any given foreign country only on the sufferance of the chief of mission. That's our ambassador or, if the ambassador is out of the country, the deputy chief of mission. If they really want to go by the rules, they could assign an embassy control officer to escort you during your meetings."

"I've been through that before," I said. I couldn't have an embassy control officer escort me to my meeting with Benny. Benny would be as silent as a dead fish. "Couldn't you do something?" I almost begged.

"Well," said David, "if you're just dropping in and can operate under the radar, you might get host-country clearance in three days."

"I'm sure you could do better than that, David," I said, relying more on hope than on fact.

"OK," he said, relenting. "Express me your filled-out travel forms. I'll sign and distribute them for approvals. Call me tomorrow for a possible green light. And let me know if you need anything else."

"I will," I said, and hung up.

"If I need anything," David had said. I sure did need something; I needed to know more about DeLouise, the guy who was about to ruin the vacation in Israel I had promised my children.

Ever since I'd divorced Dahlia, my wife of seven years, I'd tried my best to spend more time with my children, seventeen-year-old Karen and fifteen-year-old Tom. A year after our divorce the children decided they wanted to live with me, so they came to the States. Dahlia hadn't put up a fight over that. She knew too well it was a lost battle; the children were old enough to make up their own minds. Because they were grown and needed only minimal housekeeping assistance, namely in rearranging their mess at home, it was easier for me to travel and leave the house chores to Amanda, my loyal part-time housekeeper.

But now I was about to go to Israel without them. I expected a major earthquake when I broke the news at home. I asked Lan to book me a flight to Tel Aviv for the following day, convinced that David would have the clearance issued quickly. I also gave her a pack of signed, blank travel-request forms. I had a hunch that visiting Israel would only be the beginning of an extensive multicountry hunt for DeLouise.

I went out to lunch and when I got back I was handed a confirmation slip for my flight out of JFK.

II

Sitting in the too-narrow seat of a TWA Boeing 747, I thought about Benny. While I'd left the Mossad three years after I'd joined, Benny had stayed on and had slowly risen to become section chief in the Tevel Division, responsible for the Mossad's contacts with foreign governments, particularly those with whom Israel had no diplomatic relations, and with other intelligence services. The "cocktail party agents," they'd been called in the Mossad. And indeed, the instructor they'd sent to give the course on foreign relations looked more like a stiff-upper-lip British diplomat than a Mossad combatant. But then, what did Mossad combatants look like anyway? Hollywood movies stereotyped them as dark and handsome, but in reality they resembled your next-door neighbor or your school's bus driver.

As for myself, things were more complicated. With my green eyes and brown hair I didn't look like an average Joe, which had always been an advantage when I was dating but a disadvantage when I wanted to blend in with the crowd during Mossad operations. My 6'4" frame was too noticeable to ignore. Recently, world travel and irregular eating had added a few inches to my waistline. I was fighting it, without too much success. I realized that brain cells come and go but fat cells live forever. But in our trade, looks are not everything. Efraim, the Tevel Division representative, was definitely not a looker, but nonetheless he was a suave guy with worldly manners and a brilliant mind. He could have been my father's law partner.

"Intelligence is a commodity traded over the world markets," said Efraim. "We trade information for other information or take a credit slip for future exchange. For example, in 1968 a Mossad combatant in France came across information that OAS, the military organization of the

French settlers in Algeria, was contemplating the assassination of President de Gaulle as a way to stop the French pullout from Algeria. We immediately alerted de Gaulle's son-in-law, who was his close confidant, and the plot was exposed. We could do that without compromising our source. In return, and not necessarily contemporaneously, in addition to political favors the French intelligence agency provided Israel with local assistance about individuals within the Arab community living in southern France who could be tied to terrorist organizations in the Middle East."

Benny excelled at his job. Employing the art of negotiation and bargaining as though he'd been born to it, he became a world dealer in information and a master in forming human contacts where political relationships were formally nonexistent. Many non-Arab Muslim countries had strong ties with Israel, although formally they were aligned with the Arab countries most hostile to Israel. Benny and I had stayed in touch over the years and had helped each other out in minor matters. I felt comfortable with him. He was loyal and discreet.

I arrived at my hotel in Tel Aviv too late to call. I was on the phone early the following morning.

"I'm here," I said. "When can we meet?"

"I can see you this afternoon at our cafeteria. You know the place."

I took a cab to 39–41 King Shaul Boulevard, a tall office building close to the Tel Aviv courts and the IBM building. Many lawyers, accountants, and businesses used the building, but the Mossad occupied more than half of it. These were the premises the Mossad had moved into after leaving the cramped old buildings located on the other side of Hakirya. The buildings' employees and the public had free access to a cafeteria on the mezzanine floor.

Benny was waiting for me. He hadn't changed much since we'd last met — only a few additional pounds around his waist and a few more streaks of gray on his mustache and on the hair that was still left on his head. With his medium build, the weight gain made him look more like a bank manager than a highly ranked executive in a world famous spy agency. The greatest part about Benny, though, was that although he was one of the shrewdest men I'd ever met, he was just an ordinary guy — down-to-earth and never condescending.

We found a quiet corner and schmoozed a bit like the old friends we were, drinking tea and coffee. Then things turned serious. Benny handed me an envelope.

"This is for you, and you only. Nothing in it is secret or classified, particularly after so many years, but it could be sensitive so let's lay down some ground rules. After you're finished, return the documents to me. No copies. I want to make sure that Israel is kept out of it if this thing ever blows up."

I was getting curious. What was he talking about? DeLouise was a common thief. Only the amount of his haul wasn't common.

"Look," said Benny seriously, as if he'd read my mind. "Let me tell you a few things, then you can go back to your room with that envelope. This person — DeLouise, Popescu, Peled, or whatever he called himself — was not an ordinary person. He was an only child born in Romania to Jewish parents who were Romanian citizens. His father was an electrical engineer and his mother a French teacher — all very normal. But Bruno was a brilliant student in high school and graduated at sixteen. He excelled in math and sciences and was accepted to the Bucharest Polytechnic to study physics and chemistry; he got his degree before his twentieth birthday.

"When immigration to Israel was allowed, he and his parents emigrated to Israel aboard a ship from Constanta, Romania. Soon after arriving in Israel he joined the Israeli Army and fought in the 1948 War of Independence. He was an excellent soldier and was cited for bravery under fire."

I could see this account would be a real test of my memory. "Go on," I said.

"He'd taken an Israeli name by then — Dov Peled — and he was sent to the officers' training academy and became a second lieutenant. The Army assigned him to military intelligence. His first job was in field security; then he was sent to advanced training. A year later Peled was promoted to first lieutenant and placed in a secret unit assigned to collect data on the Arab countries' technical and scientific capabilities."

"So far, it sounds routine," I said. "There's nothing special about him."

"Well, it was unusual. He was assigned to a secret military intelligence unit although he was a new immigrant from a Communist country. It was unusual then, and it's almost impossible today."

"I know the routine," I said. "So why did they take him after all?"

"I don't have all the facts but it seems that field security found no negative information on him. Anyway, his initial exposure to confidential information was limited because he was assigned to analyze raw data and had no knowledge where it came from or by what means. At the time Israel needed the data for two purposes: first, to be prepared if the Arabs started developing weapons rather than buying existing ones from more developed nations, and second, to steal any scientific discovery or achievement for its own use. Israel had the need, Bruno had the credentials, and the combination worked beautifully. Remember, Israel was in a state of war with the surrounding Arab countries at the time, so the information was crucial. And they weren't just looking at the military industries. For example, the Arab oil industry brought with it substantial technical know-how, from explosives to the behavior of metals under extreme heat and pressure, which could easily be applied to the manufacture of cannon barrels."

I was becoming impatient. I knew Benny; there must have been a better reason for him to make me come all the way to Israel. Had I traveled for eleven hours to listen to the history of a guy who was no different from thousands of others? I looked at him closely, trying to figure out what bombshell he was going to drop. There had to be one; I just wondered how big it was going to be.

Benny sipped his coffee, took a breath, and continued.

"I don't have a lot of information about what Peled did in that AMAN intelligence unit; I didn't ask for his military file. Although I do know well enough how successful that unit was."

Benny then paused — an actor preparing to take center stage. I waited a full thirty seconds for him to continue. I finally spoke.

"And then?"

"And then, he joined the Mossad," Benny said. It sounded as if he'd put a period at the end of his sentence. You could almost hear it.

My jaw dropped. Not exactly a bombshell, but still a shocker. The Mossad?

"Our Mossad?" I asked, slowly pronouncing each syllable.

"Yep," he said decisively. "Ours."

I leaned back to digest the news. A Mossad-trained guy stealing millions? I didn't say anything, thinking that was the end of it.

"Wait," said Benny, as if he were reading my mind again. He cautioned me. "None of what I'm telling you about the Mossad is mentioned in the documents in that envelope. It's information that I want you to hear but never repeat."

"Is there something else?" I asked in anticipation.

"Patience," he counseled. "Please understand that I trust you not to disclose this information to anyone. I don't want this to haunt us. You can draw your own conclusions and use the information to make progress, but don't put it in writing, discuss it with anyone, or reveal your source."

This must be some heavy stuff, I thought, if Benny went out of his way to tell me that. We were trained together; we knew the rules. I nodded and waited for Benny to continue.

"After his honorable discharge from the army, Peled was looking for a job. He took up teaching physics in a high school but left after one year. I guess he was bored. Then the Mossad approached him and offered him a place in the ranks, specifically the ultrasecret unit assigned to worldwide gathering of scientific and industrial information from public and, more importantly, private sources. He was assigned to the nuclear physics section. He was to collect data on the military applications of the most recent developments in the atomic energy field."

I didn't want to say anything, fearing I'd break Benny's train of thought or that he'd change his mind about telling me all this.

"He resigned suddenly in 1957 and emigrated to the United States. That's where our story ends."

"Serious stuff," I breathed. "So this son of a bitch could lead triple lives. Tack on his Mossad training, and he could disappear anytime he wanted.

"At least I've got a place to start now," I said. "But triple legal identities? I don't think I've seen that one before."

"There could certainly be some side benefits to that," said Benny.

"Like what?" I asked absentmindedly, looking up at him. "What do you mean?"

Then I saw the sparkle in his eyes.

"You could have three wives," Benny chuckled.

"But then you're punished," I quipped.

"You mean for polygamy?"

"No," I said, "You'd have three mothers-in-law."

He smiled. Benny knew marriage was a sensitive topic. Benny and his wife, Batya, had been good friends to Dahlia and me. The news that we were divorcing had stunned them. There'd been no side to take because the decision came so suddenly and the marriage ended so quickly. Even an intelligence expert like Benny hadn't seen the storm approaching. I had simply packed and left. No battles, just good but fading memories tarnished by two people growing apart. I needed a change and the United States looked like a good new leaf for me.

"Thanks for the information," I said, when I realized he had finished the story.

"Hey, what are friends for?"

I wanted to find out if DeLouise had maintained any contact with the Mossad after he'd left, but I didn't want to push Benny with further questions. I'd try to find another opportunity to ask him that. The information could be relevant to my case.

"I'll read this stuff and call you to return it or if I have any questions."

"I'll be here," he said, and with that he left.

I was tempted to open the envelope and go through the documents then and there, but I resisted. I looked around at the other diners. I could easily pick out the Mossad types. Once you'd spent time there you learned the identifying marks — like that guy over at the other table who wore his name tag tucked inside a pocket shirt, but with the clip still visible on the outside. I could still be one of them, I thought. If I'd stayed on I would now be on the same level as Benny, or even higher up, given my extroverted personality and my pushy character and ambitions. I remembered my mother telling anyone who cared to listen, and a few who didn't, that I had ambition. That was long before I even knew what the word meant.

Three years after my service with the Mossad had begun, I decided to leave. I'd had enough. The work had become too routine. Every great organization is like a Swiss watch with many wheels working in sync. My superiors had all been veterans of the old Russian school of thought. Jews who emigrated from Russia had ruled Israel in its formative years. Some of them became the legendary leaders of Israel's security services and had implemented their strict purist doctrines in their organizations.

Their idol had been the second and celebrated head of the Mossad, Isser Harel, who emigrated from Russia in the 1920s. He was a short man with jumbo ears, piercing eyes, and unrelenting dedication in his character. People who knew him said he had ice water in his veins. He'd been revered and feared. Judging from the stories I'd heard, I didn't think anyone had loved him. Admired, yes. Loved? Hardly. During his years as head of the Mossad, from 1952 to 1963, he had carte blanche on all matters of security from David Ben-Gurion, the founder of modern Israel and its first prime minister.

Harel had ruled not only the Mossad, which was primarily responsible for activity outside Israel, but also the Shin Bet, the secret internal police whose mere existence was kept a state secret until the mid-1970s. When I joined the Mossad, Harel had already been out of power for almost two years. But he continued to cast a long shadow, influencing organizational procedures and philosophy long after his departure. As in any other intelligence-gathering organization, discipline in the Mossad had been tight to prevent leaks and infiltration attempts by hostile powers. The high moral standards imposed by Harel, which had become the norm, continued to be applied. That was fine with everyone, though to be sure there was a double standard involved. When you were on a mission outside Israel, you were expected to lie, cheat, steal, or even kill. But when you returned to Israel you had to be the exemplary model worker and citizen. Never run a red light, tell a lie, or, God forbid, forget to turn over a receipt for ten bucks you spent on the job. Outside Israel we made sizeable cash payments to informers who hadn't exactly been in the habit of giving out receipts. But in Israel? Don't even think of it. Outside Israel we had had other ways to keep a receipt — sometimes on paper, sometimes on a roll of film. The backup unit used photography in the prevideo era. The recording of the "receipt" was useful not only for bookkeeping purposes. Once you had an informer on film receiving payment from you, he was yours forever.

I had been a deputy on several major operations. It was fascinating and dangerous, but at that level there had been no room for personal initiative or original thinking. I quickly discovered that my lone-wolf personality, cutting corners on my way to the target, was in direct conflict with the rigid structure of such a discipline-based organization.

Then there was a major problem. Two groups from Mossad had been sent to Rome in January 1971. I'd accompanied Alon, a blond and athletic-looking senior case officer, and a small backup unit had followed separately. The Mossad was collecting information on the hijackers of an El Al flight from Rome on July 22, 1968. The hijackers, who called themselves the Popular Front for the Liberation of Palestine, had diverted the plane to Algeria. Thirty-two Israeli passengers had been held hostage for five weeks, the first-ever hijack of a civilian aircraft by Palestinians. It was standard procedure to investigate incidents like this, no matter how many years it took. Nothing was ever shelved, no unsolved case was ever closed, until the responsible individuals had been identified and brought to justice, in public or (more likely) clandestinely.

Our target was a Libyan diplomat keener on his payoff than on his loyalty to Khadafi, the Libyan dictator who'd been in power for just one year. We planned to meet the diplomat in a café. He thought he was going to be interviewed by Scandinavian journalists investigating the hijacking, and he'd promised to bring someone along who had firsthand knowledge of the operation.

I sat at a table with Alon who held, as agreed, a white umbrella — an old trick of the trade. The diplomat arrived with a dark-skinned young man who scanned the area with piercing eyes. Then he looked at me, our eyes met, and he recognized me. The young man was Hammed, a

Palestinian who happened to work in my parents' garden as a landscaper. How did he get here? It really wasn't important. What was important was that, through an extraordinary coincidence, my cover had been blown. The moment Hammed recognized me, he snapped something to the diplomat; they turned around and left the café in a hurry.

"It's a professional risk," said Alon afterward. "There's no way to know if a person you once met as a friend might not return as an enemy."

My disappointment was acute. Not only had the operation failed, but I knew what the personal consequences would be; once identified, I could not soon again, or maybe ever, participate in clandestine operations. I would have to spend the rest of my working life pushing papers at Mossad headquarters as a researcher and analyst while watching others triumph. I couldn't stand the thought of playing second fiddle, and being out of field operations meant I wouldn't even be in the orchestra.

Even within a glorious entity, there are many unimportant ants working to give the queen her glory. Now that my cover had been blown, I would have to become one of those ants permanently. I had to make a change. I wanted to become royalty elsewhere.

My decision to leave was met with surprise. Service in the Mossad is considered a lifetime career, not a single line, however distinguished, in a long resume.

I applied to Israel's toughest law school, at Tel Aviv University. That changed the course of my life, ushering me into a new profession and a new country and, ironically, as my lunch with Benny revealed, bringing me back years later into contact with the Mossad.

I paid for the tea and the energy bar that looked like compost and tasted no better, took the envelope Benny had given me, and left the cafeteria on my way back to my hotel on Tel Aviv beach overlooking the old Mediterranean port of Jaffa, half a mile away. Sitting at the desk in my twelfth-floor room, I opened the envelope. It contained photocopies of documents. The first document I saw was obviously an application form. The top portion of the document was cut off. I guessed it was Peled's application to the Mossad. His bio details matched what I already knew about him, but there was something else that attracted my immediate attention. He had a wife in Israel. Dov Peled had married one Mina Lerer. That was a surprise, since all I knew of DeLouise so far was that he had a wife and son in California. There was only an indication of his Israeli wife's date of birth, April 6, 1930, in Romania, and her Israeli ID number. The treasures are always buried in the minute, seemingly unimportant details.

Where was Mina Lerer now? I picked up the phone and called Ralph Lampert at his home in Tel Aviv. Ralph was a private investigator who had spent many years working in the Shin Bet. I'd met him on a joint operation before I left the Mossad. In those earlier years, operations on Mossad targets carried out within Israel were always in cooperation with the Shin Bet.

Ralph was the classic ordinary person. You could pass him by a thousand times and never pay him any mind; he looked like your neighborhood butcher or dry cleaner. He was that other guy sitting next to you on the train, on the bus, on the plane, the guy you never really noticed — a definite asset in his line of work. After leaving the Shin Bet, Ralph continued doing the only thing he knew how to do: private investigations, this time for insurance companies or suspicious wives or husbands. If there was something you needed to know in Israel, he could get it for you.

What I wanted from Ralph was simple: Mina Lerer. He agreed to come over to the hotel later in the afternoon.

I pulled out the second document pertaining to Peled. It was the standard Mossad employee evaluation sheet; every employee was judged on his personality, his attitude toward his coworkers, his traits, and his success in his work. Finally there was a recommendation concerning the employee's future in the Mossad's *maslul kidum* (Hebrew for "track of advancement"). A special section was devoted to a personal interview with the employee and the supervisor's impression of how the employee saw himself, his future in the organization, and his ability to take criticism. I could tell by looking at the handwriting that throughout the four-year period, the form had been filled in by two or three different individuals.

As reflected in his supervisors' evaluations, Peled's personality came through loud and clear: intelligent, hardworking, persistent to the point

of stubbornness, and conniving. "Marked for promotion," said one comment, "but not in positions that require teamwork." For a moment I suspected that Benny had pulled a fast one on me and given me a copy of
my own evaluation form. The most recent comments on the form were
written in 1955, although Benny had told me earlier that Peled left in 1957.
Was something being kept from me?

The only other document in the envelope was a letter of appreciation
Peled received from Professor Ernest David Bergman, the legendary
founder and first head of Israel's Nuclear Energy Commission. The letter,
only three lines long, commended him for a job well done. There was no
mention of the type of work he did to deserve this letter. Why did Benny
bother to include this letter among the documents he gave me? It didn't
seem to have any relevance. Or maybe it was Benny's not-so-subtle way
of saying it did.

Ralph came to see me two hours later. We went out to the park surrounding the hotel to sit on a bench and enjoy the sea breeze. I didn't
need to keep our meeting a secret, and I wanted fresh air. Then again,
with two people with backgrounds such as ours, even an innocent
meeting might suggest we suspected the KGB was watching.

"Ralph, I need you to find a woman for me. Her name is Mina Lerer."
I gave him her ID number. "She was married to a Bruno Popescu, who
later changed his name to Dov Peled; he probably divorced her."

"How do you know that?" he asked.

"I don't, but I know of an American-born current wife. So I don't know
what last name Mina Lerer would be using now. Call me at the hotel
when you make progress. I think I'll be here for another week."

"Sure," he said, "I'll get right to work on it."

I returned to my room and stood at the glass door looking at the sea. I
was trying to conjure up Dov Peled in my mind. He must have been
pretty sharp if he was in the nuclear science section of the Mossad.
Israel's nuclear weapons policy and efforts, and the Arab countries' capabilities, were off-limits, even within the organization, except for those
actually assigned to that section. We were warned that it was the most

closely guarded secret of Israel. In the mid- and late 1960s, Israel kept its nuclear capability under a dissembling cloud while vowing not to be the first nation to introduce nuclear weapons into the Middle East. "Non-introduction" meant doing it anyway, but quietly. Peled, I recalled, had joined the Mossad in 1952 and left in 1957. I wondered what Israel's "nuclear policy" had been in those years.

A call from Ralph woke me up the next morning. I'd closed my curtains so I didn't realize how late I'd slept. It was already past 10:00 A.M. — a case of jet lag at its worst. Ralph continued our conversation as if it had stopped only moments before.

"Your Mina Lerer is now Mina Bernstein. She lives in Haifa on Allenby Street."

Half asleep, I jotted down the address, then made it a short conversation for both of us. "Thanks, send me your bill."

I washed and dressed quickly and went downstairs. I fueled my system with a little of the famous Israeli breakfast — freshly cut salad, soft cheese and olives, and fresh-squeezed orange juice — and headed for the garage and my car. Haifa was just sixty miles north of Tel Aviv on the coast, and I figured I could be there within an hour or so. As it turned out, other drivers had similar plans, and they were ahead of me. The trip stretched to almost two hours. But the great views of the sea were some compensation. The color of the water changed from emerald green to azure blue as the waves broke on the beach. Seagulls shrieked; a few fishermen were trying their luck in the shallow waters. The breeze carried a strong smell of salt water and seaweed. It all looked so serene. But it was deceptive; I knew that the undertow just offshore was strong and dangerous.

I finally entered Haifa and drove through the busy port area to a residential area of tree-lined streets winding along the hills overlooking the harbor. I found Mina's house without any difficulty. It looked exactly as Ralph had described it: a two-story stone building, circa 1920, with an iron gate and a path leading to the entrance. I went through the unlocked gate. There were three old vines and a couple of orange trees in the small yard. This house had seen better days. Neglect and disrepair were visible, but so were traces of its former glory. There were four broken letterboxes at the door, each with several names crossed out. The landlord must have had a firm short-lease policy. Unusual. On one of the mailboxes I saw the name Bernstein-Peled. I went up shabby stairs to the first floor. I found the name I was looking for on the door on the left.

I rang the bell. There was no response, and I could detect no noise inside. I waited a few more minutes. It was apparent that either nobody was home or somebody didn't want visitors. I looked at my watch. 1:25 P.M. I hoped Mina Bernstein was at work and would be back soon. I decided to sit in my car and wait it out.

A few people, mostly children, came in but not one looked like a Mina Bernstein. I knew she had to be in her sixties, but no woman of that age entered the building. Finally, after three hours, I went back into the house, up the stairs, and rang the bell. Still no answer. I turned to the door opposite and knocked lightly. A woman in her late thirties in a dressing gown, hair tied up in a haphazard knot, opened the door.

"Yes?" she asked.

"Excuse me," I said in Hebrew, "I'm looking for Mrs. Bernstein. Would you know when she is expected back? I was to meet her here about this time," I lied with a smile.

She sized me up. In the background I heard a child crying, and the smell of cooked cabbage seeped from the kitchen. She didn't seem to have much time to spend talking to me.

"All I know is that she left a few days ago. She told me she was going overseas. She didn't tell me where she was going or for how long. That's all I know." The last sentence was said in a subdued tone. I realized the woman probably thought I was a cop; her attitude was becoming defensive. I needed more information before she asked to see a badge. Let her think I was a cop.

"What about her mail?"

"I collect it," she replied and pointed to a small table with a stack of mail on it. I went over to the table and shuffled through the envelopes. Mostly junk, some bills. I pulled out the phone bill and slid it into my pocket. The neighbor said nothing.

"Do you know where she works?"

"She was a teacher, but I think she retired last year."

As I turned away she hesitated and added, "You could also ask her daughter."

I stopped. "Her daughter?"

"Yes," she said, "Ariel."

"Ah," I said. "Do you know where I can find her?

"She's a chemistry teacher at Ramot High School. You could try there. I don't know where she lives."

"Thanks," I said, and walked outside. I looked at my watch; it was 4:12 P.M. No point in going by the school at that late hour.

In my car I opened Mina's telephone bill. It listed service and other charges for two months through September 30, 1990. There were no details concerning any local calls — just a flat fee. But there was one line that attracted my attention. It was a collect call made to Mina Bernstein from Munich, Germany, on September 26, 1990, from number 004989227645. The duration of the call was 5 minutes 11 seconds.

I drove back to Tel Aviv and called my office in New York from a pay phone just outside my hotel. "Please do a reverse search on this little item," I asked Lan, and gave her the Munich telephone number. Not much, but it was a start. I hung up and called Ralph.

"I thought it would be easy," I said.

"Well, did you find her?"

"No, I found her apartment, but she's been gone a week or so. The neighbor said she went overseas, but I want to make sure it wasn't the neighbor's assumption. How about checking to see if she actually left Israel."

"And," I added, in an exaggerated dramatic tone, "Mina has a daughter, Ariel, who teaches chemistry at Ramot High School in Haifa. I don't have a last name. It could be Peled, but she could be married and using her husband's name. Check her out, will you?"

"No problem," answered Ralph. "I'll get back to you."

Israel maintains a very efficient computerized system at the Ministry of the Interior, controlling all exits and entries across its borders. The information, available to the police and other law enforcement and intelligence agencies, was retrievable pretty much any time. At that late hour the ministry's offices were closed, but Ralph, with his connections, could do it over the phone in no time.

The phone rang in my room. It was Ralph. I looked at my watch — it had been twenty minutes since I'd called him.

"Writing this down?" he said.

"Go ahead."

"Mina Bernstein left Israel on El Al flight LY 353 to Munich on September 28 and has not returned. There is no record of her leaving Israel during the preceding seven years."

"Thanks," I said, "I owe you."

"Unfortunately, not that much," he chuckled.

"Have anything on Mina's daughter, Ariel?"

"Still working on it. I'll get back to you," he said and hung up.

This was getting more and more intriguing. Two days after receiving a collect call from Munich, a woman who was not in the habit of going abroad had suddenly decided to travel to Germany, which was not exactly a tourist attraction for Israelis. Something important must have caused Mina to make that trip. I didn't know when she had separated from Peled, but it must have been many years ago. DeLouise's son by his second wife in the United States was at least twenty-four years old.

From where I sat, Mina was just a road sign, not a destination. Did DeLouise keep in touch with her during all these years? On the other hand, why would her visit to Munich be connected with DeLouise at all? I had no answers, only questions.

With nothing more to follow up on, I sat at my desk in my hotel room, pushed the papers aside, and glanced at my watch again. It was 6:45 P.M.

I called Gila, an old friend of mine. She and I enjoyed each other's company for the time we were together, but there were never any strings attached. We didn't talk much. It was . . . comfortable.

The next morning I awoke to the sound of the rain pounding on the sliding door. I opened the heavy curtains and looked outside. The sea was black except for the foam-capped waves that broke on the shore. The city was under a heavy rainstorm. No one in the streets, only cars with head-lights on and windshield wipers working at full speed. The streets would soon be like canals, minus the Venetian charm.

It was time to talk to Benny again. I called his office.

"Benny," I said, "we need to talk. Care for lunch on Uncle Sam at my hotel?" It was either my place or his, and in the pouring rain, I'd rather it be mine.

Benny never said no to good food as long as it was kosher, and all hotel restaurants in Israel keep kosher, for the most part to satisfy the observant Jews among the tourists.

Benny showed up precisely at 12:30, as agreed. We went downstairs to the hotel's restaurant and sat at a corner table, both with our backs to the wall. Realizing that, we exchanged a maven's smile.

Abie, one of our Mossad Academy instructors years ago, had taught us operational tactics. "When you enter a public place, what is the first thing you do?" he had asked with his Yemenite accent, his wide-open mouth showing us perfect white teeth. He obviously enjoyed asking the question. No one answered, so he continued, "You look for the way out! Always be ready to leave, under favorable or unfavorable circumstances. You came in from one end, so that could be your exit, but look for other ways out as soon as you go in. Then you look at the people around you. See if you can identify something unusual. Never stare or let them know you are looking. Make it seem as if you are looking through them and not at them. See how many exits the place has, and which one is best to use in case of emergency. When you check out the place, look for the unusual, something out of the ordinary that could mean trouble. That, in fact, very rarely happens, but when it does, you'd better be ready. The second piece of advice is always to sit with your back to the wall so nobody can surprise you from behind. Be ready to turn the table over and be on the move."

We ordered lunch. Benny looked at me pensively.

"What's on your mind?"

"Benny," I opened, realizing that I needed to select my words carefully, "was Peled ever in contact with the Mossad after he left? I mean recently."

Benny gave me a long look. "I'll have to get back to you on that," he said. Already I didn't like the sound of it. For the first time ever, I felt that Benny was holding out on me. But if he wanted to be evasive, why was he helping me? And if he was helping me by giving me copies of documents from DeLouise's file, why was there no information about DeLouise's last two years in the Mossad? Why the contradiction? I needed to find out why Benny was being vague. There was a pause.

"Any progress since you've been here?" Benny asked.

I sensed he felt my surprise and disappointment and wanted to change the subject.

"Not much," I said, handing him back his envelope. "I saw that Peled was married to a Mina Lerer, so I tried to find her."

"Any success?"

"No. She's gone to Munich." I looked him in the eye. "Any idea if her departure is connected to Peled?"

Benny said nothing. He took a special interest in his sandwich. Maybe he doesn't know, I thought, trying to find a brighter side.

"I don't know," he finally said, with his mouth full. "But remember, Peled was trained like me and you. That stays even after we leave the shoo shoo business." He used the old slang for clandestine activity. It had been a long time since I'd heard that.

"So, if Peled wanted to keep things undetected, and if her departure is connected to him, you'll have to find out independently," he concluded. "I've got to go."

I looked at his plate in amazement; he had devoured a New York–style hot pastrami sandwich in ten minutes. "But I'll ask someone in the office to do a search — just as a favor. I'll call you if we find anything."

His promise sounded useless, a token gesture. I said nothing.

I went upstairs to my room. The telephone was ringing as I entered. It was Ralph.

"Well, at least the neighbor wasn't lying. Ariel, the high school chemistry teacher, is Ariel Peled; she's DeLouise's daughter with Mina Lerer. She'd asked the principal very suddenly for a few days off to take care of an 'urgent family matter.' Said she'd be back in three or four days, but it's been much longer than that already and they haven't heard from her. They're worried. Ariel isn't married and has no children. She leads a quiet life and doesn't have many friends at the school."

"Do you know when she asked for the leave?"

"The principal said he thought it was on September 23, but I spoke to him at his home so he couldn't verify the exact date."

"Ralph, I need to find these women. Get a border-exit run on Ariel as soon as you can. I just want to make sure she hasn't disappeared like her mother."

More than a week away from school during the school year. That was unusual. Events were unfolding so quickly that I felt as if I were playing catch-up. "I'll call you as soon as I can," said Ralph, picking up on the urgency in my tone.

Twenty-five minutes later he rang.

"You were right; she's gone too. Left on September 24. Guess where she was headed?"

"Munich," I stated flatly.

"That's right," he said approvingly, and gave me the flight details.

A few moments later a fax message from Lan was slipped under my door. It read: "The number you gave me is a pay phone located in the Grand Excelsior Hotel in Munich, Germany."

Three road signs leading to Munich: the pay phone and Mina and Ariel's sudden departures. Clearly Munich was my next stop. And I had to get there in a hurry.

III

The next day I boarded Lufthansa flight 693 to Munich Airport's Terminal C. The New York office had made the travel arrangements and I'd contacted our embassy legal people. My man, Ron Lovejoy, would be on duty when I got there.

When I arrived, it was almost 7:00 P.M. and raining lightly. A BMW waited for me at the Hertz counter with a note, as Lovejoy's office had promised. I drove to the Omni Hotel on Ludwigstrasse.

I checked in and then headed over to the Grand Excelsior Hotel, where the trail to Mina Bernstein went cold. She'd accepted collect charges from a pay phone located in the Grand Excelsior's lobby.

The hotel was one of those pre–World War II landmarks with plenty of Old World charm and prices far above my budget. I still remember the startled look one of the bean counters in Washington, D.C., had given me when I'd tried to explain why my bill from a Tokyo hotel ran four hundred dollars a night. "Frankly, the place looked like a youth hostel," I'd said with feigned exasperation, "but with the yen so strong against the dollar that's what you pay there." He had not been amused.

The first questions I had to answer were whether it had been DeLouise who'd called Mina in Israel and whether he had been a guest at the Grand Excelsior.

I went to the desk and asked for Raymond DeLouise. They had no such guest. The response was too pat, I thought. But then, he wouldn't have used that name. How about Mina Bernstein? No. I left the desk disappointed. Then I turned around and made yet another try.

"I'm sorry, is there a Dov Peled?" I asked.

The reception clerk hesitated, and then said, *"Minute!"* and disappeared into the back office. She returned a minute later with another man, obviously senior staff.

46

"I am looking for Mr. Dov Peled. Can you give me his room number?" I repeated. The clerk's action told me I was getting close.

"I'm sorry," said the man, with somewhat fraudulent solemnity. "We were notified this morning that Mr. Peled has died."

"Died?" I repeated after him in disbelief. "What happened?"

"We don't know," said the man. "The police just told us that he is in the city morgue. That's all we know."

"Are Mina Bernstein or Ariel Peled registered? We were all to meet here," I asked, adding feigned shock to the real thing.

He looked at the woman next to him. She shook her head. "No, I'm sorry sir, we have no such guests," the man replied.

I thanked them, turned around without another word, and went to my car.

I had my answer. Yes, he had been a guest at the hotel under his old Israeli name, but had he been the one to use the pay phone at the hotel to call Mina in Israel? And if so, why use the pay phone?

I juggled the various plausible answers around in my mind. Whoever had called didn't want the call to be traced to him or her or else was already afraid that any telephone associated with him or her was being monitored.

If it was DeLouise/Peled who had called, who or what was he afraid of? No answers. Not yet, anyway. But given his probable horizontal position in the city morgue, his concerns had been justified.

A visit to the morgue confirmed that Popescu/Peled/DeLouise wasn't going anywhere. I had to find Mina and Ariel; they were my only viable leads to DeLouise's money. Where were they? Munich could be just their point of entry to Europe. They could have taken another flight to Timbuktu in the sub-Saharan desert or driven to Finland. And come to think of it, why was I using the plural form: they? Why should I assume that Mina and Ariel had met in Europe?

I didn't know where to start, although I had a hunch they weren't far away. I decided to stay in Munich for a serious looksee. I suspected that Mina and Ariel must have been here and had left their mark. Did they have anything to do with DeLouise's death? Or were they potential victims?

Lovejoy left me no information about whether he had contacted the German police. It was too late to call him, so I decided to go to the local precinct and find out what I could. If DeLouise died of natural causes then the police would not be involved. But I had to find out what they knew. I asked the man at the desk if I might speak to the officer in command. My basic workable German, even if not fluent, could help. A few moments later, I was shown to a small office.

"Good afternoon," I said as I entered, in the friendliest tone I could muster and politely showing my ID. "My name is Dan Gordon, and, as you can see, I'm with the U.S. Department of Justice. I have an interest in Mr. Dov Peled, who I understand is in the Munich city morgue. Is there a police investigation into the cause of his death? Could I help you out with anything?"

The officer looked at me with ice-cold eyes, as if I had just vomited on his best suit, and said in excellent English, "I am sorry, sir, this is a German criminal investigation. If your government has a relevant and parallel criminal investigation, I am sure it can find out more through INTERPOL when I send my report to my superiors." The sarcasm virtually seeped through his pores.

Hell, I thought, he was right. You wouldn't get a different answer from an American police detective investigating a homicide in Cleveland or Miami. But national sovereignty or not, I had to know Raymond DeLouise's movements and activities after he had left the United States. Besides, the officer confirmed that there was a criminal investigation. I left the police station and returned to the Grand Excelsior.

A mild-looking, middle-aged man dressed in a ridiculous uniform, too much pomp and circumstance, stood behind the cashier's counter. I told him that I'd come to settle Dov Peled's hotel bill. I sensed he was not about to object.

"By all means, sir, by all means," he said quickly, and rattled the keyboard to get the printout.

The printer started spewing out a surprising number of pages. The clerk stapled them and handed me the lot.

"Twenty-one thousand, six hundred thirty-two marks and seventy pfennig, please," he announced coolly.

I put the packet in my briefcase and said casually, "Thank you, I'll forward it to the family's attorney for his review," and walked away without waiting to see his astonished look.

The bastard probably thought I was about to pay this hefty tab. That's all I needed: give the bean counters in Washington yet another reason to climb all over me.

On my way out I calculated the dollar equivalent. It came to roughly fourteen thousand dollars. I tried to figure out how long he'd had to stay there to amass that charge, given the hotel's top mark rate. Quite a tab for a short stay. It would be interesting to see the details when I reviewed the bill.

Back in my hotel I started working on my loot. On the top left corner of the invoice appeared his name: Herr Dov Peled. No address. Citizenship: Israeli. Date of check-in: September 20, 1990. He had taken the Bavarian Suite at a rate of one thousand German marks per day. Payment method: cash. Manager's note: "Herr Peled is a VIP who has patronized our hotel in the past. He insists on his privacy. Do not discuss this guest with anyone inquiring about him."

The invoice listed charge items for minibar use, restaurants at the hotel, dry cleaning service, and more than one hundred phone calls. I pulled out my laptop, keyed in my user name and password, and went directly into the investigative telephone database. People usually have a pattern of calling. If you analyze it you can discover amazing facts. Identify all the numbers called, then let the software pick up the pattern. It's simple but clever. I had designed the application myself on an existing software platform.

I started with the tedious work of typing in the numbers I'd first highlighted on the invoice. Some of them were local German numbers, but many were international. An hour later I had finished logging them all. I plugged into my room's telephone line and uploaded the data into my office computer in New York. I attached a note to Lan. "Please do a reverse lookup for these numbers."

It was late, and I was tired. I shut off the laptop and lay down, satisfied that promising results awaited me the next day and that my investigation was progressing nicely. I fell asleep then and there, street clothes and all.

Next morning I went back to the Grand Excelsior, avoiding the reception area. I took the elevator to the third floor. A housekeeper was hard at work on the carpet.

"Excuse me," I spoke in German over the hum of her vacuum cleaner, "Where is the Bavarian Suite?"

"It's on the seventh floor," she replied in strongly accented southern German, and went calmly back to work.

I took the elevator to the seventh floor. Another housekeeper's service cart was in the hallway, and the door of the Bavarian Suite was open. I walked in. A young waiter was checking the minibar.

"Excuse me," I said nonchalantly, "I think I must have left something in the room before I checked out." He did not respond.

I looked around. The two-room suite was empty of any personal belongings and already made up. The police must have removed Raymond DeLouise's stuff. I opened the closets and went through the walnut chest-of-drawers, but I couldn't find anything unusual. Finally, I knelt beside the bed and looked under it. There I saw a small yellow Post-it. I grabbed it, put it in my pocket, and left the suite. The waiter never even looked at me.

In the elevator I checked the note. There was a handwritten telephone number without an area code and a name written in Hebrew: Hans Guttmacher, and a scribble that looked like 2:00 P.M.

I returned to my own hotel room and called the hotel operator.

"Excuse me," I said apologetically, "I received a message to call a Mr. Guttmacher, but I don't know who he is, and I don't want to offend him by calling him back and asking him all sorts of questions. I may have simply forgotten him, and it's quite embarrassing."

The operator listened and responded immediately with "No problem, sir, let me have the number. I'll call and see if it is a private residence or an office. Maybe that would help you remember."

I gave her the number and a few minutes later she rang me back.

"Well," she said, "I think I can help you. Mr. Guttmacher is the manager of Bankhaus Bäcker & Haas. This is a bank here in Munich." Sometimes luck is better than smarts, and this time I was lucky. I'd done a research job on this very bank in connection with another case.

She gave me the address, which I wrote down on the pad on my night table. I hung up and removed the three blank pages under the sheet on which I'd written. Another old, hard-to-break habit for preventing others from finding out what you'd written on the top sheet by rubbing the one underneath with a pencil. Although I didn't think I had any rivals in this game, caution was never a bad thing. I picked up Peled's Grand Excelsior Hotel bill, scanned through it quickly, and nodded in satisfaction as I spied Guttmacher's number.

Bankhaus Bäcker & Haas, located in the heart of Munich's business district, occupied a three-story office building. I went directly to a counter and asked the teller to exchange a hundred dollar bill. Without comment, she passed the bill through a machine to check its authenticity. I suppose she was checking to make sure I wasn't offering her a banknote I'd printed earlier in my basement. She must have been satisfied with the result because she quickly and efficiently handed me 156.77 German marks. I looked around. The place looked old-fashioned, with wood paneled walls and a slight smell of stale carpets mixed with a strong cigarette odor. I took two brochures off the counter and left.

Outside, I looked at them. They were routine, describing all sorts of financial services the bank offered. Their logo had the German eagle and the words "Ganz Privat und Sehr Personlich," which translates as "Totally private and very personal." I went to a pay phone at the street corner and called the bank.

"Bankhaus Bäcker & Haas," announced the receptionist in an abrupt voice.

"Good afternoon. I'm an attorney from the United States," I said in a professional manner. That much was true. "I need to talk to someone at the bank concerning a new investment. I need a banker to assist me."

"What is the size of the investment? I need to know how to direct your call, Herr . . ." she paused, waiting for me to give my name. "Wooten," I said, "Peter Wooten, and the amount is quite large, in seven figures."

"Just one moment, please," she said swiftly. "I'll connect you with our director, Herr Guttmacher."

Good, I thought, I'm getting the head man immediately. I guess the sum I had mentioned was high enough.

A few more seconds and a man's voice came on the line.

"Guttmacher," he said. I felt as if he were expecting me to jump to attention and click my heels. "What can I do for you?"

"I'm looking for a bank to assist me in investments my client is considering making," I said, repeating my story.

He said nothing, so I continued. "Can we meet to discuss your services? I'll be in town for only a few days."

"I shall be glad to see you," he said. "How about this afternoon at four, if you have no other plans." Herr Guttmacher was my only plan for that afternoon, so I quickly agreed.

"Always plan ahead when meeting with potential sources," I recalled Alex, my instructor at the Mossad Academy, repeating time and time again. "Although they may or may not be your adversaries, they could snap and become hostile at any point. Therefore, your planning should cover all ends. First comes your own security. Identify the potential risks you are taking in making contact, then set the meeting in a place you are the least likely to be hurt and leave tracers behind you. Make sure someone knows where you are going, whom you are meeting, and at what time you are expected back. And finally, set your goals before you make the appointment. Know exactly what you are trying to get from the source, what you are willing to give in return, and the mechanism for the exchange." He paused dramatically, looking at us as though he were an attorney offering the jury his closing arguments in the most important case of his career. "A mistake could cost you your life, then and there or later. You'll never know what hit you."

I knew this was only a money chase, not terrorists weaving nets in Europe, recruiting local help and eliminating competition at all costs. I wasn't concerned about my personal safety. I wasn't carrying a gun. What would the banker do: toss a checkbook at me? I had researched the bank's history from publicly available sources when working on that previous case. So much for planning ahead.

Bankhaus Bäcker & Haas was founded in 1932, after the great inflation of the 1920s and early 1930s had destroyed Germany's economy. Two German bankers who operated out of Zurich decided it was a good time to open a branch of their bank in Germany, where most of the banks had not survived the hyperinflation and had folded. Although the bank offered commercial banking services, the heart of its business was private banking. Bäcker & Haas catered to high-net-worth individuals who needed an astute banker to manage assets and hedge against market trends. Above all, such people needed discretion. With a few conspicuous exceptions, rich people don't like to be flashy with their wealth and attract tax collectors, charity solicitations, and sudden new relatives.

I had also come across rumors, all unsubstantiated, that money launderers favored the bank because its managers looked the other way, ignoring suspicious movements in accounts that would have triggered the attention of more reputable bankers. After the original owners died, the heirs sold the Swiss main office to a group of Saudi investors but kept the Munich bank.

For starters, I planned an initial interview with Guttmacher in order to study him and his attitude toward borderline financial transactions. I had to see whether he would be a good candidate to lure into my den. I wanted to know how DeLouise had used the bank, and I wanted to glean that information from Guttmacher.

"Hastiness is of the devil," Mussa, our Arab customs and manners teacher, used to tell us at the Mossad Academy. "Patience! Arab nomads used to say 'I waited forty years for my revenge, and when it finally came, I said to myself, perhaps I was too hasty.' Have patience, my friends. Never approach a potential source and expose your time constraints. Always behave as if this thing is not that important, that you have all the time in the world." He had been referring to Arab sources, but I later discovered the universal application of this wisdom.

I arrived at Guttmacher's office at the designated time and gave his secretary my business card. It's part of the "legend" I usually prepare before going out of the country on assignment. The business card read "Peter Wooten, Attorney-at-Law," and gave an address in New York. The information on the card wasn't completely inaccurate. The name was phony and the address was that of a front office used by the Justice Department in decoy operations, but the profession was genuine. The business card was the only physical window dressing I had. The remainder of the legend was in my mind.

The office was located at the southern corner of the second floor. A long corridor with cherrywood paneling led to his spacious chambers. The wide planking on the floor was covered with a handsome Oriental rug. Landscape paintings hung on the walls. It was obvious that the bank made every effort to make this office reflect stability and old-time respectability.

I was shown to Guttmacher's inner office. He was a man in his late fifties with a full head of iron-gray hair. I noticed that he had green eyes, although he avoided looking at me when we shook hands. Guttmacher was wearing a conservative suit with a red vest. I sat down on a brown leather couch, surprisingly well-worn for such grand surroundings.

"Thank you for agreeing to see me on such short notice," I opened.

"It is never a problem," he said, a broad smile revealing a gold tooth. My first impression was that Guttmacher has trained himself not to reveal himself in any way. I thought I knew why. "What can I do for you?"

"I represent a group of investors from the United States led by one individual. They want to diversify their investments and need a discreet German banker who can assist them in their search for solid opportunities as well as maintain absolute confidentiality." I paused, looking him in the eye. I had emphasized the word discreet.

"Any particular area of investment?" asked Guttmacher.

"In the United States, my clients made their money in fuel delivery and concrete plants, but they're not limiting themselves to these areas. They might consider other profitable ventures, as long as the investments are safe and discreet. The initial investment is approximately thirty-five to forty million dollars, but if your bank turns out to be what they're looking for, that amount could grow substantially." I paused, drawing out the silence.

"Let me put it this way," I continued, reasserting a modest pose. "Although my clients assure me that their money is legal, there could be some tax problems in the U.S. and, therefore, they must insist on complete confidentiality."

I hoped I wasn't laying it on too heavily, watching Guttmacher trying to control his excitement. But his body language said it all. He worked very hard at controlling his fidgets; he coughed and swallowed a bit nervously and moved to the edge of his chair. I had expected Guttmacher to sit impassively, to not betray any expression. But he didn't. Apparently his greed had overcome his caution.

"I need to know more about your clients," he said. "We have established procedures that require we understand our clients' specific needs."

"I can't reveal their identity yet; I need to get their permission first. Once you provide me with a plan, I'm sure there will be no problem in identifying the clients."

"And what would be your role?" he asked.

I had a sense of cat and mouse here. But which one of us was the cat and which one was the mouse?

"Liaison," I said curtly.

My earlier fears that Guttmacher would grill me or throw me out suspecting I was there to trap him were exaggerated. He was still guarded but visibly eager to move ahead. Finally, he managed to say, "I'll be happy to assist your clients. Our bank has a long tradition of strict confidentiality, rivaling that of Switzerland."

He'd definitely gotten the message.

"How do you rival the Swiss banks, which are known to be the most discreet in the industry?" I asked, pushing him a bit more.

"It's not just the banks," he explained, "it's also the governments. You see, the U.S. has a treaty with the Swiss government that forces them to disclose certain things to the U.S. government agencies. Details about financial activities of suspected criminals, such as money launderers and drug lords. So the Swiss government is actually acting as an arm of the

FBI whenever there is such suspicion. The U.S. government forces the banks, through the Swiss officials and the Swiss court system, to disclose information, which the banks then give the Americans." He smiled genially. "In Germany, the situation is different. Our courts are much more protective of the privacy rights of our clients and the stability of our business relationship. Therefore, such things don't happen here."

I listened attentively to his speech. Of course I knew what he was saying; I had been involved in numerous cases in which the Swiss government was helpful. I also noticed that Guttmacher had conveniently forgotten to mention that, under the centuries-old international custom called letters rogatory, as well as through MLAT, a bilateral treaty between governments for mutual legal assistance, the United States and Germany could request and obtain much the same sort of banking information from one another for use in criminal investigations and prosecutions. But the subtext of the conversation showed me that Guttmacher fully understood that the money involved was the fruit of criminal activity. This was a good sign for my evaluation of his corruptibility. If DeLouise had used Guttmacher, he had probably conducted a similar assessment.

"While communicating with a potential source, and during the development process of your relationship," Alex had told us, "you may wish to make your party feel that he's being let in on a secret. That attitude bolsters the trust between the two of you and gives your party a sense of pride. Obviously, you never disclose a real secret." We all nodded. "Simply invent something that may sound plausible to your party, act as if you're confiding in him. Ask him to keep it a secret. Here, we build a good cover story or a plausible excuse in six months of training and endless exercises. Just keep in mind — if your cover is blown, you're next."

"You see," Guttmacher continued in his flowing lecture, "Germany does not have a law against money laundering and, therefore, what is not illegal here cannot become illegal just because the Americans want us to think it is. The war is over, you know," he ended with a grin, again exposing his gold tooth. Guttmacher struck me as a person who lays his cards on the table but has at least another full deck up his sleeve.

"No money-laundering law?" I repeated.

"No," he said with satisfaction.

There was truth to what he said, and that was promising because he showed me his dishonesty: a required trait if you want to be considered as a banker for stolen money. I knew that Germany was dragging its feet in passing a law intended to fight multinational crime. A draft of the law was being discussed in the German Bundestag but hadn't yet passed. I remembered having read the draft proposal before leaving the States.

The guy knew what he was talking about, I thought, giving Guttmacher an appreciative look. He must have been deeply involved in shady transactions if he knew the ropes so well. I didn't mention that I knew that Switzerland had just passed money-laundering laws, albeit limited in scope, thus both bowing to and resisting pressure from the United States.

"How do you want to proceed?" I asked Guttmacher, showing him I was satisfied with his answers.

"Where is the money now?" he asked directly. The man had all the sweetness of a funeral director.

"It's available immediately, if I see the right investment," I answered, avoiding his unexpectedly direct question.

He smiled. "Fine. I'll prepare a plan for you. Where would you like it delivered?"

"To my New York office," I answered. "You have my card."

We shook hands, and he escorted me to the door.

I decided to walk back to my hotel. I had to see if there was an indication on my guest registration that I was with the U.S. government and either remove it or check out. I strolled a few blocks in the chilly air and found myself in Marienplatz, the center of life in Munich. I looked in my guidebook. I could do this. I could be a tourist for a moment, at least until I could fully absorb the meaning of my meeting with Guttmacher.

Marienplatz, the guidebook said, was named after the three-hundred-foot gilt statue of the Virgin Mary that stands in the middle of the square. At the north side of the square is the Neues Rathaus. Built at the end of the nineteenth century, it is best known for its glockenspiel. Once a day, its army of enameled copper figures performs the Scheffeltanz, followed by a reenactment of an event that celebrated royal weddings in the fifteenth century. At the end of each session, a mechanical rooster crows.

Legend has it that, after World War II, an American GI concerned by the deteriorating condition of the figures "borrowed" some paint from his unit's storage area and gave it to the building's caretakers. As a show of their appreciation, the caretakers allowed him to ride one of the horses in the jousting scene, earning cheers from the people gathered in the square.

After taking in the sights for a bit, I stopped into a café for a cup of tea. I sat looking through the window at the buildings and at the people going by, but not really taking anything in. I decided to walk back to my hotel, preoccupied with Herr Hans Guttmacher. He'd obviously snapped at my bait. He'd proven easy to draw in to corrupt dealings, and that could have been a good reason for DeLouise to hire him. I was anxious to learn, though, whether DeLouise had used Guttmacher. If he had, would he have been Peled or DeLouise?

At the hotel I found a message from Lan waiting for me at the front desk. "I have the numbers you requested. How do you want them forwarded?" it read.

I stuffed the note in my shirt pocket and headed up to my room. Lan was always prompt, discreet, and intelligent. She could sense what I meant even if I gave her a seemingly indecipherable hint. I knew very little about her personal life. She was half-Chinese and half-Vietnamese. She'd worked at the U.S. Embassy in Saigon until the last days in 1975 but had stayed behind when the embassy's diplomatic staff left. After things calmed down, however, she was granted a U.S. visa as a token of appreciation. She came to the States and married a Vietnamese journalist in D.C. Her husband died several years later, when she was in her midforties. She'd never remarried.

I called Lan and asked her to forward the data through the secure connection to the legat at the American Consulate General in Munich. I was always amused at the double-talk in the U.S. Foreign Service: legat, short for legal attaché, isn't always a lawyer but is always an FBI special agent. In the intelligence community, use of these titles is termed light cover;

deep cover is reserved for positions outside the embassy or consulate, such as in trade companies or in other businesses in which international travel and contacts would seem normal. CIA jargon for the position is NOC, nonofficial cover. The Soviets used to call their deep cover agents illegal, because they didn't work out of the embassy or in a company connected with their country.

As usual, I had planted a decoy magazine and a telltale hair when I'd left my room and, when I walked into the room, I went directly to the safe to check on them. The hair was still in place. I took a bottle of good German beer from the minibar and watched TV until I fell asleep out of sheer boredom.

The following morning I drove to the consulate's compound at Königinstrasse and went to see Helga, the legat's secretary. She looked particularly lovely. "This came for you this morning with the diplomatic pouch," she said with a smile, handing me an envelope.

She led me to a small conference room, where I read the memo from Lan.

> October 6, 1990
> To: Dan Gordon
> From: Lan A. Tien
> I've attached the telephone numbers you forwarded with the names and addresses of the subscribers. There are ten numbers that we could not identify, even after running the numbers on the investigative telephone database as well as the reverse listing. Please let me know what else you need.
>
> Lan

I looked at the list. There were calls to three Japanese restaurants, two jewelry stores, several calls to what appeared to be private residences in Munich, and six calls to Bankhaus Bäcker & Haas, the bank of my new pal Guttmacher. I compared the numbers on the log with the number on the business card Guttmacher had given me. Different. I picked up the telephone and called the number on the log.

"Guttmacher," replied a voice at the other end. I hung up. So he'd given DeLouise his direct line. But he hadn't given it to me. I guessed DeLouise was a bigger fish for him. With six calls to Guttmacher identified, the likelihood that DeLouise had more than one contact with the banker had been upgraded from a suspicion to an assumption, but not a fact.

A separate page showed fifteen international calls made from DeLouise's hotel room: three calls to Switzerland; two to Luxembourg; seven to the United States, all to California; one to Italy; and two to Israel.

Israel again! The lines next to the two numbers in Israel were empty. "Unknown subscriber" was written in the comments box.

I looked at the numbers. There were two calls to the same number. I didn't need to look twice to realize it was a very familiar number: the Mossad's clandestine headquarters on King Shaul Boulevard in northern Tel Aviv, across from Israel's Pentagon.

"What the hell!" I thought excitedly, but then I slowed down. Why would DeLouise call the Mossad thirty-three years after he had left it? For that matter, had he really left it? Had he forgotten the elementary rules of security, which forbid making a traceable phone call from a hotel room?

I grabbed my notes and put the list back into the envelope. I stuffed it all into the inner pocket of my blazer and went back to Helga's workstation. She was out, but Ron Lovejoy was sitting at his desk with his office door open.

"Good afternoon, Ron," I said, from the doorway, "Can you spare me a minute?"

"Sure," he said, "come right in."

I sat in a chair across the desk from him. Lovejoy was a well-built, clean-shaven man in his late forties with gray hair and rimless reading glasses. He must have been a jogger or maybe spent a lot of time at a health club. The thought made me feel rather guilty. When I'd joined the Israeli army, I had barely 175 pounds on my 6'4" frame. And now? Well, never mind. I knew I had to do something about it and kept promising myself to change things. But somehow, between cases and trips, I never really got around to it. If I were three inches taller, my weight would be OK. I'm not overweight, I told my friends who'd criticized my few extra pounds, I'm just short.

"Well, the clues I dug up in Israel led me here, and I'm hoping I'll find an ex-wife and the daughter, Mina Bernstein and Ariel Peled."

"So you haven't found DeLouise yet."

"Yes, I did. He's dead." I realized I had not yet shared this information with Lovejoy. He'd left his office before I'd called David Stone in Washington with the news.

He didn't react when I told him about my visit to the morgue. Sitting behind that consulate desk didn't expose him to those kinds of stories; it was probably his field service in the FBI that made morgue visits sound routine.

"How long would it take to get a copy of the German police report?" I asked.

"Well, it depends. Usually they don't share their investigations with us unless they need our help. When that happens, we insist on getting all the details before we send Washington a request for FBI assistance."

"Is there a better way?" I asked.

"Frankly, though it sounds convoluted, the easiest and fastest way to get that report is for an FBI agent working the bank investigation in the States to send a message through INTERPOL mentioning the U.S. criminal investigation of DeLouise and asking urgently for a copy. Make sure he asks for a faxed copy of the complete report in German — ask INTERPOL specifically not to translate it. If the Germans and INTERPOL are willing, that will speed things up. The Bureau can get it translated once it arrives."

"I think my retirement could come up before we see this report travel through channels. Have they asked for your assistance?"

"No," he said, "at least not yet. I didn't even know he'd died until you told me. But give them time; they work slowly but meticulously. But at least, if they send a request to the U.S. through INTERPOL, they usually come and ask me to have the Bureau get them the same thing. I'm sure they'd like to have his criminal record, if there is one. Plus a background check to discover potential enemies. All that takes time."

"That's exactly why I'm trying to work concurrent to the criminal investigation," I said. "If the German police insist upon completing their criminal probe before telling you anything, my own chances of making progress here are slim. His assets won't wait for the Germans to finish what they're doing. Assets of the dead have a tendency to dissipate and disappear quickly. And the assets of someone who might have been killed because of them vanish even faster."

Lovejoy looked at me. "Homicide investigations take precedence over civil matters. You know that."

I knew that, but the criminal investigation was German while the civil asset chase was American. However, I wasn't about to argue with him or wait for things to run their course. Under the rules, the legat is the representative of the U.S. Department of Justice in the country, and even if not an attorney, he or she outranks DOJ lawyers temporarily in country. So, in fact, Lovejoy was my superior in Munich. I had a feeling that unless I moved fast, the assets would. But give a little to get more. I had to share more information on DeLouise with Lovejoy.

"There is a slight twist to this story. The person in the morgue is Raymond DeLouise, a U.S. citizen, but he was registered at the hotel, and probably elsewhere in Germany, as Dov Peled, an Israeli citizen."

"And why is that?"

"Dov Peled is the legal name he had while living in Israel in the 1950s. Shortly before his assassination, he was hiding in Europe from disgruntled minority shareholders of his bank and from U.S. law-enforcement agencies, hoping that his resurrected name would shield him."

"Apparently, it hasn't," said Lovejoy sarcastically.

"I guess not," I agreed. "We have to let the German police know about his double identity if we want their assistance. Otherwise, why would the American Consulate become interested in the murder of an Israeli citizen with no apparent ties to the United States?"

"Are you sure Peled is DeLouise and vice versa?" asked the legat.

"As sure as I can be from comparing the face in the morgue to the passport photo the Justice Department gave me."

"OK, I guess I can call my contacts at the police. I'll simply tell them that Peled was a U.S. citizen who also legally used the name DeLouise, and that he was a fugitive from U.S. justice, so we'd appreciate details of their investigation."

I nodded. "Can you do that now? I need to see what they have so far. Maybe they won't be so formal."

"I can try," said Lovejoy, "but don't hold your breath. These guys go by the rules."

"Could you also ask them about Mina and Ariel? I'd like to know whether their names appear on a missing persons report."

"That's easy," said Lovejoy. "I'll call you when I have something."

"Thanks," I said. "I'm going to head back to my hotel now."

I picked up a message from the reception desk and went to my room. I reached into my pocket for the room key and out came the car keys as well. I had forgotten about the rented BMW, still parked outside the consulate. I was getting absentminded, this time not true to my Mossad training.

I opened the message envelope and read: "Ron called and asked that you return to his office immediately. He has important information."

I went straight back in a cab. An opportunity to retrieve the forgotten BMW had just been handed to me.

Back at the consulate, I went quickly through security checks and up to Lovejoy's office. He was on the phone. He looked up and waved an invitation to sit down.

A minute later he hung up and smiled at me. "Welcome back. It's been a while, hasn't it? Anyway, I've got some news. A bit too special for a phone conversation. And not about DeLouise. I told the Germans about our man's multiple identities and asked for their help. I still don't have an answer on that, but not too long after they called and told me something that may be helpful to you.

"Apparently, Ariel Peled appeared at the police station downtown here in Munich to complain that two men were following her. When the policeman, a Sergeant Baumann, went outside to see them, as she insisted, he couldn't find anyone. So he brushed her off. Later that day, the owner of a motorcycle garage complained that two men attempted to steal a motorcycle parked outside his garage. When he noticed them through his window he went after them, and they escaped on a different motorcycle — apparently the one they came on. Sergeant Baumann described them as young, in their early thirties, with darkish skin, black hair, and medium builds. Could be Hispanic, Turkish, or from the Middle East. The garage owner got their motorcycle's plate number."

"And?" I asked anxiously.

"It had been reported stolen the day before. The description of these guys matched the description Ariel gave of the men who followed her."

"Did she leave her address with the policemen?"

"No. As I said, he thought she was imagining things, so he didn't write a report or anything. But he remembered her name and that she spoke English with an accent, and that she looked shaken up."

"And he let her go?!" I asked in disbelief.

"Yes, I guess so. He didn't have any reason to question her or anything."

"Did she say anything else?" I pressed.

"I don't know. Why don't you go there and ask him? No investigation is pending, so he might cooperate. Tell him you're a boyfriend or something."

"Thanks Ron," I said. "Surely worth a special trip from the hotel. Now I'll need a secure phone for a couple of minutes. Can you provide?"

"No problem," Lovejoy replied, and promptly showed me into an adjoining office.

"It's all yours. We're here to help."

I had no trouble reaching Benny in Tel Aviv. "I'm in Munich. I found our guy, mostly thanks to you."

"What do you mean?"

"He registered at the hotel under his Israeli name, that's why we couldn't find him earlier. And it was you who gave me his previous identity."

"Don't mention it. Is he still in Munich?"

"Yes, in the morgue. He was assassinated in the street before I came."

There was a pause, then Benny responded. "Well, that I didn't expect." His reaction didn't sound convincing. He continued, "Any information coming in on who might have pulled this off?"

"No, the German police are working on it now. By the way, since he was registered here as an Israeli citizen, I'm sure the German police notified the Israeli Consulate. So maybe the foreign ministry would have more details than I do at the moment."

"Thanks for telling me," said Benny.

"I'll keep in touch," I said, and hung up. Was I the last to know? Something was happening, but I was out of the loop.

I left Ron's office and drove to the police station.

It smelled of cigarette smoke and muddy water. A man with a glazed look was mopping the floor. He looked like a prisoner serving his term. I went to the desk and asked for Sergeant Baumann. I was directed to an office in the back. Sergeant Baumann was a very short and portly policeman in his early fifties. He looked like a man who'd seen and heard it all.

"Sergeant Baumann?"

"Ja," he said, looking up. When he realized I was an American, he added, "I don't speak English too well."

"My friends at the American Consulate told me that you saw my fiancé, Ariel Peled."

He gave me a puzzled look, and I continued. "She's from Israel? She came to complain about two guys following her?" I hoped it would ring a bell in his shrinking brain.

He paused for a second. *"Ja, Ja,* I remember now, nice girl from Israel," he said, scratching his head.

I tried to speak slowly. "You see, I came from the United States to meet her, but she didn't show up for our meeting, and now I don't know where to look. Did she tell you where she stayed?"

"There are too many questions about this woman," he said, as if he knew more.

"What do you mean?"

"Well, first, this morning. Two other persons with a funny accent (he said "ak-tsent") came asking about her. Now you. Tell me, how many fiancés she had?" he asked sarcastically. He hadn't believed a word I'd told him.

I wanted to punch him, but I reminded myself that I wasn't Ariel's fiancé after all, so as a substitute display of hurt emotions, I gave him a look to show how vexed I was by his sarcasm. He didn't seem to care.

"Did she say where she was staying?"

"No."

"Did you notice any more details about her?"

"No," he said. "She told me that she left Mielke Bank on the next street and saw two guys. At first she thought they were trying to," he paused, searching for the right word, "you know, to meet her. But then when they did not come closer and just followed her, she was afraid that they were trying to rob her. So she stopped and asked a person in the street where the police station was, and she came right over. We are just around the corner."

I tried to remain calm. "Mielke Bank," I repeated. "Where is it?"

"On Marsstrasse," he answered, "It's just around the corner. I walked with her outside. I couldn't see them and told her that she should go home and if she is still followed, then she could call the police again."

"Did you ask her name?"

"Yes, she told me at the beginning that her name was Ariel Peled and that she was a tourist from Israel. She thanked me and left. She was dressed in a black pants suit with a white shirt. That's all I remember. Later on during the daily activity review session in our station, I heard that two men tried to steal a BMW motor-tsykel." I nodded. He continued, "I told my officer that the description I heard from the woman was similar to the description of those men who tried to steal the motor-tsykel."

I left the station. Police sergeants are all the same, no matter what language they speak. But it was another break for me. I placed another call to Israel, this time to my private-investigator buddy Ralph Lampert.

"I need something unusual," I said.

"Go ahead. I'm an adult, you can ask me anything."

"Good," I said, "I need an official-looking power of attorney, signed by Ariel Peled, giving me general banking powers on her behalf. See that it carries the authentication of the German Embassy in Tel Aviv."

"Do you want it real or funny?"

"I just need it, as soon as possible, but it must be dated before September 24, 1990. Make sure the date won't be on a Saturday, Sunday, or during Jewish or German holidays — the embassy is closed then. You can obtain a sample of Ariel's signature from her ID card file at the Ministry of the Interior."

"Then it must be a custom-made repro," he said. "Do you want me to use Tibor?"

Now that was a name I hadn't heard in a long time. Tibor was a document artist at the Mossad. A Holocaust refugee from Hungary, he'd escaped to Israel, where the Mossad soon spotted his talents. Tibor could fake any document with such perfection that even the original creator would not be able to tell the difference. "Official" documents were his specialty.

"Is he still alive? Last I saw him he was about to retire, and that was ten years ago."

"Alive and kicking. He looks his age, but his hands are steady as ever."

"Good, I'll call you tomorrow. Just push it."

On my way back to the hotel I passed the Mielke Bank. It looked like any other. I decided not to tell David about the homemade power of attorney; sometimes "need to know" includes keeping even your own boss in the dark.

I entered the hotel restaurant and ordered the biggest veal schnitzel they had. A schnitzel as big as a carpet came with potatoes and cabbage. It set me up for a good night's sleep.

Early morning on the following day I called Ralph. "Well?" I asked.

"It's ready. The old man worked on it last night; it's just one page. Where do you want it delivered?"

"Send it by DHL to my hotel, but do not indicate your name or return address on the envelope. Pay them in cash."

The envelope came in the next day. It was too early to go to the bank, so I drove the streets of Munich trying to reconstruct DeLouise's movements and what had happened to him. I went to the street corner where he'd been shot. A professional job. The hitman had selected a congested area where an experienced motorcyclist would have no problem disappearing while any police cars in pursuit would be caught in the traffic.

That was clever. On the other hand, I was reluctant to give him that much credit. After all, he had shot DeLouise only once and my training had emphasized that to be absolutely certain that your victim is dead, more than one shot is needed, especially if you retreat immediately and cannot return to complete the job. "Death verification" was the chilling term. He hadn't done that, so I downgraded him to semiprofessional.

It was time to go to Mielke Bank. I went through revolving doors and asked to see the assistant manager. A heavy woman with eyeglasses on a chain over her ample bosom approached me. "I'm the assistant manager," she said sternly, "yes?"

I showed her my power of attorney.

"I'm attorney Dan Gordon," I said. "I have a power of attorney signed by your client Ms. Ariel Peled. I need to get copies of her records."

The assistant manager looked at the power of attorney I gave her and snapped, "Please wait." She walked away, the paper in her hand. She seemed so regimented that I was sure that when she walked into a room, mice would jump on chairs. She returned ten or fifteen minutes later.

"Problem. Miss Peled has only a safe-deposit box at the bank but no account."

"Good," I said, ignoring the negative beginning of her statement.

"But under the bank's policy, we need a special power of attorney. That's a form our bank issues. We can't accept this document," she ended, returning the power of attorney I had given her.

I couldn't believe my luck, even if it outwardly looked like a rejection.

"At this time I don't need to open the safe-deposit box," I said. "She moves between Israel and Germany, but all I have is her Israeli address. So let me see what local address she gave you. I'll leave a message for her to come in and sign the bank's form. I am an attorney working for her in an estate matter. As you can see, she signed this document before the German Consul in Tel Aviv and I don't know if she's still in Israel or here. I must return soon to the United States. It was entirely my mistake not knowing your procedures. I'm sure that the power of attorney I have is enough to see what local address she gave you."

"Wait," she ordered, looking annoyed, and walked back into her office.

I had aimed low when I'd asked for the address, but for my current purpose, that's what I needed to help me trace Ariel.

The assistant manager came out a few minutes later.

"The manager allowed me to give you the details you wanted, but you cannot see the actual signature card or open the safe."

"That's fine," I said, thinking it was better than nothing, particularly when it was just what I wanted at the moment.

She pulled out a white sheet of paper and read it to me.

"Ariel Peled rented a safe-deposit box at our branch on September 27, box number 114, and has not opened it since. On her signature card she gave her address in Haifa, Israel. Do you have it?"

Was she testing how much I knew?

"I have the one on Allenby Street," I said. "Which one do you have?"

"11–36 Weitzman Street, Haifa."

"Yeah, that's her new address," I said knowingly. "Allenby is her mother's address. Did she give you an address in Munich?"

"No. But she wanted her mother to be a signatory also."

"Yes, I know that." I quickly added, "Has Mrs. Bernstein been in yet?"

"No," she said. "Miss Peled told us that her mother would come at a later time to sign the card."

"Was there anything else?" I asked.

"No. That's it."

I thanked her and left the bank. This was at least solid proof that Ariel had set foot in Munich.

So what did I know so far? Ariel had come to Munich and had rented a safe-deposit box to be jointly owned with her mother. Her father was murdered here. I didn't need to be a rocket scientist to see that there might be a connection. But that was only a possibility, not a fact.

During our training at the Mossad, we were taught the art of report writing. NAKA was the acronym in Hebrew for uniform writing procedure. "You must always bear in mind that the reader of your report has only the paper before him. He doesn't know you and cannot and should not read between the lines. So when you mean to report about seeing a bird, and another combatant at the other side of the world wants to report seeing the same type of bird, both of you should use the same word bird and not one use bird and the other use fowl. The analyst reading your report would be confused: are both reports describing the same bird? Next, establish the level of security of the document. 'Top secret' is applied to information which, if disclosed, could be expected to cause exceptionally grave damage to national security. 'Secret' is information which, if disclosed, could be expected to cause serious damage to national security. 'Confidential' is applied to information which, if disclosed, could be expected to cause damage to national security.

"Now, how do you define national security and the level of damage it could suffer without irreparable harm?" We had spent two weeks on that. The list of topics that had to be classified included military plans, weapons systems, or operations; foreign-government information; intelligence activities (including special activities); intelligence sources or methods; cryptology; foreign relations or foreign activities of the country, including confidential sources; Jewish emigration from economically or politically distressed countries; scientific (including nuclear), technological, or economic matters relating to national security; programs for safeguarding nuclear materials or facilities; and vulnerabilities or capabilities of system installations, projects, or plans relating to national security.

In Alex's words: "Once you've done that, select the degree of reliability of the information it contains. Remember, it is not your reliability that is being reviewed but that of the information you are providing. So don't beautify the facts. If you do that, then your credibility would really be put into question. If the information is obtained from a single source, tell that to the reader, on the top of your report in bold type. The source may be your own mother, but mothers can be wrong too, you know. And finally, always distinguish between an assumption, a lead, a suspicion, an opinion, and a fact. A fact gets the highest degree of certainty, so the word is to be used only if the data provided is worthy of that definition. Preferably it would be based upon all-source intelligence; that is, information accumulated from various available sources."

Accordingly, all I could conclude was that Ariel Peled had rented a safe-deposit box. That was a single source fact. Still, somebody posing as

Ariel could also have done the same. That she put something she felt needed protection in the box was an assumption, not a fact, because the box could still be empty. But if it was Ariel who rented the box and put something in the box, I figured it was connected to her father. That was definitely a suspicion.

Back at the hotel, I went through my papers again. I looked at the identified phone numbers Lan had sent me and compared them with Peled's hotel bill. I examined the line on the bill where the charge was made for the two calls to the Mossad headquarters in Israel. The first call was made on September 22 and lasted twenty-nine minutes; the second call was made on September 24 and lasted thirty-six minutes. Since the calls came into the Mossad's general switchboard, I couldn't tell to whom DeLouise had directed his calls or whether both calls were made to the same person. I looked at the other numbers. The California numbers were easy — two calls to his wife, three calls to his son, and two calls to his attorneys. The three Swiss numbers were made to the Credit Suisse private banking branch in Geneva.

He's no different from the others, I muttered to myself, half in contempt. People who take off with large sums of money are typically repetitive in their conduct, and therefore their actions are fairly predictable. The calls to the private banking branch of Credit Suisse indicated that DeLouise was very likely to have had some banking relationship with them. But it was too premature to take any vigorous legal action to find out. I didn't know for sure that he was the bank's client. I also didn't know what name or legal entity he used. If the U.S. government filed papers with Swiss officials attempting to force Credit Suisse to disclose all records pertaining to Raymond DeLouise, the Department of Justice would have to wait six months until the bank responded. Only then would one discover that a target might have used a different name or a company or a trust to hide his assets or might have cleaned out the account and hidden the booty elsewhere. We would have lost not only important time but also the element of surprise. I'd seen cases where unscrupulous bankers tipped their clients off about the U.S. request for bank records or a law-enforcement inquiry, thus enabling them to move their money to a different location.

The Italian call was made to a company in Rome called Broncotrade SPA. I wrote a note to check that one out. The calls to Luxembourg were to Bank Hapoalim, a branch of Israel's largest bank. Then came the local calls. First on the list was a Herbert Oplatka. I dialed the number.

"Oplatka Travel," said a young woman, "How may I help you?"

"I was left a message to call you."

"And you are?"

"My name is Peter Wooten and I'm a partner of Mr. Raymond DeLouise. I don't know whether your message was meant for me or for him, because it was left on our voice mail."

"Let me check," she said, and put me on hold.

"Nobody here left any message for you or Mr. DeLouise, but it could be someone from the morning shift who called you," she informed me a moment later.

"Would you please check your computer and see if Mr. DeLouise's reservations are confirmed?"

It was the longest shot in the dark I'd fired in a long time.

"Yes," she replied after a few seconds.

Bingo! A hit.

She continued. "I see now. His flight tomorrow on Lufthansa from Munich through Frankfurt to Moscow is confirmed. I also see that he hasn't picked up his tickets yet, so that could be the reason for the message. Please ask him to pick them up, or maybe you want us to deliver them to his hotel?"

"I'll ask him to get back to you. Thanks."

This was my lucky day. I went back to the list and picked up the next number, a Sonja and Ernest Bart. I called the number; an elderly man answered.

"Pension Bart."

"I'm sorry, please say that again," I asked.

"Pension Bart," he repeated.

"Ah yes, thanks," I said, recognizing the word finally. "May I have your address?"

He gave it to me and I went down to my car and got underway.

I was getting excited now that I was at long last warm, if not hot, on the trail. The pension was in a residential area, surrounded by evergreen trees and apartment buildings with small balconies. Flowers grew in pots on many of the balconies. Everything looked neat and clean.

IV

I walked inside and approached the desk in the hall just beyond the door. Behind it stood an elderly man with white hair and a small mustache. A fireplace crackled across the hall, filling the air with the pleasant smell of burning hardwood. From the kitchen behind the counter floated the smell of home cooking. The ambience was cozy.

I tried to think of the best opening line, but what did I want to know? DeLouise wasn't staying here, he only called. But whom did he call? This guy wasn't about to show me his guest list.

Without thinking it through I took a flyer and asked directly, "Is Mina Bernstein here? My friend from Israel."

"Israel? Oh, yes, we have Mrs. Mina Bernstein here, and she is from Israel."

"Exactly," I said in huge relief, this time genuine. My gamble had paid off. "Is she in?"

"I think so, let me call her room," and he went to the telephone. He returned a moment later and said, "She'll be right down."

I moved to the small lobby, enjoyed the fireplace, and waited. A woman of medium height came in — blue eyes and gray streaks in her hair, dressed in a wide flowery skirt and a white blouse.

I got up. "Shalom, I'm Dan Gordon," I greeted her in Hebrew.

"And I am Mina Bernstein," said the woman in a subdued voice. "You are looking for me?" she continued in our shared native language.

"Yes, I need to talk to you about a family matter."

"A family matter? Do you have news about my Ariel?" she asked with a mix of apprehension and hope.

A small sitting room adjoined the lobby. I motioned her along, delaying my answer to her question.

As we sat down Mina looked at me with soft, deep blue eyes. I could tell she'd once been a beautiful woman.

"The reason I am looking for you is that I believe you, and possibly Ariel, could be in danger."

"Who are you?" she asked in a frightened voice.

"All I can say now is that we share a common background, and I want to help you."

"Are you from the — Office?"

I nodded. Misleading her was enough; I didn't want to tell her lies more than was absolutely necessary. Yes, I was with the Office, but not the one she assumed. "Office" was the code word used among Mossad employees to describe their workplace. You'd never hear the name *Mossad* from a true Mossad person. I was dragged into a typical false-flagging scenario now — hiding my true employer — without the ordinary preplanning, without the time to develop a good cover story. The fact was that many successful Mossad recruitment operations of Arab informers were made possible only because the informer, "a source," was convinced the recruiter was working for NATO or for some European country and not for Israel.

"Tell me, why did you come to Munich?" I asked.

"Ariel called," she answered.

"What did she tell you?"

"I must say it was a bizarre conversation. She said I must come to Munich immediately, and that I should not tell anyone."

"Did she give you any reason?"

"She hinted that it had something to do with her father's past, so I must keep it a secret. Ariel said I should stay at this pension. She didn't answer my questions and only asked that I come as quickly as possible. But when I arrived, she wasn't here, although her luggage was in her room."

So we had a missing persons case in addition to the homicide. If the events thus far could have been described as questionable, they had now been upgraded to strange.

I asked Mina if she was aware of any previous irregular behavior of Ariel's that could explain her disappearance.

"No," she replied, "she has never given me any cause for concern. Ariel always used good judgment. She's not the kind of person to disappear all of a sudden for no reason."

"Has Ariel been in contact with her father lately?"

"I don't know for sure. She used to call him now and then, and he also called her at least once every month or so and sent her money. I don't know about recent calls. She's a grown woman and leads her own life. But then, there were hints in our last telephone conversation that she's here in connection with her father. So I don't know what to think."

"Did you call the police?"

"I intended to do that today, unless I hear from Ariel. I was also thinking about calling Dov, but I have no idea where to find him. He moves between California, Europe, and Japan. Does he know that Ariel is missing? We should notify him."

So Mina didn't know that her former husband had been murdered. I suspected that the sad chore would fall to me.

"Mina," I said, "it's a very complex matter and I don't want to burden you with the details, not just now anyway, but we must find Ariel. You'll also have to tell me about Dov's work in the past; I think Ariel's disappearance has something to do with that."

"I thought you know about his past work," she said.

"Yes, I do, of course. But I need you to tell me exactly what he told you about his work, the kind of things that are not reflected in his file, particularly if you know whether he attempted contacts with the Office recently."

I had almost slipped. I needed to know if there was a continued connection with the Mossad, as Dov's two phone calls to their Tel Aviv headquarters indicated. For a split second I even considered the theory that DeLouise had kept his Mossad contacts. Then was the disappearance of the ninety million dollars also connected to the Mossad? Was it their way of financing a slush fund? If my suspicions could be verified then it might have a surprising effect on my asset chase, not to mention Israeli–American relationships. I quickly brushed it off as complete insanity. But still.

I had said "Office" in a lower voice. Use of the epithet was meant to instill further confidence in my relationship with Mina. She could fill in the blanks.

"Why do you need to know? Couldn't you find out about this in his file? You could also call him."

I had to tell her now. Perhaps it was better to do so even without preparation. Bluntly.

"Dov was murdered a week or so ago," I said quietly, "and Ariel's disappearance might be connected to that. So everything concerning Dov's background is now important. You may know things the file is lacking."

There was a long pause. Mina was clearly stunned. And just as clearly working to keep her emotions under control. "Murdered! Why? How?"

"The why I don't know yet. It happened here in Munich; someone shot him. It looks like it was deliberate, more like an assassination. The German police are looking for suspects and motives. So now you can understand why I said that you and Ariel could also be in danger. I didn't realize that you weren't aware of Dov's murder. So until the killer is caught, you must exercise caution."

Mina looked away for a moment but I saw the tears begin to slide down her cheeks.

"I'm sorry," I said. "I had no idea I was going to be the first to tell you."

"There was no one else to tell me," she whispered. "As I said, I haven't seen Ariel and no one else here knows that I was married to Dov."

Although I was hungry for information, I could see that Mina Bernstein needed a moment to compose herself. I stepped across the hall and asked the old gent if he could find us coffee and tea for two. He turned, walked toward the back of the house, and in a minute, to my surprise, he presented me with a tray, cups, a pot of coffee, a pot of tea, sugar, and cream. I carried the tray back to the sitting room.

Mrs. Bernstein reached gratefully for the coffee cup, and I got back on track.

"Let's talk about your marriage to Dov," I suggested softly, trying to be compassionate. I had a job to do, and expressions of human empathy would serve that purpose. But I have been trained to focus on my goal. "You must always be target oriented," said Alex, my instructor. "Be a nice guy after hours, but when you do your job you do your job, and if being nice advances your position, then be a nice guy. But only to the extent needed at that time."

Mina wiped her eyes, took a sip from her cup, and took a deep breath. "I married Dov in 1955, when he was already in the Mossad. He used to work very long hours and I barely saw him. We tried to have children, but I had problems. Dov only told me that his work involved collecting scientific material. He loved science, especially physics. Then one day he told me that he was being sent to France to work on a project that would take a long time. He said I couldn't come with him because that was the requirement of the Office, but he would come for visits. I guess they sent him to France because he spoke French fluently. In Romania, it was almost a second language for him. His mother was a French teacher and she frequently spoke the language with her son."

While Mina drank her coffee, I asked, "Do you know where he worked?"

"Yes, in the French Atomic Energy Commission installation in Saclay, near Paris."

"Did he tell you what he was doing there?"

"Not much. He said he became a paper pusher. He worked in the procurement department where they were buying their materials and supplies. He used to return to Israel every two months, sometimes just for the weekend and sometimes for a whole week. We never had time to be a real family. During his visits I noticed how nervous he had become. Dov had started smoking. We had arguments. He refused to talk about his work. I was not allowed to call him. I didn't even have his number. His salary went directly to my bank account and every month someone from the Office came to see how I was doing. Sometimes they would bring me letters from Dov, and once or twice a small present. At the beginning I thought that the Office sent Dov to work with the French government or something. He told me that several Israeli scientists were working there for the French government in planning the first French reactor. I don't know if you could remember because you look too young, but the relationship between Israel and France began to warm up during that period.

So it seemed natural to me. I discovered later that he never spoke Hebrew with any of the Israelis and nobody even knew he was an Israeli. I don't even know under what name or nationality he worked in France. Even when he flew to Israel, he never arrived from France; it was always through a third country."

"How do you know that?"

"I saw once or twice his airline tickets. He'd also buy me presents in duty-free stores in various European countries on his route to Israel."

I tucked that away in my mind. Was it possible that Popescu/DeLouise/Peled had a fourth identity supplied by the Mossad?

Mina sighed. "Then my world collapsed. During one of his longer visits to Israel we had a fight. I think I was already pregnant with Ariel but didn't even know it. I felt lonely. I needed him, and I wanted to have his attention. Dov exploded. He said that I should stop whining because he was under great pressure." She looked at me sadly. "I still remember his words: 'If they catch me I'll end up under the guillotine!' 'They?' I had asked him, horrified, 'Who are they?' 'The French government,' he answered. 'What do you think they do to people spying on their nuclear shopping lists?'"

Mina paused and looked at my face, expecting my reaction. I sat motionless; I couldn't appear to be surprised. I searched for words to show that I understood her feelings, but I didn't want to interrupt her.

Mina soon continued. "I cried nonstop for two days, until he left. I didn't know. I simply didn't know. I thought he was working with the French, not stealing from them. Dov called a few days later telling me he wanted a divorce. He said he was going to change his life completely, and that included being free from his marriage too. I didn't tell him that I had just found out that I was pregnant. I was in a cloud, in a bubble. I lost contact with reality. I didn't know what was going on with me. The people from the Office made the arrangements. Dov delivered me a Jewish divorce through the Mossad's chaplain and it was over. Dov returned to Israel for a week or so, but the tension between us was so strong that I couldn't tell him about the baby. He said he was leaving the Office and moving to America to start a new life."

I needed time to think. What Mina was saying dropped on me like a bomb. In the middle of the 1950s, Israel had planted a Mossad operative to be its agent-in-place in the most secret center of the French government. He had never been caught and nobody had found out about it. Only a wild imagination could fathom what the French government's reaction would have been to such a revelation. Mina said that her husband told her he was stealing their shopping lists. That explained why he was planted in the purchasing office of the French. Apparently Israel wanted to know what was being bought and from whom, in case the official French aid dried up. So it was not espionage proper, although I don't think the French would have appreciated Dov's real purpose if they'd found out.

In those early years the Israeli–French relationship was softening under the unrelenting efforts of Shimon Peres, who was then Ben-Gurion's deputy in the Ministry of Defense. France had realized that it and Israel shared a common enemy: the Arab world was supporting the Algerian rebels in the same manner it had always supported the Palestinian fight against Israel. In late 1957, France agreed to supply Israel with essential material for a second nuclear reactor, which Israel then secretly built in the Negev desert near the town of Dimona.

"It's a textile factory," Israel had claimed, when the skeptical American government had raised questions. But aerial photographs made by high-flying U-2 planes told a different story. The U.S. military attaché at the U.S. Embassy in Tel Aviv had collected additional information, enough to confirm the American government's suspicions. Israel was building a nuclear reactor with a capacity to manufacture weapons-grade plutonium.

"What did you do then?" I finally prompted her.

"I had some money saved up and Dov had given me his share of our apartment. I was pregnant. What could I do? I stayed at home feeling sorry for myself until Ariel was born."

"Did you ever hear from him?"

"He used to send me cards on my birthdays, sometimes with a few words about himself. I guess he wanted me to know how successful he had become. For years I suspected that his move to the U.S. was a part of a Mossad plan to plant him there. But I guess I was wrong. He really left the Office. Only when Ariel was three or four months old did I write him a letter telling him he was a father. I didn't hear from him for a month. Then he called me and said he had just returned from Japan, where he had a real estate business, and read my letter. I expected a shouting match for not telling him earlier. But he was nice. He asked for Ariel's picture. He started sending me money to help raise Ariel and about three months later he came to visit. Since then he has been a good father and kept in touch with his little girl. When Ariel was eleven years old she went to the United States to visit him and his new wife, and she returned thrilled. Not with the new wife, but with Disneyland. For her that was more important. Through Ariel I heard he had made it big in America. He sent newspaper clippings from time to time describing his growing empire, the bank he bought, and his successes. The clippings were sent to Ariel, but I knew he wanted me to see them."

"Why did Dov leave the Office, do you know?"

"I only know what he told me, that the French government was satisfied with his work and wanted to promote him by sending him to their purchasing office in the United States. He'd always wanted to go to America but his controller at the Office said no. I don't know why. Maybe they wanted to keep him in France, close to the source of information. I know he had a big fight with his Israeli boss and then told them he was resigning."

"When did Dov change his name to DeLouise?"

"He told me that in the United States he felt some anti-Semitism coming from his coworkers and decided he needed a new identity. So he chose a name that wouldn't sound Jewish but that would be foreign sounding, explaining his accent. He told people that he came from France. He spoke excellent French, so DeLouise sounded right, I guess."

"And now your name is Bernstein? Did you remarry?"

Mina lowered her eyes and blushed. I almost smiled; it was such a girlish gesture for a grown woman.

"Yes," she replied, "Two years after my divorce I met a wonderful man who worked in the Israeli Navy as a radio operator. His name was Rafi Bernstein."

"Was?" I asked.

"Yes," she said sadly, "he died two years after we married. I wanted Ariel to have a father in her life, but he died when Ariel was only four years old, before she could really remember him."

Mina then looked up at me. "Now you know it all. I still don't know how all this could be connected to Ariel's disappearance. Can you help me find her? I was afraid to go to the police because she insisted that I not talk to anyone about this. 'It's a matter of life and death,' she said. Now I understand how right she was."

I had a long laundry list of questions, but I held back.

"I'll help you find Ariel," I said.

"Thank you so much," she said, "I need your help. There's just no one else."

"So let's get started," I said. "Do you know if Ariel had a bank account in Europe?"

"No, she didn't. She made me a signatory in all her bank accounts. I would have known that. She only banks in Israel. Why are you asking?"

"Because sometimes people just take off. If she had a bank account here, we could see if she withdrew money lately and see any unusual movements in her account. You said that her father sent her money?"

"Yes, from time to time. He also bought her an apartment in Haifa and a car. He wanted Ariel to have a comfortable lifestyle. Anyway, Ariel never really cared too much about money."

I wanted to ask Mina to let me have access to Ariel's bank account in Israel. If DeLouise had wired her money also from his foreign bank accounts, it would be a beautiful lead. But I couldn't ask for it now. Not just yet.

"Let's talk to the receptionist here. Maybe he knows something," I said.

"Did I miss any messages during my stay here?" Mina asked the man behind the desk.

"No," he said, "but someone asked about you."

"Who?" asked Mina.

"I don't know," he answered. "It was a man with a foreign accent and he did not leave any message."

Mina looked troubled.

"He'll probably call again," he added in a comforting voice, when he saw Mina's obvious confusion. "It's the same person who called for you twice just a few days ago."

Mina looked at him and snapped: "No one told me that people were looking for me. Why wasn't I told?"

"There was no message to deliver," he said apologetically, with a half-embarrassed smile. "I asked him if he wanted to leave a name or number, but he said that you'd soon know."

"Soon know what?" asked Mina confusedly, as we went back to the sitting room.

"Did you get any mail here?" I asked.

"No."

I knew I had to intervene. I asked Mina to wait for me in the lounge and returned to the reception desk. I didn't want her to know that I had checked out the phone calls DeLouise made and that, in view of Mina's account of her conversation with Ariel, it was obvious he had called the pension to speak with Ariel.

"Mrs. Bernstein and I are trying to find Ariel Peled. Has she actually checked out?"

"Excuse me," said the man firmly, "could you tell me who you are?"

"I'm a friend of the family," I responded. "Ariel Peled is Mina Bernstein's daughter."

"I see," said the man relenting. "That explains why my wife let Mrs. Bernstein move Ms. Peled's luggage to her room."

"Are you Mr. Bart?"

He nodded.

"So Ariel Peled never checked out?"

"No, she just left. Sometimes people do that. Her room was paid for, so I guess we weren't concerned about the bill. Why are you asking? Is there a problem?"

"Her mother is worried because she hasn't heard from her yet. Tell me, who made the reservations for Ariel's room?"

"We don't keep formal records of these things, but let me look."

He leafed through his book and said, "Yes, just as I thought, the room was paid for in cash. I remember now; a man called and made the reservation. When I asked for a credit card to guarantee the room, he said that he'd send a messenger with cash. Sometime later somebody came with an envelope with cash. It was odd, because most people send in personal checks or charge the room to a credit card."

I was convinced DeLouise had made these arrangements to distance himself from Ariel. But why? He must have felt the heat. In the end, he'd been justified.

"Do you keep a record of messages or phone calls? Mrs. Bernstein is very upset about missing these calls."

"No," he said, and added in a defensive tone, "we are a small pension, only twelve rooms. We give our guests their messages and we don't record them."

Mina had left the sitting room and was coming to join me. When Mr. Bart saw her he said, "Mrs. Bernstein, this has just come in for you," and handed her an envelope.

Deftly, I grabbed the envelope out of his hand. There was a typewritten line in the center: "Mrs. Mina Bernstein, Pension Bart." There was neither a stamp nor a return address.

"How did it come in?" I asked Mr. Bart.

"A boy on a bicycle gave it to me moments ago and said a man in a car stopped right outside the pension and gave him a tip to bring it in."

"Are you expecting any mail here?" I asked Mina.

"No," she said. "Nobody but Ariel knows where I am."

I bent the envelope to see if there was any object inside other than paper. It bent just fine. I looked for signs of oil stains, which could indicate explosives. There were none. Mina followed me as I went outside the building to open it carefully. There was only one sheet of paper inside. I carefully pulled out a typewritten letter.

We have Ariel. If you want her
back alive, do not contact the
police, or we return her in

pieces. We want the papers
DeLouise gave her.
Call 900-5593 every evening at
7:00 P.M. until we answer. This
is your only chance. The goons
can't help you.

I handed the letter to Mina. She went pale and held it with a shaking hand. "She was kidnapped!" Mina said dazedly. "It's all because of Dov's dirty business. I'm sure of it."

"What do you mean?"

"It wasn't enough that his work ruined our marriage! Now it has to hurt our child too!"

"What work?" I asked, hoping to hear something new she might have held back from me. "It couldn't be the Office — he left it more than thirty years ago. Was it his banking activity, or was there other work that affected Ariel that you haven't told me about yet?"

"Look at the note and see for yourself. These people don't want ransom money. They want something Dov gave her. I have no idea what it might be." She sounded desperate.

"Come," I said, "let's go inside." We returned to the sitting room. Mina sat down, cradling her head in her hands. I looked at my watch. It was 6:55 P.M.

Puzzled about a line in the letter, I turned to Mina and asked, "Goons?"

She was surprised I'd asked the question. "You know, the men from your Office. They came here three days ago after I realized that Ariel was missing and decided to call them and take advantage of her father's old job. Isn't that how you've come here to see me?"

I felt my stomach turning. The Mossad was here? I almost asked but luckily didn't. Mina thought I was with them and I had failed to deny it. A real mess could be brewing.

"There is no time," I said, and almost pushed her to the telephone. "Call this number," I demanded, giving her the number that appeared on the ransom note.

She dialed. The phone rang ten times but nobody answered. "Try again," I ordered. Obediently, she dialed again.

Mina signaled me with her hand. I put my ear close to the receiver she was holding next to her ear; I heard a voice say, "Hello?"

In broken German, Mina asked, "Excuse me, I was asked to call this number, can you tell me where it is?"

The person on the other end, in a very youthful sounding voice, said, "It's a pay phone at the corner of Schillerstrasse and Bayerstrasse, right here in Munich. I just came to the phone to call my mom and you were on the other end. I didn't even start to dial." He sounded timid.

"Is there anyone else waiting near the phone?"

"No," he said. "This place is empty."

Mina hung up.

"We need to get the police on it," I said decisively.

"Absolutely not!" she exclaimed. "They'll kill her."

"Do you know what papers they refer to?"

"I have no idea," she said in despair. "I haven't seen or spoken with Ariel since I came here. I have her luggage in my room, but there's only clothing in it. Maybe she received papers from her father?"

This was also my assumption. Ariel probably received some papers from her father and put them in the safety deposit box at Mielke Bank. That's why she rented the box. That's what they were after. And the Mossad? They could either be after the same documents or simply be trying to help an ex-Mossad operative in distress. The people who kidnapped Ariel must be very desperate to get the papers. They could be the ones who killed DeLouise. But I didn't want to jump to conclusions. Clearly, a person who had multiple identities could also have multiple enemies.

In the Mossad Academy we had received several lectures on hostage taking and negotiations. "Set your priorities," the psychologist had told us. "You want to enter a vineyard and steal grapes, but the guard is in your way. You must decide what's more important: to wrestle with the guard and force yourself in, or sneak around the fence and eat the grapes."

If the people who kidnapped Ariel had murdered DeLouise, they must have feared something more than a loss of money. This was not simply a dispute over stolen money. The prize in this case could be the papers at Mielke Bank. If that was true, then by killing DeLouise they had revealed that they knew he no longer had the papers. The kidnappers believe that Ariel was now holding the papers or could be traded for them. So why had DeLouise been killed? Suspicion and speculation abounded, but no facts.

I wanted to ask Mina about the Mossad operatives who came to see her, but I couldn't do it. That would have blown my false-flag tactic. I had to keep Mina away from them and get her to Mielke Bank.

One thing puzzled me though. Who had called Mina at the pension? Why hadn't the caller been persistent enough to try again or, like me, come to see her? Why hadn't the Israeli Consulate told her about DeLouise's murder and asked her to identify the body? Inefficiency, perhaps. Or maybe Mina wasn't telling me everything. I'd have to find out.

It was clear that the Mossad operatives had decided to keep the German police out of the loop. Otherwise there would have been swarms of German police at the pension. A weird theory crept into my mind: the strange disinterest of the Israeli Consulate could indicate that they knew where Ariel was and that they believed she wasn't at risk. However, it could also be a simple case of bureaucratic stupidity or apathy, or both. Or — the absurd thought crept in once more — maybe the Mossad was in cahoots with DeLouise after all. I brushed it off again.

Some things were starting to fall into their logical places in my jigsaw puzzle, but new and far more complex questions kept coming up. I thought of Greek mythology, of Tantalus, king of Sipylos, son of Zeus. The gods punished Tantalus by putting him in an underworld lake where he couldn't reach the water when he wanted to drink, and, when he wanted to eat, the grapes above him disappeared. With each forward step I made, DeLouise's money seemed farther away than ever.

It was clear to me that I had to keep the competition away. Somehow I felt that there was more than one client bidding for DeLouise's assets in this crowded marketplace.

"Ariel should be safe," I concluded to Mina, omitting the words "for now" that were on the tip of my tongue. "She has something that these people want — the papers her father gave her. They won't harm her until they have them. I still think you should call the police."

"No, they'll harm her. I don't trust the police here. I can't be certain that they'd put Ariel's interests first." She looked determined.

"In that case," I said, accepting her decision against my better judgment, "we have to make contact with these people and understand what it is they want. We must insist on talking to Ariel." What I didn't say was that we had to make sure she was still alive, despite my assurances to her that Ariel wouldn't be harmed while the kidnappers thought they needed her. "Maybe she could tell us exactly what papers these people want."

Mina looked at me appreciatively. "I see that you have a lot of experience in these matters." She gently squeezed my arm, "I trust you." This compliment was totally undeserved. In actuality, I was hoping that by acquiescing in Mina's determination not to involve the German police, I wasn't harming Ariel.

"Go to sleep," I said. "I'll pick you up tomorrow morning. Have your passport ready." To my surprise, without any resistance, Mina nodded and went upstairs. I was troubled by that. Mina had just found out that her ex-husband had been murdered and that her only daughter had been kidnapped. She refused to call the police, and then retreated obediently to her room. That was it? I knew I didn't have the whole picture.

I started walking toward my car. Then I returned to the pension and walked around the block, approaching my car from the other direction. Just a little precaution. The street was empty. I drove back to my hotel. There were no messages and only second-rate movies on TV. I laid down to think about the amazing labyrinth I had wandered into. Only two weeks had passed since David assigned this case to me, but it felt like eternity. I was completely focused on DeLouise, putting aside almost everything else. It was time to call my children in New York.

"Tommy is with some friends playing video games," said Karen, when she answered my call. "Dad, when are you coming back?" There was a ring of concern in her voice.

"Soon, honey, I hope soon," I said, not knowing whether I was telling the truth or speculating. "Is there a problem?"

She paused, "Not exactly, but you've never left us for such a long period. We miss you."

A mixture of guilt and pride flooded me. "I miss you too, sweetheart. It won't be long, I promise."

I was angry at myself for being so preoccupied with DeLouise. I fell asleep vowing to wrap things up as soon as I could.

The following morning I called Mina and picked her up at the pension. "Where are we going?" she asked, as I navigated through the narrow streets.

"To a bank," I said. "Ariel rented a safe-deposit box."

Mina's pleasant demeanor turned to suspicion. "How did you find out?" she asked, narrowing her eyes.

"A combination of legwork and good luck, I guess," I said briefly. "Trust me," I added, attempting a bit of comfort. I couldn't tell her more, certainly not until I found an explanation for her unexpected reaction last night. I looked in my mirror to see if we were being followed. Nothing unusual, though there are several ways to set up a tail without detection. Certainly, if the same person follows you then you can eventually recognize him or her. However, you can be tailed in a relay; each follower tracks you for just a short stretch, then you're "picked up" by the next.

Then there's the ultimate trick: each follower stays where he is but keeps an eye on you as you pass. When you've gone a certain distance, he radios ahead that you're approaching. The next guy watches you pass, radios ahead, and so on. It takes a lot of people to pull off this leapfrogging act, but since no one actually follows, except by eye, it's highly unlikely that the subject will notice he's being watched.

During my Mossad training we spent two weeks learning how to shake off, or "dry clean," followers, but I'd never had the opportunity to practice it in real life. I had always been the pursuer, not the target. Was I becoming one now?

As we entered the bank I gave Mina her instructions: She should ask to be added as a co-owner of the safe-deposit box and then appoint me as her attorney-in-fact to allow me access as well.

"Why would they listen to me?"

"Because Ariel left instructions concerning you."

"So why do you need to have signature rights as well?" she asked.

"Ariel is still away, and her safe return may be dependent on these documents. If only one other person, namely you, has access, it could be complicated." I didn't want to say *dangerous*. My earlier statement to Mina that she and Ariel could be in danger wasn't exaggerated. If Ariel's captors had also killed DeLouise, they would not hesitate to harm Mina, if that's what it took to get what they wanted.

She looked at me carefully, then reached her decision. "All right, I trust you." She touched my arm again. The drill-sergeant assistant manager who saw me a day earlier wasn't there. Good, that would save me a lot of squabbling. In her stead we saw another woman who looked a bit more kindly. She checked Mina's passport, went to her office, and returned with Ariel's original signature card.

"Yes, I see here. Miss Peled informed us that you'd be coming to cosign." She handed Mina a pen and she signed the card.

"Is that all?" she asked, looking around at us.

"No," I said, "I'm here to be appointed as an attorney-in-fact for that box. Can you please prepare the paperwork?"

She looked at Mina as if to obtain her approving look.

"Yes, of course, Mr. Gordon is helping us," said Mina.

There were forms to be filled out. I showed my Israeli passport, then I asked her for a key.

"That takes a few hours to process." She went back to her office and returned with a grim face.

"I'm sorry but there is another problem. My manager tells me that joint permission of all owners of the box is required to give a power of attorney to another person. Therefore, you'll have to bring Miss Peled to sign her consent to let you have access to the box."

"This presents a problem," I said. "Miss Peled is not available at the moment."

Of course, I could give up and let Mina open the safe, remove its contents, and give it to me. But I didn't want her to see what was in the box or to take it. It could be what the kidnappers wanted, but it could also be what I wanted — DeLouise's banking information. Clearly, I had to be the first person to see what was in the box. And then again, I don't give up that easily. I had to do something before Mina made her logical move.

"May I speak to the manager?" I said in an annoyed voice.

"I'll ask," she said, and went to an office in the back.

When she came back she told me that the manager was busy, but they would process the paperwork and have the key for Mina later that day. Meanwhile, they would check with their legal counsel on my appointment.

"Fine," I said. As I guided Mina outside, I said, "I still think you should contact the local police."

"Please, not yet. I don't want my daughter harmed in any way. Let's wait at least until we make the first telephone contact with them." She sounded determined. Reluctantly, I agreed to wait.

"If that's the way you want it," I told her. "Why don't you go back to the pension and wait for my call. I'll pick you up later and we'll go back to the bank together." I hailed her a cab and sent that tough little lady on her way.

It was time for a small audio-video surveillance operation. I was far from an electronics expert, but I'd had enough training in the old days to bug your everyday phone booth. I found an electronic gadget shop not far off, bought what I needed, and headed back to the street corner. I managed to set things up without observation — not too easy in Munich, but I was lucky once again. I then crossed the street to an apartment building opposite the phone with my just-bought camcorder in my briefcase. The second and third floors looked most suitable for my plan. I went to the second floor and knocked on the door of the apartment I guessed would overlook the street. The name on the door read "Landau."

An elderly woman opened the door. "Excuse me," I said in my most polite voice, "do you happen to speak English?"

"Yes," she said, looking at me curiously. "What do you want?"

"I'm working for an American consulting engineering company. We are looking for a homeowner who would agree to rent a balcony for five hundred dollars a day for a few days."

"Rent my balcony?" she asked in disbelief. "For what?"

"Well, ma'am, we are hired to conduct traffic congestion surveys throughout Europe and we need to measure the flow of traffic in certain areas to help plan for the coming traffic growth. Of course, we are surveying many other junctions as well. We need your permission to put a camcorder on your balcony to take continuous video shots of the intersection. We must know how much traffic passes through here and when it peaks. I can pay you five hundred dollars now, if you agree, and set up immediately. I have my equipment with me."

"All you want is to view the street? But you won't actually be here; it'll be automatic, right?"

I nodded. "Just let me see your balcony."

She walked me to her balcony, which had a direct view of the street and the pay phone. It was a perfect location.

"Excellent. The location suits our needs perfectly. May I set up the machinery?"

"Yes," she said. "Why not?"

I attached the camcorder to the tripod, hooked the power cable to the wall outlet, set the speed to slow, and set the timer to 5:30 P.M., to run two hours.

"It's all set." I gave her five hundred dollars in cash. "I'll prepare a receipt later and will ask you to sign." She took the money and counted it.

"Five hundred dollars a day," she said, confirming the arrangement.

"Yes," I said, "but please don't touch the camcorder. I'll be back tomorrow and we'll see if we need your balcony for additional days."

I looked at my watch; it was 2:30 P.M. I decided to return to the bank before picking up Mina Bernstein. Fortunately the same assistant manager was still on duty.

"I'm sorry," she said. "The bank's lawyer was unavailable, so you'll have to return tomorrow. Please tell Mrs. Bernstein that her key is ready."

I left the bank and called Mina.

"There's been a change of plans," I said, neglecting to mention my visit to the bank. "I'll be at the pension before six tonight. I want to be there when you call the pay phone again."

I decided to defy Mina's wishes. The police had to be in on this matter. I went to the American Consulate and looked for Ron Lovejoy. I found him getting ready to leave for the day.

"Ron, things are getting complicated. I need help." I told him briefly about Ariel's kidnapping, the safe-deposit box, and the ransom note. I didn't mention that the Mossad had contacted Mina. I didn't know if it was relevant and it might have complicated things even more.

Ron listened to me and asked, "These women are Israeli citizens who encountered a problem on German soil; what's the U.S. government interest in this matter?"

"Ninety million dollars," I said flatly. "The documents in the safe-deposit box could be connected to that money."

"Your assumptions may or may not be correct. This thing may blow up in your face, and ours too, if you stick your hand too deep in this shit."

"I know that," I said. I wasn't about to argue with him now. "That's why I came to you for help. You'd have a lot more leverage with the police than I would. And we need action."

Ron said, "Let's go into my office. I'll call my contact." Ron made the call and thirty minutes later we both were sitting in police headquarters in Arnulfstrasse.

"You'll have to let us handle this matter our way," said Polizeidirektor Karlheinz Blecher, head of KRIPO, the criminal investigations department. He didn't leave me with any choice, but I still had options of my own. I decided to hold on to them.

"That's fine; you do what you have to do. But bear in mind that Mina Bernstein may refuse to cooperate with you; she's desperately worried about her daughter. That's her only concern. She doesn't care about anything else. I'm actually a bit surprised that she trusts me, and it's a slender trust at best."

The chief turned a shrewd eye on me. "Mr. Ron Lovejoy tells me you work for the American government. Does this matter concern the United States government?"

"In a way it does," I said, "But our main interest is in Raymond DeLouise, aka Dov Peled."

"You mean the man who died in Munich the other day?"

"You mean 'was murdered' the other day?" I corrected him. "Yes. You see, Ariel Peled is his daughter and Mina Bernstein was his first wife."

Blecher leaned back in his chair. He kept his cool — just. I could see how astounded he was by my statement.

"I see," he finally said. He turned to one of his three telephones and snapped a few orders in German.

"I'm getting the hostage rescue team ready and we put our intelligence unit on the alert. You can come with me to the pension. If you want to, of course."

I wanted to. I climbed into an unmarked police car and drove with Blecher to the pension. Ron went back to the consulate.

"I'm out of here and out of this," Ron told me, essentially washing his hands of the whole business.

I followed Blecher and his four plainclothes detectives into the pension. I expected Mina to be angry, but I could no longer obey her wish to keep the police out of the situation. Blecher went straight to the reception desk. As I approached, Blecher turned to me and said, "The woman has checked out!"

"Are you sure there's no mistake? I spoke with her earlier today and we agreed to meet here at 6:00 P.M. Did she leave a message?"

"No. The receptionist just told us that an hour ago two young men came to see Mrs. Bernstein. She was waiting for them in the hallway with her bags packed. They helped her to their car where a third man was waiting with his engine running, and then they drove off. Obviously she was not forcibly taken."

"It just doesn't make sense," I said. "Would you ask the receptionist if Mrs. Bernstein made or received any phone calls within the past three hours?"

Blecher looked at me. "Herr Gordon, we know our work." He was unsympathetic.

"Of course. I know that," I said quickly. Alienating him was not wise. While we were talking, two detectives went up to Mina's room. They returned to report that the room was clean. The occupant had left no belongings, suspicious or otherwise.

Something was happening. "What's going on?" I asked Blecher as I moved toward him.

I was sure the two men who took Mina away were Mossad operatives. Mina wouldn't have left the pension without telling me or leaving a note behind, unless she thought I was part of the operation, or Ariel had been found.

"How did she settle her bill?" I asked Blecher.

He went to the front desk and returned with the answer. "In cash. American dollars. She apologized for not having enough German marks."

"This is more proof that her departure was sudden and unplanned," I said. Blecher nodded in agreement. I looked at my watch; it was 6:15 P.M.

"I've got to leave now, but I'll call you later? I'm still with you on this case."

Blecher looked at me, thought for a second, and said, "Fine. You can go, but if I need to talk to you, where do I find you?"

"You can contact me through Lovejoy or at the Omni Hotel."

I drove back to my hotel, parked my car, and went up to my room to check for messages. Nothing new. Down again quickly, I hailed a cab to go to Bayerstrasse. I got out one block from my favorite corner, on the sidewalk opposite the pay phone. There was no one in sight. I looked at my watch: 7:18 P.M. I crossed the street to the pay phone. I took up the receiver to fake a call as my other hand searched for my tape recorder under the box. It was still there. I quickly replaced the tape and put the used one in my pocket. I hung up the receiver, crossed the street again, again went up and knocked on Mrs. Landau's door.

"I came to pick up the equipment," I said, and walked directly to her balcony. I disconnected the camcorder from the wall outlet and folded the tripod.

"Our experts will analyze the material and then a decision will be made if we need to use your balcony for additional days," I said. "May I call you again tomorrow morning if we need more footage?"

"Oh, yes, of course," she said, apparently liking the idea of making another easy five hundred. I gave her a paper and asked her to confirm that she received $500.00 from Peter Wooten. I still had to satisfy the penny-pinchers back at the office.

——

Back in my hotel room I slid the videocassette into the VCR on the TV set and waited for the action to start.

Each time someone used the pay phone I froze the frame. I watched tensely. A woman in her seventies who walked her dog made a short call; two giggling teenage girls were on the phone for approximately thirty minutes. A man dressed in painters' overalls stopped his van near the curb, jumped out, and made a two- to three-minute call and drove away. Then two men in their late twenties walked up. I held my breath. The clock on the camcorder showed 6:58 P.M.

I tried to look closely at their faces, but the damn dome over the pay phone blocked my view. They were on the phone for six or seven minutes. I saw one of them take a coin and give it to the other. A few minutes later they left.

I didn't lock myself on the two guys, at least not until I'd listened to the audiotape.

I pressed the "play" button on the tape recorder and listened. Each call started with a set of touch-tone signals created by the dialer. The sound quality was good and identifying the numbers would probably not be too difficult. The first four calls were in German and did not seem relevant. One guy was letting his friend know he was running late. My calculation showed that it was the man in the painters' overalls. Then there was a ring for an incoming call.

"That's it," I said to myself. After one ring the receiver was lifted and I heard the conversation.

"Hello," said a woman's voice in English. "You left me a message?"

Strange, I thought, it didn't sound like Mina Bernstein. This woman had a deeper voice than Mina's and her tone was far more aggressive. It was definitely not Mrs. Bernstein. But who would be impersonating her, and why?

"Yes," said a man with an accent I could not immediately identify. "Who are you?"

"I'm Mina Bernstein. Where is my daughter? I want to talk to her."

"She's OK," said the man, "but you must give me what I want first."

I still couldn't place his accent.

"What do you want?" asked the woman.

"DeLouise gave Ariel an envelope. I want it," he said firmly.

"But if he gave it to Ariel, how can I give it to you?" asked the woman. "Tell me what it is, or if you know where it is, I'll look for it."

"Ariel says you have access to it."

"I don't understand. Let me talk to Ariel. Maybe she could explain it to me. I haven't received anything from Ariel; I haven't even seen her in Germany. This must be a big mistake. Let me talk to her. If I have what you want, I'll give it to you. I promise." With the same breath she added, "Where can I meet you?"

"You can't meet me. Call this number again tomorrow at the same time. And if you call the police, Ariel will die," he said abruptly and hung up.

I waited a few seconds then heard his voice again as he spoke to the person next to him, and I finally placed his accent. It was Spanish.

"*La putana!* Ariel was lying to us. I'll kill her!"

"What did the woman say?" asked another voice.

"She said that she doesn't have any papers from Ariel. We'll have to go back and squeeze the little bitch."

"Wait," said the other voice. "Let me call the boss first. We can't call from the apartment."

Then I heard another series of touch-tone beeps. A man's voice answered the phone, "*Ja?*"

"It's me," said the voice in English. "The woman called. She says she has no papers but she wants to meet."

A pause. "Are you sure she didn't contact the police?"

His voice sounded familiar but I couldn't place it. He also had an accent — German, if anything, surely — it certainly wasn't Spanish.

"She never mentioned it and she was very anxious to see Ariel. She isn't stupid enough to do that."

"OK, get back to the apartment and I'll call you there."

"Yes, boss."

The boss's accent came through again. It was clearly German. Was I just imagining that the speaker sounded familiar?

The tape ended. I turned off the recorder, marked the date and time on the cassette label, and put it in my pocket.

I sat at my desk thinking through next steps. The first move was easy; speaking of bosses, I had to report to Stone.

I went out to the street, found a pay phone, and used my prepaid phone card to call Washington.

"David," I said, "things are getting hotter here."

"I guess you don't mean the weather."

"No," I smiled, "the German weather is cooling but our climate is warming. I have a safe-deposit box I suspect contains papers my target gave his daughter in Munich before he was killed. It's possible that he had already felt the heat. Next, the daughter called her mother in Israel. The mother came to Munich looking for her daughter, who shortly was kidnapped. It didn't make the papers."

David listened attentively, as always. "Are the German police on the kidnap matter as well?"

"Certainly," I said. "I'm also trying to help them. They don't seem to appreciate it, but you know me. I hang on anyway."

"Don't create a turf war."

"Well, some kind of war is already on," I countered.

"What the hell do you mean by that?"

"Something is brewing but I'm not sure exactly what it is. Just to identify one player, I suspect the Israelis are in on this matter as well. I mean the Israeli government."

Stone let this one hang for a moment, then came at me. "What do you make of it? These are your people, after all."

"Well, our friend was in their service more than thirty years ago, but I don't understand their current interest. Assistance could come now for old times' sake, or maybe he had something they wanted as well."

"So where is the war?" puzzled David.

"I'm guessing they're not the only ones following my target's trail; there seem to be others."

"What others? Do you know who they are? You should always know who you're up against."

"Take it easy, I'm working on it. The problem is that I'm not sure each player has the same goal. The people holding the daughter have a distinct agenda. They want to get some papers her father gave her."

"Do you know who they could be?"

"Could be Latinos. I suspect that in addition to the Latinos and the Israelis, there are others. I'm walking in a fog, and every now and then I bump into something."

"Don't let me lose you," said Stone with genuine concern. "Is the legat helping you?"

"As much as he can, I guess. Don't worry; I always land on my feet. I'm more concerned with what's going on around my dead target."

"With all the international interest in this guy, I'm surprised he managed to live sixty-three years."

"The whole thing is a mystery," I agreed. "There are too many players, and all of them seem somewhat in the dark."

"I'll have to report this to the State Department," said Stone, somewhat reluctantly.

"I guess so," I said. Scandals in foreign lands are their territory. Since I was working out of the consulate, Ron Lovejoy was kept in the loop. It was his job to keep the ambassador informed. Then it was the ambassador's job to do the same with the State Department. But I knew David — he covered all the bases.

I went back to my room, looked at the yellow pad on the desk, and drew several square boxes. In the middle box I wrote "DeLouise." Then I drew a line to another box and wrote "Ariel" in it; next to it, in a separate box I wrote "Mina." I drew five additional boxes on the side and inserted in each a different name: "Mossad," "German police," "U.S. Department of Justice," "Latinos," and finally a question mark, for all others yet to emerge.

I looked at the pad again and tried to identify each group's interest in DeLouise.

The German police: That was easy. They wanted Ariel, and to prosecute anyone involved in her kidnapping and in her father's murder.

The U.S. Department of Justice: That was a two-pronged effort. I was after DeLouise's money, but that trail now seemed to pass through Ariel and Mina. So I was stuck with them as well. And the criminal division, through INTERPOL, was trying to locate DeLouise so that it could request his extradition to the United States for trial. Although INTERPOL does handle requests for police interviews of witnesses, many countries, including Germany, require either an MLAT request under a Mutual Legal Assistance Treaty between the countries or a letter rogatory — a formal request from a court in one country to the appropriate judicial authorities in another country — for such interviews and have such questioning done by (or, less often, supervised by) a *magistrat*, with a *greffier* — a legal assistant of the court — making a *procès-verbal* of it.

If the person to be interviewed abroad is a suspect or the target of an investigation, the matter becomes sticky. The United States would not send Germany a letter rogatory for the questioning of an actual defendant. And there's no international criminal-law mechanism for compelling a person to return to the States just for questioning. Although DeLouise was dead, rendering this issue irrelevant, I still wanted to know if Germany had commenced with an investigation following a request through INTERPOL. In that case their findings could become handy for my investigation. I made a mental note to ask David to find out.

Finally, the Mossad: If they were in on this, as I suspected, I had no idea what their objectives might be. To get Ariel? To help Mina? To get something DeLouise gave Ariel? Did they want the same thing the Latinos wanted? What documents could DeLouise have held that could cause such havoc?

I went out to the street again to call Benny at the Mossad. It was cold and drizzling. I was going to catch pneumonia just so I could maintain confidentiality. There had to be a better way.

There was no answer on Benny's direct line. I left a message on his voice mail asking him to call my New York number. I called his home. No answer there. I called Blecher at the Munich police headquarters but a detective told me that he was gone for the day.

I went up to my room, activated the touch-tone-identifier software on my laptop, and replayed the audiotape recording of the call the Latinos made from the pay phone. The identifier quickly interpreted the touch tone beeps into numbers: 2-3-5-9-9-0-9. This was probably a local number, since no area code was punched. I called the police station again, asking them to trace Blecher for me. Where were all these guys when I needed them? Nobody called me back and I fell asleep.

The next morning I woke up in a belligerent mood. A delay in my efforts here meant more guilt for being away from my children and increased pressure from David to produce results. After spending most of the morning writing my report, I took a cab to Mielke Bank. I was determined to get access to the safe-deposit box. If Mina was with the Mossad guys, she might tell them about the box. They would ask her to open it, and I would be chopped liver.

At the bank I asked to talk to the legal counsel. He wasn't available. I asked to talk to his assistant. A slim young man with short blond hair and rimless glasses showed up.

"How may I help you?"

"My name is Dan Gordon," I said and handed him the Tibor-made power of attorney. "I'm here about the safe-deposit box rented by Ariel Peled, and . . ."

"I already know the details, Herr Gordon," he interrupted me mid-sentence, "but I'm afraid there is nothing to be done without Ms. Peled's signature."

"Look," I said aggressively, "I am an attorney from the United States. I have a power of attorney from an owner of a safe-deposit box, signed in Israel before the German Consul. A few days ago the bank refused to honor it, telling me that it must be signed on a bank-issued form. Then the owner of the box came to Munich and signed your damn form here at the bank, in front of the assistant manager. Hours later I was told that since there were two owners of the box, I needed authorization from both owners." I paused and added venomously, "Nobody bothered to tell us that earlier."

"That's precisely what the rules say," said the lawyer, looking a bit startled at my belligerence. "Well, I don't think so," I said, my anger brewing. "Look at the signature card of the bank, which was generated when the box was rented." He looked at it. "Now tell me, can each owner open the box without the presence of the other?"

He looked at the form again and said faintly, "Yes."

"Now," I continued, like a teacher in a school for the intellectually challenged at the end of a long day, "as I am sure you know, a power of attorney is a delegation of power by the principal appointing another person or entity to act on the principal's behalf, having the same powers as the principal has or those he has delegated, right?"

He was starting to get the picture.

"So, if Mina Bernstein could open the box independently of Ariel Peled, and empty it, she could also give me that same power. And, sir, your games," I spat, finally letting my rage burst, some real and some inflated, "are causing my client severe financial damage, which I intend to recover from the bank and from anyone involved in this delaying tactic!"

I was following the advice Alex had given us. "Always aim your veiled threats against the person standing in your way in an otherwise indifferent bureaucracy; make it personal. The bigger the organization, and the smaller the hurdle you are trying to pass, the more chances the person will yield. He or she wouldn't want to be blamed for creating a legal mess. Who'll defend them if they are personally named in a complaint or a lawsuit?" This time, no veil disguised the threat. It was unequivocal and direct.

"Wait here," said the assistant. He seemed pleased to walk away.

I must have sounded convincing because he didn't give me an argument. I sank into the soft leather couch next to the legal counsel's office and looked around. Moments later he returned and said, "OK, I checked the power of attorney Mina Bernstein signed, and it seems to be in order. I'll take you to the vault."

"Thank you," I said, "but I don't have a key. Yesterday the assistant manager prepared the keys but I never received them." Then as a second thought I added, "Do you know if Mrs. Bernstein received her set of keys before she left?"

"No," he said, "I have the envelope with her keys." That was a relief, since it meant that Mina hadn't opened the box.

"I'll take the keys and give them to her," I said, holding out an open hand.

He hesitated.

"Remember, I have full power of attorney," I reminded him.

He relented and gave me the envelope. "At this time we are honoring only the power of attorney Mrs. Bernstein signed here. Here is the one signed in Israel. Please ask Ms. Peled to come in and sign our own form."

He returned the power of attorney Tibor had prepared.

Frankly, I couldn't have cared less why he was yielding, as long as I could get access to the box. I followed him to the lower floor, went through a chrome-plated, metal-barred door, then a ten-inch-thick steel door, and finally into the safe-deposit box area. I opened the key envelope, took one key and read the number — 114. The box was in an upper row. I inserted my key and my guide inserted his master key into the slot. The box opened.

"I'll wait here until you're finished," he said, moving into the adjacent room to allow me privacy.

I composed myself, resolving to be businesslike. But excitement overtook me. Here was the information I'd been looking for, and it might give me new insight into Dov Peled. The safe-deposit box door opened and inside was a white envelope. I took the envelope, put it in the inner pocket of my jacket, locked the box, took the key, and left the room. I looked at my wristwatch; it was 1:15 P.M.

The main door of the bank was closed and I was directed to a side door. As I stepped out, I noticed a shadow to one side. I felt a hard, sharp blow on my head. Then blackness.

The first thing I heard when I came to was the sound of an elevator door opening and footsteps. Then I felt the thick, sweet taste of blood in my mouth. My blood. I was half sitting on the floor, breathing heavily. I was dizzy, disoriented. My head was a ball of pain. I felt wetness. Darkness, more pain. There were voices around me, speaking in German. Where was I? The darkness began to clear and I saw the blurred figure of someone trying to help me get up.

"Mein Gott," I heard a man's voice say, coming through the pain. "He is bleeding."

I lifted my left hand and touched my face. It was sticky and warm.

There was blood coming from my nose and forehead. I raised myself slightly and leaned against the wall.

My head began to clear. I realized I'd been hit — hard. I reached into the inner pocket of my jacket. The envelope was still there. That was all that mattered, but I knew I'd better move out of there fast.

"Please help me get up," I asked the person standing next to me. I didn't even know whether it was a man or a woman.

"No," he said. It was a man after all. "You must to wait for the ambulance." I couldn't allow that. Whoever had attacked me might come back. I had to leave. I got up, despite my dizziness. I was as nauseated as if I were on a bobbing boat on the open sea without any air. Air! Yes! That's what I needed most.

"Thank you," I said in the man's general direction and walked slowly outside, my knees weak, my vision foggy. The crisp October wind blowing in my face had had never felt better. My vision was slowly coming into focus, but my head hurt even more as the shock wore off. I looked down. My shirt and jacket were spattered with blood. Somehow my overcoat had escaped the flood. I buttoned it over shirt and jacket. I wiped my face with a tissue I found in my pocket.

I was still breathing heavily, trying to inhale every bit of air I could into my aching body. "That guy must have used a blackjack on me," I thought with the one small part of my brain that wasn't aching.

I hailed a cab. It would really say something about Munich taxi drivers if one stopped for me in the shape I was in, I thought grimly. But one did stop and I slid into the backseat and asked the driver to take me to the Omni Hotel.

Then a thought struck me. What if they — whoever "they" were — were waiting for me at the hotel? They wanted something I had, clearly. The envelope! Again I checked my pocket; the envelope was still there. No, I couldn't go back to the Omni.

"Driver," I directed, "I've changed my mind. Take me to the Sheraton." Without a word, he turned the car around, and within minutes I was at the door. The doorman helped me out, visibly shocked by my bloody face. I walked into the lobby praying they would give me a room.

I went to the reception desk. "I need a room for one or two days."

The receptionist looked at me and asked in genuine concern, "What happened to you? Do you need help?"

"Thanks, no, I'm fine. I had a car accident. I wasn't badly hurt but I need a room immediately to rest."

"But there's much blood on your clothes. Are you sure? I could call our doctor."

"I'm fine. The blood you see on me is actually the other passenger's. I helped him into an ambulance."

I placed my American Express card on the counter. In five minutes, I was on my way to the twenty-second floor and a clean and spacious room.

Even through the pain, a nagging sense of responsibility intruded. Breaking the rules, I picked up the telephone and called Lovejoy at the consulate; a phone call by an American citizen to his consulate could be regarded as benign. "Ron," I said wearily, "I have a small problem. I was attacked leaving the bank. I managed to get away."

"Holy shit," said Ron, "do you need help? Are you OK?"

"Yeah, I'm OK. In this business, the fleas come with the dog. I have a little bleeding and a lot of headache. I didn't go back to the Omni because I don't know what or who is waiting for me there. Would you send your men to my room and check it out? I'll call you later."

"Where are you now?" he asked.

"I just checked into another hotel. I need to lie down. I'll call you later." I'd broken the rule of leaving traces but I simply didn't want anyone to disturb me. I didn't mention the envelope. I needed to collect my thoughts first.

V
─────

I took off my bloody clothes and got into the shower. Even though the gashes on my head stung like hell, I stood underneath the hot water for ten minutes. I was going to have to do without stitches, whether I needed them or not. I wrapped myself in the thick terry-cloth hotel robe and slowly sat on the bed. My head was still throbbing. Any sudden move felt like a million needles pricking me from all directions. I suddenly remembered the envelope. Had they gotten it?

I reached over and took it out of my jacket pocket. It was an unsealed standard white envelope. Four folded sheets of ordinary writing paper were inside. It was a letter handwritten in Hebrew.

September 13, 1990
My Dear Ariel,
I hope this letter finds its way to you. I left it with Mr. Bart at your pension with your name on it, in case we do not meet.

I know I wasn't much of a father to you, and I can't change that now. It may help you to know you are the only person I can trust. There are a few things I want you to know before you hear about them from others.

I had to leave the United States because my bank, First Federal Bank of Westwood, was failing. The real estate market collapsed in the late '80s, and soon afterward commercial developers who had already borrowed money from the bank could not repay their loans because the real estate market was dead; they made no sales and had no cash flow. Soon enough the value of property was lower than the value it had been appraised for when we made the loan. This was happening all over the country. Federal regulators demanded that banks' owners bring more capital, but who wants to throw good money after bad? So the federal government started seizing banks by the hundreds, including mine. The federal regulators who swarmed the bank told me that there was more than $90 million dollars missing. I knew I couldn't win any battle against them since most of the $90 million had financed my personal transactions; a complete violation of the law, I admit, particularly when some of those transactions went sour. I was already fighting off several civil lawsuits by investors who claimed they'd lost their money. I heard rumors that the U.S. Attorney's Office was about to bring criminal charges against me. I was removed from my position as chairman and chief executive officer of the bank under the order of the federal regulators. I knew I couldn't endure a battle with them for the next five years, spending millions of my own money on lawyers. So I moved to Europe to put an end to it all.

Between 1957 and 1990 I had accumulated substantial assets in Europe and Japan but I couldn't move them to the U.S. because there was no way I could explain these assets to the U.S. government after I'd neglected to report them all along. Frankly, I didn't feel like paying the hefty American taxes on income unrelated to the United States, generated from businesses I started before I became a U.S. citizen.

But my troubles with the government were not my only problems. Other issues followed me to Europe because of a bad decision I made. I had depositors in the bank who were wealthy businessmen from Colombia. They deposited more than $75 million with the bank. They always told me that they were in the tobacco and coffee businesses. I even visited them once in Cali, and they gave me red-carpet treatment. They hinted that they wanted to keep their money outside Colombia to avoid paying income taxes. I had no problem with that. However, I later discovered that the source of their money was cocaine, not coffee, and that they were using my bank to launder their dirty money.

I admit that even when I discovered that, I did not stop taking their money; it was a very good source of income for the bank. Practically speaking, I couldn't stop working with them. Although they never threatened me, they made sure I understood their ruthlessness. So I kept copies of some of their money-transfer documents in case something went wrong. It was my insurance policy. I also found out that they were making "campaign contributions" to four politicians and three judges in the U.S. In Cali they'd shown me the politicians' autographed photographs along with "thank-you letters." "They'll help us on a rainy day," the Colombians told me.

When things got worse and the federal regulators auditing the books at the bank increased their number from three to fifteen, I smelled trouble. They told me that I was undercapitalized and, unless I acquired fresh money, the FDIC would have to seize the bank. So I called Ignacio Perez, the Colombian businessman, and asked him to convert some of his deposits into capital by purchasing shares of the bank. That would have solved the capital-shortage problem and driven the regulators away. He refused. I told him about the transfer documents I kept elsewhere. He did not lose his composure; he told me that I'd made a mistake, wished me well, and hung up. I have not heard from him since. Once I'd left the bank, and with the cloud of pending criminal investigation hanging over me, I thought I'd be better off in Switzerland. I settled in a Geneva hotel where I hoped I could put the recent past behind me. But lately I've begun to suspect that Perez's people were following me. So I left Geneva. I didn't tell anyone where I was going. I drove a car to Munich.

Now I'm coming to the important part: I never told you about it, but I'm sure your mother must have revealed my distant past to you. For more than five years I served in the Mossad. I was sent by them to France to work in a French nuclear research facility. But when hiring me, the French government didn't know that I was also working for the Mossad. You may call what I did spying, but Israel needed the information badly and the French had it. I wasn't damaging France by helping Israel. Later I left the Mossad over a serious disagreement with my superiors. I had not been in touch with them for many years, but I still remembered one or two of the old guard who served with me, and I'm sure they know my name. Now that things were becoming complicated I needed help. I couldn't ask the Swiss or the German police for protection from the Colombians; I had to assume that they'd report my whereabouts to the United States through INTERPOL or the FBI. I'd be arrested and extradited to the United States for trial.

So I turned to the Mossad for assistance. I knew I'd made a mistake by threatening Ignacio Perez and telling him about the documents I had, so I asked the Mossad to protect me. I didn't think they'd do it just because I was an operative thirty-three years ago, but I was sure they didn't want me to be captured by anyone who could get out of me what I knew about Israel's espionage in France. I'm thinking of asking them to call you, to ask you to come over, so I could talk more freely with you and guarantee your future. I didn't want to call you directly and expose you. I have sufficient financial reserves to cover the missing $90 million. But that is not the problem; I have a plan to relieve me of the criminal charges. I'll tell you more when I see you. If anything happens to me, see Mr. Hans Guttmacher, the manager of Bankhaus Bäcker & Haas, a banking institution in Munich. I left him an envelope with documents for you. There is enough there to compensate you for my not being a father to you all these years.

Although I have seen so little of you, I love you with all my heart. Remember the nickname I started calling you when you were five years old? Be sure to tell it to Mr. Bart, the pension's owner. He'll laugh hearing it.

The letter was signed All my love, Your Father, Dov Peled

The name was written at the bottom of the last sheet in those round Hebrew letters. I felt as if I had invaded his privacy.

It was too much for one day. "The son of a bitch," I said loudly, not knowing whether I meant Benny or DeLouise. Benny had hidden the most important part of the story from me. DeLouise, Dov, or the devil knows what other names he used, wasn't just a scientific researcher at the Mossad; they had planted him in France to spy. Mina wasn't exaggerating or bluffing. So did DeLouise blackmail the Mossad to provide him with protection when his blackmail attempt on the Colombians backfired? If that was the case, how did the Mossad react? Was he telling Ariel the whole truth? It seemed as if, to preserve his daughter's memories of him as an honorable man, he was not being entirely forthcoming in this letter to her; that he'd fudged some facts. Did DeLouise let the Mossad in on his hidden assets to smooth his way out of his problems, with their help? Is that why Benny had kept me in the dark?

The most important thing was that DeLouise had told Ariel to see Guttmacher. He was the money keeper. Finally — a breakthrough in my own chase. I felt satisfied; I forgot the pain in my head. I was only tired, very tired. I called housekeeping and left my clothes outside my door to be washed and dry-cleaned. I lay back on the bed, asleep before my head hit the pillow.

I woke up suddenly. My head was numb with pain. I went to the bathroom and looked at the mirror. I looked like a second-rate boxer. There was an ugly slash on my forehead, covered with clotted blood, and a potato-sized lump on my cheek.

There was a scratch at the door. I opened it warily and was relieved to see my dry-cleaned clothes hanging on the knob, wrapped in rustling plastic. I shaved with the help of the hotel kit in the bathroom, dressed, and went to eat breakfast. I had no appetite, but I had to kill time until Lovejoy arrived at the consulate.

At eight thirty I decided to head over without advance warning. I called through to Ron's office from the guard station and got a quick OK. Ron looked me over and asked, chuckling, "Are you sure it wasn't some jealous husband that knocked you down?"

I was in no mood for jokes, and I still had a headache.

"Listen," I said, "I did some investigating and I think I have a lead on Ariel's kidnappers."

"Do you know something that the German police don't?"

"I don't know what they know. But now I know plenty. Remember, this guy Blecher isn't too generous with information. He has his duties and I have mine."

Ron didn't even ask me what I knew. He called Blecher.

"Polizeidirektor Blecher," said Ron, "Gordon is in my office now."

Ron handed me the receiver.

"Hello, Mr. Gordon," said Blecher in a slightly friendlier voice, perhaps feeling that I deserved better treatment after his city had caused me the mother of all headaches. "Are you OK?"

"Yes, I'm fine. What I really need to do is find out who attacked me and why."

"Do you have any ideas of your own?" asked Blecher.

"I don't know, I could simply have been the victim of a smash-and-grabber looking for cash."

"Or could it be that he was after you personally or after something he thought you had?"

"I don't know, I was hoping you'd find out."

I decided not to tell Blecher about the safe-deposit box or the envelope I had retrieved.

"Mr. Gordon," said Blecher, "I'm sorry that you received the wrong kind of hospitality in Munich. We will continue with our investigation. Do you remember any witnesses?"

"No," I said. "I left the bank but while still inside the building was hit on the head with a dull object, a club or something. That's all I know. There were people who saw me on the floor and tried to help, but I don't know who they are or whether they saw who did it."

"Can you come to the station so that we can take your complaint?"

"Yes," I replied, "but not just now." I had more important things to do.

"Yes, I understand you need some rest. Call me when you feel better."

"Polizeidirektor Blecher, I thank you for your concern, but I also must tell you that I have information that can't wait. Ariel Peled was taken because her kidnappers thought she had something they badly want. I can give you some help in your investigation."

"Go on," he said.

"You know that Mina Bernstein received a ransom note at her pension, with a number to call for further instructions. It's a pay phone. I have the men who took the call on videotape, though from a distance. I also have another telephone number called by the two people, probably Latinos, after they thought they had spoken with Bernstein."

"Thought they had?" he repeated, wanting to make sure.

"Yes, I recorded the conversation, and it was not Mina. It was some other woman. There are at least three suspects you should look for: the two persons who spoke with the woman who said she was Mina and their boss. I suspect that the boss is in a separate location from 'the apartment' they mentioned as the place where Ariel is being held."

I decided not to tell him about the envelope Guttmacher was holding for Ariel. I wanted to get it first.

But I did tell him how I had recorded the conversations and gotten them on videotape. "I'm leaving the tapes here in this office. Please arrange for a pickup," I said, and I also gave Blecher the telephone number they called. I thought he'd be appreciative.

"This is all very nice, but why didn't you seek the assistance of the police?"

"Because Mina was adamant that the police be kept out of it. Her only concern was her daughter, and her captors demanded in the note that she not call the police. I notified you about the kidnapping against Mina's instructions."

I hung up and turned to Lovejoy. "You can handle this, can't you?" He looked almost too cool.

"Of course," he said, but it was clear that he was trying to stay as far away as possible from the whole affair.

I left the consulate and decided that my next move would be to visit Herr Guttmacher. Blecher could wait with my complaint. I had to see Guttmacher before the police finally found out about DeLouise's letter to Ariel. I went to the bank and asked the receptionist to connect me with the gentleman. I gave her my name and Guttmacher was on the line like a shot.

"Mr. Guttmacher, I'm sorry to come unannounced, but I have just spoken to my clients and I need to see you immediately."

"I'll be happy to meet with you," he said. "How about tomorrow at ten?"

"No, I mean today. Now."

There was a pause. "Let me check my calendar," he said. I thought he was pretending some reluctance. "I can see you in thirty minutes."

I sat down next to the annoyed receptionist. I couldn't have cared less. Twenty minutes later I went upstairs to Guttmacher's office. His secretary showed me in. Whoever invented whiskey sour did so after seeing her face.

"Hello, Mr. Wooten," said Guttmacher, getting up to shake hands.

"I'm pleased to see you again," I said. "Thanks for finding time for me on such short notice."

I got straight to the point. "My American partners just told me that a leading member of our group is missing in Munich and that you were his local contact."

His smile froze. "Who is he?"

"Raymond DeLouise. They told me that he made some arrangements with you." I emphasized the word *arrangements*.

That was it. I'd put my best cards on the table. If Guttmacher had a better hand, he would win. If DeLouise had introduced himself under any other name, I was finished with this guy. I couldn't do here what I did in the Grand Excelsior, when I had managed to get three bites of the apple until I discovered that DeLouise had used the name Peled.

"Yes, yes," said Guttmacher absently, looking like he was collecting his thoughts. Then he said, "You never told me that you were connected with Herr DeLouise."

Bingo.

My cards were better than his, but since I had no immediate answer, I ignored his question. "We're from the same group of investors. He was the first to come to Europe with some of our capital. I need to continue from the point he left off. Let's work on it," I suggested.

Guttmacher was no fool. "Excuse me," he said trying to take over the conversation, "but I need to be convinced that you are his partner. He never mentioned your name."

"In our operation, we work independently, but the money comes from the same source. You can relax, Herr Guttmacher. I can give you details about certain activities that only you and DeLouise know. This should show you that he shared secrets with me."

"And what details are those?" asked Guttmacher.

"DeLouise gave you an envelope for Ariel Peled."

Guttmacher was weighing the information.

"Where is Herr DeLouise now?" he demanded.

"I don't know. DeLouise may have taken off with some young German woman for a beach vacation in North Africa for all I care. But business is business, and we must continue. You and I know the rules." I hoped I sounded conspiratorial enough.

Guttmacher didn't seem to be convinced. "Please understand," he said, almost begging, "I believe you, but German law requires that I get some written proof."

The schmuck! *Now* he cared about the law.

"Fine," I relented, "what do you need?"

Guttmacher looked gratified to have regained some control. "I need something to show, like a power of attorney from DeLouise or the lists we gave him for the materials and equipment."

Something to show? To whom? Materials? Equipment? What was he talking about? Was there a transaction going on? I couldn't ask, of course.

"I have a power of attorney he gave me in New York a year ago. It was notarized, would that do?"

"Notarized? Yes, yes, I think so."

"OK, I'll have it faxed to you right away." Another quick task for Tibor in Tel Aviv.

"Thank you, Mr. Wooten. That will solve the problem, I'm certain."

This guy looked to me like he was pissing in his pants — Guttmacher's body reactions were weird. He was beside himself. But why? He must have feared something he thought I knew, or he viewed me as a threat to his interests. There had to be a reason for his fear. If I found it, perhaps I could use it as leverage to get Guttmacher to spill some information about his dealings with DeLouise.

═══

I returned to the consulate and set up shop in a small conference room next to Lovejoy's office. Three hours later I had a fax with the power of attorney. The cover letter said that the "original" was being mailed next day to my hotel. I sent the paper on to Guttmacher and called him moments later. "Yes, yes," he double-talked again, "it's OK. So, I can tell you that the meeting is scheduled for this afternoon. I'm glad you are substituting for Herr DeLouise, whom I couldn't find. These gentlemen don't like to wait."

"Yes, tell me about the meeting," I said. "Who is attending?"

"Cyrus Armajani and Farbod Kutchemeshgi as well as Roberto DiMarco from Broncotrade."

"Anyone else?"

"Just you and me."

Broncotrade. I'd heard that name earlier. Where had I heard it? And those other names. Who were those guys?

"At what time?"

"My office. Two o'clock."

I wracked my tired memory. Then it came to me: Broncotrade's telephone number had appeared on DeLouise's hotel bill.

I burst into Ron's office without so much as a knock. "Ron," I said, as he raised his head from his desk in surprise, "have you heard the names Cyrus Armajani, Farbod Kutchemeshgi, and Roberto DiMarco from Broncotrade?"

Not surprisingly, he came back immediately.

"Broncotrade is an Italian trading company suspected of supplying embargoed materials to the Iranians. DiMarco is president of the firm. The other names don't ring a bell, but I can check with the Company upstairs." He meant the CIA.

"Please ask them. I need to know."

"I'm not sure they'd tell me without knowing why I need the information."

"Turf wars again?"

"No," he said, "plain vanilla procedures."

"I'm about to participate in a meeting, as DeLouise's substitute, with a German banker and these guys. I have no idea why the meeting was scheduled, but I couldn't ask because I was supposed to be in the loop, being DeLouise's business partner. The German banker who arranged the meeting apparently doesn't know that DeLouise is dead — or, if he does, he's a good actor. If he or any of the other participants of the meeting know about the DeLouise murder and had something to do with it, then I'm walking into a trap."

"Why?" asked Ron. "You could still be the partner who doesn't know about the murder."

"Because if these are the guys who murdered DeLouise, they could conclude that I'm as dangerous to them as DeLouise was. They don't know what DeLouise may have told me. If DiMarco's connection to Iran indicates that the other two men are Iranians, then I'm sure you know that human lives are cheap for these guys, and if they have any doubts, they eliminate you without prior or further notice. I'd like to live; I still have unfulfilled plans."

"Let me run upstairs and see what they have on these names."

I waited in Ron's office. Ten minutes later he returned with another man.

"This is Eric Henderson, Chief of Station, CIA," said Ron, introducing a balding tall man in his forties who wore rimless eyeglasses over shifty blue eyes. "He's interested in hearing more about your meeting."

Hell, I thought, I came here to get information, not to share any.

"What do you want to know?" I asked, slightly annoyed.

"Everything you know about the participants in the meeting and its purpose."

I started from Genesis and went right through to Deuteronomy, the whole story of my mission up to this point. When I finished I looked at his face, waiting for a muscle to move. No go.

Eric kept up the sphinx act for a moment and then said, "I'm not sure it's a good idea to let you go to the meeting by yourself. Cyrus and Farbod are Iranian agents on a purchasing mission for nuclear materials and missile technology. DiMarco is one of their fronts for the actual purchase and shipment arrangements. Now that Iraq has invaded Kuwait, and the U.S.

and its allies are sending threats in the Iraqis' direction, the Iranians in general and their intelligence services in particular are on high alert. This whole thing is a matter of national security. I ask that, until otherwise instructed, you do not attend the meeting. I need to call Langley."

He got up and left the room without another word. I was puzzled and fuming.

I looked at Ron. "Do I take my instructions from this guy who can't make a move without calling headquarters? Does he always stick his 'No's' into other people's business?" I punned.

Ron didn't answer. Maybe he didn't get it either.

I picked up the phone and called my man in Washington, D. Stone. He wasn't in yet, so I left an urgent message to call me back at Lovejoy's office at the Munich Consulate. I was angry and frustrated. I thought I was running my own show, and now this guy Henderson was trying to take over.

Thirty minutes later the phone rang. Henderson walked back into the room as I lifted the receiver.

"Dan," said David Stone in his soft voice, and then continued without waiting for my response, "they say it's a matter of national security. I want you to cooperate."

"David," I said trying to keep my composure, "this guy is rocking my boat. I'm making good progress. He's talking principles but acting on interests."

"I can understand your frustration," said David. "As always, you continue to take your instructions from me only. But don't make any unnecessary waves."

"OK, David," I put the phone down quietly. This was no time to refuse my boss's instructions.

"You can go to your meeting, but we want you to wear a wire," said Eric.

"What for?" I asked innocently, already knowing the answer.

"We've got to get a record of that meeting. We don't have enough time to bug the place, so it's up to you."

I decided to use this opportunity to score some points for my side.

"Look, if you're putting me into one of your operations, is there something else I should know? I can't go in there wearing your wire without some back-ground. I'd be a sitting duck if something went wrong. Now that I know who these guys are, this whole meeting might be a trap. If Guttmacher or his friends were involved in DeLouise's murder, I'm next."

"You already know all you need to know," said Henderson in a conde-scending tone. "You made up the story about being attorney Peter Wooten, DeLouise's partner, so stick with it."

"Look," I said trying to control my mounting rage, "I don't understand what your problem is. You obviously know what's going on, so why not tell me? I can continue just so far with my fake story about my partner-ship with DeLouise. If I don't come up with more credible information, I'm finished."

"I thought you were going to the meeting before I asked you to wear a wire."

"True. But going there to learn more about DeLouise's connection to the bank is one thing. Wearing a wire that could connect me with the Iranians' worst enemies if they find it is something entirely different. It's my neck that's going to be on the line in that room. Unless you give me more information about these guys and what they're up to so I can have some control of the meeting, I'm not wearing your damn wire. And you can even call the president."

Eric was a bit taken aback at my unexpected outburst. He wanted to have his cake and eat it too, but I guess he realized that there was no point in alienating me after all.

"All right, here's the deal. We don't have much time so I'll try to give it to you briefly. There are several things going on at the same time, so be patient. The things I'm about to tell you are a mixture of public informa-tion, information that is still unknown to the public but isn't classified, and, finally, some classified pieces. We have no time to sort it out, so treat all of it as classified."

I nodded.

Eric pulled out a folder with a few printed pages and looked at them while talking to me. "Tehran is secretly building weapons of mass destruc-tion. That's no secret. However, that requires a vast industrial base because it's an extremely complicated process. So these guys are looking to buy materials and machinery. We must know what they need."

He'd finally gotten my attention. I nodded for him to continue.

"Fine," said Eric, "here is the next issue: now we're facing a new problem. Many members of the Soviet military are feeling the earth moving underneath them, after Gorbachev gave up East Germany so easily. They don't know what's next, and they fear the unknown. Their morale is very low and their wages are meager, when they're paid. Same goes for their nuclear scientists. We hear that they're looking for ways to make money off their own missile and nuclear development. We also know that Iranian agents are intensively working in Soviet Central Asia searching for nuclear material. There is a planned meeting between a source in Kazakhstan and Iranian agents. We think that the Iranians take that opportunity very seriously and plan to send a technical team, which includes U.S.-educated physicists, to check the goods."

"Who are their contacts?" I asked, appreciative of the quality of the intelligence.

"Never mind," said Eric. "The important thing is that there are scientists and maybe government officials who are willing to sell Iran nuclear materials. We need to look closer into the vibrations we're getting from that direction. See if anything is mentioned concerning the Soviet Union, or more particularly Kazakhstan and the other Central Asian republics. See if you could develop it further without arousing suspicion."

"Anything more specific?"

"Just bear in mind that the Iranians are launching an accelerated effort to increase their supply of weapons-grade plutonium to build an atom bomb. Originally the program was meant to put Iran on the nuclear map and help crown itself as the superpower of the Islamic world. But now that their archenemy Saddam has invaded Kuwait, finding himself at odds with the U.S., the Iranians feel it is a good time to accelerate their nuclear program in order to deter the U.S. from attacking them while they are in the vicinity. Being a local superpower also gives a thick hint to the other oil-rich countries in the Gulf to obey Iran's directions concerning production and pricing of oil. They want to be the guys with their hands on the spigots."

"So you are not quite certain what the Iranian agents are up to?" I asked.

"No. Although I'm strongly convinced that Armajani and Kutchemeshgi's mission is to continue with their leaders' original plan to get the weapons-grade plutonium and other compounds, I'm not sure about that. They could be on a mission to get missing parts for their missile program. Therefore, you should try to get as much information as you can on their mission. If they're on the missile program, see what they still need. And if they are buying nuclear stuff, I need the list of compounds and equipment they are looking for."

"Obviously," I said, "it's a known fact that the current members of the club make it especially difficult for more countries to join the nuclear race."

"Right," said Eric, and continued. "We know that Iran is encountering serious problems with the development of a nuclear weapon, but, still, they could be only a few years away from producing the first Islamic bomb using indigenous facilities. They can always lower their standards by using plutonium-239 and weapons-grade uranium. There are uranium deposits in Jazd province that contain 60 grams of uranium in every 100 kilograms of ore, sufficient to produce a small stockpile of nuclear warheads in four years.

"The Iranian government wants the world to believe that their only nuclear facility is a nuclear power station in Bushehr. But, as always, they are deceitful. They have several top secret nuclear programs, none of which are for peaceful purposes. One such facility is in Natanz, one hundred miles north of Isfahan. They claim that the reactor is intended for peaceful purposes only. Their cover story is that it is meant to eradicate the desert by creating enough energy to desalinate seawater for extensive agriculture."

"I think we are considered desert, for their purposes."

Eric gave me a rare smile. "Right. The facility is currently being built near the old Kashan-Natanz highway in the village of Deh Zireh. They fenced an area of four hundred square miles to deter intruders. The installation will have more than one thousand employees and when completed will be mostly underground, with ten-foot-thick concrete walls wrapped by an additional concrete buffer. Once the installation is operational, Iranians would be very difficult to stop. Remember the name 'Kala Electric'; they use that company as a front for purchasing equipment abroad. The name could surface during the meeting. They are establishing eight additional companies to disguise the true purpose of these facilities."

Eric looked at me like a teacher who is about to give up on a stupid student. "Do you follow?"

"Yes," I said. I had a few questions, but I was getting tired of his patronizing tone.

"The other planned secret facility is in Arak's Khondaub region, on the banks of the Qara-Chai River. It will probably be used for cooling purposes. The front company for that project is Mesbah Energy Company."

I nodded, memorizing the name.

Eric continued. "Now see the connection between the two facilities," he said as he wiped his rimless glasses. "Natanz will be a uranium-enrichment plant. That's a sensitive nuclear site, much more than a fuel-fabrication installation. If exposed, their pretext would probably be that they are building it to produce low-grade uranium to be used as reactor fuel. We know that with a little effort these plants could be converted to make weapons-grade uranium. Our sources tell us that if plans go ahead as scheduled, the Isfahan uranium-conversion plant will convert yellowcake into uranium oxide, uranium hexafluoride, and uranium metal. While there could be peaceful uses for the other materials, we are concerned because they clearly plan to use uranium metal."

"Why?"

"Because uranium metal has very few civil uses, but it is a basic component in nuclear weapons."

"Anything nearing completion?"

"Yes. The uranium centrifuge program has been secretly operating since 1985. Next year Iran's laser-enrichment program will be fully functional. Both programs use technologies for making fissile material for nuclear-power plants or weapons. During the past two years Iran also made plutonium at the Tehran Nuclear Research Center. Plutonium production means one thing: they have a nuclear-weapons program. I have no doubt that they are building a nuclear bomb. They plan to install centrifuges at both sites as backup should the other one be bombed."

"Do they already have enough fissile material?"

"No. But we estimate that Iran will have a total of almost 19 kilograms of fresh 80 percent enriched uranium in two to three years from now. They could use the irradiated fuel from their reactor and supplement it with import from other countries, with or without their governments' knowledge."

"You mean stolen?"

"Yes. Look around. We are in a buyers' market. Someday, somewhere, someone will be greedy enough to sell it to the eager, oil-rich Iranians."

"How many bombs could they build with what they'll have soon?" I asked.

"Just one. All they need is 18 to 20 kilograms of uranium," said Eric. "We suspect that Iran, after the Iraqi invasion of Kuwait, intends to use all their highly enriched uranium and even continue enriching portions of it. They are probably planning a final weaponization process to deter the U.S. from attacking them while they're in the neighborhood."

Eric continued, "We think that once the Iranians complete the bomb construction, they'll have two options: the first is to test the bomb in the Iranian desert. The world would then treat Iran as a local power with a nuclear capability. Then, their tacit control over neighboring oil-rich countries would be tolerated, albeit opposed."

"And the second?"

"Their first bomb would be too big to launch with the obsolete missiles the Iranians currently have. Our friends at the Mossad say that the Iranians could try to detonate a bomb near Israel. All they have to do is put it on a boat entering Haifa harbor. They couldn't send an airplane because any unidentified plane approaching Israel's airspace would be shot down immediately."

I knew what Eric was referring to. There were rumors that Iranian-backed terrorists had maintained all along that it was possible to cause devastating destruction in Israel by using a boat carrying even a primitive atom bomb.

"But wait," I interrupted. "Didn't you tell me earlier that the Iranians need the materials their agents are looking for to boost the destruction capacity of their bombs? I don't understand why, because even a small A-bomb would be enough to change history."

"We don't know why. Their attempt to obtain these boosting materials could be psychological warfare to scare off the West, or it could be a part of a bigger plan. I don't think the Iranian fanatics limit the area of potential use to the Middle East. There could be other targets. The United States for example."

"OK," I said, "I got the picture. Are the threats imminent?"

"No. Unless they buy or steal ready-made bombs. Otherwise they are approximately ten to twelve years away from a homemade A-bomb."

"Got it," I said.

"Next, have you heard of Gerald Bull?"

"The Canadian engineer hired by the Iraqis? Yes, what about him?"

"He was a brilliant weapons-research specialist. In 1961, Bull convinced the Pentagon that large guns could be used as launch platforms for nose cones for orbital reentry. He started Project HARP — for 'High Altitude Research Program' — to study high-altitude ballistics and large guns. For political reasons his financial plug was later pulled. Bull transferred HARP's assets into his private corporation and worked as a consultant to foreign armies on issues of artillery.

"In the mid-1970s the South Africans were in conflict with the Communist government of Angola. Bull, with a silent nod from the CIA, helped South Africa design a new 155-mm howitzer with a range exceeding that of any other known cannon. With the new guns, the South Africans had no problem stopping the Angolans.

"However, by the time Jimmy Carter was elected president, apartheid South Africa had lost favor, and Bull was caught in a legal quagmire and charged with illegal arms dealing. He pleaded guilty and served six months in U.S. federal prison in 1980. When he got out, Bull was devastated personally and financially. His reputation was ruined, he was kicked out of his facility in Quebec, and his company went bust.

"Bull left Canada and settled in Brussels. He looked for work everywhere and found consulting work in China and Iraq. Entangled in a bloody war with Iran, the Iraqis bought hundreds of Bull's howitzers from Austria and South Africa. The guns were very efficient on the open fields of the border between Iraq and Iran, where no protection was available for the Iranians from the Iraqi shells. Bull became a celebrity for the Iraqis, who increased his pay and code-named their Bull-managed new weapons systems 'Babylon.'

"Bull knew that Israel would not tolerate an Iraqi-built supergun that would put Israeli cities within its range. Therefore, as an insurance policy he secretly double-crossed the Iraqis when he contacted the Mossad and provided them with information on Babylon, thereby hoping to spare his project from an Israeli attack. Bull then deceived the Israelis *and* us. He managed to divide the project into small portions and had the pieces of the project manufactured quietly. Even his own family was kept in the dark.

"Israel became concerned because Bull also designed highly accurate navigational systems for the Iraqi missiles. First the Mossad tried to warn Bull and make him stop. His apartment in Brussels was burglarized several times, but nothing was taken. He misread the Israeli tenacity and ignored the not-so-subtle message. So on March 22, someone was waiting for him outside his apartment and shot him five times. He died on the scene. No one was ever caught."

"This is not a clean war," I said.

"No. And it works both ways," said Eric. "After the Iranian Islamic revolution of 1979, the Iranians physically started eliminating their opponents under the command of Hojjatoleslam Ali Fallahian, their intelligence minister."

"Has anything happened recently?"

"Yes. Dr. Elahi, deputy leader of Derafsh Kaviani, an opposition group fighting the Islamic Republic, was just assassinated in Paris by an unidentified killer. We think it was done by Fallahian's agents."

I touched my neck. It was still there.

"Get the picture?"

"Yes, when you actually explain things to me slowly, I understand very quickly," I said, as mildly sarcastic as he'd been condescending. It must have escaped Eric, though. He didn't respond. Eric continued. "OK, then there's the Mossad's continued silent war against suppliers of war materials to the Iraqis."

"But the meeting is with the Iranians, not the Iraqis," I said.

"I know that," said Eric. "With Saddam busy, and Bull dead, the Iranians are looking to scavenge the remains of Bull's projects for the Iraqis. They know firsthand how efficient Bull's guns were, and they're hoping they can pick up what Bull left behind. Anyway, everyone in our trade is extremely cautious these days. Keep your eyes wide open. By the way, the Mossad could be interested in this meeting as well, as outsiders or even insiders."

"What do you mean by 'insiders'?"

"Well, any of the participants at the meeting could double as a Mossad agent or informer."

"OK," I said, "I'll do my best. Any security instruction?" I asked, feeling that the participants in the event I was about to attend could have my head on a platter.

"Frankly," said Eric, "I find it odd that professional Iranian intelligence agents would agree to meet these days with an American, any American, to discuss their purchasing plans. Therefore, the whole thing could be a simple scam, or a trap. Any way you look at it, it doesn't feel right. So I think you should appreciate the bug we're attaching to your back. It'll give us an idea of what's going on during the meeting, but it will also alert us if something goes wrong and you become a target."

I nodded. "Obviously," I said, "this is a game of interests. I want to use Guttmacher to find DeLouise's assets and Guttmacher is using me for something, which I haven't identified yet. I don't think he swallowed my story about being DeLouise's partner, but still, he's deeply afraid of me for some reason. Otherwise there's no basis for him to let me continue playing my act."

"And the Iranians?" asked Eric.

"I don't know if they're players or spectators. Apparently, if they know I'm coming, maybe I have something they need."

Henderson didn't answer. I thought I should tell him about DeLouise's flight reservations to Moscow and Baku, Azerbaijan; it could be connected to the meeting there Henderson mentioned earlier. But just as I was about to tell him that a technician entered the room. It was 1:00 P.M. and time to get ready. He asked me to take my shirt off.

The technician attached a transmitter on my lower back with adhesive tape and asked me to put on my shirt.

"How does it feel?"

"Cold." I put my shirt and tie on.

The technician attached a pin-size microphone behind my jacket's right lapel.

"The pin is both a microphone and a low-output transmitter. It picks up anything said within a fifteen-foot range and transmits it to the transmitter on your back. That one can resend the signal as far as one thousand feet. Even if they discover the transmitter, it doesn't look like a radio transmitter. We designed it to look like a massage vibrator, the same one that is used to alleviate lower back pain. Only an expert could tell it's in fact a transmitter. In the unlikely event that you'd have to explain the device, make up a story about lower back pain. Additionally, the unit acts like a bug detector. It sweeps the area to discover any listening devices or recorders. If one is detected, a warning vibration is sent to your back, and the transmitter automatically operates as a recorder only and, in order not to be detected, emits only minimal, mostly undetectable radio output. The pin microphone looks like a regular pin only slightly bigger. Again it takes an expert to tell. Remember, the battery on the pin microphone is limited to sixty minutes, so we are giving you one other device."

"And what is that?"

He gave me a ballpoint pen, the kind you can buy for ten dollars a dozen.

"It's a high-power UHF transmitter," said Eric. "'Ultra-high frequency' is used in a range that causes no interference from other equipment, such as aircraft or taxis. The frequency is preset so no tuning is necessary. Even when closely examined nothing unusual can be found, yet the pen conceals a hidden transmitter that will pick up the slightest whisper and transmit to our dedicated UHF receiver up to a distance of fifteen hundred feet away. Of course, it is also a fully functional pen, in case Guttmacher tries to use it."

With a chuckle, he added, "You can simply 'forget' it in Guttmacher's office, anywhere around his desk. The pen has a solar battery, which feeds itself from any source of light, even a lamp, so leave it where it would be exposed to light. That would assure continued transmission long after you leave the room."

"It's all very nice," I said, "all these gadgets, but do I get any protection if they find out that I'm a walking spy-electronics store?"

Eric nodded. "We'll be out in the street. Remember, we hear everything, so if you're in trouble we'll come and get you."

We went downstairs to Lovejoy's car. Behind us were three others, each with three passengers. The delta barrier was lowered and we drove off. I looked back but didn't see any of the other cars.

"They're taking alternate routes. We don't want it to look as if you're coming in a motorcade," said Ron, reading my mind.

I was dropped off two blocks from the bank, following standard operating procedure. I walked to the bank and went directly to Guttmacher's office. It was 2:00 P.M., right on the button. Although it was not the first time in my job that I have gone into a situation in which a physical threat might be present, I felt that the forthcoming encounter would be different. I was not nervous; I felt tense and focused.

VI

Guttmacher welcomed me, took my coat, and went to his closet to hang it up. I pulled out the pen Eric gave me and casually put it in the pen and pencil holder on Guttmacher's desk. I looked over my shoulder; Guttmacher was busy hanging my coat and didn't notice.

Guttmacher came at me, all smiles, and said, "They're all here." He opened a set of sliding doors and we entered a connecting conference room. There were three other people waiting: a short European-looking man dressed straight out of a fashion magazine and two darker guys in their forties with very short beards. They did not look like muscle to me but more like businessmen. Both wore business suits and had clever black eyes.

"This is Mr. DiMarco, president of Broncotrade," Guttmacher introduced him first, "and these are Mr. Cyrus Armajani and Mr. Farbod Kutchemeshgi from the purchasing mission of Iran's Atomic Energy Commission." We shook hands. As they got up I noticed that they had potbellies. I sat around the table and Guttmacher started.

"I told my Iranian friends and Mr. DiMarco that you are substituting for Mr. DeLouise. How is he?"

"I don't know. Raymond has always been a ladies' man and used to disappear at times for a few days whenever he met a suitable girl to keep his nights active. This may be one of those times." I decided to take that avenue in case they knew that DeLouise was in fact dead.

"The problem is," continued Guttmacher, "that DeLouise was working on some transactions in Moscow when he disappeared." I sat silently.

"There's another small matter. We gave Mr. DeLouise a two-million-dollar advance. Now he and our money are missing," said Armajani, in a heavy accent.

So DeLouise stiffed them for two million. Was that why they may have sent him to the morgue? I wondered.

"I'm willing to go along and continue from where DeLouise left off, but frankly, I don't know where that was. Perhaps you could help me," I ended, turning to Guttmacher. "Let me review with you the stuff DeLouise left to bring me up to speed. I know we could help you in Moscow; our contacts there are extremely good. But I must know what you need and when."

Roberto DiMarco then said, "We gave DeLouise a list of equipment and supplies we need. And now he's disappeared. As his partner, we're expecting answers from you."

The two Iranians looked at me impassively waiting. I had to show that I was in the loop or the meeting would end there and then. The only card I had was my knowledge of DeLouise's Moscow plans; I had to share that knowledge with them. Otherwise, why on earth would these guys believe a complete stranger?

"DeLouise had plans to go to Moscow tomorrow, he'd already made airline reservations on Lufthansa. He may have left earlier, I don't know. He didn't leave me any instructions."

DiMarco stared at me. "Anything else? Have you talked to DeLouise recently?"

"No," I conceded, "when I arrived I couldn't find him either." Some truth wouldn't hurt, I thought. "However, if you're really interested in moving this thing forward, you'll have to help me do it. I don't have DeLouise's lists. So one option would be to wait until DeLouise shows up. The other option is to work with me. All I have is my sincere wish to go along with you, so I suggest we stop playing hide-and-seek."

When no negative reaction came, I took the initiative.

"Mr. Guttmacher, would you please bring copies of the documents you gave DeLouise?"

All eyes turned to Guttmacher.

Guttmacher moved in his chair, his eyes shifting from me to the Iranians to DiMarco and back. Armajani nodded to Guttmacher in approval. Guttmacher got up and went to his office. I heard the sound of metal drawers opening and closing. In a moment he returned to the conference room with a file folder. We watched his movements.

"This is the DeLouise master file," he said and threw it on the conference room table.

I was the only one who reached for it. The folder was almost two inches thick. I opened it and started to quickly run through its contents. It had several pages of correspondence between DeLouise and Broncotrade, a ten-page document in English on onionskin paper with a letterhead in Arabic script, and photocopies of bank statements and wire transfers.

"That's enough," said Farbod Kutchemeshgi, after less than a minute. He reached for the file folder. It was the first time he'd opened his mouth or moved.

"For example, take lithium-6 compounds, palladium, and beryllium," Armajani's voice caught me off guard. "They are on the top of the list. Do you have any answers?"

"No," I conceded, "at least not yet. I need to go over the list and try to follow DeLouise's lead." I didn't like the situation or the suspicious way they were looking at me.

"This is it, for now. You are not taking any lists from this office. DeLouise received information from us, took our money, promised progress in Moscow, and disappeared. That will not happen again." The implied threat in his voice was obvious.

"How long would it take you to find out?" asked Farbod Kutchemeshgi, ignoring what Armajani had just said.

"I don't know yet, but I understand the urgency." I thought it was a reasonable response that would have been acceptable in any business circumstance. Evidently, it was unsatisfactory here.

"Look at me," said Armajani slowly, in a whispering tone that echoed across the room. "We haven't got much time, and the same goes for you. We need results; we need answers. DeLouise fed us his bullshit and we have no patience for yours! The only way you could prove that you're indeed DeLouise's partner is by delivering on his promises. Otherwise . . . " he didn't finish the sentence, but I got the message. I could feel cold sweat traveling slowly down my spine.

"We gave DeLouise an advance on the Russian delivery and we want results. Now!" He raised his voice a couple of levels. I looked at Guttmacher. He was pale. The poor schmuck was visibly unnerved.

"I came here to help you out. So I don't think shouting or threatening me will get you anywhere. I'm willing to continue from the point DeLouise left off, but I must know what it is."

They waited for me to continue.

"You say that you need lithium compounds, palladium, and beryllium. I need to know quantities, payment, and delivery arrangements. You don't buy this stuff by mail order, do you? If you can't tell me now, I'll look for DeLouise and his files and get back to you with my answers if I ever find him." This was a good time to see if my last sentence triggered their attention. If they had anything to do with DeLouise's murder or if they knew about it, I could expect some human reaction. When none came, I had to conclude that either they were not human or they knew nothing about it.

I remembered what Eric told me about the Soviet scientists looking to make an extra buck and the mention of Moscow by Armajani, so I added, "If you hold your cards so close to your chest, you make it difficult for me to help you."

"What do you mean?" asked Kutchemeshgi.

I was making progress. After the mental battle, logic and necessity won out over suspicion, though not by much.

"I mean that DeLouise got your money but I don't know if he made any payment to the Soviets. You're not telling me, DeLouise isn't around to tell me, how am I supposed to know? You may end up paying double, or not getting the goods at all, just because you're stubborn. How can you expect me to work for you while you blindfold me?"

"What guarantee do we have that you won't disappear on us like your friend DeLouise?" And when I thought he was finished Kutchemeshgi added, "How do I know you're not an American spy?"

"You don't," I said, regaining my confidence. "You've told me nothing, I never received any money from you, I owe you nothing, but I'm still agreeing to help you. And if you believe I'm a spy, we can end the meeting right now. This may assure you are not divulging any information to a spy but will also guarantee you the dead end you were faced with before I arrived. Besides, what's espionage got to do with it? Everyone knows that Iran is trying to make commercial purchases in the world's markets. Why the secrets?" I remembered what Alex had taught: "At a certain juncture in this kind of negotiation, make a show of frankness." I wasn't sure it would work with Iranians, whose national heritage and tradition is to negotiate. But apparently my approach worked.

"All right," answered Armajani, although I looked at Kutchemeshgi. "We'll go along with you for now. Here is your first mission: I want you to retrieve the file DeLouise was holding. Then we'll talk." Another cold chill went down my spine. "But we'll be watching you."

I got up and left the room. I didn't even offer a handshake. I had achieved a few things though; they'd agreed to talk if I found the file.

Back on the street I kept my eyes open for Lovejoy or any of Eric's goons. I knew they wouldn't try to make contact with me, but I also knew they were close by. I picked up a cab and told the driver to take a detour or two, then headed back to my hotel, thinking hard.

I tried to put the pieces of the puzzle together. The people in the meeting didn't seem to know that DeLouise was dead. Either that or else they were worthy of Oscar nominations. But given what I had just heard in the meeting, DeLouise's disappearance had stalled their efforts. So, I concluded, the Iranians hadn't killed DeLouise. It must have been somebody else. On the other hand, as all lawyers like to say, if the Iranians *had* killed him that meant that he was expendable. As always, surprises were possible and expected.

In the cab I scribbled the names of the compounds I had seen on the list before Armajani had taken the file from me. I went straight to my room and was met with one of those surprises — a well-built stranger of a man. Before I could open my mouth, he said, "I'm Tom and I work for Eric. He has asked me to bring you over to see him."

Although Tom looked and sounded American, I needed more proof.

"How do I know that you work for Eric?"

"Eric, Ron, and the technician are waiting in the safe house to get that equipment off your back."

That was enough for me. "Let's go," I said. "How far is the apartment?"

"A ten-minute ride. I'll go out first. You follow in a few minutes. I'll be driving a German taxi; when you see me, flag me down."

Our three friends were waiting in a third-floor apartment. I stripped off my jacket and shirt, the technician removed the gadgets, and I handed Eric the notepad I had used in the cab to jot down the names of the few materials I could remember after glimpsing the file.

"You'll want to look at this," I said. He took the pad and quickly scanned the list, then put it aside.

"The bastards are raising the stakes after all."

"What do you mean?" I asked.

"The materials you mentioned tells us the direction they're heading. Small details sharpen the total picture. Langley could estimate exactly the direction of their program. On a more urgent level, I hear that the Iranians only need you to get DeLouise's file. I don't know what he did or said to gain their trust, but apparently he conned them. So now their heads are on the line. If the Iranian government finds out that their agents gave such sensitive material to somebody who disappeared with it, I wouldn't want to be in their shoes. If I were Armajani or Kutchemeshgi, I wouldn't buy green bananas because I wouldn't be around when they're ripe."

"And maybe I'm right on the other front," I said. "Guttmacher was only passively involved in the meeting. Right now it seems to be the Iranians versus DeLouise. Guttmacher and his bank are only the battlefield."

"So it looks as if you're staying on the job; you've got to go on with the game to find out what you need to know about DeLouise's business," said Eric, pretty much taking me for granted.

I decided to ignore his statement. "So what are these chemicals used for, and why do the Iranians need a covert operation to buy them?"

"Chemistry and physics not your strong points, huh?" snapped Eric.

"Nope," I replied, "I skipped every single class."

He grabbed a chair and said, "I guess I'll have to educate you." And proceeded to give me a short lecture on nuclear energy and how it works.

"OK, let's get back to present-day reality," I said, when he'd finished giving me the basics of nuclear fission. "You probably picked up from that funny transmitting pen that Guttmacher has a file in his office with substantial information on Iran's purchasing plans. This is the one I got a quick look at. I'm convinced that they have additional files with documents concerning the Iranian purchases. Once I retrieve DeLouise's file, I don't think they'd expect me to supply them with the radioactive compounds that they paid Raymond DeLouise to obtain. Frankly, I don't think we would get that far, because what they're concerned about are the lists they gave DeLouise that apparently have gone missing with him. I'm sure they're not convinced I'm DeLouise's partner. That's why they demanded that I first produce the file they gave DeLouise. I don't know what happens if I do produce the file. It could go either way."

"What do you mean?" asked Eric.

"Well, if I succeed in retrieving the file, they could think I had something to do with DeLouise's disappearance and connect me to some foreign-intelligence service. Or they could be convinced, and my legend sticks that I am, after all, DeLouise's business partner. Under both theories, they'd have the file and then could choose what to do with me. But since the file was not among the items DeLouise left behind, this is all just guesswork."

"How do you know that?"

"Because I saw the police report that came with the body to the morgue. There was no mention of any such documents in his room or on or near the scene. But I do have some ideas about the Iranian files Guttmacher keeps in his office."

"I'm listening," said Eric.

"Why not copy the files? Or simply remove them altogether."

Eric looked at me. "Tell me more," he said. "We didn't realize the Iranians let Guttmacher keep their files in his office."

I wondered why Eric hadn't thought of this. Why did I have to be two steps ahead of everyone else here?

"It's worth the effort. The files could be very helpful to you with the amount of detail they have."

"Is Guttmacher's office part of the bank's security setup?"

"That's my guess. I didn't see any metal doors between his floor and the main business floor. Looks to me like his office is less secure than the rest of the bank."

"Do you know where he keeps the Iranian files?"

"No, and I didn't see any file cabinet or vault in his office. When I left the conference room the file was still on the table."

"OK," said Eric. "I need a report from you on anything you saw in his office. And we'll need a floor plan. Once I see your report, we'll take it from there."

It was clearly time for me to leave. Tom drove me back to my hotel.

I went to the restaurant to get a bite of good German schnitzel. When I returned to my room, the phone was ringing. It was David Stone.

"Dan," he said, "Call me from the outside."

I went out to the street and called him from a pay phone.

"Dan," he said, "I just finished a phone conversation with friends at the Company. They were satisfied with your performance. What have you done this time?"

"That's nice, but I haven't made any progress on my real assignment. I still haven't clearly identified our guy's asset-protection scheme. The stolen money is my top priority, not playing spy games with mean-looking Iranians."

"Really?" said David, with a grain of sarcasm. "I get the impression that this is exactly the kind of operation you enjoy."

"I do," I conceded. David was familiar with my Mossad past and knew me well enough to pick up on my zeal to close the case.

"They want you to continue in this game," he said.

"You know me," I said. "I won't be the problem."

"I'm sure of that. It seems that you could be part of the solution."

I went back to my hotel. There was a message from Eric waiting at the front desk. I couldn't call him from my room, so downstairs I went out to the street once more.

Eric got right to the point. "We need to talk," he said in a tone that, as always, sounded like an order. "Wait outside; Tom will pick you up in fifteen minutes." I knew what he was going to say; David had just told me the CIA wanted me to continue. My hunch was that the topic would be the break-in.

"I'll be back outside in fifteen minutes," I said and went upstairs to change. I wondered at my sudden burst of energy. Maybe it was the spirit of the chase kicking in.

Ten minutes later, as I prepared to leave, my old in-field training came into focus. The Iranians were in the picture now, and knowing their aggressiveness I had to assume that they'd be watching me, as they promised. I had to raise my level of caution and alertness. I went to my suitcase, looking for anything that might have a connection to Israel. I checked all my clothes for Israeli laundry labels. I emptied all my pockets, removing coins, business cards, and receipts. I put all my receipts from Israel into an envelope. I opened my briefcase and removed anything that had to do with Israel or with my work for the U.S. government. The bulk of it was already in the hotel vault but I checked again anyway. Then I went to my laptop. I deleted all the files with an Israel connection. I transferred anything to do with my work to a new directory and protected it with double-entry passwords. Finally, I installed a new ten-character password to enter the entire system. Although I was sure that neither Guttmacher nor the Iranians knew where I was staying in Munich, I left the room carrying the laptop and the envelope with me. I turned the TV on and put the "do not disturb" sign on my door. I had also marked the door with a hair. I'll run out of hairs soon, I thought. I should develop some new tricks.

I went outside to my car. A day earlier I'd removed it from the hotel parking garage and parked it in the street. If I was under surveillance then the car was also being watched. By parking it publicly, it was easier to spot watchers without letting them know that I was aware that I was under surveillance. The car was where I'd left it. I gave it a quick look and walked on by. I went into a bakery, bought a pastry, and watched the street while the clerk made change. I spotted a dark fellow who seemed to have his eye on my car and decided to take no chances.

I left the bakery and continued walking to a bus stop. When the bus came, I got on and stood next to the door. I got off at the next stop, crossed the street in front of the bus, and went up a one-way street, against traffic. No one seemed to be on my trail, so I went through a convenient shopping arcade and then back onto the main street. Everything looked normal. I caught a cab and went back to the hotel. Tom was waiting patiently.

Eric was already nervous when I walked in.

"Where were you?" he demanded, as if I were his teenage daughter coming home at dawn with smeared lipstick and a wide smile.

"There was a watcher on my car," I said quietly. "I don't know whether he was just a lookout or if he was going to follow me."

"So what did you do?"

"I went on a short trip, made sure I wasn't followed, then went back to the hotel for the pickup."

Lovejoy walked in, and I handed him the envelope containing my ID and odds and ends, including a spare key to my hotel room. I asked him to send the stuff to my New York office with the diplomatic pouch and to keep my laptop and the spare key in his office.

"Dan," said Eric, "I checked with the Company. They want the Iranian files in Guttmacher's office." He looked at me for a reaction, but I simply sat waiting for him to continue. "We reviewed the audiotape of your meeting at the bank. It's obvious that the Iranians won't let you walk with even one file. The only way to get the files would be through a break-in." He paused again. I continued to play the calm, attentive listener.

"There isn't much time. And under ordinary circumstances it would take a while to organize it properly."

Was he telling me that the job couldn't be done? Why bother?

"So what are you going to do?"

"There is another country closely monitoring the Iranians," said Eric, as if he were revealing a secret. "Israel."

I saw what he was getting at.

Eric continued, "We know that right now there are some Mossad people in Munich making preparations to approach the Iranians."

"Approach?" I asked.

"Well, you know what I mean, either lightly or deeply."

"Do you mean steal their information?" I called a spade a spade.

"That's light," he said, leaving me with a clear understanding that "deep" meant elimination.

I was too familiar with Mossad procedure to believe that Eric had received such information from them. It was unlikely that the Mossad would ever alert another foreign-intelligence organization of its intention to eliminate a rival. It would stand in violation of basic operational rules and could cause serious legal and political problems. Any cooperation between intelligence organizations, even of friendly nations, is always based on an "honor him but suspect him" basis. Operational or intelligence cooperation, yes, but information on assassination plans — never. I wondered how Eric had found out. Did he have a mole inside the Mossad? It was a question that would remain unanswered.

"So you want the Israelis to do the job?" I asked, doing my best to seem surprised.

"Almost," said Eric. "With our active assistance, of course. Langley has already contacted Mossad headquarters in Israel and they've sent here a senior representative to discuss it."

Eric looked at my face, but I didn't react. I was sure now that he knew about my past. Langley would never have authorized my unrestricted access to the details of such an operation unless they'd first reviewed my file, and if they'd authorized my involvement it must have been in spite of my past rather than because of it. Yes, Eric knew, but I wasn't going to give his smug ass any satisfaction by looking guilty for not telling him earlier. Strictly a need to know basis — and he didn't need to know this detail about my past.

"Fine," I said unconcernedly. "What do you want me to do?"

"The Israeli government agreed to discuss the matter, but they didn't promise they'd send their people in. This is where you come in. You were there, you met the Iranians, you saw the lists, you know what catastrophe it could wreak on Israel, and you can help their representative get all the facts." And then he added nonchalantly, "And you've worked with their representative so you should know how he thinks."

Now he did surprise me.

"Who is he?" I asked, ignoring Eric's revelations and thereby affirming them.

"He's right here," said Eric and, with a total lack of drama, opened the door. Benny Friedman entered the room.

"Greetings, Daniel, long time no see." I tried to keep a straight face, but Benny knew me better than that. "Gotcha!" he smiled at me.

Of course! Benny was the head of the American desk at Tevel, the Mossad's branch in charge of cooperation with foreign-intelligence services. That made him the right person for this meeting. How did they know I knew Benny? I couldn't ask now, but I would have to find out. Were the Langley boys watching me as well?

There were only four of us in the room but it was already too cramped.

"Mr. Friedman," said Eric solemnly, "let's not waste time. You know why we're here, but there have been some alarming developments. Through Dan and other sources we hear that the Iranians are planning to increase substantially the destruction power of their yet-to-be-built atom bomb. They plan to insert a few grams of tritium and deuterium directly into a plutonium warhead. The result is a huge boost of power. That process allows the Iranians to reduce the amount of plutonium, which is, as you know, heavily regulated and expensive to manufacture. Now, add that to our mutual knowledge of the progress the Iranians have made in their missile program and their threats against Israel, and you get the bottom line: the Iranians have the intention and could have the means to destroy Israel. They've shown their aggression against U.S. allies by sponsoring terror attacks. It is typical of Iran to use proxies for its dirty war. The Iranian government rarely sends its soldiers but instead uses their state-sponsored terrorist organizations, such as Hezbollah in Lebanon or Al Dawa in Iraq, to do the job. Even the capture of the U.S. embassy in Tehran and the taking of the hostages was not carried out by the Iranian army or police, but by so-called 'revolutionary students.' The Iranian fanatics won't hesitate to use doomsday aggression against another U.S. ally, Israel, through one of their clandestine terrorist organizations, and then offer their help treating the surviving victims."

Benny scratched his head and said, "And do I know what all this adds up to?"

"Of course you do, it's written all over your face," said Eric. "First, the file Dan saw at the bank would tell us exactly what they expect him to do and allow him to continue with his charade. And second, that file and hopefully the others kept at the bank would give us an insight into their capabilities. Our scientists would be able to predict how advanced the

Iranian development of the bomb is and how long it would take them to join the nuclear club. That could give us several options: hit the suppliers, the buyers, or both. You hit the Iraqi nuclear reactor at the last minute, just before it became 'hot.' I don't think Israel would want to wait and risk missing an opportunity with the Iranians."

Eric looked at me, waiting for me to fill Benny in with further details and comments.

"Hey, I'm here for DeLouise's money," I said. "That's my prime mission. I need to bring ninety million dollars back to the U.S. Treasury. When this thing is over, I'm back looking for the assets."

"Hang on," said Eric, "there could be some dividends for you from this matter." Then turning to Benny he asked, "What do you think?"

"Do you need our manpower for the break-in, or do you just need intelligence?" asked Benny.

"Well, I was about to suggest Israel could actually do it with our active assistance. Israel has a lot to gain from the operation and a lot to lose if we let the Iranians continue with their plans. Besides, I think you have a score to settle with the Iranians."

Benny gave him his brown-eyed shrewd look in anticipation.

"I need to bring this matter to the head of the Mossad," said Benny. "But before I can do that, I need to collect essential elements of information, what we call EEI, and risk assessments on both political and operational levels. Based upon the results of these evaluations, the director of the Mossad will decide whether we're in or out."

"That's good enough," said Eric. "Although it'll be an Israeli operation, we'll have joint investment and joint profits."

Benny nodded to show he'd heard Eric, but knowing him I knew it didn't necessarily mean an approval. "OK, let's roll up our sleeves and do some research. The results, whether we play or not, should be useful to you."

"Fine," said Eric.

Benny continued, "I took the liberty of bringing two of our men with me. One is an expert in break-ins and the other is a logistics man. Do you have anyone here you want to attach to them while they look around?"

"How long do you think your EEI will take?"

"We'll be done here in one or two days, but that could change based upon the operational needs and risks evaluation. Then we'll continue in Israel with the political risks review. Finally, I don't know how long it will take for the director to decide once we submit the report for his review and approval. Bear in mind that even if he approves, he might want to consult with the prime minister."

"Give me a time frame for your country's decision," insisted Eric.

"A week," said Benny.

"Good," said Eric. "I have three men available to join your EEI team."

Benny turned to me and said, "Well, Dan, you didn't think we'd ever work together again."

"No," I admitted. "Life is full of surprises."

Benny pressed me. "Tell me what you think. You were inside the bank."

I thought for a moment. "From an operational point of view, I don't think there will be a problem breaking in to the bank. Guttmacher's office is not physically protected with bars on the windows or with a safety door. However, there could be some invisible protective device such as a sonic or infrared alarm system. Although I didn't notice any, that doesn't mean they don't exist. The EEI would give you all the facts you'd need to make a decision."

"That's enough for a start. Let's get our teams organized. I'll be working with Shimon, my break-in expert. What about you?" he asked Eric.

"Tom and Jeff," said Eric. "And, I think, Dan Gordon." He looked at me for approval.

"Sure," I said, "I'll be glad to, but I need to work alone."

"On the logistics assessment side, we'll need help," said Benny. "I only have one man with me to survey the needs and I don't know if you have the technical means here. If not, we'll have to bring them in from our European center in Brussels."

"Let's see the list of what you need," said Eric. "We could do that after the operational team recommends a course of action."

"OK," said Benny.

"Who handles the German police?" I chipped in.

"We'll treat that as part of the EEI," said Eric. "We'll consider the

German police from two angles. First, we'll fake an event and monitor their radio to hear if an entry to the bank was reported by an individual or automatically by a silently triggered system.

"Second, we'll work on a contingency plan in case the police stop a member of our team before, during, or after the operation. We need an immediate cover story, a plausible explanation, and a political decision about what nationality to claim if caught."

Benny nodded and turned to Eric. "I expect your team to do the drill on the German police. You have the right equipment for that. As to the cover story, I suggest we handle that in Tel Aviv as part of the operation structuring."

"That's OK with me," said Eric.

Benny added, "During the EEI period, even before we go into planning, we'll need a native German from this area, preferably someone who understands police jargon. I need to study the police routine here."

"I can take care of that," said Eric. "We'll record one or two days worth of police-radio activity. You could take it home with you for analysis."

"What about a cover story during the EEI period?" I insisted.

"We'll fabricate something. In fact my men are working on it as we speak," said Eric.

"Good," concluded Benny. "Are your men here? Mine are outside."

Tom and Jeff were called in, and Benny brought in Shimon, a skinny, dark Israeli with a wide smile. He looked as if he could infiltrate a keyhole.

Eric pointed to his guys. "They'll do the intelligence first, and Dan will join them."

Benny nodded and said "OK, Shimon, what about you?"

"I'll do some research on my own. I'm a burglar, remember?"

"I guess we're set for now," said Eric. "The next meeting will be here later today. Let's make it at eight tonight."

I went outside and Tom drove me back in his cab. I knew what I wanted to do. I'd been a lone wolf for a long time. As a child I had learned the Jewish sage's wisdom: "If I'm not for myself, who will be for me? And if not now, when?"

"Tom," I said, "change of plans. Take me to the bank, but let me off before we get there. I want to check out a few things."

Tom looked like a serious Robin Williams. "What do you mean?" he asked.

"Well, I've been inside the bank twice, so I know my way. I can wander around and get a better view of the security arrangements. The bank is open for business, so my presence shouldn't raise any suspicion. I'd be just another customer."

Tom said, "I don't have to remind you that if you're caught, you're on your own. Even so, I think you should talk to Eric about it; you could risk the entire operation."

"Don't worry," I said. "I intend to go back to the second floor to see what the visible security arrangements are and anything else I can learn. I met with Guttmacher, including one unscheduled meeting, so if I'm stopped I can always ask to see Guttmacher again."

He said nothing and dropped me off a block from the bank as requested. I entered a café across the street and went to the pay phone at the back where I searched the Munich yellow pages for a "spy store," one of those shops that sell gadgets to real and wannabe detectives and spies. That kind of place would have a wide array of electronic surveillance equipment. There were two such stores listed. I wrote down the names and left the café.

The first store on the list turned out to be only a short walk away. I noticed that dark clouds had begun to gather, and it had suddenly gotten a lot colder. I didn't have my coat with me and I ended up dashing the last few blocks as rain began to fall.

I browsed around the shop for a bit and finally bought ultraviolet powder and two ultraviolet light bulbs. Ultraviolet long-lasting detection powder is designed for the detection and identification of stolen items. The substance is invisible to the eye, and even when a small amount is applied on any surface its particles attach to the hand or object that touched it. Just dusting it can mark an article. When exposed to ultraviolet light, the item and anyone who touched it are easily identified. This is an excellent tool for small objects such as currency, paper, clothing, and any other surface.

By the time I left the shop, it was pouring and chilly. "Where the hell did I leave my coat?" I grumbled to myself as I hailed a cab to get back to the bank. Then I remembered where I had left it.

During the ride, I opened the powder bottle and sprinkled some on a paper napkin I had taken from the café.

At the bank, I went straight to the second floor. Guttmacher's sour-faced secretary was there. "Good afternoon," I said. "I was here yesterday, and I'm afraid I left my coat in Mr. Guttmacher's office. I gave it to Mr. Guttmacher when we went into the meeting, so it should be somewhere in his office." My forgetfulness was very helpful now. I decided that I'd unconsciously done it on purpose.

"Mr. Guttmacher is not in, but I can look for it," she said, and opened the door to his office. I followed her and quickly checked out the room. The radio pen was still in the holder on Guttmacher's desk, as neat and clear of paper as one would expect.

There were no cameras or blinking red lights on the ceiling or walls. "Herr Wooten," said the secretary, opening a closet, "there are several coats here. Please help yourself."

I looked in the closet. Three coats were hanging on a rod, including mine.

"That's mine," I said, and as I took it off the hanger I saw my prize: a steel vault on the back wall of the closet. I wanted to kiss the secretary, or my coat, but neither deserved it. I pulled the paper napkin from my pocket and surreptitiously smeared the vault's lock as I put my hand through my coat sleeve. I made sure Sour Puss didn't see.

"Thanks so much," I said as I walked out, "You've been a great help." I waited for a few minutes on the ground-floor hallway near the side exit to the street, until the place cleared out for a moment. I then quickly replaced the bulb in a wall light next to the exit door with the UV bulb. With some luck, if I were standing in the right position outside the bank my powder trick would work. I could spot anyone who touched the vault and used that exit.

I crossed the street and waited, leaning against a wall, pretending to read a newspaper. Two hours went by but no luck. Also, the newspaper was in German, of which I understood little, in print anyway. I was about to give up; I like cold climates but not when I'm dressed for spring and exposed to the relentless European autumn weather. But then suddenly the bank's exit glowed. A woman walked out the door with shiny hands. I took my camera and snapped her picture, then crossed the street just in time to see her catch a bus. I couldn't get a clear view of her but I was sure that it was not Sour Puss. I looked for a cab to follow her. The rain closed out that plan. The bus was long gone by the time I found a cab.

I went back to my hotel. As soon as I walked into my room I caught the unmistakable odor of cigarettes. Anyone who'd ever smoked and quit, like I had, would recognize that stale and bitter smell. Someone had been in my room and whoever it was had been smoking. People don't recognize that they leave odors behind. The smell had been on their clothes and now it was in the air. I checked the bathroom and the closets. All empty. I bolted the door and checked my room safe. The hair was missing. I froze. Then I opened the safe. My magazine was still there. I closed the safe. I took the credit-card-size bug detector Eric gave me and attached it to my telephone. The readings were negative. I couldn't trust the test as conclusive, though. Telephone PBX systems in offices and hotels sometimes send false-negative signals to bug detectors. I went with the bug detector around the room; near the television, the paintings on the walls, the drapes, the lamps, and the desk. Nothing.

I then checked my luggage; it was obvious someone had been through my things. Whoever it was was apparently more interested in my luggage itself than in its contents, because I saw that the rims of my luggage were slightly opened. I checked it with the bug detector. Nothing.

Although I still had a few hours before the 8:00 P.M. meeting at the safe house, I thought I should leave my room immediately. Obviously I was being watched, and I couldn't use the phone until I was sure it was safe. I dusted the safe and my luggage with the UV powder and left the room.

VII

I went outside to check the surroundings. I thought I saw the same Middle Eastern–looking man I'd seen earlier. I went into a café across the street and used the house phone to call Eric.

"It's Dan. I'm across from my hotel. My room was searched and the room safe was opened. There are other developments."

"Do you want to move?" asked Eric.

"No. I don't think that would be a good idea. Disappearing from the hotel would only let these guys know we're on to them. It would be wiser to continue playing the unsuspecting lawyer."

"OK," said Eric, "but I'll have to move the meeting tonight. The safe house we used earlier may have been compromised."

"What's the new location?"

"Jeff will be driving a different cab — it will be a beige Mercedes and will pass by the same location at 7:45 P.M. He'll take you to the meeting."

"I'll be there," I said. I hung up, then dialed another number at random and hung up once more. Just to keep any follower off the track.

I glimpsed at my watch; it was 2:20 P.M. I had a few hours to kill. I hailed a cab and went to the Oplatka Travel Agency. Even if the Iranians were following me, it could easily be explained as my effort to find DeLouise for them.

When we got there I asked the driver to park and wait in a nearby lot; a twenty-mark bill did the trick. There were five workstations in the street-level store with clients talking to the agents at four of them. I went to the only available desk, operated by a woman of indeterminate age; she could be a young-looking fifty-year-old or an old-looking thirty-five-year-old. I was never good at determining a woman's age. She raised her head and flashed a pretty smile.

"Good afternoon. I called this office earlier concerning flight reservations for Mr. Raymond DeLouise for Moscow?"

"Just a minute," she said and clicked on her computer.

"Yes, I see the reservation," she said.

"Has the ticket been issued?" I asked.

"No. It was never picked up, so we canceled. It also says here that a Mr. Wooten called concerning your flight and promised to get back to us on the delivery of the ticket. Apparently he didn't," she said, turning back to me. She must have thought I was DeLouise.

"I apologize," I said, hoping to sound embarrassed. "I'm Mr. Wooten. Raymond DeLouise is my partner. He couldn't make the flight; he is in the hospital even now as we speak." Alex's words were in my mind. "Be humble, show human emotions, give your subject some information to convince her that it's OK to give you the information. Make it sound like it's only a technicality that you don't have the correct account number or the information you are seeking. Don't sound conniving or sleazy. The door will be slammed in your face."

"I'm sorry to hear that," she said. "Is he all right?"

"Not quite," I said, remembering how pale and motionless he had been, stretched out on that slab in the city morgue.

"What can I do for you?" she asked.

"Well, since Mr. DeLouise is not in a condition to speak, I wonder if you could help me. I need some information."

"Sure," she said, waiting for me to continue.

"Did he pay for the ticket?"

"Yes, he used his American Express credit card, but we credited his account after the cancellation of the ticket." Seeing me holding my pen and a pad, she gave me the credit card number. I wrote it down.

"Did you also make a copy of his card?" I asked. "May I see it? We have several subaccounts of this card and I want to see to which one the credit note was sent to."

She went to the file cabinet and gave me the copy. "You may have this, I suppose, since we canceled the transaction."

"Thank you," I said, putting the copy in my pocket.

"Come to think of it," I said nonchalantly, "Did Mr. DeLouise make reservations for any connecting flights from Moscow? I may have to cancel them too."

"Yes," she said looking at her monitor, "I see here that after a three-day stay in Moscow he was booked on an Aeroflot flight to Baku, Azerbaijan, and from there back to Leningrad. We canceled these tickets as well."

"How about hotel reservations — did he make any? I'd like to avoid a late cancellation fee if at all possible."

"Yes, but only in Moscow, at the Cosmos Hotel. You'll have to send them a fax to see if they charged you any cancellation fee."

"You're very helpful," I said. "Our business is in such chaos ever since Mr. DeLouise was taken to the hospital. I have one final question. There is a young lady associated with our company who was working with Mr. DeLouise on their project; I don't know whether she also made the reservations through this office."

"Do you have her name?"

"Yes. It's Ariel Peled." I had my fingers crossed.

She clicked the computer's keyboard and said, "Yes. Ms. Peled booked the same flight number to Frankfurt connecting to Moscow, but it was not on Mr. DeLouise's scheduled flight date."

"Really?" I said, sounding surprised. "I thought they were traveling together."

"No, she booked it to leave just four days ago."

"Bingo!" I shouted in my head.

"Of course," I nodded, "I see. I should get in touch with her and tell her that Mr. DeLouise won't be coming to Moscow. She must be looking for him. Did she also reserve a room at the Cosmos?"

"Yes."

"When did Ms. Peled make the reservations?"

"Oh, it was a night before her departure. I see that the ticket was picked up here."

I thanked the agent and left.

This was my lucky day. I had a lead on Ariel. I went over the dates in my head. Had she been kidnapped at all? Maybe she'd been kidnapped and released. Maybe she'd escaped. Why did Ariel go to Moscow? Was she still there? Was the person traveling under Ariel's name in fact DeLouise's daughter or was it someone else assuming her identity? I didn't have a clue. At least not yet. As I walked down the street, I reviewed my findings.

First, I knew that there was a vault in Guttmacher's office. I suspected that the Iranian file — and there was probably more than just one file — might be in the vault, and I suspected that Guttmacher's office did not have an independent alarm system or monitoring cameras, but I had nothing to corroborate either assumption. I needed to find out the identity of the woman who'd left the bank with the UV powder marks on her hands; she might get us access to the vault's keys. Second, a smoker had paid a visit to my room and had gone through my things and might have planted something in my luggage. Third, from my visit to the travel agency I'd learned that DeLouise had never made the flight to Moscow. Well, I'd already known that. Also, Ariel may have taken the flight to Moscow and stayed at the Cosmos Hotel. She could still be in Moscow. Finally, as a small prize, I had a photocopy of DeLouise's American Express card. I pulled out the photocopy of the card. It was a Platinum Corporate American Express card issued to Triple Technologies and Investments, Ltd. The name of the cardholder was R. De Louise. The first four digits of the card showed that it was issued by an American Express center in Europe, but to derail a computer search he'd made it De Louise, in the French style.

I stopped at a stationery store near the travel agency and faxed the copy of the credit card to Lan, asking her to have the U.S. Attorney's Office issue a subpoena to American Express for the records of the card. Since there were pending proceedings in California against DeLouise, the government could exercise its subpoena power and force American Express to disclose all the transactions made with the card. Hopefully it would also lead me to Triple Technologies and Investments Ltd. and to the nature of its relationship with DeLouise; it could be his company but it could also be a company owned by a friend who let him use the company's name.

I went back to the parking lot and the waiting taxi. "Take me to the Sheraton Hotel. And go the long way. I'd like to be late for a meeting." I wanted to be sure I wasn't being followed. Driving through residential areas would make it easier for me to detect unwanted company.

I called Ron Lovejoy from the hotel lobby and told him about the search of my hotel room. "Did you report it to Eric?" Ron asked.

"Well, I called him earlier so he moved our meeting to another location. I don't even know where it is." I told Ron briefly that I might have traced Ariel's footsteps to Moscow. "Either she was kidnapped and escaped or was released, or the whole thing was a hoax. I don't even know by whom and for what purpose. We should also be prepared for a more sophisticated twist."

"What do you mean?"

"Someone could be traveling under Ariel's name. How do we know that this person is in fact Ariel Peled?" That was a conversation stopper, and I hung up.

Next, I called David Stone in Washington from another pay phone using a prepaid phone card. "David, I hope that this side matter won't delay my real job."

"It's a question of priorities," said David. "What you are doing now seems more urgent than your original assignment. That can wait for a few days."

"OK. I plan to go to Moscow immediately. I don't want to wait until we're done with the other business."

"Why?" asked David.

"The young lady's tracks lead to the Soviet Union. I don't know if she actually made the trip or whether her visit is connected to my matter or something else. I don't even know for sure if it's who we think it is. Either way, I want to find her. She's the main lead now in my scavenger hunt. Her father trusted her and left her written instructions. I'm sure finding her is vital to my investigation and I want to reach her before she makes any other moves." Without waiting for an answer I said, "I'll call you later."

"Not so fast," said David. "If you think it's a nuisance getting embassy and host-country clearance from Israel or Germany, try the Soviet Union! I could never get it this fast, especially not these days. So you'll have to wait or think of something else."

Well, I would have to come up with another plan. I had to use this narrow window of opportunity; I couldn't wait for the bureaucrats to move their asses. Moscow! I hadn't been there for a while. The spillover from the former Eastern Bloc countries and the fall of the Berlin Wall was shaking up the Communists, and chaos was spreading through the whole country. Moscow would not be the ideal place to visit just now. But being in the information-gathering game and not the travel business, I went wherever the goods were sold, not just where the friendly sun was shining.

Jeff came driving by in his cab at 7:45 P.M. sharp. I hailed him and got in without a word. Twenty minutes later we arrived at an apartment building, large but undistinguished except for a circular driveway and four entrances. Just the place for a safe house.

Jeff let me off and directed me to the nearest entrance. "Apartment 7F. I'll park the cab and meet you there."

I got in the elevator at the end of the lobby and went to the eighth floor, walked down one flight, and knocked. Eric opened the door.

The place had a big living room with a wide glass door leading to a balcony. There were three black leather sofas and a dining table with six chairs. Although the apartment was fully furnished, I could tell no one lived there. There were no flowers, photographs, books, souvenirs, or other personal items that would have transformed an apartment into a home. Benny, Shimon, and Tom were already present. Jeff arrived a few moments after me.

"OK, we're all here so let's begin," said Eric. "We all had homework, so let's see some interim findings. Who wants to start?"

Benny turned to Shimon and nudged him. "Go on."

Shimon grinned and went to the center of the room, where an easel was standing. He unfolded a roll of paper he was holding and put it on the easel. A large color photograph of the bank building displayed amazing clarity and detail.

Shimon stood next to the easel. "The building has three entrances." He pointed to the main business entrance in front. "This is where the public enters during business hours. There is a side entrance for employees, which is mostly used when the main entrance is closed and at all times for the employees working on the second and third floors. I assume it's a shorter way out. It is also convenient to the elevator."

Shimon removed the photograph and put up a second photograph taken from the rear of the building. He pointed to an entry shown at the bottom of the photograph. "The third entrance to the building is at the back and is mainly used by the superintendent of the building, by technical support staff, and for delivery of supplies and, very likely, cash and securities. A small truck can go up to the door.

"The bank building has three floors above ground. The main business floor is on the street level, the management uses the second floor, and the third floor is used for filing and storage. The building also has a small basement, mostly occupied by one big walk-in vault. There are no safe-deposit boxes for rent to customers. Metal bars protect the windows on the street level. These windows are also protected by an obsolete alarm system, the type that reacts to broken glass or vibration. I don't know yet whether that alarm system is connected to any central monitoring system in the building or elsewhere.

"The main entrance door is a heavy double door, probably made of metal sheets plated with a thin layer of copper. The lock is not a problem. However, use of the main entrance is ruled out because the bank is situated on a street that is active most hours of the day, and any forced entry from the front entrance is likely to be detected. The door used by the employees is also facing the street, though it doesn't look like a part of the bank building and may attract less attention."

A true professional, I thought in appreciation.

"Look at the back door," Shimon continued, pointing his finger at it. "I think it's the most suitable for a silent entry, if we opt to use a door. You'll soon see that there are other options. I did not detect any alarm systems in the hallway of either the side entry or the back entry; however, the doors themselves are protected with a rather primitive and outdated alarm system that should not cause us too much concern. I did not risk entering the second and third floors at this time."

We listened attentively. Eric was taking notes. Benny, reading our collective thoughts asked, "So, how do we get in?"

"At this time, our best way in is through the roof," said Shimon, pointing to the photograph. "See here, there is a tree in the backyard that extends all the way to the roof of the bank. I could climb that tree, pass onto the roof, and lower myself to a third-floor window, and from there go through the bank corridor and down the stairs to the second floor. But I'm not done with my end of the EEI, so let's not lock ourselves into that option. I'm still working on other possibilities."

Shimon paused, as if he were waiting for approval. He then turned to me. "Dan, you were there so you'll have to draw me a floor chart showing me where Guttmacher's office is."

"I shouldn't have a problem doing that. Besides, I think we are getting the floor plan from the city's building department. It's a public record available to anyone; you go and pull out in a central hall of archives the volume needed from a flat metal drawer, pay a small fee, and make a photocopy."

Shimon paused, waiting for comments, and when none were made he added, "Then there's the final question: Where is the file?"

"I have the answer to that one. I went back to the bank and discovered a small vault hidden in Guttmacher's office. My guess is that's where we'll find the file."

"And how did you arrive at that guess?" asked Benny.

"A case of a lost coat," I said, and then gave them the details, including a description of the vault.

Shimon smiled, and Eric turned to him.

"Could you do the entry?"

"I think so, if I'm given the word. I'll need support staff, backup force, security arrangements, and some equipment."

"If we are convinced that the file is in the vault, we still need to make a decision how to open that vault," said Benny.

"What do you mean?" asked Eric.

"We'll have to decide whether to detonate the vault's lock and leave the scene with the door blown away or try to open it and take out the file without being noticed. Once we have the file do we remove it and leave or make copies then and there, returning the file to the vault? If the latter option is taken it increases the chances that the entire operation will remain unnoticed, but it also increases the level of danger because copying will take time. From Israel's perspective minimizing risks is very important. If something goes wrong, I don't think my government wants to be connected to a bank break-in in Europe, even if the goal is important."

I knew what Benny was referring to. In fact, I'd wanted to say just that when Benny interrupted me. Covert operations, by definition, always had to have a built-in deniability factor. If the operation was exposed, the original operational plan must contain several levels of deniability to minimize the likelihood of positively linking the operation with the Mossad. Even when Israel releases the results of covert operations, the sources and methods utilized remain classified to protect sensitive assets.

All the Mossad's operations outside Israel are secretive and denied by the Israeli government. But there are denials and there are *denials*. When the Mossad kills a terrorist in his bedroom somewhere in Europe or North Africa, although Israel denies any connection Israeli officials leak the story to a foreign newspaper. This is how Israel kills two birds with one stone. The government denies any involvement so that there will be no protests by the foreign country whose sovereignty was violated by Israel. But the message is clear that Israel will pursue terrorists anywhere and under any circumstances. Then there are denials that are meant to distance Israel from any covert missions outside its borders. There are no leaks of operational details and in fact Israeli agents outside Israel spread "distracters" or "blowbacks," false information aimed at sending investigators on a wild-goose chase. That happens in "black operations," when Israel will stand to lose if it is connected to the operation. In the cost-benefit equation, the damage outweighs the projected gain from the exposure.

Benny continued as if he'd heard my silent explanation. "I believe that, although stealing the Iranian's nuclear materials purchasing list is important, Israel would not like to be implicated. So," concluded Benny, "if you want my recommendation for an Israeli participation in the operation, I'd suggest that the break-in be silent, the vault secretly opened, and the file copied and returned."

Eric sounded disturbed. "Opening a vault without explosives needs special equipment and additional professionals. It could take me up to two weeks to bring them over and orient them, and we may not have that time. Time could be of the essence; the file may be removed if we sit on our asses and wait for others to do our job."

You could cut the tension with a knife. It was clear that Benny was controlling the meeting. He was far more senior in the Mossad than Eric was in the CIA; he was also older and more experienced. I sensed that Eric was torn by his urge to tell Benny to play second fiddle or get lost and his knowledge that he couldn't do it without Benny, at least not as fast. I also suspected that Eric had a contingency plan if the operation was exposed and people were caught. He could always spin the media to put the blame on the Mossad.

"I need to add something," I said. "There could be a solution to the problem, but I'll wait for my turn." I looked at Eric.

"There's no need to wait. Go ahead and give us what you've got."

I poured myself a beer and began. "Earlier, I told you that I located a vault hidden in Guttmacher's office. I'm pretty confident that the Iranian–DeLouise transaction file is kept there, because I vividly remember hearing metal clicking when Guttmacher went from the conference room into his adjoining office to bring the file. It definitely sounded like a vault being opened. I suggest you check the audio; it must have picked that up. Now, here is the part that you still don't know: I have a snapshot of a woman who touched the lock of the vault today. I don't know anything else about her, but I think she could easily be traced."

"How did you get that?" asked Eric with surprise.

I told them about the UV powder and the UV lightbulb.

"You son of a gun," said Benny, "you remembered that trick? I think you and I were on the same team that rehearsed it ages ago."

"You're right," I said, "I remembered. I also used the powder to dust my hotel room. I had visitors today while I was away."

"The Iranians?" asked Tom.

"Possibly. They told me in the meeting with Guttmacher that they'd be watching me."

"Is your room clean?" asked Lovejoy.

"Yes, I sanitized everything. There's nothing in my luggage other than clothing. Everything else is in the hotel's central vault or at the consulate. They didn't remove anything, and all my stuff checked benign. But they may have planted some devices in my room or my luggage: audio, video, the works. I also noticed someone scrutinizing my car outside my hotel."

"OK," said Eric, "we all stay away from Dan. He's contaminated. He cannot be seen with any of us until further notice. Dan will continue living in the hotel, but communication with him is limited to calls from pay phones to our special secured line."

"I'm excluded from the quarantine," said Benny. "I'm a foreigner, nothing links me to Israel or to our meeting today, and I'm leaving tomorrow through another European country."

"Avoiding me may not be necessary," I said. "I have other plans. I traced Ariel's footprints and they lead to Moscow. I'm going there."

"What do you mean?" asked Eric. "She got away?"

"I don't know yet," I added, and told them about the airline reservations under Ariel's name.

"So you don't know if she actually made the flight?" asked Jeff, opening his mouth for the first time.

"No, I don't," I conceded. "And furthermore, I don't even know if the person traveling is in fact Ariel Peled. I simply haven't had the opportunity to work on it; I've only just learned this information. I was planning to call the Cosmos Hotel in Moscow to see if she checked in."

Eric went to the telephone, dialed a number, exchanged a few terse sentences, and hung up. "The office will do it for us."

"Since I have become a security burden, you won't mind my Moscow plans. I think you'll survive without me for two or three days."

"We'll talk about it later," said Eric, reassuming his control over the meeting.

"So what are your conclusions? Is the bank job doable?" asked Benny.

Eric thought for a minute. "We transcribed the recording transmitted from the pen Dan left on Guttmacher's desk. The metal clicking suggests a vault. I'm fairly convinced that Dan is right. The file could be in the vault. I also suspect that Guttmacher may have plans that he has neglected to reveal to his Iranian clients."

We waited for Eric to continue. Only Tom and Jeff sat back. It seemed as if they already knew what Eric was about to say.

"Guttmacher is somehow connected to the Latinos. We don't know how. We don't know if he's in bed with them or in competition with them. There were some angry exchanges on the phone between Guttmacher and someone. They spoke English, but Guttmacher paused twice to shout at his secretary to look up a word in the dictionary. In both instances it was a Spanish word. We know that as late as yesterday the file was in his vault because we heard him order a woman named Gertrude to bring the file out and we heard the vault click from a close distance."

"So then," I interrupted, "the woman in the photograph is likely the very same Gertrude."

Eric gave me the look reserved for teachers showing displeasure toward a failing student. "We know that. There are several other pieces of information we obtained from the transcription. One is that Guttmacher planned to go to Moscow soon. The second is that he's probably blackmailing DiMarco to split some of the commissions the Iranians are paying. Guttmacher threatened DiMarco that unless he agreed, he'd simply be bypassed."

"Is that all?" I was hoping my contribution to the operation would bring me closer to my original objective. While it was very exciting to participate in planning the operation against the Iranians, my main assignment was to locate and retrieve the missing ninety million dollars. The spy stuff was nice, but it was no longer my game.

"No," said Eric, "we have plenty more, but it's being transcribed now. However, Guttmacher doesn't spend much time in his office. There is no question that he's a serious money launderer. I wouldn't be surprised if most of his business is built on dirty money."

"OK," said Benny, "I need Avi, my logistics guy, to confer with yours. I'll attach his findings to my EEI report."

"Did you get the building plans?"

"Yes, I did," said Jeff from his corner seat. "It was built in 1936 and no modifications have been made since. We are preparing the floor charts on three different small plastic sheets that glow in the dark. So Shimon, or anyone else, could read them. But I need Dan to go over the plan of Guttmacher's floor, in case they made changes that do not need a building permit."

"No problem," I said.

"Good," said Shimon, smiling and exposing his perfect white teeth. "The plastic map is a good idea. But just in case, I use a night-vision scope that lets me see in the dark like a wildcat. Avi, show them our toy." He looked at the Mossad's logistics man, a tall slim guy with a military crew cut. He opened his attaché case, pulled out a scope with a strap, and handed it over to Jeff.

"This little baby enables you to see anything in pitch dark. It's the latest technology, made in Israel," he added with unconcealed pride. "This is a compact, lightweight, handheld night binocular combining night vision with a laser range finder and a digital compass enabling accurate azimuth and inclination and elevation measurements."

Eric gave it a brief, slightly jealous look and said, "OK, let's continue."

"What about the utility company's junction box?" asked Shimon.

"It's next to the fourth building down the road. We could yank it off in no time," said Tom. "It'll black out the entire block. The switch is mechanical, not electronic, so we can't make it look like the power failure originated from a different location. I think their repair team could be on the scene within thirty minutes of the power failure. We'll give them a drill later on tonight in another location to check their response time."

"Shimon, under the worst-case scenario how long would it take to enter the bank building in the dark and with the alarm system immobilized?"

"About ten minutes if we take the roof-entry option," said Shimon. "I'll climb the tree to the roof and, from there, to the third-floor window. If there are any alarm systems they could have a battery backup, so they could still be working. But in my experience many alarm systems go off in a blackout, so people are kind of used to it. Anyway, we'll try to shut down the alarm when we go in."

Jeff added, "We also planned a decoy operation in another bank down the block, Bayerische Hypotheken und Wechsel Bank. We're trying to learn how to trigger their alarm system. It's electronic and linked to a monitoring control center. We want them to think there's a break-in and send the police in that direction. The street leading to that bank is not directly connected to the street on which Guttmacher's bank is located, and any police-car movement would be in the opposite direction. The sirens would also tell people that the police are on the way without knowing that they're on the wrong way. We'll monitor their waveband."

"Now we're getting somewhere. Avi, you and Jeff need to talk logistics," said Eric. "You two can work at the dining table. Speaking of which, is anyone hungry?"

"Good timing," I said. "I'm starved. I haven't eaten all day."

I grabbed Benny by his arm. "Let's you and me be the pickup and delivery boys." We made a quick list of orders and left. It was time for Benny and me to talk.

VIII

The rule was to leave the apartment one by one, making sure nobody was in the hallway, and then use different building exits. We met and talked only a block away after checking for watchers.

"Let's find a kosher place," I said to Benny. He said nothing but I knew he appreciated my suggestion. He kept kosher; he wouldn't eat otherwise.

"I know a good one on Reichenbach Street," he said. Although it wasn't far, we took a cab. The place was bustling, many of the men wearing yarmulkes and beards. I saw Benny's eyes widen when he ogled the plates full of mouthwatering, cholesterol-laden delicacies. We placed our orders for takeout.

Benny caught me off guard. "I think you're angry at me for withholding recent information about DeLouise," he said in a tone that indicated it was all right with him.

"No, I'm not angry, I'm surprised or disappointed. More of one than the other. I'm not sure which."

Benny gave me his no-nonsense, sharp-eyed look.

"I couldn't tell you that Dov Peled, aka Raymond DeLouise, made a surprise contact with us after thirty-three years. You know the rules. Need-to-know basis. Even if you were still in the organization, I couldn't have told you unless you needed to know."

I sat there silently. I knew he was right, but somehow I had hoped that our friendship and common past would be stronger than these rules. I had to realize that even a strong friendship was a matter of degree in this business.

"At least can you tell me if you have Mina Bernstein? I hope that isn't information classified on a need-to-know basis. Even if it is, I need to know."

"No need to be sarcastic, Dan. Yes, we do. We sent her back to Israel. The lady wouldn't be safe here until Ariel was found."

I was moderately relieved. Lack of any elaboration by Benny showed me that maybe Mina didn't tell them about the safe-deposit box. Otherwise he would have asked me for a copy of its contents.

"Why did DeLouise call you?" I asked.

"He didn't call me personally. The duty officer forwarded his call to the unit controlling agents operating on foreign lands."

"What did he want?"

The waiter called our number and we went back to the counter to pick up the order. It smelled great: *brathächen* (fried chicken), *klopse* (meatballs), *bratkartoffeln* (the German roasted potatoes), *apfelmus* (thick applesauce), *doboschtorte* (a seven-layer cake with mocha cream), and bread rolls, which in southern Germany are called *semmeln*. At the last minute Benny ordered *kalb schnitzels*, breaded veal cutlets on rolls.

I had an instant recollection of my mother's kitchen. These were the same mouthwatering smells, only without her smiling at me and saying, "Come, I prepared your favorite dish, sit down and enjoy."

"Let's go," I said. I wanted to continue the conversation outside the restaurant. We stood at the street corner. I zipped up my coat. The sky was clear and the light wind chilled the air.

"What did DeLouise want?" I asked again.

"He needed help. He said that a Colombian drug cartel was after him for some documents implicating them in massive money laundering in the U.S. He said he couldn't call the police because he was wanted by the U.S. Justice Department over the failure of his bank and he was afraid of being extradited to America if he contacted any European police."

"Couldn't he use his Israeli identity? The U.S. wouldn't have had INTERPOL broadcast an international lookout for someone named Dov Peled. INTERPOL was looking for Raymond DeLouise."

"Apparently he wasn't sure whether the U.S. government knew about his additional identity. He couldn't risk it."

"Why did he think the Mossad would help him?" I became curious.

Benny hesitated as a cab drew up. "Let's get in," he said, in a transparent effort to cut the subject off.

"No, let's walk; it's only a mile or so. We need to clear this up before we get back to the others. Did it have anything to do with his service for the Mossad in the French nuclear installation?"

Benny turned. "Fine, let's walk if you insist. I need the exercise."

We went on for a while, but Benny said nothing.

"So?" I urged.

"I see you know about his past. So why are you angry at me?"

"Because I thought we were friends. You could have tipped me off about his phone calls to the Mossad."

"That's the whole point. I couldn't because it might have compromised other things. You know that. Don't forget I wasn't talking to my friend Dan Gordon, I was talking to Dan Gordon who works for the American government."

"I don't have conflicting loyalties," I said. "What I learned in the Mossad I keep a secret, and what I learn during my service for the Justice Department I give the same level of confidentiality and loyalty. In my line of work there's no conflict between Israel and the United States; on the contrary, there's a joint interest."

"I respect your integrity," said Benny, perhaps feeling that he'd hit a raw nerve. "I'd never doubt that. There's no need to be defensive."

"So DeLouise was cooperating with the Mossad? Is that it?" I continued, satisfied with Benny's clarification.

"No," he said decisively, "definitely not. He said that if he was caught by the Colombians they'd kill him, and if the Americans found him first he might be interrogated and the fact that he was planted in France by the Mossad could surface."

"So he wanted the Mossad's help in return for his silence? Is that all?"

"Generally yes," said Benny, relieved that I seemed to be satisfied by this. "He was subtly blackmailing the Mossad. We weren't going to be blackmailed, not by him or anyone else." Benny sounded determined.

"My God. So you people terminated him," I said in disbelief.

"No," countered Benny, "of course we didn't. We don't do our own people, you know that."

"So what did you do?"

"We told him that we couldn't protect him, but if he came to Israel he would be safer from the Colombians."

"I must say I understand him. There's no absolute safety and I guess he didn't want to be living in Israel or anywhere else in constant fear of the Colombians." Israel, like most European countries, does not extradite its own citizens, so at least he'd be safe from that. "But, come to think of it, he was born in Romania of Romanian parents, so he could have obtained a Romanian passport. Why couldn't he use it to go to Israel or anywhere else?" I pressed.

"He said that he risked himself once going abroad because he felt that it was unlikely that anyone would think he'd be using the name Popescu again. The potential benefit was substantial: getting enough on the Iranian plans to allow him to trade this information for the termination of any criminal charges against him in the United States. This was a decisive move, which he took in view of the potential benefit. But using the Romanian passport just to escape would have rendered him a fugitive. Only a question of time before he was discovered."

"A calculated risk," I concluded, when the information had sunk in.

"Anyway, his suspicion of Guttmacher was growing, and DeLouise felt that his problems should be resolved at their root so that he could return to the United States. He understood that his stay in Europe under Guttmacher's protection was short-lived. Trading on the Iranian secrets was a better choice, because it had the potential to totally extricate him from his problems."

"What did DeLouise say to your offer to return to Israel?" I asked.

"He said he couldn't because he was afraid to use an airport. He was sure that INTERPOL had every patrol on every border looking for him. Airline records and passport control could have exposed him to the authorities and to an immediate arrest and extradition to the United States."

"There are many ways of entering and leaving a country without letting the border control know about it," I said matter-of-factly.

"Of course," confirmed Benny, "but DeLouise was reluctant to come out of hiding and trust a smuggler who could blackmail him or simply sell him out. Although he never said so, I suspect he wanted us to do the job.

Extricate him from Germany, bring him to Israel, and give him a new identity."

"Did you do it?" I asked, wondering how many more identities DeLouise had.

"Certainly not. From our perspective there was no justification for that. Particularly when facing the risk of confronting the U.S. and Germany. We are not in the business of hiding people who run from the law, even if they were in our service thirty-three years ago."

"Did you tell him that?"

"In a way. I told him he was on his own. So, as second best, he asked us to send his daughter, Ariel, to Munich to help him. We agreed to pass on his message."

"Is that all you did?" I asked. I didn't quite buy his answer.

"No, of course not," said Benny, with the small smile of a cat who'd just licked the forbidden cream.

"I'm listening," I said, encouraging him to continue.

Benny looked at me hesitantly. "And this time I need to know," I insisted.

"Well, we had two of our guys in Germany watching him. More to see what he was doing rather than to protect him."

"You mean your men witnessed his murder?"

"Our instructions were to give him some room, unless they were the only ones who could save his life. And he was attacked when they were across the street more than fifty meters away. Too far to step in."

"Did your men identify the killer?"

"No, they were wearing helmets."

"They? The police report said there was one killer."

"No, there were two of them on a motorcycle. Remember, our guys are professionals and they'd been watching DeLouise, while the bystanders who testified to the police were alerted to the event only after they heard the shooting. The one who sat on the backseat of the motorcycle got off, approached DeLouise, and shot him, while the other waited five meters away on the motorcycle with the engine running."

"Come on, tell me what you know. Don't make me cross-examine you," I said impatiently. "I guess you discovered who the killers were."

"No, we didn't. That's a job for the police. We had no direct interest in it. Since DeLouise was no longer a security risk for us, who killed him became a secondary issue. Hey, life's tough."

"Oh yes," he added, as if he had just remembered something. "Here's something we couldn't give the police because we didn't want to be connected to the crime scene." Benny took a spent shell out of his pocket. "These guys who killed DeLouise may have looked like professionals but they weren't; just a couple of sloppy thugs who left this behind."

I took the shell and inspected it. It was a .38 caliber and had no manufacturer's name on it. Benny was right; a professional would never have left this behind. It's the same as leaving your fingerprints. If the gun were found, the shell could be connected to the gun and its owner to the crime.

I put the telltale shell in my pocket and turned to Benny, "Thanks, did you pick up on all his European and Soviet escapades?"

Benny didn't answer.

"Go on," I said, "It's important for our joint operation, and I know you have more information. I need the whole picture before I go to Moscow."

"Why do you ask? You mean Eric didn't tell you?"

"Tell me what?"

"We told him what we knew. I was sure he gave you that information."

"No, he didn't," I said bitterly. "I don't like that jerk. He sits on important information like a dog on a heap. He only likes to get information, not to give any. It seems that the only thing he'll share with me is a communicable disease," I said sarcastically. "Tell me what you gave him."

"It's not a big secret that we've been chasing the Iranians in Europe trying to figure out what they are planning next. We know that ever since our jets leveled the Iraqi nuclear reactor in 1981 they've been suspecting that their nuclear capacity would be our next target."

I had no argument with Benny.

"It's obvious that the Iranian ayatollahs are fanatics and will not hesitate to wipe out Israel," Benny went on. "Our research department believes that the Iranians are deliberately leaking the news about their nuclear capacity. They are signaling the U.S., which is now planning an attack on Iraq, to stay away."

It was time to shift the conversation back to what I needed. "What about DeLouise and the Iranians?"

"We still don't know if he tried to con them and make a quick bundle, as he told us, or if he, in fact, intended to deliver on his promise and broker a sale of nuclear materials from one of the republics of the Soviet Union. We don't know for sure yet; we are working on that now."

"So I guess the Mossad would recommend that the joint operation with the CIA be authorized? It would be a good opportunity to share information and move a step forward in finding out what the Iranians still need."

"I don't know," said Benny. "There are so many factors in the decision-making process. The prime minister would be the one to decide, although the head of the Mossad has the same authority."

"Well, at least he has some understanding of how these operations work," I said. "After all, didn't he head up European operations working out of the Paris station?"

Benny took out one schnitzel from the bag and ate it while we walked. "Now you see why I insisted that the break-in be silent," he said. "That's why I interrupted you. I knew what you were about to say. But I wanted Eric to hear it first from me."

Benny had learned how to be a politician too.

"We can't let the Iranians know we have their shopping list or that we are able to identify their suppliers."

"Why?" I asked, although I knew the answer.

"Because they will take protective measures. We don't want that to happen. You saw what happened to the people who didn't listen to our friendly advice to stop shipping deadly materials to Iraq. Remember what happened to Gerald Bull. But I can offer you the flip side of it," he added in a serious tone. "If the break-in becomes public, as well as the list, the suppliers will panic and might halt further shipments before we have exhausted all the benefits from the intelligence. They know that having their names on the front page of every newspaper in the world could be detrimental to their health, not only from Israel or the U.S. but also from unexpected directions. Think of the green environmentalist organizations; they are an emerging power in Europe," he concluded with an ironic smile.

Of course I remembered. Israel had suspected that a TZ1 nuclear reactor built by the French for the Iraqis in the late 1970s, allegedly for "research for peaceful purposes," was in fact a crucial leap forward in Saddam's dream of an Iraqi A-bomb. Israel knew better than to attribute any peaceful intentions to Saddam. Israel had complained publicly, but the French had refused to listen. The transaction was too financially lucrative. So on the night of April 6, 1979, at a factory in La-Seyne-sur-Mer, a small French village on the Mediterranean forty miles east of Marseille, a group of men penetrated the warehouse where the core of the nuclear reactor designed to hold the fuel had already been crated for delivery to Iraq and blew it up. Someone had then left messages at the news agencies attributing the detonation to the "French Ecologist Group." Nobody had ever heard of the group before, nor has anyone heard of it since.

As a result Saddam had had to wait almost two years for the next shipment. Again, Israel wouldn't allow it, and Israeli jets flew one thousand kilometers and destroyed the reactor site in Iraq just shortly before it became "hot." As usual, political hypocrisy went into operation, with public rebuke of Israel but a silent satisfaction that the Israelis had done the dirty work of others. "It was a world-class 'bang and burn,'" I said.

"Yes, but anyway it's not for me to decide if Israel should participate in the planned break-in into Guttmacher's office," Benny continued, taking the last bites of his sandwich and bending forward, trying to keep the oozing sauce from staining his pants and then throwing the paper napkin into a garbage can on the street corner. "My recommendations would come only from the operational perspective. We should let the politicians make their own decisions, or mistakes. Do you remember the MOG rule?" No, I hadn't forgotten the rule governing break-ins, commonly referred to by its Hebrew acronym. But Benny answered the question anyway. "Operations and incursions must be approved by the prime minister. Although I believe that the planned break-in is not included in the list of activities requiring preapproval, in the 'cover your ass' atmosphere I wouldn't be surprised if the head of the Mossad would nevertheless seek an approval."

"You still haven't told me what you know about Raymond DeLouise and the Soviets," I persisted.

"Let's talk inside. Eric must clear it first. I don't want to be caught in a turf war here."

We took separate entrances and went to the seventh floor.

"Food is here. And it's about time!" said Tom, when he opened the door. I noticed that although we were expected, Tom had a .38 in his hand as he opened the door.

We went to the table and distributed the food.

"Eat," said Benny to Eric, Tom, and Jeff. "Probably your first shot at kosher food. Enjoy it!" It was only the second time I saw Eric smile.

Eric's mouth was full now, so it was a good time to ask him about the information that the Mossad had given him on DeLouise's contacts with the Soviets. After he heard what I was about to say, he'd choke — an outcome that was not undesirable in my book. "Eric, I was under the impression that while I'm here to help you, you would also provide me with some information on my own case. I am aware that Benny shared information with you on DeLouise and I've been the last to find out about it. Last time I checked, you and I work for the same government."

"There was never any such understanding," said Eric coolly. "The Justice Department had agreed to attach you to our operation because of your familiarity with DeLouise's affairs and your initial contact with Guttmacher. I don't know of any agreement in which I give you what I have. You're the one who's giving, not me."

I couldn't believe my ears. The guy had more nerve than I thought. My mother used to call it *chutzpah,* and I was about to call it quits. I got up and said, "In that case, I'm leaving, and you can call the Justice Department if you don't like it." Although I had started this tirade as partly genuine and partly staged, I now felt real anger surging in me. Benny, who sensed the storm coming, quickly said, "I'm sorry, it's my fault. I told Dan that I gave you what we have on DeLouise's European activities and his Soviet and other connections. I didn't intend to create a rift. We all need Dan in this matter."

Eric swallowed his food. "We do work for the same government, but I can't allow you to use the same information we are working on and potentially risk CIA operations."

"Look," I said, "you have no monopoly on information. The fact that the Mossad has given you whatever they gave you means only that they have that information. I could have developed it independently, and I'm sure others have it as well. I'll run my business, and you'll run yours, but you can't stop me from doing my job. In my asset-recovery work, when I come across information that could be useful to another U.S. government law-enforcement agency, I relay it on. Nobody has ever tried to control me the way you do. You want to work together? Fine. You don't? That's also fine, but I've had enough of your little games."

Eric looked almost guilty, conceding that he'd overdone it. He didn't need me walking out on him, reporting to Washington about his tactics and making him look like someone who couldn't coordinate a multi-agency operation. That wouldn't look good on his efficiency report. After all, I wasn't asking him for confidential national-security information. I didn't even ask him to reveal his sources; the source was sitting in the same room with us. So why the bullheadedness?

"Look," said Eric, in his best conciliatory voice, which wasn't much to begin with, "I wouldn't mind giving you more information on DeLouise, but you'll have to agree to coordinate with me so that you won't accidentally expose our other sources or interfere with our operation."

"I have no problem with that. But *coordinate* should mean what it really means. Don't expect me to take orders from you when it concerns my work."

Eric didn't answer.

"I'm waiting," I said. It was now or never.

"Fine," said Eric. "Benny, you can tell Dan what you've told me."

Benny opened his briefcase, pulled out a yellow pad, leafed through the pages, and began.

"First I want you to know that substantially all of the information you're about to hear is single-source information. And you know what that means. The single source is DeLouise himself. We interviewed him after he had asked for our help. So if you intend to rely on this information, you should corroborate it from other sources as well. Use it as intelligence, not facts or evidence."

"I understand that," I said. "Go on."

"When DeLouise left the United States, he thought he wouldn't be gone for long. It seems that his attorneys knew federal banking law but not enough about federal criminal law, and they assured him that the storm would soon be over."

"I've heard this before," I said. "I've seen how even experienced civil lawyers might simply not understand that their clients had committed federal white-collar crimes. One of them once even said to me, 'That's just the way we do business.'"

Benny went on. "So in mid-1990 he settled at the Noga Hilton in Geneva, using his DeLouise name. He was busy having a good time. But as the weeks passed he began to understand that his problems were far from over. First he heard from his attorneys that, once it filed, the U.S. government was likely to win a ninety-million-dollar civil suit against him unless he was present to testify and fight it. Next he heard that the indictment had come down, and he knew that within hours INTERPOL might have every police force in every country in Europe looking for him."

"How did he hear that?" asked Ron. "Grand jury deliberations are confidential. He was a fugitive, so the indictment would undoubtedly have been sealed. There'd be no public announcement of it and no public record. Did he tell you that someone was leaking that information to him?"

"I don't know," said Benny. "We didn't ask and he never told us. Anyway, he then realized that a Colombian drug cartel was also on his back, and finally he realized that your office was looking not just for his money but for him as well."

That was a surprise. I was sure my office maintained tight field security to prevent our targets from knowing we might be after them. I'd have to report this to David and our security officer. Benny paused for a moment, as if he'd read my mind.

"The last straw was a call from the hotel porter at the Hilton telling him that two men were asking questions about him. DeLouise withdrew $250,000 in cash from his account at the small Credit Suisse branch in the hotel; that was all the cash they had on hand at that time. But he couldn't wait for the bank to replenish its cash, and, therefore, he took only cash. I guess he didn't want to take a bank check that could be traced back to where he cashed it; that would have revealed his new location. He took a cab to a used-car lot in Geneva and bought a Mercedes. He drove directly from the car lot north toward Germany. He didn't even check out of the Hilton, since he didn't want to be seen leaving the hotel with luggage; departing without checking out had its advantages. Anyone looking for him would assume he was still in the area because his hotel room was still under his name. By the time the hotel, or any of his pursuers, had figured out that he'd gone, DeLouise would already be hundreds of miles away. As you know, there are very few border checks within Europe. DeLouise had a U.S. passport and a respectable appearance, so I guess the German border police didn't bother stopping him. He drove through Germany looking for the right spot. Through a recommendation of an acquaintance that had previously used Guttmacher's bank for untraceable money transfers, DeLouise made contact with the bank.

"The match was perfect. He needed a seasoned banker who wouldn't ask too many questions and who could help him move his money from Switzerland to other locations without making any waves or attracting attention. The complexity lay not only in moving the money out of Switzerland to another country without leaving a traceable paper trail but also in moving it into accounts held under different names.

"For Guttmacher, too, meeting DeLouise was a blessing. Not only did this new client bring a potentially huge fortune to his bank, he also brought his personal business savvy. Guttmacher was doing business with DiMarco, the Italian purchasing agent for the Iranians. Doing business Guttmacher-style meant moving some of the transactions through Bankhaus Bäcker & Haas as well as hiding DiMarco's fat commissions both from the Iranians and Italy's internal revenue service. Apparently the Iranians didn't realize that in addition to the hefty fees they were paying DiMarco, he was collecting commissions from the suppliers. Their contract with him specifically forbade that."

Benny continued. "DiMarco complained to Guttmacher that he was having difficulty supplying the Iranians with the missile technology and the nuclear machine tools and materials they ordered. Many vendors in Europe were reluctant, for various reasons, to deal with the Iranians. There were significant trade restrictions imposed by the U.S. government and many European manufacturers had subsidiaries in the U.S. Therefore, fearing they would have to explain their ties with Iran, they simply gave up. When after a tedious search the Iranian agents found a good source of supply they negotiated the transaction, and then DiMarco was brought in to do the actual placing of the order, masking the identity of the real purchasers. But nothing went smoothly, and the Iranians were blaming DiMarco for the delays caused by bureaucracy. The export-control laws of some of the industrialized nations made it difficult to purchase and ship what the Iranians wanted to the places where they wanted it to go. This wasn't the kind of stuff you'd buy out of catalogues or off the shelf. These were materials and machinery that were complex, expensive, heavily regulated, and easily detectable in border crossings.

"Hearing DiMarco's gripes, Guttmacher suggested two solutions to help the Iranians and DiMarco. To answer the growing need for suppliers who'd look the other way when Iranians orders were placed, he suggested they look for contacts in the Soviet Union. The shake-up of the Soviet empire during the previous year had opened new opportunities if you knew where to look for them, he told him. Another possibility was North Korea or China, but Guttmacher told DiMarco to concentrate on the Soviet Union first. The second piece of advice was to use private businessmen to front all the nonnuclear orders, to distance Iran even further from the transactions. The Iranians were impressed with Guttmacher and suggested he locate the kinds of businessmen he'd described. When Guttmacher met DeLouise and sized up both his international business experience and his flexibility, he asked DeLouise whether he was available to participate in some 'interesting business transactions.' DeLouise, smelling money and needing the available cash, said yes without knowing what he was getting into. How long could he live on the meager $250,000 he carried with him and the one or two million he managed to extricate from Switzerland? That was small potatoes for him."

Benny paused to take a drink and I answered for him. "Not too long if you're living the lifestyle to which DeLouise was accustomed."

"Exactly," said Benny. "His big bucks were stuck in Switzerland, where the Colombians, disgruntled minority shareholders of his collapsed bank, were still looking for him. He also needed to remove his money from Switzerland as quickly as possible, before the U.S. government found it."

"At this point Guttmacher threw out the bait. He told DeLouise that the government of Iran needed to buy machinery and spare parts for its oil and pharmaceutical industries but the West was giving it a hard time. Therefore, said Guttmacher, the Iranians were looking for private businessmen to front and 'facilitate' these transactions. Many of the products and machinery had dual purposes and could pass as benign. If the government of Iran buys steel with military specs, it's a suspicious transaction; if Raymond DeLouise, a private businessman, buys it, it's legitimate business.

"Also, the Iranians needed U.S. computer technology for the development of ballistic missiles and nuclear weapons; their shopping list included graphics terminals to design and analyze rockets, and U.S. law prohibited export of this hardware to Iran and other nations known to sponsor terrorism. But it looks as if DeLouise thought that he could at least order the terminals, supposedly for end users in an acceptable country but actually for clandestine transshipment to the Iranians."

Ron said, "I've handled parts of some of these cases. European law can be far more accommodating than U.S. law about shipment of dual-use equipment and materials to nations on the State Department's list of states sponsoring terrorism — which of course includes Iran."

"They forget their morals when it's time to do business. But that will change," said Benny. "Terrorism knows no political borders, and terrorists, like extortionists, know how to identify weakness and use it for their own benefit."

"Anyway," Eric stepped in, trying to distance himself from politics, "Guttmacher's deal sounded like a good business opportunity to DeLouise. He was no fool, and with his education and background he immediately understood what kinds of deals the Iranians were trying to make in Europe and why they wanted advanced U.S. computer technology. He thought he could bilk the Iranians while also gaining access to their covert activity in Europe and the U.S."

Once an agent, always an agent, I thought. But was DeLouise working only for himself?

"So DeLouise took a step forward, showing Guttmacher he understood what the transactions were really about, and offered his contacts in the Soviet Union," Eric said.

"Did he have any?" I asked.

"Apparently not. But he read the papers and saw what was going on in the Soviet Union, and that gave him an opportunity to take a lead in a transaction rather than simply lend his name to a shady deal and collect a limited commission. He wanted more than that. Instead of being just a straw man, with no influence or knowledge of the ins and outs of the Iranian purchasing frenzy, he wanted to play center stage. It was riskier but more lucrative, and the leverage he expected this to give him with the U.S. government would be commensurate with the risks: he hoped to trade intelligence on the Iranians' nuclear program, and their attempts to get prohibited U.S. computers, for a sweetheart deal on his criminal charges."

"I would think that DeLouise would have needed a viable U.S. criminal case against someone else, which he could then give up to a federal prosecutor in exchange for a plea bargain," said Ron.

"He had it," answered Eric. "There was an Iranian attempt to acquire proscribed U.S. computer technology."

"I don't know who gave him that idea," said Ron. "Certainly a defendant could trade intelligence data for a plea bargain, but, from my own experience, it seems far-fetched. For one thing, the CIA wouldn't let the federal prosecutors know how good the defendant's intelligence had been, so the prosecutors could not make representations to the court about the usefulness of the defendant's cooperation — thus, there'd be no adequate basis for the court's acceptance of the plea. The prospective plea bargainer almost certainly would have to give up persons whose activity clearly contravened U.S. criminal law."

"I don't think it's the case here," said Benny, "but DeLouise had his hopes; he must have thought that the information he was willing to trade was so valuable that his case would be the exception. In any case, DeLouise's words were music to Guttmacher's ears. But he demanded proof that DeLouise had the right connections before he agreed to discuss anything with him. DeLouise had to deliver, and the nuclear materials were first on the list. So DeLouise made a few phone calls and went to Berlin. Berlin is heavily populated with Russians who have escaped the Soviet Union and are hungry for any kind of business, legal or not. It took DeLouise only a week until he came across Vladimir Tkachenko, a wheeler-dealer in everything, who promised that he had the right contacts in the Soviet Union. DeLouise challenged him to prove it, asking for trace residues of lithium-6. Within two weeks Vladimir delivered the goods wrapped in a plastic bag, stored in a lead container. Happy, DeLouise went back to Munich with the proof. From then on, things moved quickly."

"Was it that simple?" I asked, finding it hard to believe you could buy nuclear materials so easily on the open market.

"No," said Benny, "not quite. Let's take one step back. First DeLouise wanted to see if Guttmacher was for real — to make sure his offer wasn't a scam, or worse, a sting operation by a law-enforcement agency. So he hired a retired agent of BND, Bundesnachrichtendienst, the German federal intelligence service, to do a background check for him on Guttmacher."

"Do you have his name?"

"Yes, Kurt Hansa. He operates out of," Benny looked at his pad, "Kaiser Wilhelm Strasse number 311, Munich."

I jotted down the name and address. Benny continued. "Hansa reported to DeLouise that Guttmacher's bank was legitimate but that Guttmacher himself had been under increased attention from Germany's federal police over his connections with the Iranians."

"I guess Hansa reported to his former employers, the federal police, about DeLouise's inquiries, and from there the information flowed to the CIA and the Mossad," I said.

Eric and Benny smiled the kind of a giveaway smile that says I ain't talking.

"Anyway, Hansa's report to DeLouise that the bank was a genuine institution and that there was no conclusive negative business information about Guttmacher was all DeLouise needed. Apparently Hansa never told DeLouise about the secret ongoing investigation of Guttmacher. DeLouise called Guttmacher and told him that he had the samples that Guttmacher had requested earlier as proof. Now it was quid pro quo time: DeLouise demanded that Guttmacher show his hand and bring his clients in for a meeting. Guttmacher called DiMarco in Italy and quickly arranged a meeting with DiMarco, plus Cyrus Armajani and Farbod Kutchemeshgi, the Iranian agents."

"Here in Munich?"

"Yes, in Guttmacher's office. At the meeting DeLouise gave them the proof: a detectable trace of lithium-6. The Iranians were apparently gratified."

"So the meeting ended with DeLouise having the deal he was hoping would extricate him from his problems with law enforcement?"

"Not exactly," said Eric. "The Iranians wanted to make sure that they weren't walking into a trap of some sort. They knew that every Western intelligence service was snooping around them. They interrogated DeLouise about his personal background, his business and family connections. They asked him to prepare a family tree, telling him bluntly that they'd first check the accuracy of his family tree and if DeLouise didn't deliver or was discovered to be an agent of any foreign government, they would kill his relatives."

"DeLouise couldn't give them his family tree," I said. "He has family in Israel, and that would have revealed his Israeli background."

"Precisely," said Benny.

"So what did DeLouise do?"

"We don't know exactly," said Eric, "but we think that DeLouise told them to forget the whole thing if they wanted to become so personal with him. Apparently he managed to persuade them to lower their level of suspicion."

"How?" I asked.

"I don't know," conceded Benny. "We know that he suggested that the delivery of whatever he could arrange be made to a country friendly to Iran. That was one way of insulating the Iranians from the transactions. I'm sure there were other guarantees."

"Did they agree?" I asked, finding it hard to believe that they were so unsophisticated.

"I guess so," said Benny, "since apparently there was some sort of an agreement. DeLouise received a list of materials and equipment the Iranians needed, and an advance of two million dollars."

"Without collateral?" I asked.

"No," added Eric. "Guttmacher's bank guaranteed the advance to the Iranians, and in return DeLouise gave Guttmacher a letter of assignment, through two correspondent banks acting as intermediaries, for a deposit of $2,050,000 that a company named Triple Technologies and Investments Ltd. had in a Swiss bank. I guess Guttmacher was satisfied with that guarantee."

I felt like I'd been hit by lightning. I tried to hold my composure.

"Do you have further details about this company, the deposit, or the bank's name?"

"I guess we might have it somewhere," said Eric, indifferently.

Was he a complete idiot, or was he so self-centered that he didn't see the obvious even when it was right under his nose? I needed that information. Triple Technologies and Investments was the name of the company on DeLouise's American Express card.

I said, "It might tell us where the DeLouise money is hidden." I wrote the details on my pad and asked, "How long have you known about this?"

"About what?" asked Eric.

"About the bank account."

"I don't know. We developed the information the Mossad gave us, and the results are somewhere in the file," said Eric, tossing it off. "I wasn't really interested in the financial details."

I looked at Eric, trying to decide if he was pretending, or if he was indeed the dumbest CIA agent I'd ever met. "I repeat," I said at a snail's pace. "I'm here to find DeLouise's stolen assets. The U.S. government took over his collapsing bank and paid the depositors. The government sent me to recover that money. What you've just told me indicates that DeLouise had control over a company called Triple Technologies and Investments Ltd. that had at least two million dollars in its bank account. Do you get it?"

I took a gulp of beer because my throat was dry, but it didn't calm me down.

Eric still didn't seem to grasp the significance of what he'd just told me. I continued, "You know everything but understand nothing. Guttmacher is not a fool; he wouldn't have given the Iranians his bank's written guarantee unless he was sure that the letter of assignment DeLouise gave him was valid. That means he checked the Swiss account first. Banks do that, you know. He must have received the Swiss bank's written consent for the assignment of the deposit. So that brings the level of certainty concerning this information to a new high. Pay attention also to the fact that there were two intermediary banks. That shows that DeLouise must have insisted on using them as a buffer between the Swiss bank and Guttmacher's bank to avoid detection of the ultimate beneficiary."

Eric finally realized what was going on. "We've only had the information for a few days now," he said with some mild embarrassment.

"I'd like to see the actual copies of the documents."

"Tom will get them for you; they're in our office."

"Any other revelations that you've forgotten to give me?" I asked. Eric didn't answer.

"There is one final thing," said Benny. "DeLouise knew that the only way to show he was working on the deal was for him to travel to the Soviet Union. But he was reluctant to use his U.S. passport, because he figured that there must be an INTERPOL lookout for him and border officials generally check these. He couldn't use his Israeli passport under the name Dov Peled either. Israeli citizens need a visa to visit the Soviet Union. He couldn't ask for a visa without attracting law-enforcement attention, uniformed or plainclothes. He also knew the Iranians would be watching him to make sure he didn't betray them. Therefore, the likelihood of their finding out that he traveled with an Israeli passport was too much of a risk. DeLouise knew what happened to those who betrayed the Iranians."

"So he needed a third passport," I said ironically.

"Exactly," said Benny, ignoring the fact that I already knew about this part. "DeLouise aka Peled was also known as Bruno Popescu; that's his birth name. So he travels to Bonn, goes to the Romanian embassy, and asks for a Romanian passport under the name of Bruno Popescu. Traveling to the Soviet Union with a Romanian passport has another advantage: he doesn't need a visa, a privilege left over from the time Romania belonged to the Eastern Bloc countries."

"Did the Romanians give him a passport?" I asked, tacitly agreeing to play Benny's game of hiding from Eric that he'd already shared some of these details with me.

"Yes, although I think DeLouise helped the consul's personal fund for needy families, meaning his own, with a few hundred dollar bills. In spite of the extremely slow bureaucratic process, a passport was issued to him within forty-eight hours. DeLouise-Peled-Popescu returns to Munich, buys a ticket to Moscow, and then before he leaves — boom — a bullet to his head." He pointed his finger to his temple.

"Something isn't right here," I said, remembering my earlier conversation with Benny. "Do you know who his Soviet contacts were?"

"We are working on it right now," said Eric. "I presume they should be in Moscow and Baku, Azerbaijan."

"It doesn't sound right to me," I said again. "On the one hand you say that DeLouise was reluctant to use his U.S. passport or openly appear in an airline reservation system, for fear that INTERPOL was looking for Raymond DeLouise — then he makes reservations to Moscow and Baku under that very same name? I know for a fact that he made reservations to travel to Moscow under the name DeLouise."

Eric and Benny looked at each other. The room was silent.

I continued, "How could he enter the Soviet Union with a ticket carrying a name other than Popescu that appears on his Romanian passport? He couldn't even get on the plane to begin the journey."

Benny was the first to respond. "We don't know for sure, but with his skills, he could have bought another ticket to Moscow carrying the name Popescu."

"I can suggest another theory," I said.

"Enlighten me," said Eric, his eyes focused on me.

"Well, one explanation could be that the reservations to Moscow and Baku were a decoy perpetrated by DeLouise. We all know that when you want to confuse those who are watching you, you make three, four, or five airline reservations to different destinations under different names and times. Then you use only one or none at all. Bear in mind that DeLouise was trained in covert activities, so he knew the tricks of the trade."

Eric turned red. "Tom, call the office to cable Langley to check all airline reservations for the period around DeLouise's murder under the three names DeLouise used."

"Remember that there were more than eight or nine days between DeLouise's murder and the expected departure to Moscow with the ticket he bought under the name DeLouise," I went on.

"I wouldn't be surprised if DeLouise had intentionally made the reservation under his own name to show the Iranians, Guttmacher, and anybody else who was watching his movements that he was indeed leaving for Moscow to take care of business. However, he also made other reservations, to go to Moscow or elsewhere, as Popescu, well before the date he was supposed to fly as DeLouise. With such a plan he could achieve several goals: one, he leaves for Moscow with everyone else thinking he's still in Germany; two, his departure doesn't alert INTERPOL because he travels under a name that it doesn't have. I also think that just before his purported day of departure to Moscow under the name of DeLouise he planned to cancel the reservations, because he had already returned from Moscow. He probably planned to be invisible for a few days and then call Guttmacher and pretend he had just returned from Moscow." Everyone in the room looked at me in silence.

My confidence in my own theory increased. "The more I think about it, the more I'm convinced that he had already traveled to Moscow even before he called the Mossad or his daughter."

Benny gazed at me for a moment, reflecting on my theory and then said, "If he in fact did that, it was a brilliant plan."

"Your theory is inconsistent with your own logic," said Eric. "If we agree that DeLouise was loath to use any airline, fearing the discovery of his whereabouts, then why did he make reservations under his own name, even if he never intended to take the flight? That would have placed him in Munich, and the police could then narrow in on him."

Eric wasn't stupid after all. "Well," I continued, "my theoretical answer is that such a maneuver may have been an indication that DeLouise had no intention of staying in Munich on his supposed day of departure to Moscow. If I read him clearly, his plan was to return from Moscow and either disappear or continue working for the Iranians but from a new location where they couldn't threaten him personally. If he planned to run with the money, that could mean that the collateral he gave Guttmacher was bad; on the other hand, if that was good money, he probably planned this maneuver to transfer the money from Switzerland. Remember that DeLouise received two million and gave collateral with a slightly greater value. Now, if DeLouise takes off, he keeps his own two million advance, and Guttmacher collects the $2.05 million collateral. So, in effect, DeLouise gets his own two million: money he couldn't reach earlier because it was stuck in Switzerland. I don't think that the collateral was bad, because that would have caused Guttmacher to reimburse the Iranians from the bank's own resources. An unwise move for anyone who had significant additional business with the bank."

Benny interrupted my train of thought. "I tend to believe that theory, even if it does seem far-fetched. Since the Colombians also spotted him in Munich, there was no point in staying here, and he could find a more convenient location with better weather."

"Let's wait for tomorrow's results. Langley will tell us if your theory holds any water," said Eric.

"Do we have any other business?" asked Tom. "I guess not," he concluded when nobody answered.

"OK," said Eric, "enough for today. We have some work to do in the office. Benny, what's your next move?"

"I'm leaving for Israel tomorrow and will discuss my findings with my director as soon as I see him."

"Good," said Eric. "You know the rules of dispersal from this location."

We did. We left one by one, using different exits and no loud English conversation or attention-attracting movement.

Tom took me back to the Omni Hotel, driving around town to make sure he had not grown a tail. Although I was tired after being out for almost eighteen hours, I was alert. But as I walked down the carpeted hallway a sense of threat seized me. Perhaps it was the feeling that I was returning to my room for the first time since someone had searched it, or that I was participating in planning an exciting operation involving both my birth country and my home country. I felt my muscles contract and my vision go into hyperfocus. Was I subconsciously sensing imminent danger, or was there extra adrenaline pumping into my bloodstream from the events of the past two days? The hallway was empty and there were no noises on an early Sunday morning.

I slowly inserted the magnetic card into the reader and quietly opened the door. The room lights were on. A man was kneeling next to my safe. He was a slim, medium-tall, light-brown-skinned guy in his thirties. He turned his head, startled. He stood up and looked around quickly, either evaluating the situation or seeking a way to escape the inevitable confrontation. There was no chance for that. I was almost twice his size and blocked the doorway. The windows were closed. But even if open, it was still the thirteenth floor. I guess he was superstitious because he didn't try to jump through the window. Instead he pulled a knife and came at me — clumsy and tentative for a man his size; clearly not a hand-to-hand expert. I shifted my weight and kicked out with my left foot, hitting him squarely in the groin. As he bent forward, gasping in pain and surprise, I grabbed his curly hair with my left hand, raised my knee with some force, and smashed his face directly onto it. I heard the crack as his nose broke and the gasp of pain escaping from his clenched teeth when he had quickly to decide which was the most painful: the high-speed meeting of his face with my raised knee, the kick in his groin, or the fact that he was caught.

I let him fall to the carpeted floor and decide for himself while I neatly slipped the knife from his hand. I pulled off my belt and secured his hands behind his back, then extended the belt to strap one leg, enough to make a move impossible. I took off my tie and used it to knot my belt to the bed frame. He was still semiconscious, groaning in pain and bleeding on my carpet, when I went to the telephone and called the police. I looked at my unwelcome guest and thought back for a moment. Amos, my martial arts instructor during special forces training, would have been proud of me. Amos was a short guy with red hair; he was cross-eyed, so you never knew where he was looking. That helped him to kick us hard when we least expected it.

"I need to speak to Herr Blecher immediately," I said in the calmest tone I could summon, despite my heavy breathing and a heart still pounding.

"Just a minute."

"Blecher," said a man's voice.

"This is Dan Gordon. I'm at the Omni Hotel. I've just surprised a burglar in my room."

"Did he get away?"

"No. I got him down and tied him up. Send your men over. He may also need some medical attention."

"Done," said Blecher.

Ten minutes later, the man on the floor was showing signs of returning to reality from the temporary blackout I'd imposed on him. I checked his pockets, searching for a gun. I found only some cash. No weapons or ID.

"Water," he said faintly. I rolled him over and looked at him. Blood was smeared on his face and neck. His nose was already swollen.

I went to my bathroom, brought back a glass of tap water, and held it to his lips. He drank and sighed.

"Who are you?" I demanded.

He didn't answer. I grabbed him by the hair again and asked him whether he wanted an encore. "Julio."

"What is your last name?"

"Rodriguez," he whispered, and asked for more water.

"What is your nationality?"

"Please, water." he repeated.

"Where are you from?"

He didn't answer.

I grabbed his hair again. "I'm going to blow your fucking brains out if I don't start getting some answers!" I was not armed, but my visitor had already experienced what my bare hands could do to him.

"Colombia," he almost shouted.

"What were you looking for?"

"Nothing," he begged. "Money, jewelry."

"How did you get in?"

"The door was open."

"I don't believe you, you son of a bitch." I yanked his head up to where I could look him directly in the eyes. "Have I given you any indication that I give a shit about what happens to your pathetic life? Give me the truth or I start messing up other body parts."

He didn't answer, and I heard steps at the door. It was Blecher and a few of his hounds.

"He's all yours," I said, and gave Blecher a brief account of the events, then went to the bathroom to wash Julio's blood off my hands.

"I don't think he was looking for money," I said when I came out of the bathroom.

"What do you mean?"

"He gave me his name — Julio Rodriguez — and told me he's Colombian. My room was ransacked earlier today. It may have been this jerk. He could be one of the gang that's after the papers DeLouise gave Ariel. I guess he thought I had them."

"We'll try to find out if Rodriguez is connected to Ariel's kidnapping," Blecher assured me. "I have just heard from the Israeli Consulate that Mina Bernstein has returned to her home in Israel. That's too bad, because I wanted to ask her a few more questions."

"I'm sure the consulate could arrange that," I said. "Anyway, I expect to have developments concerning Ariel as well. Have you made any progress?"

"Yes, we have," said Blecher, giving me a cold look. "It is most unfortunate that you have been keeping information from the German police on the Ariel matter."

"What do you mean?" I asked, sensing the grievance complaint against me rapidly approaching. "I gave you everything I had."

"Not all of it," said Blecher. "It was highly irresponsible not to alert the police that the kidnappers were waiting for a phone call at a certain location. We might have caught them."

"You know that it was the mother's decision not to call the police. But more important, I found out about the note only five or six minutes before the time she had to make the call. There was no time to call the police."

Blecher gave me a long look, trying to decide whether to believe me. "I have also just heard from the Israeli Consulate that the second call was made by another woman from the consulate," he said.

"So, what have I got to do with it? I gave you the audio and the videotapes. Didn't I mention that the caller wasn't Mina?"

"No," said Blecher.

"I had nothing to do with it, I'm sure you know that. If that was another woman who called, it must have been because they hoisted Mina back to Israel. Remember I work for the U.S. government, not the Israeli government."

"Yes," said Blecher. I didn't understand what he meant, but I wasn't interested in pressing the issue any further.

Alarm bells were ringing inside my head. Was it a residual thrill from the fight I'd just had or the intuition that I'd just made another step forward in my investigation? Obviously, I'd become somebody's target. Although Rodriguez said he was Colombian, it didn't necessarily mean he was telling me the truth or that he was from the same team that had pursued DeLouise or kidnapped Ariel. He could be working for somebody else.

By this time, two plainclothes detectives had Rodriguez up and moving.

"We're taking him downtown for questioning. We'll let our doctor see him. What did you use on him, a hammer?"

"Wait," I said, and gave the man's knife to Blecher. "It looked like he was going to stab me with this, so I had no alternative but to reshape his face." Blecher asked me to come to the station to give my testimony.

"Later," I said, stretching the leeway I had received thus far from Blecher, since I was working for the U.S. government.

I called Eric from a pay phone outside and told him about the incident. "What do the German police think?" he asked.

"I don't know yet. Blecher wants to see me in the station later. Anyway, I'm checking out of the hotel; it's getting too hot here. I'll call you from my new location."

I packed my luggage, checked it into storage, and left the hotel through the employees' exit. I took a bus for a few blocks, got off, and went into the lobby of a residential building. I looked through a window for a few minutes, checking to see if I'd been followed. The place was quiet. I took a cab to Rosenheimerstrasse in the center of town and got off near the German Museum, took another cab to the Sheraton Hotel, and checked in using the Peter Wooten name. I called from a pay phone and left messages for Eric and Ron asking them to arrange for my bags to be brought over from the Omni. Two hours later my bags showed up and I could relax. I decided to stay in my room and watch CNN and old American movies on the only English-speaking German channel. Although I understood enough conversational German to watch the German-dubbed English-speaking movies, it was still strange to hear Gene Hackman or Harrison Ford speak German. I ordered room service and ventured out only once to call my children in New York.

The following morning the phone rang. It was Eric. Yes, my theory concerning DeLouise's travel ploys had some truth in it. When he said "some truth" I knew all of it was true. He just couldn't admit that I'd been right.

"What did you find out?" I asked.

"DeLouise used his Romanian passport under the name Bruno Popescu and left on a Lufthansa flight from Frankfurt to Moscow on September 17th. In Moscow he checked into the Hotel Intercontinental. Three days later he returned to Frankfurt and probably drove back to Munich. We don't know at this point whom he met in Moscow or where he went."

"Well," I said, "it seems that you can do without me for a few days. I'm going to Moscow." I wasn't asking Eric's permission to go; I was simply informing him of my plans.

"I need you back here in four or five days. I expect to hear from Benny by then. Also, do you plan to notify Guttmacher and the Iranians about your forthcoming trip?"

"No, I have no intention of doing that. I made it clear that I owe them nothing. Although they were intimidating at times, I think they got the message."

"All right. When you're in Moscow, just in case, go to the embassy and make contact with a Charles Hart. He's my counterpart there. I'll let him know you're coming."

I called my long-suffering office in New York from a street pay phone and asked Lan to book me on the afternoon flight to Moscow and make arrangements for me to stay at the Cosmos for five days. I gave her my new numbers at the Munich Sheraton and alerted her that in Munich I'd be Peter Wooten, but in Moscow I'd return to my real name. Then I asked her to connect me with Stone.

"David," I said, "I'm through here for the moment and off to Moscow tonight."

"Did Eric authorize that?"

"Well, I didn't exactly ask his permission, but I let him know I was headed out."

"And what did he have to say?"

"Not much. He asked me to contact his station chief in Moscow."

"Fine," said David, "but I don't want more complaints from other agencies that you're too independent."

"OK, boss," I said obediently. We both knew the procedure; he gave me instructions and I followed them my way.

"How long will you be in Moscow?"

"Just a few days, looking for the daughter."

"Good," said David. "I see you're working for me again."

"Yes, I guess so. Although I'm not sure whether she had anything to do with the other business," I said, hoping David would understand I meant the Iranian matter. "Currently she's the only living link between the two."

David picked it up immediately. "Fine. In the meantime there are developments in California. With DeLouise dead the criminal investigation against him is over, but the civil proceedings can continue. The U.S. District Court out there has just entered a default judgment against DeLouise's estate ordering restitution in the amount of ninety-one million dollars and change. So we're in a position to seek European judicial assistance to enforce this as soon as you discover assets."

"Good news," I said. "Can you send over a certified copy? I could use it here to open some doors even before we file in court."

"It's already on the way."

"Thanks for reading my mind. Am I cleared for Moscow?"

"Well, I don't have all the approvals yet, but you can go. If there's any heat, I'll take it, given the urgency of your trip; I suspect we'll avoid a major storm. Have a good trip and call me when you get there."

IX

I went to the consulate of the Union of Soviet Socialist Republics in Seidlstrasse to get a visa. Although I was carrying a U.S. passport issued to government employees traveling overseas on official business, I used my personal U.S. passport. With the latest incidents and hijackings involving airlines and Palestinians terrorists, like the TWA 847 from Athens, I didn't want to have to eat my official government passport in the cramped toilet of the aircraft while a guy with a foreign accent announced, "This flight is now going to Beirut. Remain seated, stay calm, and nobody gets hurt." Besides, there was no way I could have a Soviet visa issued on the same day using an official passport, not when the KGB had to screen each application and make sure that the official visitor is officially supervised. No, I was an attorney going to Moscow on business to meet some people. No, comrade, I am not affiliated with the U.S. government.

There were about twenty people waiting at the consulate, but the line was moving rapidly. Did this mean that they were all being rejected instantaneously? I entered the consulate and filled out the visa application. The application form was in Russian and German, printed on cheap, woodpulp paper that I hadn't seen since the austerity days in Israel in the 1950s. A big red flag with a hammer and sickle was hanging above the desk of a man dressed in a uniform-like suit.

"I need an urgent tourist visa for five days," I said in English, hoping he understood.

"What is so urgent?" he replied in English.

"I have a business meeting tomorrow in Moscow."

"A business meeting?" he repeated.

"Yes."

"Then why do you ask for a tourist visa? You need a business visa."

"Fine," I said, "let me have a business visa."

"Give me the invitation letter, your round-trip ticket, money order, and passport, and come back in one week."

"I don't have a letter of invitation, and I can't wait a week. This is a sudden and urgent business meeting."

"Sorry," he said sternly. "No invitation letter, no visa."

"Well, I forgot that I do have an invitation; it's right here in my passport," I said, handing him my passport with two folded hundred-dollar bills inserted between the pages.

He took my passport, flipped through the pages, saw the money, and said "Just a minute," before he exited to a back office. Ten minutes later he returned with my passport and handed it to me without saying a word. I looked in my passport; a red visa stamp gleamed at me.

I went back to my hotel where Lan's fax message with my flight itinerary to Moscow was waiting. I left the hotel, drove to the airport, and in twenty minutes I was in my seat on the plane. Airline efficiency at work — for once.

Three hours later I was in Sheremetyevo International Airport, nineteen miles north of Moscow. The airport is connected to Moscow by a high-speed expressway, notable not only for its speed but for its pollution. Years after most of the modern world had converted its vehicle fleets to engines using only unleaded gas, the Soviet Union was lagging behind in its persistent use of leaded gas. The results were visible on the cars' dirty windshields and on the grimy houses by the side of the road. I couldn't find a cab so I took bus #551 to the Rechnoy Vokzal metro station in the center of town. I sat cramped between two old peasant women with live chickens in straw shopping bags who looked at me with curiosity. The chickens seemed to be curious as well. With my Levis jeans and windbreaker, I must have looked different to them. From there I took a beat-up cab for a twenty-minute ride to the Cosmos Hotel on Prospekt Mira, past the center of Moscow and the All-Russia Exhibition Center. The driver suggested I visit it to get acquainted with Russian culture and to buy souvenirs. It was only a matter of minutes before he volunteered to be my personal tour guide, money changer, and provider of female companionship; he used a more crude word for the last. I declined all three offers.

The Cosmos Hotel was an amazing twenty-six-story building, crescent shaped with sprawling gardens, completed in 1979 to accommodate visitors to the 1980 summer Olympics. I checked in and went with my one bag to the nineteenth floor. The room was small. It had two beds, an armchair, and a desk. The furniture was all dark oak. It was modest but clean.

I opened the curtains and saw a beautiful view of the Botanical Gardens and Lossiny Ostrov, the national nature reserve.

Near the elevator was a floor lady's post. Seated constantly at her table, she sold bottled water and could monitor who was entering or leaving each room and when. I suspected she didn't keep the information to herself.

I went downstairs and spoke to the receptionist. Although the tall blond young lady had a British flag pin on her lapel to indicate her command of English, she had difficulty understanding me, and it wasn't because I spoke American English instead of British English.

"I'm looking for Ariel Peled," I said. "Is she still staying at the hotel?"

She looked at her file index, pulled out a card, and said, "Yes, she is in room 1123." That two-sentence exchange took almost five minutes using a combination of English and sign language. I decided not to spend the rest of my adult life trying to ask the receptionist if she knew whether Ariel was in her room. I simply looked at the key box behind the desk. Her room key was not there. I decided to make a direct approach, like most Israelis would.

I used the house phone and called Ariel's room. After two rings a woman's voice answered.

"Is this Ariel?" I asked in Hebrew. If she answered in Hebrew, then she would pass the first identity test.

"Yes," said the woman in Hebrew, in an amazed tone. Moscow isn't Tel Aviv or New York, so it was obvious she didn't expect to hear Hebrew on the phone. "Who are you?" Her accent was that of a person who had been born and lived in Israel all her life. She'd passed the second test.

"I'm Dan Gordon," I said. "I'm your mother's friend. May I see you?" I had to be Dan Gordon, not Peter Wooten. Gordon was the name her mother knew.

"Where are you?"

"I'm in the lobby."

"How did you find me?"

"Please come downstairs; you'll soon find out, I promise."

She paused a moment, then said, "I'll meet you in twenty minutes at the Dariali restaurant, located on the left wing at the main lobby level." I knew that Ariel would not hesitate, because she'd recognized in my voice the unmistakable inflection and dialect of a native Israeli and would trust that. Besides, we were about to meet inside the hotel where Ariel would feel protected.

"Good, I'll see you there."

I hadn't planned on finding Ariel so quickly, so I had no plan for an introduction or how to lead the conversation. Was she friend or foe? Was she really Ariel Peled?

I decided to allow the meeting to flow naturally and let my instincts be my guide. This method left many things to chance, of course, and went against my training. If she were Mina Bernstein's daughter, I'd relax my level of caution. But then again, she would also be DeLouise's daughter; I tried to put that out of my mind.

I entered the restaurant. The place was completely empty. A mustached waiter greeted me wearing a costume typical of the Caucasus, a kaftan with two lapels in Turkic manner and a round embroidered cap laced with gold thread.

"Welcome," he said in English, "Deutsch?" That sounded bizarre.

"No," I said, "English. And I'd like a table for two."

He looked down at his reservations book and said, "I don't know if I have a table available for tonight, let me see."

I thought the guy was just a pompous ass playing games. The place was empty, so why the show? To get a tip for a stale joke?

Finally he said, "Yes, I can give you one table, please follow me."

He took me through the empty restaurant and to a table like all the others, covered with a red tablecloth and set with Caucasian-style copper plates.

"Thank you," I said, giving him a dollar. He thanked me vehemently.

A U.S. dollar went a long way in the Soviet Union, where his salary might be only thirty dollars a month. "I'm waiting for a lady. My name is Gordon; please direct her to my table."

"Of course, sir," he said.

I sat so preoccupied with my thoughts that I was surprised to hear a woman's voice so close to me, "Dan Gordon?"

I got up, smiled, and said, *"Shalom,* Ariel."

Ariel looked very much like her mother, perhaps taller and more slender but with the same blue eyes and the same smile. No further identity tests were needed; she was definitely Mina Bernstein's daughter. I was taken with her immediately. She looked younger than her early thirties. Her face was tanned and her body looked athletic in blue jeans. A close-fitting white sweater outlined her ample breasts. Her copper hair was braided loosely, falling below her shoulders.

As soon as she sat down Ariel began firing questions at me. "How did you find me? Are you one of them? How is my mother? Does she know I'm here?"

"Which one do I answer first?" I smiled.

"About my mother, does she know I'm here?" she asked in a serious tone.

"I don't know. I saw her in Munich just before she went back to Israel. She was worried about you; so frankly, I have no idea if she knows that you've escaped from the Latinos. Tell me, how did you manage it?"

She smiled. "I spoke with her on the phone from the consulate after I escaped. So, if you were with my mother before she returned to Israel, you must be from the Office!"

"I'm one of the good guys," I said, deftly sidestepping a more direct answer. "Tell me."

At that inopportune moment, as usual, the waiter came with the menu. It consisted of a sticky plastic card with an attached handwritten list in Russian, which I couldn't decipher. "Do you have an English menu?" I asked.

"No. But I can explain," said the probably fake Caucasian.

"Never mind," I said, figuring that the best way to get rid of him quickly was to ask him to decide for us.

"Don't pay attention to the menu; their selection is actually very limited," said Ariel.

"Just give us your freshest meal," I told the waiter, "and please make it only mildly spicy." Off he went.

Ariel smiled at me again. "I see that you're impatient. When did you arrive?"

"Two hours ago. So, tell me, how did you get away?"

"From where?"

"From your captors in Munich."

"How much time do you have?" she asked jokingly. She didn't look or sound like someone who'd just been through an ordeal. She sure was putting up the front of a tough cookie.

"All the time it will take. Just tell me the story."

"There were two of them," she recalled. "One who said his name was Tony, but I heard his friend call him Julio. I don't know the other's name. I'm not sure he could speak English, maybe only Spanish."

"Do you know where you were?"

"No. It was a small apartment somewhere in Munich or its vicinity."

"Did they tell you what they wanted?"

"They kept demanding that I give them some papers, which they said that my father had given me. But I didn't know what they were talking about. I told them that I had just received a personal letter from my father but no other documents. They kept on pressing me. I was petrified; I was sure I was about to die."

"Why?" I asked. "Did they hurt you?"

"They never touched me, but they threatened to kill me five times a day. But oral threats weren't the reason I was worried. I wasn't blindfolded and I could identify them. That scared me."

"Why?"

"Because if they didn't care that I saw them, that must have meant that I would never live to describe them. There was something alarming in their story that my father had kept documents that belonged to them. I didn't know if my father was looking for me, because I couldn't find him when I arrived. I couldn't take it anymore, so I told them about the safe-deposit box where I left my father's letter."

The waiter came with ten small plates of a variety of unidentified salads and a loaf of freshly baked bread with a thick crust. Ariel waited until he left and continued.

"I told them it was in the Grand Excelsior hotel safe and that only I had access to it. I was hoping that I would be able to attract the attention of somebody at the hotel to help me get away from those terrible people. But when we went to the hotel, they were so close to me, one of them holding a knife underneath his jacket telling me he'd slaughter me like a pig if I made any move, that I realized I couldn't get away. So I had to invent a story: that I had forgotten and that the envelope was in fact in a safe-deposit box at the Mielke Bank. I guess they didn't want to risk going to the bank with me as their hostage, so they demanded to know who else had access to the safe. I told them that the only other person who had access was my mother, who lived in Israel, hoping that would force them to give up the idea. I always add her name to all my accounts, as she does with me. They made me call her in Israel from the hotel pay phone and reverse the charges. They put a tape recorder by the phone to record the conversation and said that if I told my mother anything alarming in Hebrew, I would die because their people can understand Hebrew. I was totally petrified and confused, so I did what they wanted. I asked my mother to come to Munich to help me. I really didn't care about giving them the letter, as long as I got away from them. But when my mother came over, I wasn't allowed to call her."

"Did you try to escape?"

"Yes. When I understood from their conversation that my mother was in town, I was afraid they'd kidnap her too. I had to warn her. I constantly looked for ways to escape. When they left the apartment for the day they chained me to a water pipe in the kitchen with a chain long enough to let me reach the toilet. I started looking in the kitchen drawers to find a tool to break the chain — a knife, a can opener, anything. There was nothing I could use. Then I thought of a completely different angle. Under the sink there were a few bottles with detergents — cleaning stuff, you know."

I nodded.

"The chain they used seemed to be made of iron. So I looked through the detergents' labels for ingredients I could use to prepare a caustic acid that would eat the metal."

I looked at her, amazed, and then remembered that she was a chemistry teacher. But my chemistry teachers in high school never looked so good.

"Did it work?"

"Eventually, yes, I used a drain cleaner, which I mixed with other detergents," she smiled. "But the problem was that the solution I was preparing would emit dangerous gases. It would also leave a stench and, most importantly, would take a long time to consume a thick iron link. I didn't know how much time I had."

"So what did you do?" I asked. I found her, and the story, fascinating.

"I covered my face, prepared a small quantity of the acid in a glass cereal bowl, and left one ring of the chain dipped inside. I tried not to move, to keep the link soaked in the acid, but my eyes and nose were watering. I was able to keep it dipped for about an hour when my captors returned."

"Did they notice anything?"

"Yes. They noticed the smell immediately and asked me what it was."

"I said, 'It was dirty here, so I cleaned.' I guess they were satisfied with that."

"Did they use the phone?"

"I didn't see any phone at the apartment. During the night they locked me in the living room and kept me chained to the sofa bed's metal leg. When they fell asleep, snoring so loudly they could've torn a hole in the wall, I checked the link I'd dipped in the acid and it looked to me like it had been damaged, but not enough to break. The following morning they brought me an apple and a roll for breakfast and tied me back onto the kitchen pipe. As soon as they left I started working on the acid and doubled the quantity. I said to myself, better to cry now because of the fumes than have my family cry over me. Two hours later, the metal was becoming weak so I twisted it and a few drops of the acid flew on my leg."

"That must have hurt."

"Well, I have a scar now," she said, bending to show me her ankle. She came so close I could smell her light flowery perfume.

"You'll live," I said. "Tell me how it ended."

"Around noon I was able to break the link but it wasn't enough to release me. I couldn't touch the broken link because of the acid, and the broken part was not big enough to unlink the chain. I almost panicked. I didn't know when they'd be coming back. If they found what I'd done, they would've hurt me."

"So what did you do?"

"I placed the broken link between the kitchen door hinges and opened and closed the door a million times until the weak metal was flattened and then broke. Then I was free! I still had the handcuffs on my left wrist and a chain of three feet dragging from it. I ran out the door and into the street. I know I must have looked awful, but I didn't care. I stopped a taxi and he took me to the Israeli Consulate. And the rest, you know," she said, assuming that I already knew the whole story.

"You're lucky to be a chemistry expert," I said admiringly.

Ariel smiled. "In fact my education and expertise are in physics. I'm finishing my Ph.D. in nuclear physics at the Technion. I teach chemistry in high school to support myself."

The Technion, Israel's top technological academic institute, was often compared to MIT. So Ariel was following her father's path. Was she also doing it now in Moscow?

"So whom did you meet there?" I thought Benny Friedman might have been on the scene.

"It was a man named Ilan. He debriefed me and wanted me to leave on the first flight out to Israel. I refused and demanded to talk to my dad first."

Her calmness took me by surprise.

"So they told you?"

"Yes." She paused. I could see she was fighting tears; her eyes glistened. Impulsively I reached a hand out to touch hers, resting on the table.

"I'm sorry," she said. "I didn't cry then. It hit me later. They told me that they'd had to send my mother back to Israel and that she was fine. I spoke with her on the phone and she begged me to return home. But I was angry and wanted to stay. I had to see what I could do to track down my father's killers. Everything happened so quickly. I went with Ilan to the

safe-deposit box but it was empty. I guess my mother had taken everything out."

This was a good opportunity to upgrade my credibility level with her.
"In fact, it was a combined effort of your mother and me. I have the letter
in my room; I'll give it to you later."

The place had become noisy all of a sudden. I looked around. A wave
of people had washed into the restaurant. I'd been so immersed in our
conversation that I hadn't even noticed.

"Have you met Hans Guttmacher?" I asked.

"My father's banker? I know he's holding some things for me, but I didn't
get a chance to see him. When I first arrived in Munich, two or maybe three
weeks ago, I've lost track, there was no answer from my father's hotel room.
So I called Guttmacher. His name was mentioned in my father's letter. I
thought that as his banker he might know where my father was. We had a
short conversation."

"Did you ask Guttmacher if he knew where your father was?"

"I only mentioned that I hadn't been able to talk to him yet."

"Did Guttmacher say anything about it? Did he know where your
father was?"

"No, he had no reaction at all, or maybe he said he didn't know. I don't
remember."

"So you never met your father in Munich?"

"No. I first called his hotel, but there was no answer from his room. I
called him again several times and left messages but he never returned my
calls."

"Now you know why he never called you back."

"Yes," Ariel said quietly. "And I'm just beginning to accept the fact that
he's gone."

"Did you talk to Guttmacher again?"

"Yes, but only briefly." Ariel pushed away her plate. She put her head
in her hands. "I don't think I can deal with food anymore."

I signaled the waiter to clear the table. But I needed to continue.

"Why did you travel to Munich in the first place? Did your father talk
to you about that?" I found myself asking her a question to which I knew
the answer from Benny. Was I questioning his story?

"The whole thing was very strange. First I got a call at home in Haifa from someone who told me his name was Gideon. He claimed to be my father's friend and that my father needed me badly in Munich. I didn't quite believe him. But Gideon insisted and told me that my father had wired ten thousand dollars to my bank account in Haifa from Bank Hapoalim in Luxembourg to pay for my trip and expenses. So I decided to check my account and see if the money was there. I thought that would indicate whether Gideon was telling me the truth."

"And the money was there," I said knowingly.

"Yes. Exactly the way he said. I had another indication that it was my father's money because he had used that bank to wire me money from time to time. He found it convenient, since the bank in Luxembourg is a branch of my Israeli bank. But this time I noticed something different: the money came from a trust with a long German name that I couldn't pronounce, not from my father's regular account."

"Do you know who the man was who called you?"

"Gideon? No; I think he's from the Office. He never said it, but I suspected he was working for the Israeli government and that the call was connected to my father's distant past at the Mossad."

"Interesting," I said. "Did he explain why your father didn't call you directly, why he needed somebody else to call his own daughter?"

"Gideon said that my father could not call but that he had asked him to make the call to me. The man calling himself Gideon gave me the pension's name in Munich where I should stay and my father's hotel name and room number. He told me to call my father's hotel when I arrived but not to go there. I called my mother and told her briefly that I was going to meet my father in Munich and that I'd be back in a week. I bought the ticket and left for Germany." She stopped for a moment, then continued.

"I waited at the pension for one day but nobody called. I didn't have Gideon's phone number in Israel. I called the Israeli Consulate and they didn't know what I was talking about. I knew something was wrong but I didn't know exactly what. When none of my calls were returned, I went to my father's hotel and asked the manager to take me to his room. His things were there, but there wasn't even a note to tell me where he'd gone. The manager said that my father might have been traveling. He didn't seem to think anything was wrong. So I decided to wait. Perhaps my father had had to leave unexpectedly. But as I returned to my pension I had a strange feeling that I was being followed. So I went to a bank, I changed some money, and I opened a safe-deposit box and put the letter there. I had a feeling that the whole mystery of my father's disappearance was somehow connected to the people who were following me."

"That was a very wise move," I said. "But why this next move — to Moscow?" I asked, directing the conversation back to the present.

"You don't know? I thought you were working together with Ilan from the consulate in Munich, and that he sent you here to protect me." Her tone became suddenly suspicious. I knew I'd tripped; I was supposed to know. Damage control, quickly.

"I did come here to help you. I don't know everything, but isn't your visit connected to the Russian contacts your father was building?"

"Yes. So if you know, why are you asking these questions? Are you testing me? Is that it?"

"No, Ariel," I said, trying to calm things down. "I'm simply trying to pull the story together. Tell me what you've accomplished so far."

The waiter came again, cleared our plates, and opened a folding table. Whether we liked it or not, there was more food. Another waiter came carrying huge plates with a mountain of yellow rice, cubes of lamb, and grilled vegetables. It looked wonderful and smelled even better — a welcome change from stolid German food.

"I don't know if I should tell you. I want to keep it a secret. I don't need a replay of my shouting match with Ilan in Munich when I first told him I was going to Moscow, while he wanted me back in Israel."

"That's fine with me," I said agreeably.

"Mutual confidence must be built first," were the words that Alex, my Mossad instructor, had used. "Never try to kiss on the first date." I'd made a mistake by trying, but Ariel's story was exceptionally tempting. I had to play it safe for a while. Adam and Eve had been expelled from Eden for a lesser transgression.

In the back of my mind I feared that I was not being professional. These were the facts: While on the trail of plutonium-seeking Iranians I meet, for the first time, a woman who is also the daughter of DeLouise, who had contact with the Iranians. Now she suddenly mentions her research in nuclear physics. Could Ariel, with her expertise, be part of the Iranian conspiracy? According to my training, every alarm bell in my head should be going off. But they weren't. Was I accepting her story at face value? Did that mean I considered her trustworthy? Were my instincts right, or was I being lulled by my attraction to her beauty? I came to no conclusion other than to be careful, and to watch and wait.

"How long will you stay in Moscow?"

"I don't know yet, I need to see some people first."

"Tell me more about your doctoral thesis." I wanted our meeting to last longer.

Ariel chuckled, "How well do you know your physics?"

"Try me." Only when I'd said it did I realize that my reply could go both ways.

"Now, that's going to take even longer than my kidnapping story," said Ariel in a teasing tone. I didn't quite follow what she meant. It could have more than one meaning. But I kind of liked that idea.

"Go ahead," I finally said.

"I'm working on the naturally occurring changes in plutonium."

"You mean the radioactive metal?"

"Yes. Plutonium is one of the more mysterious and complex elements in nature. Although it can be found in nature, for nuclear-power purposes it must be manufactured in a process developed only fifty years ago. Have you ever seen plutonium?"

"No," I admitted.

"OK, here's a quick course for beginners," she said.

"Do I need to take notes?" I asked with a smile.

"No, and there'll be no exam at the end. Plutonium, element 94, is named after the planet Pluto. It was discovered in 1940 at Berkeley by the physicists Glenn Seaborg, Edwin McMillan, Joseph Kennedy, and Arthur Wahl."

"Was that discovery part of the Manhattan Project that created the first atom bomb?"

"No," she responded, "But it certainly led the use of plutonium in that project. Anyway, the isotope Pu-239 exists naturally in trace amounts in uranium ores. The quantity is really minute, only several parts per quadrillion."

"I'm ashamed to ask, but how much is a quadrillion?"

"It's one thousand trillions or one followed by fifteen zeros."

I nodded. "What big number comes after that?"

"Quintillion, that's one thousand quadrillion, or one followed by eighteen zeros."

I looked at her eyes. They glittered when she talked about her work.

"So, isotope Pu-239 is produced by the capture of spontaneous fission neutrons by uranium-238. Extremely small amounts of plutonium-244, the longest-lived plutonium isotope, have been detected in cerium ore; apparently surviving residues of plutonium were present at the formation of Earth."

I began to feel sorry that I'd skipped my physics classes in high school. Then I could ask Ariel an intelligent question and show interest in more than just her. That part of physics was not included in the nuclear overview at the Mossad Academy. I wasn't completely ignorant of the subject, however.

"Plutonium is produced in a process called 'breeding,' by bombarding uranium-238 with slow neutrons in a nuclear reactor. If a slow neutron is captured then uranium-239 is produced, and the compound then quickly decays into neptunium-239 and then plutonium."

I nodded because I wanted to continue looking at her. In fact, everything she was telling me was somewhat familiar from my science classes at the Mossad Academy. But in the sciences you had to run twice as fast just to hold the same ground; otherwise, the others would pass you — and I didn't run. I had to admit that I'd gotten out of the science race immediately after my Mossad training.

Ariel continued. "Plutonium is silvery in color and naturally warm. But when you expose it to the atmosphere it changes color to yellow. One of the reasons that plutonium is so complex is the great number of its stable structures. Carbon, for example, has three, while plutonium has six, each with a different density, and they change in accordance with temperature."

She paused and looked at me with curiosity. "Did you understand any of it?"

"Some," I admitted. "Does your research have any practical applications?"

"Definitely," she said. "Since plutonium changes its condition rapidly and each new version has different qualities, it is very difficult to control. You must control it if you want to use plutonium in a nuclear device."

"Such as the big A?"

"Yes. American scientists at Los Alamos discovered that plutonium is stable when alloyed with aluminum and gallium. After the smelting and the cooling off, plutonium enters its most stable condition, known as 'delta phase.' This phase proved to be very convenient, because it made plutonium behave like a normal metal. It was unbreakable, did not corrode over time, and was simple to mold."

"So what's the problem?" I asked.

"It's a problem of catastrophic magnitude," said Ariel seriously, her blue eyes intent. "For years everybody believed that plutonium with aluminum and gallium alloy was the ultimate solution to handling plutonium. But Soviet scientists repeatedly claimed that with increased temperature, plutonium might change from delta phase to alpha phase. That is alarming, because alpha phase is far less stable and might induce a spontaneous chain reaction."

"A chain reaction leading to a nuclear explosion?"

"Yes. That's why I said it could be a catastrophic problem. The world scientific community is only beginning to realize that the life span of a nuclear warhead is much shorter than previously anticipated."

"And what is that?"

"It went down from seventy years to twenty years. Can you imagine what it would do to the superpowers' nuclear stockpiles? They'll have to renew it faster than they thought and dump the old stockpiles when they still haven't figured out what to do with the existing nuclear waste."

"And you are a part of that research?"

"Yes, in a small way. I'm trying to determine the mechanism that leads to the dangerous change from the safe delta phase to the volatile alpha phase."

"Are you making progress?"

"I am, but my problem is that some nuclear scientists still do not believe they have a serious problem. I can't say I'm too popular in these circles. I'm just a doctoral candidate, and they're all accomplished scientists," she said wryly. "Soviet scientists are the only ones so far to take this problem seriously, particularly when they are concerned that, with the dissolution of Soviet Union, the question of what happens to those stockpiles looms."

"It's so interesting," I said. "You are one of the few people I know who can simplify complex issues into sentences that even a lay person like me can understand."

If Ariel noticed I was following my training, she did a good job hiding it. In the Mossad Academy, Alex had taught me the art of conversation. "You have two ears but only one mouth, so nature intended us to listen twice as much as we speak. Everyone loves talking about their work or hobby; therefore, let them talk, because they reveal themselves and it directly inspires them to trust you."

"Thanks," she said, "I appreciate the compliment." I looked at her face, her tanned skin, her copper hair and her feminine body, and let my thoughts wander.

Ariel gave me an interested look and said, "We shouldn't talk about me all the time. Tell me about yourself."

"What do you want to know? Just ask."

"Are you married?"

It was my turn to smile. "Why do you want to know?"

"Because," she said in a teenager's teasing tone, without elaborating. "Well?" she urged.

"I was."

"Not anymore?"

"No," I said with a sigh. "It's over."

"Was it because of another woman?"

I shook my head. Ariel was digesting the information.

"You never remarried?"

"Hell, no. That would be like upgrading to a better room on the Titanic."

"Is that what you think of marriage?" Ariel sounded hurt, as if we were married to each other.

"No, of course not. It was just a figure of speech. I divorced because it was over, not because there was another woman. I wish there had been."

"So you haven't been in a serious relationship since?"

Ariel was giving me the third degree. But I liked her interest in me.

"No. There wasn't anyone in particular that I wanted to spend more than a week with. So I took small bites of different apples."

"Any children?"

"Yes, two teenagers, a boy and a girl."

"Do you see them often?"

"As much as I can between trips."

We were now headed into quicksand. Soon she'd ask where they lived in Israel. What would I say? That they lived in New York? Then would come the next question, and soon enough my cover story would be blown. I started regretting allowing myself to get personal.

"Where did you go to school?"

"The routine route. Tel Aviv public schools; then Tel Aviv University, international relations; and finally Tel Aviv University law school."

"So you're a lawyer," she said. I couldn't identify her tone of voice, whether she was being appreciative or mocking. "Have you ever practiced law, I mean the usual way?"

"Yes, at the beginning, but I preferred the more exciting government work."

I was praying she would change the subject quickly, hence my laconic answers. I couldn't lie to those huge blue eyes. But at the same time, I didn't want her to stop the personal direction she was taking with me.

"I'm tired," I said, sounding like a yawning husband getting off the couch. "I've had a long day, flying from Munich and all that. Can I see you tomorrow? I want to do some sightseeing." I needed to continue our conversation. It would take more time to gain her trust and make her talk about her father's business. After all, that was the reason I had come after her, not to admire her eyes.

"You never told me why you came to Moscow. Was it only looking for me?" She was putting me on the spot again.

"Hey, isn't that the question I asked you earlier?" I teased, trying the flirtation route. "I never got an answer and now you pitch it back?"

"I don't know if I should tell you," said Ariel teasing back, inviting me to keep on asking. But I decided to take it seriously and continue to build confidence between us.

"I respect your reluctance to discuss with a stranger the details of your Moscow visit," I said. "But the same rule applies for me. I told you earlier that I'm here to help you. I've already shown you that in fact we could be working on the same project. How do you think I knew about your kidnapping? How is it I have the letter your father wrote you? Do you think I broke into the Mielke Bank in the wee hours of the night with a mask on my face and broke the lock of your safe-deposit box just to retrieve the letter? Why the suspicion?"

"I'm sorry," said Ariel, a little shyly. "So many things have happened during the past two weeks that have turned me from a naive scholar into a suspicious person."

"Do you feel you can trust me?"

"I don't know. Many of the things I believed in went up in smoke, including the speed with which I used to trust others."

"I can understand that," I said.

Ariel looked at my face and added, "I guess when I see the letter I'll feel more able to trust you."

Liking the change of wind, I called, "Waiter!" No response. More calls for help, but to no avail.

"Watch this," I said. "I'll show you the fastest way to attract the attention of a waiter deliberately ignoring you." I took my copper plate, knife, and fork and dropped them on the floor. The sound of clanking metal had the desired effect: the waiter came right over. I paid the bill and we went up to my room. I opened my briefcase and gave Ariel her father's letter.

"Here it is," I said. "I'm sorry I had to read a personal letter, but I thought it might help me find you."

Ariel took the letter and put it into her purse.

"Thanks," she said softly, "for helping my mother. I do appreciate it. Call me tomorrow." She came over, took my face in her hands, and kissed me lightly on the cheek. My heart pounded as she left the room.

I went to sleep thinking of Ariel, but I had bad dreams. I needed to make sure which side she was on. Was she continuing with her father's work or was she working with us? Could she be doing both?

Next morning I called her room. "Feel like sightseeing?"

"I have an important meeting in a little while," said Ariel. "I'll call you when I get back."

"Leave a message if I'm not in."

Blue eyes or not, she wasn't going to get out of my green-eyed sight. I wasn't going to wait for her call. I definitely wouldn't allow that in Moscow, where her father's plans concerning the Iranians' shopping list were so vague and needed to be clarified. I wasn't sure what motivated me most: my original assignment to retrieve the money DeLouise had stolen, to gather intelligence for the forthcoming joint American-Israeli operation in Munich, or, as much as I hated to admit it, my growing personal interest in Ariel.

Duty comes first, I concluded quickly but sadly.

Following a quick cup of tea, I went outside the hotel and found a garden bench where I could sit and watch the hotel's main entrance. The late October sun was shining, but there was a real chill in the Moscow air. I was wearing only a light coat, and as the minutes passed I became colder and colder. Finally, I saw Ariel in a pants suit, long coat, and sunglasses leaving the hotel. She hailed a cab. I dashed to the next one and said in English, like they did in the old Hollywood movies, "Follow that cab!"

The driver sized me up in the rearview mirror.

"Girlfriend?" he replied in English.

"Yes," I said, "and don't lose her."

After cruising through a few busy streets, still in the center of the city, the cab stopped and Ariel got out. I paid my cabbie with an extra-large tip and said, "Stick with me. There's more of the same for the whole day."

"Sure, boss," said the cabbie. "I like these games."

I watched Ariel approach a small wooden ticket booth. With a ticket and a brochure in her hand, I saw her join a group of tourists. I kept my distance. The guide, a woman in her early fifties, began her spiel in a loud tour-guide voice, then led the group off to visit Moscow's highlight attractions. I stayed discreetly to the side.

"Good morning. This tour of the center takes you to Moscow's three main central squares — Sverdlov, Revolution Marx Prospect, and Red Square — and concludes at the KGB headquarters at Dzerzhinsky Square.

"This area is called Sverdlov Square because of the three theaters dominating the northern side. Hard to imagine that decades ago it was just a stinking bog of the Neglinka River, also used as a garbage dump by rich people living in the city center."

The group continued walking to the right from the western exit of Ploshchad Revolutsii metro station around the square, looking up at the high walls.

"These walls were built by Prince Vassily III in the sixteenth century to protect Kitai Gorod, the main trading area of the city."

Ariel seemed disinterested in the tour guide's explanations. She kept looking around. That made my job more difficult, but I had to be there because I felt that something was about to happen. Ariel wasn't being a tourist. The tour guide continued her monotone narrative.

"In the center of a minisquare on the right you will pass an interesting pile of stone blocks. This was the site of the statue of Yakov Sverdlov, a comrade of Lenin and the so-called first head of Communist Russia."

I moved closer to the group.

"On the side of the square facing you is Metropol Hotel, one of Moscow's finest examples of art nouveau architecture, which at the time of its building filled conservative citizens with horror. It was built by William Walcott, an English architect also known for his imaginary sketches of ancient classical buildings." The guide pointed her finger up and said, "Look up to see the two large mosaics created by Mikhail Vrubel; they were inspired by Edmond Rostand's play *La Princesse Lointaine*. Meanwhile, look at the second floor; above it you can see an inscription of a proverb by Friedrich Nietzsche: 'It's the same old story, when you build a house; you notice that you've learned something.'" Cameras clicked, but I was too focused on Ariel.

"I'm not going to tell you about Metropol restaurants, you'll have to find this information on your own," the guide continued.

I didn't pay much attention to the tour details. I was troubled by Ariel's presence. Why had she taken the tour when she'd told me that she had a meeting? Was it her subtle way of avoiding me, or was there a place on the tour where she would meet her contact? What was she doing in Moscow? Who is she working for, if anybody? If her father was seeming to be working for the Iranians, is she into that as well? Was I asking myself all these questions to defray the possibility that she simply was not interested in my company? The group continued on and I lingered three hundred feet behind, my cabbie in the distance.

When the tour guide headed everyone toward the Maly Theatre, across Okhotny Ryad near the Metropol Hotel, a new face joined the group from the rear — an unshaven man in his thirties dressed in a long black leather coat. He didn't look like a tourist to me and apparently not to Ariel either. He looked as if he came from one of the "Stans," the Asian Soviet republics: Azerbaijan, Kazakhstan, or Uzbekistan. I saw Ariel and the newcomer make eye contact.

The tour guide continued. "This theater was designed in 1824 by Osip Bove, who was in charge of Moscow's rebuilding after the fire of 1812. Currently Maly's repertoire concentrates on historical plays in traditional dramatic style and on Russian classics."

Ariel, the newcomer, and I were no longer even mildly interested in the tour. The pair exchanged a few words and the man then left the group. Ariel turned her back to him and drifted from the group as well. My training again came to my aid or she would have spotted me. I immediately turned around to the opposite direction, stopped a passerby to ask a stupid question (only to be seen talking to someone), and turned slowly sideways so as not to lose my eye contact with Ariel. She tried to hail a cab, initially without success, then one pulled over for her. I quickly walked to my waiting driver and we got underway. I had to restrain him from getting too close to the other cab. He liked the sport too much.

It was clear I had to find out quickly if Ariel was with us or with the opposition, a process called IFF: "identifying friend or foe." I didn't like what I'd just seen. Why was Ariel taking this risk? Was she working for the CIA or for the Mossad? Was either one helping her hide her father's money in return for services rendered?

I decided to break off the chase and went back to my hotel. I needed to talk to Benny, but how? I couldn't use the hotel phone, with the KGB a likely listener. I couldn't go to the Israeli Embassy or to the American Embassy for much the same reason. It was possible that I had an invisible tail. I had had at least one in Munich, so I could expect to have another here. I was confident that the Iranians had not followed me to the Munich airport. They'd had no idea where my new hotel in Munich was and therefore couldn't have trailed me. So Moscow was a relatively Iranian-free atmosphere. Although it was possible that I was under the watch of the KGB, I believed that they did that to most foreign tourists as a measure of counterintelligence rather than as an attempt to recruit and develop new sources of information. I wasn't concerned about being either observed or subjected to recruitment attempts. But I didn't want to create an unnecessary risk when none was needed. I couldn't be sure that in addition to the Iranians and the KGB there wasn't someone else interested in what I was up to. I hadn't even begun to investigate the Colombians and their motives, and clearly they were players. If Ariel was being watched, then I could be spotted watching her and become a target as well.

I weighed my options. One was a short conversation with Benny that could answer my questions or clarify my doubts, or expose me to the Soviets as someone who was more than just a lawyer. Another was to go to the American Embassy; it was plausible for me as a tourist to do that and certainly less risky than venturing into the Israeli Embassy. I chose the former and went to the American Embassy on 19–23 Tchaikovsky Street. Surprisingly, it was easier to enter the Moscow compound than the one in Munich; perhaps American security officers thought that the Soviet perimeter security was better. I considered contacting Eric's counterpart in Moscow. But if he was anything like Eric, I didn't want to spoil this sunny day with its brisk wind and beautiful Moscow sky. So instead I showed the Marine on duty my government ID and asked to use the phone. "Secure?" he asked.

"Yes, if possible."

"You'll need to clear it first with the RSO, the regional security officer."

He directed me to the first floor. Minutes later I was talking to my children. Tommy asked me to come home. Karen was more understanding of my work requirements, which made me feel even guiltier. Then I called Eric. No, he had no idea whether Ariel worked for the Mossad; Benny hadn't said anything. And she didn't work for Eric either. Why was I wasting my time on her? It took a strong will not to slam the phone down. Waste time over the beautiful, rosy Ariel? To me it was beginning to sound like a better idea than chasing the secrets of the Iranians.

I called Benny in Tel Aviv.

"Having fun in Moscow?" Benny asked jovially.

"I haven't had time yet. Isn't there something else you forgot to tell me?"

"Such as what?"

"About Ariel, for example."

"What about her?"

"Is she on your payroll?"

"No. Whatever gave you that idea? Is she there?"

"Yes."

"Dan, I have no idea what she's doing there. I told you right from the beginning that even my interest in her father was limited and only preventive. With him gone, I have no interest in the daughter."

"Don't rush. Wait until you see her."

"Aha, does she have an admirer now? Forgot the rules?"

"No. I keep the rules, but I can still enjoy what I see, can't I?"

"Did she tell you what she was there for?"

"No. I wanted to make sure she was on our side first."

"I can double-check, but I'm certain that she is not under contract to us."

"OK. I won't ask you about developments in the other matter. I'm sure I'll hear more from Eric."

"Thanks for not asking."

I waved to the Marine in the lobby by way of thanks and went out to the street. Although the country had been disturbed by Gorbachev's consent to the reunification of the two Germanys just a few weeks previously, Moscow was surprisingly quiet.

I went back to my hotel and found a note written in Hebrew from Ariel: "I looked for you. Still want to spend some Moscow time? Call me. Ariel."

What a few words can do to improve your mood! I lifted the receiver and called her room.

"Hi, Dan," she said. Her voice was light, cheerful, and open.

"Did you have a good meeting?"

"Yes. Even though I was locked in a room full of smokers. I hated that, but the meeting was good."

"Whom did you meet, if I may ask?"

"Three Soviet scientists, something to do with my work."

"Good." I said. So big blue eyes could lie, too.

"What would you like to do?" I asked.

"I don't know," she said. "Have you been to Red Square yet?"

"No. But sounds like a good idea."

"I'll be ready in ten minutes; meet me in the lobby."

Ariel's sudden eagerness alerted the sleeping sentinels in my brain. She'd lied once; she could lie again. Was she using me now? For what purpose? If she didn't work for Benny or Eric, what was she doing here that was important enough to keep her away from her teaching job and have her tell me phony stories? Had she exposed my cover and true intentions while hiding her father's assets? Was it the investigative attorney in me asking these questions, or my libido?

When I got to the lobby Ariel was already waiting. Dressed in a dark blue skirt and a gray cashmere sweater, she looked as engaging as ever. We took a cab to Red Square. Ariel was holding a tour book and when we got there she assumed the role of tour guide.

"You see that tower? It must be the Cathedral of Vasily the Blessed." She looked at the book and pointed her finger to the next building. "That must be the monument to Minin and Pozharsky, the leaders of the people's volunteers of the war of 1612."

"Here, look at that," she said in appreciation. "This is Lobnoye Mesto," she pointed at a round stone pedestal facing the Cathedral of Vasily the Blessed. "It was built as a symbol of Calvary. There are rumors that Lobnoye Mesto was used for executions, but in fact it was used to proclaim the tsar's edicts and to hold religious ceremonies." I said nothing.

We walked toward Senatskaya, the Senate tower that rises high over the Kremlin wall. On the opposite side of the wall the Lenin Mausoleum stood right in front of Spasskaya. With the excitement of a third grader, Ariel grabbed my hand and pulled me. "Come on, look at this tower. It's called Nikolskaya, which means, of course, St. Nicholas. The tower got its name from the icon of St. Nicholas, which was previously displayed on the tower wall."

I listened and looked politely at the monuments left, right, and center, but my mind was elsewhere. What was Ariel doing in Moscow? Must it have something to do with her father? If yes, then was it possible that she worked for the Iranians? I found that impossible to believe. But if her visit is innocent, why the clandestine manner of her meeting this morning, and why her lies about it? Was DeLouise hiding his assets, or a road map to them, in Communist Russia? I was also troubled by my repeated attempt to lock myself into a theory that her visit to Moscow was related to her father. There certainly could be other reasons. I decided to continue investigating all the options. I gave Ariel a few more minutes as a tour guide, then said, "I've seen enough here; let's get some hot tea." In my dictionary that meant "Let's have a candid conversation."

Ariel looked surprised. I debated whether to confront her or to keep quiet and see what might happen.

"How long do you intend to stay in Moscow?" she asked.

"One or two more days, or until I'm told to return," I tried telling the truth. "Why do you ask?"

"I simply want to know."

"And how long will you be here?" I retorted.

"We need to talk," said Ariel, and touched me on the arm, sending shivers down my spine. "Let's find a café nearby."

We looked around. Not a café in sight. "Let's go back to the hotel. I'm sure it'll be more comfortable there." I said.

As we entered the lobby of the Cosmos, the same sense of danger that I'd felt in the Munich hotel came over me. I thought I saw a familiar face. A dark-skinned man passed me but vanished before I could get a good look at him. Were my instincts correct, or had they betrayed me? Neither the Iranians nor the Colombians could have known I was in Moscow. Did I have new rivals? Was I the one attracting the attention, or Ariel? Why was that a familiar face?

I didn't say anything to Ariel.

"Do you want to sit in the lobby?" I asked.

"No. Let's go up to my room, it'll be quieter there."

Somehow I didn't expect that our conversation would be quiet. When we entered the elevator, I saw the man again as the doors closed. When we got to the eleventh floor, I suggested, "Why don't you go ahead to your room. I'll be along shortly." Wanting to sound serious but not to unduly alarm her, I added, "Don't open the door to strangers."

I took the next elevator to the restaurant level and used the phone to call the American Embassy. With mounting security concerns, I had to forego some precautions.

"Charles Hart, please," I said when the receptionist answered.

"Mr. Hart's office," said a voice with a southern drawl.

"This is Dan Gordon. Is Mr. Hart available?"

"Hold on."

"Charles Hart," said a man in an impatient tone. Not another Eric, I hoped.

"I'm calling you from a pay phone at the Cosmos Hotel. You may have been advised of my arrival."

"Yes." There was a pause. "Of course."

"I located one of the matter's subjects here. But I believe I've grown a tail."

"Do you see trouble on the way?"

"I don't know, but one guy passed me twice today. Not a coincidence. He made an effort not to be noticed."

"Better go to your room and sit tight. I'll send my men. What's the room number?"

"I'm in 1901 but I'll be in room 1123 for the next hour or so."

I hung up. I was certain that the KGB was eavesdropping on the embassy's telephone line as well as all public phones in hotels. I didn't care if they'd listened. President Bush and the Soviets were in delicate negotiations over the Kuwait invasion; Bush was calling on the Soviets not to oppose U.S. leadership of a coalition to liberate Kuwait. The Soviets wouldn't like hostilities on their home ground over irrelevant matters.

I went upstairs to Ariel's room thinking that I had to give her some straight talk. From the corridor, I heard the sound of a scuffle. I ran toward her open door. The man I'd seen flash by me earlier had a gun in his right hand and a grip on a struggling Ariel with his left. He was clearly too busy to hear me coming. I slugged him on the side of his neck as hard as I could with the edge of my hand, fingers together, just the way they'd taught me years ago. The blow worked — the man sagged, dropped his gun, and Ariel slipped free.

"Call for help! Quick!"

Ariel ran to the telephone. "Room 1123, I need help! I'm being attacked!" she shouted in English.

Still in action, I held the guy up with an arm, got to his carotid with the other hand, and pressed until he went all the way to the floor. He'd be in a quieter world for the next hour or so. I stepped back, breathing heavily. I hadn't had so much exercise since I'd left the Mossad. Ariel moved to me. "Are you all right?" I asked.

"I'm not hurt. Just breathing a little hard."

Ariel looked at me and said, "Oh my God, you're bleeding."

I touched my shirt. It was soaked with blood, but I didn't feel any pain. "No, I think it's his blood. I'm OK. I'm not hurt."

She came closer to me. "I'm really frightened." I hadn't heard those words in Hebrew from a woman for such a long time. They softened and invigorated me at the same time.

I held her close. She leaned her head against me, almost as if she was listening to my heartbeat. We held each other for a moment, then parted, embarrassed at our sudden intimacy.

Two men burst into the suite, clubs at the ready. Both were big, over six feet tall, with blond hair. Physically they looked like American college football linebackers, but their facial features betrayed their Slavic origins: high cheekbones and high foreheads. They got a quick grip on the situation and asked me a question in Russian. I tried to respond in English but apparently they spoke none, so I couldn't have explained anyway. They quickly searched the man on the floor, taking from his pockets his wallet and a couple of sheets of paper. One linebacker handcuffed him while the other barked into the phone.

"We'll be safer in my room," I said, holding Ariel's hand. I approached one of the Soviet security guards and said, "We'll be in room 1901." To make sure he understood, I wrote my room number on a piece of paper and gave it to him, gesturing that I was leaving but would return.

I took Ariel to my room. She was still visibly shaken. I made sure there was no surprise waiting for us, then headed straight for the minibar and gave her a shot of vodka.

"Here, drink this. You're safe now. I'll be right back. Just don't open the door to anyone."

I had to move fast. Charles Hart, the resident CIA station chief, was about to send his men to Ariel's room. But if the hotel security men had already left, her room would be empty and they'd likely come to my room. How could I explain their presence to Ariel? I also wasn't too comfortable leaving her in my room. If we'd been seen together, they — whoever *they* were — might look for her in my room. I had to take her elsewhere, and as quickly as I could.

I quickly ran to Ariel's room and saw the two security officers standing next to the man on the floor. With a mix of broken Russian, some English, and mostly sign language, I explained to them that we are both hotel guests and needed a new room for Ariel to protect her until the police arrived.

"It's too dangerous for her to remain in this room. We don't know why this person tried to kill her and whether he was acting alone."

They got the message, and one of them escorted me to a vacant room on a different floor. He also signaled that he'd have housekeeping move Ariel's luggage to the new room.

"No." I shook my head, "don't do that. I'll take care of it."

I didn't want anyone else at the hotel to know where Ariel's new room was. I quickly returned to my room and saw Ariel standing next to the window looking at the beautiful botanical gardens.

"Come," I said, "I have a new room for you; I want to move your luggage."

Ariel gave me her hand. I held it tightly; my heart accelerated its pace. I didn't stop to think if it was only because I had just fought to save her.

I opened the door of her new room and said, "Please stay here until I return. I must make sure that they took away the guy who attacked you. Do you know who he is or why he attacked you?"

"I have no idea," said Ariel. "When I entered my room he was there. He tried to grab me and put a piece of cloth to my mouth. I smelled chloroform. I'd recognize that smell anywhere, we used to handle it at the university lab; it would put you to sleep in seconds. I struggled and grabbed an unopened bottle of soda from my night table. I tried to hit him with it, but it slipped from my hand and dropped to the tile floor. The bottle exploded. I managed to pick up the narrow end of the bottle and stick it to him at least once. That's when you came in."

"Have you ever seen him before?"

"I don't know. I didn't get a good look at him. The room was semidark and I was so startled. He didn't say anything, he just grabbed me."

"Do you know of any reason why anyone would try to attack you like that?"

"This is the second time," she said in despair. "Since the first attack on me in Munich was connected to my father, I guess this one could also be somehow connected to him. And to my visit to the Soviet Union," she added after a short pause.

"We'll talk about it later," I said, caressing her cheek. "I'm going over to your old room now. Please stay here. You knew how to protect yourself well; I just hope it won't be necessary again."

"Dan, I served in the Israeli Army; self-defense is something they teach us during basic training," she said, bridling.

I went back to the scene of the assault. A third security officer was there. Thank God he spoke English. I asked to see the papers the attacker had in his pockets. They handed me two sheets. On one of them there were a few typewritten lines in English.

> Ariel Peled, age 33, female, Israeli citizen. Height: 1.68 m. Weight: approximately 58 kg. Blue eyes, copper-brown hair. Speaks Hebrew, English, and a little French. Very intelligent. Expected to stay at the Cosmos Hotel for about a week, hoping to be contacted by scientists working for the Soviet government concerning sale of nuclear materials. Does not know what the contact looks like. Caution is recommended because she may be protected from a distance.

The paper had no date, letterhead, or a signature. On the second piece of paper there was only one handwritten line: "Cosmos Hotel, room 1123."

The security man told me that the police were about to arrive. I didn't think I should waste my time waiting; I'd learned all I could at this point. I gathered up Ariel's things and went back to my room.

I knocked on the door carefully. She opened it with the chain on, then all the way when she saw me.

"Are you OK now?"

"Yes, I think so." She seemed more calm.

"The police should be here any minute. They'll want to interview you. I think we should talk first." I had to be more businesslike than I felt.

She sat down on the bed and waited for my questions.

"Ariel, I think you should tell me the real reason you came to Moscow," I said. "Don't hold back. We should be past that."

She paused for a moment, looked at me trying to decide whether or not she agreed with me. Finally she said, "I think I can trust you now, Dan. The truth is that I had two letters from my father, not one."

I waited for her to continue. But when she paused again, I asked, "You mean Pension Bart kept two letters for you?"

Ariel nodded.

"But there was only one letter in the safe at the bank. What happened to the other?"

"I knew my mother could have access to the safe and if anything were to happen to me, the sentence about the envelope Guttmacher was holding for me would lead her to him. Remember, I was clueless in a foreign city. My father was missing, strangers were following me, and the police treated me like a daydreamer."

"How would your mother know to go to the Mielke Bank and open the safe-deposit box?"

"That's simple. I told her that during our telephone conversation when my captors made me call her."

I was puzzled. Mina Bernstein had looked surprised when I'd told her I'd found Ariel's safe-deposit box. So she had kept this information from me. I felt disappointed. I thought Mina had told me everything. But why would I be angry with her for withholding information from me while I was deceiving her concerning my motives and my employer?

"What was in the other letter? Do you still have it?"

"No. I couldn't put it in the safe-deposit box; I was kidnapped that same day."

"So they took the letter with them?"

"Oh, no! Earlier that day I burned parts of it but kept the important stuff."

"Why did you have to burn it?" I asked. I had a suspicion, but I wanted Ariel to tell me first.

"At the end of his letter my father told me to burn it, but I was afraid that if I burned it completely I'd forget the things he wanted me to do."

"What was in the letter?"

"The letter described my father's contacts with Guttmacher and the Iranians. There were lists of materials and equipment that the Iranians wanted to buy with names of suppliers and other technical information."

I hoped that the blood rushing to my face didn't show. "Do you still have that list?"

"Yes," she nodded, "I copied part of it."

"Where is it? Can I see it?"

"I have it in my luggage. It's just a list of compounds and such details. I did not copy the supplier names and all other details. I left what's left of the original with all the details in Munich."

I needed to reassure her that she had done the right thing before I ventured further in asking her to get the lists.

"You took a great risk by moving around with the list."

"Not really," she smiled. "Don't forget that I have the perfect explanations for that if I'm ever asked. I'm a nuclear scientist, a doctoral candidate, and my scientific articles were published in several professional magazines. I'm on my way to meet scientists in Moscow."

This information was so important I wanted Ariel to continue without interruption, but she was waiting for my questions.

"Did your father describe his relationship with the Iranians? It's a pretty surprising alliance, I must admit."

I'd hit a raw nerve.

"The answer is so obvious that I'm surprised you're even asking. He wasn't about to trade with them. Not ever. He was after two things: his freedom and their money. You don't think that with his background he'd do anything to help the Iranians and hurt Israel. Never. He was planning to get their money and then extricate himself from his troubles with the American government by giving them a complete file on the Iranians."

I listened, mildly stunned. Ariel had just repeated Benny's account. DeLouise was trying to kill two birds with one stone. Although he was about to make a bundle off the Iranians, he hoped to rid himself of his problems by bringing this extremely valuable information to the CIA. Then the path to any deal he could make with the regulatory banking agencies would be smoothed by the compliments showered on him by everyone from the White House down.

"So your father had actually prepared a file?"

"Yes," said Ariel, and I sensed that she was proud that he had.

"Where is it?" I asked, trying to contain my excitement. I hoped she wouldn't notice my eagerness. "In Munich," said Ariel, apparently missing my reaction to the revelation. "I couldn't take it with me to Moscow."

"Is it safe there?" I asked, hoping she'd tell me where it was.

"Yes. It's safe," she said. "Well, I hope so," she added.

"Is it bulky? I guess it contains many documents."

"Well, there are bank records, contracts, even a few documents in Farsi."

"So the file came with your father's letter?"

"Yes. Everything in one big envelope."

DeLouise must have sensed what might be coming, so he'd left a trail. I silently thanked him for that.

"You still haven't told me all the details about why you came to Moscow," I pressed.

Ariel paused a moment and squared her shoulders. "I felt I had to complete my father's job and get back at the Iranians who killed him. I wanted to expose their plans and their Soviet cohorts. The Iranian fanatics should not be allowed to get an atom bomb. As a scientist I know the devastating consequences the device could bring, and as a citizen of Israel I fear for my country. The Iranians have threatened Israel repeatedly and promised destruction of Israel. They should not be allowed to have the means to carry out their plan."

"Why do you think the Iranians killed him? Do you have any proof?" I wondered whether Ariel knew something I didn't.

"If they didn't, then who did?" she retorted.

"There could be any number of bad guys. The Colombians, for example. Aren't they the people who kidnapped you?" It seemed clear, in the end, that Ariel knew nothing about her father's murder.

"I thought of that," said Ariel, "but they killed my father in the street. If they wanted any documents from him, they'd have kidnapped him like they did me. Besides, the Colombians weren't necessarily working for the cartel; they could have been working for the Iranians."

"Well," I said, "criminals act under different logic than yours or mine. Everything is possible." She had a point though, I conceded.

"Anyway, I was convinced that that was what my father had wanted me to do by leaving me the file and the letter with the materials lists. So I decided to go to Moscow to try to meet with his contacts; they could tell me about the sale of the nuclear materials to the Iranians. Nuclear materials are familiar territory for me."

"So what did you do?"

"There was one name, Igor Zurbayev, with a Moscow address and a telephone number in the file that my father left me. I called him and arranged to meet him in Moscow."

"For what purpose? Were you going to buy the nuclear materials and give them to the Iranians?" I said in disbelief. "The whole thing doesn't make sense to me." I was beginning to tire a bit. It was all crazy and stupid. There must be a different agenda here — Ariel could not be that irresponsible.

Ariel looked at me and saw my expression. "I know I was foolish," she said. "I stood to gain nothing, but I was so angry I wanted to take just another step, complete the information in the file and then expose the Iranian nuclear efforts as well as the Soviets who were helping them. I would give it to the media or the Mossad. I haven't made up my mind yet. Now that my father is gone and there is no need to strike a deal with the Americans, I could still give the file to the Mossad. Israel would know what to do with it."

I wanted to put a lid on that. I'd heard enough and didn't want to sound too critical, so I moved on.

"You made travel arrangements through Oplatka Travel. Why did you choose them?"

"You know everything," said Ariel smiling. "I found their receipt in the file my father had left me."

"So did you meet Igor Zurbayev in Moscow?"

"I called him several times, but as much as I could understand from the woman who answered his phone in Russian, he was away. I gave her my name, but I'm not sure she understood much of what I said. So I met my scientists for one day and then just toured Moscow waiting to be contacted. Finally, I was able to speak to someone at that number who spoke a little English and I repeated my message to Igor. Today someone made contact with me while I was out on a tour, but I haven't met Igor yet."

"How did they know where to find you?"

"They called at the hotel yesterday and asked me to take the tour today. So I did."

Now I was getting nervous. Ariel was dipping her unprotected hand into a snake pit. It was only a question of time before she would be bitten. What she was doing was amateurish and dangerous. Any number of groups could be behind Igor: rogue Soviet scientists or members of the military. It could also be entrapment by the KGB trying to apprehend the culprits. Whichever group Igor belonged to, Ariel did not belong with him, particularly when her story was so illogical that it made me suspicious.

"By the way, did you mention to Guttmacher the file your father gave you or the second letter?"

"No. Just the first letter, why do you ask?"

"So Guttmacher didn't know you were going to Moscow to continue with your father's project?"

"I did tell him, and said I'd be at the Cosmos Hotel and that I'd be in contact with him when I returned."

I had heard enough to realize that danger was no longer just a possibility, it was imminent.

"You're in over your head now," I said decisively. "You must leave Moscow immediately. I'll come with you. Now! On the first flight out."

"You're frightening me. What do you know that I don't?"

"Lots. I'm going to my room to pack my stuff, please stay here."

I ran to my room and opened the door. Everything looked intact.

There was a knock on the door. I knew who it was. "And about time," I thought, as I went to answer the knock. Two guys were standing outside.

"Are you Dan Gordon?" asked one of them in the most stereotypical Brooklyn accent I've ever heard.

"Who are you?" I asked, just to keep up the charade.

"Charles asked us to see if you need help. I'm Brandon and this is my partner Sean."

"I need to leave Moscow immediately with my companion. Just let me pack up and we'll leave. She's in room 1405; let me call her first."

I picked up the phone and called Ariel's new room.

"Ariel, I'm sending a friend of mine to bring you over to my room. I'm packing, and we should leave immediately."

"OK," said Ariel. "I didn't know you had friends in Moscow. Are they from the Office?" She was surprised.

"I have friends everywhere. You just need to know where to look."

I turned to Hart's men. "One of you should go to her new room and bring her over here. There was an attempt to kidnap her today. We don't know who is responsible, and finding out who's behind it is, in fact, second priority until we leave Moscow safely. Things are getting too warm around here — even for Moscow in the fall. Please avoid all her questions; she doesn't really know who I am. Just bring her here safely."

Sean said, "I'll go," and left the room.

I had to call an airline for the first flight out but decided it'd be too risky to leave traces. I emptied the closets and changed my bloodstained shirt for a clean one. I put all my clothes into my duffel bag and zipped it up. Sean returned with Ariel. I looked at her face. She was pale and confused. It was all moving a bit too fast for her.

"You didn't tell me that your friend was an American," she said in Hebrew.

"Let's go." I said; I didn't think I had to explain any further.

"Guys," I said at the elevator, "why don't you take our things with you and bring your car to the front. I don't want to be seen leaving the hotel with baggage. We'll leave without checking out."

"What about the bill?" asked Ariel.

"Don't worry about that. I'll leave money with my friends here," I said. "After we take off, they'll settle up."

It all went smoothly. Sean and Brandon walked out, Ariel and I followed. When we saw a Pontiac Grand Am pull up, we got into the backseat and we were on the way to Sheremetyevo, with Brandon behind the wheel.

"How far are we from the airport?" asked Ariel.

"It's twenty miles to the airport," said Sean. "With the current traffic conditions I expect that we'll be there in forty minutes or so."

As we entered Prospekt Mira Street just outside the hotel, going northeast, I looked back. I did not like the sight. "Brandon," I said, "we have company. Backup from the Office?" I used the code name that would let Ariel continue to think I was with the Mossad.

"No," he answered.

"Do you recognize them?" asked Sean in a cool voice.

"No, their headlights are blinding me, but they have been behind us for about five minutes."

"Let me see," said Brandon and changed lanes. The car behind us did the same.

"It could be the Soviet police," said Sean, "and in that case we have nothing to worry about." Nonetheless the tension was palpable.

Brandon looked at the rearview mirror again. "They don't look like police to me. Soviet police can't afford to buy a black Mercedes."

"Radio the Office and alert them to the situation," said Brandon, and Sean pulled out a two-way radio and reported it. Brandon changed lanes again and the followers' car was again on our tail.

"There are three of them," said Brandon, after looking back through the side mirror. "Ladies and gentlemen, please fasten your seatbelts, we are about to take off." The Pontiac's engine roared as Brandon accelerated; we were pulled back by the velocity. Ariel squeezed my arm. I took my hand and held hers. "We'll be in the airport soon," I said.

A red Mercedes appeared from nowhere and came dangerously close to us on our left. A man in the front seat signaled to us to pull over; his gestures and expression were not friendly. Brandon ignored him. The red Mercedes broadsided our car from the left, ramming us over to the right lane. We barely escaped colliding with a light truck.

"Son of a bitch," said Brandon. "I'll show you what high-risk driving is" and pulled hard to the left just as the red Mercedes was trying to pass us, pushing it to the divider. The screeching metal of the collision between the metal barrier and the red Mercedes sent sparks into the air. The black Mercedes, which had been on our tail throughout, accelerated and tried to rear-end us.

"Sean, get your gun," said Brandon, "and radio the office that we are under attack." Sean pulled out a short barrel .38, opened the side window, turned around, and fired one shot at the black Mercedes behind us, hitting its radiator, which immediately spewed white steam. He fired another shot, blasting their windshield into a million pieces. The noise created by the wind blowing through the open window prevented me from hearing the barrage of gunfire aimed at us. It hit the rear window, shattering it, covering me and Ariel with glass fragments. I bent down and pulled Ariel to the floor, seeking cover.

"Give me a gun," I shouted. Sean handed me a .38. I raised myself and through the splintered rear window shot the driver of the black Mercedes directly behind us. I could see his face take the hit and his head drop on the wheel. The black Mercedes lost control and rolled over the divider.

"Hold on," said Sean in his cool voice, "we're getting into Moscow Ring Road in about one minute. Let's get the other son of a bitch before we make the turn — it'll be more difficult to shake them once we are on the highways with its heavy traffic." Passing cars were doing their best to avoid this gunplay, scrambling to get out of the way.

The red Mercedes was still on our left, again trying to broadside us but failing each time due to Brandon's skilled maneuvering.

"Let me get him," I said, "he's on my side." I opened the left side window and shot at the driver but I missed and hit only the right door. Brandon swiveled our car to avoid being smashed by the Mercedes.

"Slow down," I shouted, "slow down!"

"Why? Are you hurt?" asked Sean.

"No, just slow down and let him pass us a bit, I can get a better shot." Brandon slowed and I finally got a good look at the passengers of the Mercedes. They were all light-brown-skinned men in their thirties. One of them in the backseat was aiming a shotgun at me. "Goodbye," I said, and pulled the trigger, hitting him in the neck. I saw a gush of blood flooding his chest. I pulled the trigger again at the passenger next to the driver, but missed.

"Hold on, I'm making a sharp turn to the left," shouted Brandon as we entered the expressway. I looked back; the red Mercedes was still after us. I aimed hard, holding the .38 with both hands, and squeezed; that was my last chance, and it was also the Mercedes driver's last minute on earth as the bullet hit his forehead. The Mercedes collided into a passing eighteen-wheeler and burst into flames.

"Let's get the hell out of here," said Brandon, as we merged into the hectic traffic.

"Are you OK?" I asked Ariel, pulling her up from the car's floor. She was confused and shaken. "Yes," she mumbled and cuddled into my arms. "Just hold me."

I put my arm around her. "Do you know who these guys are?" asked Sean.

"I can only guess, she was being watched by several different groups. I can't tell you who our pursuers were, but I do know we need to leave immediately before another smart-ass pops up from nowhere."

Sean radioed the office and tersely reported the events, keeping his cool.

"I'm sorry to leave you with the mess," I said.

"Don't worry," said Sean. "We'll clean it up."

I handed the gun back to Sean. "Thanks!"

"Nice shots," said Brandon in appreciation, "Where did you learn to shoot so well?"

"I'm a hunter," I said, "I hunt a lot." I didn't mention that my usual prey was money launderers, not animals, and that I hunted them with my brain, not with my gun. Ariel was still cradled in my arms. I wanted it to last, but we saw the glittering lights of the airport approaching.

"Which airline?" asked Sean.

"I don't know yet; let's go to the main departure area. I want to take the first flight out, preferably to Germany, but any other major European city will do."

"I'll come with you into the terminal," said Brandon, as Sean brought the car to the curb.

"Go ahead, I'll join you in a minute," said Sean. "I'll get rid of this car first. Be careful, others could be waiting for you here."

We entered the departure hall and I looked at the big board. It was 8:15 P.M., and the next flight out was British Airways 875 to London leaving at 9:35 P.M. No further precaution was necessary; the place was full of police in uniform and probably just as many in plainclothes. If word of a highway chase came to their attention we'd have a lot of explaining to do; we'd miss the flight, and I'd miss the break-in to Guttmacher's bank. I could not allow that. We needed to hurry; in this case, even the rigid Soviet bureaucracy might move quickly enough to stop us.

I ran to the British Airways counter, bought two one-way tickets to Munich via London's Heathrow, and checked in our luggage. I'd fight the bean counters in Washington later over the extra ticket. I held Ariel by her hand and rushed to passport control. Brandon joined Sean as they stood at a distance waiting for us to clear through the police passport inspection.

"Did you get rid of the car?" I asked Brandon.

"Yes, I dumped it. It won't lead to us; the registration is under the name of a nonexistent person. But I don't think it'll get to that. I left it in an area that car scavengers love. In one hour it'll be taken apart as if it never existed. As far as we're concerned, this entire incident never happened."

I stepped forward with Ariel to the passport-control counter, manned by a grim-faced Soviet officer wearing green military uniform. "Are you family?" he asked.

"No," I said. "She is my friend and she is not feeling well, and she does not speak Russian or English, so I'm here to help."

"Very nice of you," he said without the smile I expected. "Step back."

Ariel remained standing before his counter and signaled me that it'd be OK.

A few minutes later, which felt like eternity, I heard the sound of stamping and Ariel walked away to the gate. I approached the counter. The officer raised his head and looked at my face, which was losing its blood supply fast. He said nothing. He flipped through my passport and looked at some papers on his counter that I could not see.

"Please step aside," he finally said and buzzed a button. *That* I saw. Two men in plainclothes approached me. "Please come with us," they said firmly.

"Why? Have I done something wrong?" I asked, hoping they couldn't hear the tremble in my voice. They did not answer. I was led to a side room. "Sit down," said one of the men in an unexpectedly polite tone and pointed at a metal chair next to an empty desk. I sat on the chair. I saw my duffel bag in the corner of the room. I'm in deep shit, I thought.

"Can you explain that?" asked the man as he showed me my blood-stained shirt. "Airport security discovered it in your luggage."

I needed to come up with a quick explanation or I was doomed. "Oh, that," I said, showing them how relieved I was, and I was indeed. "There was a car accident on my way here; you must have heard about it, I was in a car just behind it. A car collided with a huge truck on the Moscow Ring Road and I rushed to help the injured. It was a terrible scene, I'm glad I could help until the ambulance came, and then I had to leave because I didn't want to miss my flight. I hope the passengers were all right; when I left they were in an awful shape." My interrogator went to the phone in the corner and dialed a number. Moments later he returned and said something in a Russian dialect I did not understand to the other guy.

"OK," he said, "your story about the accident checks out. It was nice of you to help a stranger. Are you a doctor?"

"No, but I was a Boy Scout and took some courses in first aid." I'll never know how I came up with that one.

They handed me back my passport and escorted me to the gate. Ariel was at the gate when they announced last call for our flight. When she saw me her face lit up. It was all worth it, I thought.

Five minutes later we were seated in the cabin of the Boeing 747, just like a couple of tourists. "Was there a problem?" she asked.

"No, just routine bureaucracy," I said. Ariel squeezed my arm. "I'm always nervous during takeoff," she said apologetically, and smiled.

The plane left the gate and taxied to the runway, moving faster and faster until it abruptly stopped. I saw two stewardesses running to the front of the aircraft. My heart was beating fast again. Had they found out who I was and tied me to the shooting? I looked out through the window. There was no activity around the plane and no explanation from the cockpit as to why we'd stopped. Ariel didn't seem to notice my concern. A few passengers got up from their seats to look through the windows. "Please sit down," said the stewards politely but firmly. I thought I should tell Ariel to call David Stone in Washington and inform him of my forthcoming arrest. I wrote down David's name and number.

"Ariel . . ."

She looked at me with the deep blue eyes I'd grown so fond of in the past few days. She said nothing. "Ariel, in case of trouble, I want you to . . ."

The PA system came on strong. "Ladies and gentlemen, this is your captain speaking. I have to apologize for the delay. There has been a severe weather warning, and air traffic control was not sure we would be allowed to take off. Now it seems that the storm is about twenty minutes away to the east, and we could avoid it if we leave immediately. So please fasten your seatbelts again. Thank you."

The plane accelerated down the runway, as did my heart in relief. In two minutes we were airborne.

"What did you want to say?" asked Ariel.

"Nothing, just nothing." I took her hand. She smiled.

We didn't talk much and my lovely companion was asleep as we approached Heathrow. I gently touched her shoulder. Ariel opened her eyes. "Time to wake up," I said. "We're almost in London."

"So soon?" she asked, and stretched like a cat after an afternoon nap.

"Everything passes quickly when you're asleep," I said. "We need to stay near the airport; I don't think we should try to get to Munich at this late hour."

"Munich?" asked Ariel. "I thought we were going back to Israel."

"No, I need you in Germany. You should see Guttmacher, and," I paused, "you promised me your father's file."

"You're right. I'm still sleepy," she said, and leaned her head against my shoulder.

We took a local airport bus to the Hilton Hotel at the airport. I took adjoining rooms for us without asking Ariel what she'd prefer. And like a tourist pal, she pecked my cheek goodnight.

The following morning featured typically English weather, rainy and foggy, but our flight to Munich was not delayed. I was sitting at a table in the dining room when Ariel walked in wearing blue jeans and a T-shirt. Many eyes were on her, including mine.

"Good morning, Dan," she smiled. "Did you sleep well?"

"Like a log," I said. "How about you?"

"I had nightmares," she said as she sat down at the table.

"So why didn't you knock on my door?" I asked jokingly, masking my disappointment.

"Dan, people are asleep when they have nightmares," she said in a tone that very much reminded me that she was a teacher.

"Our flight leaves at noon," I said, "so let's take our time." We had an English breakfast and perused the top story in the morning paper: yet another English sex scandal involving a cabinet minister.

We finished our breakfast and went through the hotel's lobby. I stopped at a television set broadcasting BBC News. With a mix of astonishment and relief, I heard the breaking news about the weather in Moscow. A sudden blizzard had swept the city, dumping two feet of snow. The next item was of similar interest; "With continued political unrest in the Soviet Union, there are growing fears of gang wars in the Soviet capital after a high-speed shoot-out on a major artery of Moscow between two gangs from the Asian Soviet republics left three dead. The Soviet Internal Security Minister said that the police were investigating. 'We vow to keep these hooligans off our streets.'"

Approximately two hours after takeoff we were back in Munich. The skies there were gray also but the air, although cool, was clean and crisp. The foliage was gone, leaving the trees bare and ready for winter.

I suggested we go to the Hotel Intercontinental. I didn't think returning to the Sheraton or the Omni was a good idea. I would explain the sudden cost hike as a security requirement. I still didn't know how to budget Ariel's airline and hotel costs. Sundry expenses? I'd worry about that later.

I checked us in, again with adjoining rooms. I was a bit more comfortable now that we were out of Moscow. We agreed to meet in the lobby in twenty minutes. I sensed that I was nearing the end of my search and wanted to get on with it. I needed that DeLouise file. ASAP.

"It's at Pension Bart," she said as we met and in answer to my query. "I left it there for safekeeping with Mr. Bart."

Ariel didn't realize it, but she was holding the key to some big questions: who killed DeLouise and where his money was. I badly wanted to see the file and substitute hard facts for my suspicions and gut feelings. Obviously, the file was expected to contain vital information that both Eric and Benny could use. Would the file live up to any of my expectations?

We took a cab to the pension. "Let me go in first," I said. "Stay in the cab."

"Why?"

"Just routine security. I want to be sure we have no surprises." I went inside. The place was empty, but Mr. Bart was behind the counter. I returned to the cab, and she followed me to reception.

"Hello Mr. Bart," said Ariel. "Remember me? I was a guest here about two weeks ago."

Bart looked at her and said, "I'm sorry, I don't recognize you. Did you forget something?"

"Not exactly," said Ariel, "I left an envelope here for safekeeping; it came earlier from my father, Raymond DeLouise."

Bart was apologetic, "You'll have to excuse me, but I don't remember ever seeing you or receiving any envelope for you. Is your father a guest here?"

I felt the chill of reality creeping all over me. Had Ariel been lying to me?

Ariel looked confused and looked at me in embarrassment. "I don't understand," she said to me quietly in Hebrew.

"Mr. Bart, will you please check your records and see that I was a guest here two weeks ago. Let's start with that," Ariel said firmly. Mr. Bart shifted his eyes from Ariel to me and back. There was silence. I got the message. I was in the way. "Let me check something outside," I said, and walked out. I quietly returned to the space near the entry door and looked inside through a window. I saw Bart giving Ariel a thick envelope.

So Ariel was leading me on, after all, I thought in deep disappointment. But why? Being double-crossed by Ariel was not something I'd wanted to entertain, although the possibility of it lay dormant in my mind. Frustrated, I walked back inside.

Ariel walked toward me, visibly relieved, and handed me the envelope. "Let's go," she said, sending my mood up like a rocket.

"What happened?" I asked.

"Bart knew me and knew I'd been kidnapped. He wanted to make sure you weren't part of the gang that kidnapped me and that you were coercing me to give you the envelope."

"Smart move," I said. "But Bart should have remembered me as a person helping your mother while she was here. I don't understand it."

"He only said that he didn't know who to trust anymore, and until I assured him that all was well, he'd pretend to be a senile old man."

"Let's go in again," I said.

"Don't be mad at him; he was trying to help me," she said.

"No. I want to thank him."

"This gentleman was asking about you some time ago," said Bart with a small smile, pointing at me. "I see that he found you. Or was it you that found him?"

Ariel smiled. "Actually, it was a little bit of both."

We sat in the lobby as I sifted through the papers. My intuition had been correct; I'd stumbled on a treasure trove — so much information I didn't know where to start. This was DeLouise's entire file on his dealings with Guttmacher and the Iranians. I hoped it contained the lists the Iranians had given DeLouise. If that hope materialized, it would be my first-class ticket into the Iranian transactions, just as Cyrus Armajani had demanded.

"This is too much to digest here," I said finally, masking my deep satisfaction. "Let's go back to the hotel. I need some study time."

We went back to the Intercontinental and up to my room. I sat at the desk with my legal pad and computer ready. Ariel sat quietly nearby, looking at me.

The first important document was an agreement between Triple Technologies and Bankhaus Bäcker & Haas. Under the agreement, Triple Technologies assigned a Credit Suisse certificate of deposit in the amount of $2,050,000.00 to Guttmacher's bank. The nice thing about it was a confirmation at the bottom of the document by Credit Suisse that they consented to the assignment. They also confirmed that DeLouise was a director who had sole power to sign for Triple Technologies. That could serve as some proof of the connection between DeLouise and Triple Technologies, in case we decided to try to pierce the corporate veil and show that the company was in fact DeLouise's alter ego. If I could show that DeLouise had commingled his assets with those of Triple Technologies and that there was really no separation between DeLouise and his company, it might convince a Swiss judge to attach the company's assets to satisfy the huge money judgment against DeLouise.

The next document was an agreement between the Italian Broncotrade and Tehran Nuclear Research Center (TNRC), Tehran, Iran. Under the agreement Broncotrade committed to act as the TNRC's liaison for the purchase of machinery, materials, and consulting services from European companies. Broncotrade received a monthly payment of $150,000 for its efforts and was promised a bonus of five million dollars when its mission was successfully completed. The agreement detailed the various services Broncotrade had agreed to provide to the Iranians. There was reference to a list of materials attached as exhibit to the agreement. I searched, but the attachment was missing from the file.

I was surprised that DeLouise had gotten his hand on this contract. He wasn't supposed to be in the loop concerning the relationship between Broncotrade and the Iranians. I guessed that DeLouise had "borrowed" a copy from Guttmacher's file, as part of his effort to build a dossier on the Iranians.

The file also contained confirmations of money transfers, through Guttmacher's bank, between Broncotrade and three accounts in other European banks. These were identified only by numbers, with no names of holders. These could be numbered accounts of individuals wanting to hide their identities.

Ariel approached and handed me a cup of hot tea and a small chocolate cookie. I found her presence very distracting. I didn't want her to see me looking through the material in the file and taking notes. After all, I was after her father's money. Not that I thought that Ariel would attempt to take the stolen money and run; she didn't seem impatient to get the money at all. If she was, she'd have been picking up from Guttmacher the envelope her father had mentioned in his first letter. Still, I wasn't professionally comfortable with Ariel leaning over my shoulder. Personally, it was another story.

Clearly it was time to call Stone and Henderson to tell them what I had. Hot stuff and plenty of it. But I couldn't do that with Ariel listening. I closed the file and turned to her. She had moved to the loveseat in the corner and was flipping through a magazine. I loved the silences between us. She didn't seem to need to fill them with useless talk. I liked that quality in a woman; she was comfortable with herself and me.

"I'm hungry," said Ariel. "How about dinner?"

"I'd love to, but not just yet. I need to make some phone calls first."

"OK," said Ariel, "I'll go to my room to freshen up and meet you back here in an hour."

"Good," I said, "but remember — no phone calls, not one. We've got to be careful until we find out who's after you."

"I'll be a good girl," promised Ariel. I didn't know if she was being face-tious, sardonic, or yielding.

I went to the lobby and locked the file in the hotel safe. For the umpteenth time I used a pay phone in the street to call Stone in Washington.

"Dan, where are you? Still in Moscow?" came David's friendly voice.

"No, David. I'm back in Munich. I made real progress. Things look promising, in both areas — Eric's and ours. But first I need to study some documents I've just received. I simply called to report that I'm back in Munich at the Intercontinental. I'll call you soon with another report."

And before David could comment, I added, "I have Ariel with me."

"Good," said David, "is she cooperating?"

"So far, so good," I said, "but she still doesn't know who I really am, and that bothers me."

"It never bothered you before," said David.

"It's different this time. I hope to be able to explain — to you, to her, and to myself."

Next I called Eric. He wasn't available. I left a message. I'd done my part. I retrieved the file from the safe, went back to my room, and con-tinued going through its contents. Then I saw it — a handwritten note: "Cyrus Armajani, Schwanthalerstrasse 122, Munich. Tel (089) 555-6765." That must be Armajani's private residence and phone number. There were many more documents that I was curious to read, but Ariel called and asked me to meet her downstairs for dinner. I took the file with me and back it went into the hotel safe.

We went casually into the hotel restaurant, almost as though we were going out on a date for the sixth or seventh time. We didn't talk about work, or about anything meaningful. Ariel spoke with her body. She liked to touch me with her hands. She touched my arm occasionally, my cheek, or my hand. This was her way of saying things and I needed to learn her language. I didn't want to miss a sentence, or even a single word.

After dinner we took a short walk. The streets were fairly empty and it was cold. This was no way to relax, with me having to constantly be on the alert, so back we went to the hotel.

"You must be tired," I said. "We've had a long day."

"Not really," she countered, with, I thought, an invitation in her voice. But I couldn't ask her to my room again. Self-control was the order of the day, but it wasn't easy. I had to separate my work from all else.

"I'll see you in the morning," I said.

"And I need to arrange a meeting with Guttmacher," she reminded me matter-of-factly.

"Not just yet. Please. This is important and I've got to check some things out before you call him. Trust me."

I couldn't tell her that I had to speak to Henderson first, clear her meeting with Guttmacher, and hear how the break-in operation was progressing. I went on.

"I'll see you for breakfast at eight. Is that too early?"

"No. That's fine."

"Remember," I repeated, "no phone calls."

I stepped over to her, held her arms, and said, "We'll have a lot to talk about when it's all over, so forgive me for being a bit cool. I'm simply focused on my work, and it's not easy when you're around."

It was the most direct statement I'd ever made to her.

She came closer, rose on her toes, kissed me lightly on my lips, turned around, and left without a word. I went to the lobby, took the file from the hotel safe, and asked the receptionist to let me do some photocopying. "The business center is closed now," she said. "Why don't you try in the morning?"

"I can't wait; these are medical documents that are needed for an emergency surgery. I must send them out with a courier to the United States."

That must have convinced her, and she unenthusiastically showed me to a back office. An hour later I was done. I returned the original file to the safe. I still had to satisfy my curiosity with respect to Armajani's Munich address, so I took a cab to the building and surveyed it. Upon my return there was a message waiting from Henderson. No need to wait. I called him back from the lobby.

"I need your report on Moscow," said Eric. He must have had some advance warning from Hart.

"I think we should talk in person," I said, "as soon as possible."

"I'll send Tom around to pick you up. Be ready in thirty minutes."

Eric was in the safe house when we arrived. "Benny came to Munich last night, and he called ten minutes after we spoke. I told him about this meeting. He'll be here shortly."

"Good timing." And, I thought, Benny's presence always instills sanity into a conversation. I proceeded to brief Eric on my Moscow trip, omitting the important details. I wanted Benny to be around to hear those.

A few minutes later Benny arrived.

"Greetings, friend. Looks like we coordinated our return to Munich."

"Like clockwork."

We sat down at the table and Eric began. "Benny came with a positive answer from his government. So the Mossad is in."

"Great," I said.

"There are certain conditions attached," said Benny. "This will be a joint operation. We share everything — means and information. As to the operation itself, we condition our participation on silent entry without the use of explosives at the vault."

"Does that complicate matters?" I queried.

I meant for Eric to answer, but Benny responded. "Not really. I think we solved that problem, largely thanks to you."

I was flattered. "What did I do to deserve the honor?"

"You remember the woman you caught on film after she left Guttmacher's office?"

"Yes, I remember. So tell me more."

"I had her followed during her lunch break. While she was having lunch in a restaurant, our guys picked her pocket and took her keys, went outside, made an electronic imprint, and returned the keys to her purse."

I laughed, "And she didn't catch on?"

"No. My guy is an expert; he could strip you of your underwear while you're wearing your pants."

"Tell him not to try." I laughed. "So you have the vault keys now. But will Shimon still need to enter through the roof?"

"No. She had keys to the back door of the bank as well. We checked them already. Our copy works fine. But I don't know if the vault's copy will also work. Obviously we couldn't test it."

"Talking about matched keys," I said, "you may want to consider an additional target: Cyrus Armajani, the head of the Iranian's nuclear purchasing mission in Europe."

"And where do we find him?" asked Eric.

"Right here in Munich."

"And we call information to find his address?" asked Eric sarcastically. "We've been looking for him for months now."

"Your search is over. Here's the address. I checked out the building; it's purely residential. It could be his home address in Munich." I gave Eric the address I copied from DeLouise's file.

"How did you find it?"

"A present from hell or heaven, depending on where you think DeLouise is now. He left some documents behind and the address was among them. But that could be a stale address, so check it out."

Eric didn't even blink when I gave him the information. "So you suggest we break into Cyrus Armajani's home?"

"Yes. Verify and break in. Since the Iranians don't seem to have an office here, I guess he'd be keeping some hot stuff. I'd plan it for the same night as the break-in at the bank."

"Why?" asked Eric.

"Because if we do just one break-in and they suspect that the documents connected to him are the target, they'll move them from his place for sure."

Eric gave me a long look and made some notes.

As usual, he demanded more. "Anything else I should know?"

"I prepared a copy of the complete file. See for yourself," I said, and pushed the papers in his direction.

Benny sensed what was going on.

"You certainly were on top of things, weren't you?" said Benny. "Now tell us how you got the file."

"DeLouise left it for Ariel. I found her in Moscow, and it's some of what I got for my trouble." I looked at Benny and figured he was wondering what else I got.

"Tell me more," said Benny. "I know this guy," he said to the others. "He needs to be asked."

"Ariel said she went to Moscow on her own, after reading the letter her father had left her with details of his scheme. Apparently he felt that his rivals were closing in on him. Your earlier theory about DeLouise's ploy checks out. Ariel gave me the same story. He was definitely planning to double-cross the Iranians. He was going to rip them off and trade the information they gave him for a sweetheart deal with the U.S. government. He hoped that the material he'd turn over to the U.S. would be so good that they'd forgive him and allow him to go back to the States with only a slap on the wrist, rather than prosecuting him on felony charges and sending him up for a long prison term. I think that the documents I found confirm his expectations."

"So what about Ariel?" asked Benny. "How does she fit into this?"

"Ariel said that after she learned that her father had been murdered she was certain it was an Iranian plot and decided to expose them, their Soviet suppliers, and their nuclear plans. I have doubts about that story, though."

"Who put it into her head?" asked Benny.

"The connection was detailed in her father's notes, and for Israelis, all Iranians are villains," I said. "Anyway, to carry out her plan she needed to meet with some Soviets who were willing to sell nuclear materials to the Iranians. But while Ariel is a very smart lady, she is an amateur in intelligence operations and basic security, and before long there was an attempt to kidnap her in Moscow." I didn't raise the possibility that I was the intended target of the car chase and the shoot-out. "I think it was only the beginning," I continued. "My suspicion is that she attracted the attention of at least two groups of bad guys. Frankly, I don't even know if the attack was connected to her father or to her own plan. I didn't need to find out; I simply got her out of Moscow that same evening."

"What proof do you have that there were two groups after her in Moscow?" asked Eric.

"I don't," I corrected him. "That's why I said that I have suspicions, not proof. One of them could be a group of rogue scientists, probably backed by the Russian Mafia, and the other could be the Colombian group, although I don't know if they still have their original agenda."

Benny chipped in. "If the Colombians are the ones who chased Ariel to Moscow and made the kidnap attempt at the hotel and later during the car chase, then it might indicate that their original goal when they kidnapped her in Munich was not achieved. We could also assume that the papers they were after are so important that they'd send somebody after them all the way to Moscow."

"I think so too," I agreed. "On the other hand I didn't like what I heard from Ariel about her connection in the Soviet Union. Based on her description of her local contact, and maybe also the guy I manhandled, it's possible that they are from Azerbaijan, Kazakhstan, or another neighboring Soviet Asian republic. These guys shoot first and ask questions later, and then you don't understand what language they used. It's possible they either wanted to hold her for ransom or to get a better deal on their goods. Under any circumstances I concluded that she had no business being there."

I handed Eric a short report I had written about Igor. "These are the details. You may want to do something about it."

I caught Eric off guard. "Who?"

"Igor Zurbayev, the contact of DeLouise whom Ariel called in Moscow."

Eric nodded, said nothing, and put the report in his file.

"Next on the agenda is Ariel's meeting with Guttmacher," I said. "She wants to see him, and I need your input on that."

"Why?" asked Eric.

"According to DeLouise's letter to Ariel, Guttmacher is holding documents for her, supposedly a road map to her father's money. I don't trust this guy, and I think he has his own agenda. That's why I need to hear your thoughts about a meeting between these two before the break-in."

"What do you recommend?"

"I tend to think that Ariel should not be allowed to meet him. Not now. She's not safe here, she's already been victimized three times, and until this matter clears up, I think she'd be better off at home in Israel."

"That's her interest," said Eric. "What's ours?"

"That should be obvious," I said, trying to hide my anger at his callous attitude toward her safety. "A meeting with Ariel could alert him. She could talk, mention me or the new kidnap attempt — she might scare him off. Once she goes to meet him, she's out of our control. I don't think Guttmacher should be given a reason or opportunity to review the DeLouise situation now. He may remove the file; take it home, what have you. There's no urgency in having Ariel meet Guttmacher just now, so I suggest that she return to Israel and meet him another time."

Eric said, "Benny?"

"I think Dan is right. We don't need any distractions here. She might talk. Send her home."

Although Eric eventually agreed with Benny's and my conclusions, I still didn't like his attitude. He was the kind of person who'd throw a drowning man both ends of a rope.

"OK, guys," I said as I got up, "I'm tired; I'm going back to the hotel. Call me when things get hotter."

Eric managed to surprise me. "The operation is scheduled for Saturday night. The center of command will be located in a suburban safe house. Be ready at your hotel at 4:00 P.M."

"OK," I said, not showing my excitement. I turned to Benny and said in Hebrew. "Call me later," and left.

I went back to my hotel room and fell asleep easily. I'd gotten a lot off my chest.

The following morning I saw a note inside my door. A single sentence written in Hebrew: "Where are you?"

I went to the dining room and saw Ariel waiting for me. She was a knockout in a close-fitting dark blue business suit with a white blouse.

"Good morning," I said as I sat down next to her. "Sleep well?" I paused a moment. Her clothes told me where she thought she was heading, so I had to make a move.

"Where are you going so dressed up?"

"To meet Guttmacher," she said.

"You haven't talked to him, have you?"

"No, you said no phone calls. Is there a problem? I need to see what my father left with that man."

"Yes, there's a problem." I turned serious. And I meant it. "I've spoken to some people and they don't think it would be a good idea for you to remain in Munich, even for one day and an important meeting. Remember, you were already kidnapped once, and we know it's connected to your father. There were two more attempts in Moscow, and we don't know who's responsible for that either."

"What are you saying?" she asked, with mounting anxiety.

"I'm saying you must pack and leave Munich now. Go back home; you'll be safe there."

"And what about you?"

"I'll stay here until we resolve all the questions. Please, go back. Believe me, it's the only way — for now."

"Did you know this when we were in London? I guess you only wanted me here to get the file. And I was stupid enough to think that you had other reasons."

"Please, Ariel," I said. "You couldn't be more wrong. I led you here because I was too blind to see the risks you're exposed to. I admit I wanted the file. I wanted you near me as well. You know that, don't you? But now I've got to think only of your best interests. I'm sorry if you think I misled you; I meant well. Please bear with me. There are only a few remaining pieces to the puzzle and then we can put this whole thing behind us. I promise."

There were tears in Ariel's eyes. She didn't offer any words and I didn't know what else to say. If she was upset at me for using her to get to the file, it was just a passing shower before the storm I'd be caught in when she found out the real truth about who I was and why I had looked for her.

"When do you want me to leave?" Her voice was tight.

"Right away. I think there's an afternoon flight to Tel Aviv — let's finish breakfast and call El Al." I could do nothing to fill the sudden blankness between us.

Later we rode in tense silence in the cab on our way to the airport. I had a lot on my mind and a few words to say, but it wasn't the time for soul-searching, or for the truth for that matter. I hoped she'd understand. But judging from her reaction, I'd need more than just hope; I'd have to make it happen.

There was no dramatic good-bye scene at the airport. Only more silence. Before she disappeared through passport control and into the departure hall, though, Ariel turned to look at me and smiled a shy smile.

I went back to the city feeling empty. Why did I have to put my work first, above everything else? I knew the answer — my training. But they never taught me how to overcome human emotions like the ones I had now. I knew I'd just done the right thing, personally and professionally. I was protecting Ariel by sending her back to Israel. At any cost she had to be kept away from Guttmacher, the Iranians, and the Colombians. This didn't make it any easier to take, however.

All of a sudden I found myself with nothing to do. I had to sit and wait. It was maddening to go from frantic, busy days to a day of nothing, much less two or three. I called Lan. No, the responses to the subpoenas served upon American Express concerning the R. De Louise credit card had not arrived yet. I had to give in. I had two days to kill but no idea what to do with them.

I had been out of the loop during my Moscow trip. I hoped that the planners of this sensitive covert operation had a firm understanding of the bureaucratic process of conducting a joint operation with another intelligence operation. I had never participated in such a joint venture. But my experience had taught me that the very nature of bureaucracies' hierarchical structures limited the degree of their operational success. Just as the speed of light is the ultimate speed, government bureaucracies cannot move effectively beyond a preset operational timetable. Rules must be followed; memoranda drafted and, at every level up the chain of command, signed by someone with the authority to sign; reporting and approvals must be obtained, and all that takes time. While each bureaucratic level in turn complies with all its requirements, the operational deadlines slip. The result is fatal holdup. If the operation is civilian, the damage is mostly financial. But if the operation is in either the military or intelligence categories, heads could roll. Therefore, if you want to run a successful covert operation, the person in charge on location must have full, decentralized authority to initiate actions as changing circumstances require.

Since this was a joint effort, these problems were now doubled. If Eric was going to need approvals from both his boss at the CIA and from the Mossad each time a departure from the original plan became necessary, the operation was doomed. As a rule, operational cooperation between two foreign intelligence services is complex. There's a built-in distrust embedded in organizations in which "suspicion" is the motto. The difficulty here was greater because the CIA, much larger and more rigid, had to cooperate with the smaller and more flexible Mossad.

X

By Saturday noon I was anxious and tense, the same kind of feeling I had before I went on incursion across the Israeli-Syrian border or on subsequent Mossad assignments. Failure here was not an option. Tom came on time as usual to pick me up. Again, he was like a monk who'd taken a vow of silence. We drove to a safe house in Gernlinden, on the outskirts of the city. I'd lost count of the number of Munich safe apartments I'd been in by now, but I was sure that there'd been more than ten. This time the neighborhood looked similar to that of Bart's pension. The two-story villa was secluded and surrounded by shrubs and birch trees.

Tom opened the metal gate with his remote and we drove into the courtyard. Two other cars were already parked in the yard near the entrance. Three young men were not in very active guard mode, sitting inside. They looked as if they might be U.S. Marines just out of boot camp, crew cuts and all.

I followed Tom upstairs and to a door at the end of the hall. One of the two guards on duty checked us out quickly and let us in.

A huge room occupied most of the second floor. Two dozen people were sitting or moving around in complete silence. Heavy curtains covered the windows and fluorescent lights focused attention on the desks, the maps, the telephones, and the computers. Large photographs of the bank, taken from different angles, covered the wall next to a huge street map of Munich and its surrounding suburbs. Two smaller maps showed the two target areas. It was a charged atmosphere where words were barely audible. The neighbors couldn't possibly complain that we were disturbing their afternoon naps.

Eric, expressionless as usual, was clad in jeans and a sweatshirt. He was wearing a headset. He noticed me come in and nodded. Two distinguished-looking men in business suits sat next to him, both with headsets as well. Needless to say, I was curious about them. Somehow, they didn't seem to me like technicians. Benny, Shimon, and Avi, the Mossad's logistics men, were very much on the scene. Computer and telephone operators were behind workstations; technicians were completing some wiring. A stocky guy in jeans approached Eric, gave him a note and said, "We've got the codeword: Bonanza."

Eric looked at the two men next to him, showed them the note, and they nodded in approval.

Eric got up and faced the small crowd. "Folks. We've just received final authorization to go ahead with the mission. From now on, no private talk or security violations. We've done all the rehearsing we have time for. This is the real thing and I'll go over it once more. I'll act as the director of operations for both incursions. This guy on my right is Eugene, the stage manager. He'll report to me and oversee the operational stage to make sure all conditions and contingencies are considered. In particular, he'll take the point of view of the German police, the Iranians, and casual observers, to make sure we're invisible." Eric paused, looked at us, and continued.

"There will be three operational groups, each headed by an action officer. Team number one, headed by Shimon and assisted by Yuval from the Mossad, will hit Bankhaus Bäcker & Haas. Team number two, headed by our Brian and assisted by Gary, will hit Armajani's residence, and team number three, headed by Tom and assisted by Jeff and Larry, will act as decoys at the Bayerische Hypotheken und Wechsel Bank and handle the power failure. There are three rescue teams waiting in three separate safe apartments near the target areas, in case the walls crash in on us. There are also two backup teams to replace any of the operational teams, and two technical support backup teams. If all goes well, you'll not be seeing any of them. There are almost seventy people involved in this operation.

"Team number one will leave Gernlinden at 4:30 P.M. in the blue Volkswagen. Team number two will leave at 4:45 in the green Fiat. Team number three will leave at 4:35 in the Volkswagen van. Remember, this is Europe; this is Germany. People here obey traffic lights and rules within the city. They go wild only on the expressway. Don't burn up the road. You could blow the entire operation with a stupid moving violation. The license plates are genuine, but the registrations are under phony names. It will survive a police check, but a thorough inspection will raise unnecessary questions. It's getting dark earlier now; use your headlights.

"Make sure there's nothing on you to give away your identity. One last time, will each team member please inspect his partners' clothing, pockets, laundry labels, everything."

Each team member checked the others' pockets, shoes, and shirt collars, anything that could give identity away.

I knew what Eric meant. In these operations, in case of apprehension the first police report and the initial press coverage leave the longest imprint on public opinion. "Two burglars caught in a Munich bank" gets a mention inside the local papers and that's the end of it. On the other hand, "two burglars caught in a bank and in an apartment in Munich, one is a Mossad agent and the other a CIA agent" gets the front page of every newspaper in the world, with continued coverage throughout the investigation and trial. And that's only the news coverage. Then come the columns, the commentaries, the speculations. The bottom line: in addition to the political quagmire, public pressure would make it very difficult to extricate the agents from a prison term. However, if operatives were caught as anonymous foreign citizens, a quiet understanding with the friendly government of Germany would spring them loose fairly quickly.

"Clean," announced each team member after the inspection.

"Good," continued Eric. "Under no circumstances are you to use your weapons against any civilians or the German police. Keep your gun loaded but with the safety on. Use it only if you are in imminent danger. Although we don't believe there's anyone in Armajani's apartment, there could be surprises. Armajani, his wife, and their daughter are under surveillance in Milan for the weekend. We've also staked the place out for the past week and know the apartment to be unoccupied. Same goes for the bank — if you're surprised inside, don't use your weapons unless your life is in danger. Simply knock the guy out. Remember your cover stories: if stopped before you enter the bank, then you're tourists from South Africa. The passports you've left behind in your hotel rooms are genuine fakes. Memorize your new names. You entered Germany two days ago through Austria and you're on a trip to Switzerland. If you're caught during the operation, make no excuses and give no explanation whatsoever. You're regarded as burglars and nothing else. If you're rolled up after the operation, stick to the burglary story: you came for cash but found only papers. If there is cash in either location, take it. If the vault was full of cash and you're stopped with only papers, your cover as a burglar would only look ridiculous. Do not even think of asking to see a U.S. or Israeli consul if you're arrested. The police will treat you in their usual manner — not gently. Endure that. The police must not know who you are. After you've dieted on their food for a while, we'll figure out a way to exfiltrate you. Be patient.

"Next, maintain radio contact with your partner only if absolutely necessary and use the codes we rehearsed. I don't want some German ham-radio enthusiast to call the police after hearing suspicious talk. Your radio is on UHF band and therefore it's very difficult to trace. But still, the last thing we want is the German police on the case. If you do hear the code word on the radio alerting that the German police are closing in, just get the hell out of wherever you are. We'll jam their communications in the area for at least twenty minutes. That'll give you plenty of time."

Eric then went on to review the operational details one last time.

"There we are. Now, just do what you did during the drills and I'll see you later. Team one in safe house number one, team two in safe house number two, and team three in safe house number three. Only the backup unit returns here after all teams report to their safe houses; we'll dismantle all these installations. This place should be empty no later than 8:00 A.M. tomorrow. Any questions?"

No one spoke.

"Good luck."

Team one picked up their equipment and went out the door. Five minutes later team three was on the way. I stopped Shimon and wished him well.

"Thanks," he said. "Don't worry, we'll pull it off."

Ten minutes later team two was on its way.

I stood behind Benny at the monitor showing a street map of Munich. A yellow arrow and a red arrow, one for each car, showed their progress. Each car had a small transmitter allowing our direction finder to know its position and direction at any time.

Prudent planning, I thought, not to mix the teams. Each organization would hit a different target. That would reduce the risks of confusion due to language and cultural barriers.

I looked at my watch; they should be on target in about fifteen minutes. The curtains were down so I couldn't see outside, but at this time of the year Munich would already be dark and there would be almost no people outside in this part of town, which was why we could begin operations relatively early in the day.

The radio hummed.

"Team one five minutes to target," said a young man next to the computer.

We waited silently for the next report.

"Team three, five minutes to target."

Eric seemed calm. Only his frequent glimpses at his watch revealed any tension. I was holding a bottle of water, sipping every couple of minutes to keep my own nerves under control.

"Team one, on target," said the computer operator.

"Team three, on target," said another computer operator.

"Power is off in the entire block."

"Give team one the go-ahead," said Eric.

The computer operator spoke into the mike.

There was silence for a few minutes and then the operator reported, "Team one inside target. All is well."

"Team two inside target, all is well."

That's it; the floodgates were open. The operation was on and there was nothing we could do but wait.

"Team one reporting that the safe is opened, documents have been removed, and photocopying started."

I gulped more water. Nerves again.

"Team two has recovered documents, expects to leave premises within ten minutes."

"Great," said Benny in a low voice standing next to me. "That's what I want, and that was fast."

I noticed that the back of my shirt was wet. I looked at Benny; I could detect sweat even on cool Benny's forehead. The temperature outside was near freezing, but the heat in the room was almost palpable from our excitement and the warmth generated by the computers and other equipment.

"Team one reporting that the volume of documents in the vault is enormous; there's no time to photocopy it all."

Eric looked at Benny. "What do you think?"

"Ask him if there's any cash in the vault."

Eric nodded to the operator who relayed the question.

The coded answer came in quickly. "Yes, 200,000 to 300,000 German marks."

Benny thought for a moment, and said, "How many documents have they already photocopied and how many more are left?"

"They say that they copied just one file, but there are more than sixty."

"Tell them to focus on anything that looks to be connected to the Iranians; we don't need anything about other sleazy money-laundering operations. Can they do that?"

"Yes, they think that for sure there are fifteen files connected to the Iranians."

"How long would it take to copy those?"

"They still couldn't make it by morning."

Nothing was said about DeLouise's files. I had initiated the operation and my objectives were being overlooked.

Benny turned to Eric. "Here's what I suggest. Let them continue with the copying until 5 A.M. That's almost two hours before sunrise, so they could still leave in the dark. Then tell them to remove all the cash in the vault and the files that haven't been copied."

"Fine with me," said Eric. "I suggest we send Dan to join them; he could help them sort out what files to take. After all, these are the bank's files and he is familiar with that kind of paperwork." Encoded orders were relayed.

"Go ahead, send Dan, there's plenty of work for anyone coming to help."

"Dan?" said Eric.

"I'm ready, who'll be driving me?" I was already having *reise fieber,* the German word for hectic excitement in anticipation of travel.

Andy, a young man in jeans, drove me to the bank in a white Ford Taurus. An observer standing on the outside signaled Yuval, who was inside the bank, and the side door was opened for me. Nobody seemed to notice. There was barely any traffic in the street during the blackout and the entire process of my entry took less than two minutes. A bigger problem waited for me inside. It was completely dark; I had no flashlight and nearly fell off the stairs. "Dan?" I heard a whisper in Hebrew. "Come here."

"Nice idea," I said, "but I can't see a damn thing."

"Wait, I'm coming to get you." Yuval came closer to me holding a flashlight. His face looked odd when the only source of light that illuminated him came from below. He gave me a pair of plastic gloves. "Put them on," he ordered. He also gave me cloth-covered rubbers to put over my shoes, giving me the look of a surgeon going into the operating room. Finally he gave me a wool cap to put on my head to prevent any hair from falling out and leading to me — if they happened to have my DNA.

"We don't want to leave any prints or marks around," he said. We climbed the stairs into the executive floor and passed the secretarial workstation into Guttmacher's office. The closet was wide open. A flashlight was mounted on a tripod and Shimon was busy taking photos of files. "Hi," he raised his head. "Welcome to our studio. Here, look at these files and see which are the best for us. There is so much we could photocopy. To me they all look the same. So pick up what's important."

I quickly sifted through the pile. There was so much there that I felt lost at first. Then I developed a method. I picked a file and searched for key words inside, such as *Iran,* or *nuclear,* or *chemicals.* I immediately identified six such files and I gave them to Shimon. "Make photocopies of these," I said. "But use discretion; we don't need every piece of paper, such as postal receipts or copies of documents when you have the original. The German secretary seems to keep many documents in triplicate, God knows why; don't repeat her mistakes."

I progressed very slowly, reading each file under the ineffective light of the flashlight. I separated the files into two piles: the first for files containing significant information, the second for files that were unimportant. I was thirsty but didn't want to waste time by looking for water. The pile with interesting stuff grew taller. The amounts involved were significant. It seemed that the Iranians were willing to pay big bucks for the best machinery, parts, compounds, and chemicals. Most of the vendors were German, Austrian, and French, but I also identified Belgian and Swiss companies. The use of offshore companies was substantial. There were addresses of companies in Liechtenstein, Cyprus, Jersey Islands, and the Cayman Islands. Obviously the goods purchased from these companies hadn't been manufactured in these tax havens, which were most likely used to mask the true origin of the goods.

Many of the files had no connection to Iran. A quick look revealed that they documented substantial money movements during a period of two years, clean words for dirty work: money laundering for private individuals who had difficulties sharing their fortunes with others, be it their government's tax authority or their creditors.

Two hours went by, and Shimon with Yuval's help worked relentlessly in photocopying with their two state-of-the-art document cameras. "Did you see the DeLouise files yet?" I finally let my curiosity get the better of me.

"Yes," said Shimon, "I think I did two already."

A call came in from the outside. "Report progress."

"We have more files than we could photocopy by the deadline," reported Yuval.

The official word came from Benny in a coded message. "Continue with the copying until 5 A.M., which is almost two hours before sunrise, so you can still leave in the dark. Then remove all the cash in the vault and the files that haven't been copied." I thought it was a smart move. When the break-in was discovered the bank would realize that, apart from the money, the burglars also took a few files to sell, to capitalize on them later.

I knew what Benny was plotting. We'd done it before. After the removed files had been copied Benny would anonymously engage underworld figures, who'd have no knowledge of what had gone on, to contact Guttmacher and offer to sell him these files. That move could help convince the Iranians that the break-in was perpetrated by thieves and not by a foreign-intelligence service. If Benny wanted to expose the Iranian clandestine nuclear-purchasing mission, his men would then tip off the police about the forthcoming transaction. All involved would be arrested and publicly exposed.

We barely exchanged any words. I finished going over the pile. "I'm done," I reported. "What do I do? Wait for Yuval and Shimon until they finish, or return?"

"Sending a car for you," came the response. It was a good move, reducing the number of people leaving the bank, thereby reducing the chance of being spotted. I was no longer needed at the bank, because only Yuval and Shimon had cameras.

"See you later," I said, and started on my way down, escorted by Yuval carrying his flashlight. I got to the side door and tried to open it. It was locked. I put my ear to the door to hear if any noise was coming from the outside before I made another attempt. It was quiet. I tried the door again; there was no question it was locked, not jammed. I looked at Yuval, "You try."

He did, but still we could not open the door. We quickly went upstairs to alert Shimon. "Where are the keys?" I asked. "The damn door is locked."

Shimon raised his head in surprise. "The keys work only from the outside, and on the inside there is a latch that you have to turn."

"I did just that but the door wouldn't open."

Shimon went downstairs with us and tried the door. "You're right, it's locked, not jammed. I can break it, but I need to know if there is anyone on the outside who might hear me."

Yuval radioed the sentinel, who was positioned in a rented office across the street.

"The coast is clear," came the answer.

Shimon ran upstairs and brought a small toolbox.

"What are you doing?" I asked.

"I need to pick this lock, the mechanism seems to be stuck," he said. "In a normal deadbolt lock, a movable bolt or latch is embedded in the door so it can be extended out the side. This bolt is lined up with a notch in the frame. When you turn the lock, the bolt extends into the notch in the frame so the door can't move. There are pins inside that are pushed correctly if you have the right key." He took a long pick that curved up at the end out of the toolbox. After several attempts, the door was still locked. Precious photocopying time was being lost.

"Yuval," said Shimon, "why don't you go back upstairs and continue copying while I try to unlock this door." Yuval took his flashlight and climbed the stairs. I was standing next to Shimon. We took from his toolbox a tension wrench and a thin flathead screwdriver. We tried several more tries, to no avail.

"OK," said Shimon, "I can break the door, but we risk being discovered and we'd need to leave as soon as I break it because we can't leave the bank broken open and continue to work upstairs. It'd be only a question of time before the police get our asses. We need to go to plan B."

"Which is?"

"The one I thought of before we stole the keys: through the roof. We go out through a window on the third floor, or directly climb the roof if there is a way, and lower ourselves to a tree in the backyard of the bank."

I wasn't thrilled with the idea. I never saw myself performing as a trapeze artist in a circus.

"Do the three of us need to do that?"

"No," said Shimon with a smile, sensing my reluctance. "I'll do it and then try to open the door from the outside. Once in the street I can see if danger is looming."

"Let's try it then," I said.

We went upstairs, alerted Yuval on the change of plans, radioed central about the problem, and climbed the stairs to the third floor. The entire floor was used for file storage and was rather cramped.

Shimon lighted the ceiling with his flashlight. "Here, there are wooden stairs to the roof," he said, "I can go through there. That will save me from climbing from the third-floor window. Wait here, I'll be right back." He went downstairs and returned with a rope and tied it around his waist. "When I give you the word, tie the end of the rope to this column," he pointed to a concrete pillar in the middle of the floor. "Once I'm on the ground, I'll pull the rope three times to signal you to pull back the rope. Then go downstairs to the door and wait for me there. Here, keep that for me," he said, and handed me the rubbers from his shoes, his gloves, and his cap. "I wouldn't like to explain if I'm stopped wearing these," he said with a smile.

Shimon climbed the wooden stairs to the roof, opened the latch holding a small wooden door on the ceiling, and pushed himself in. After five minutes, which seemed like eternity, I felt the rope tugged three times. I quickly pulled back the rope and hurried downstairs, waiting for him at the door. I was tense and restless. I waited for a few minutes but nothing happened. I didn't hear any activity next to the locked door. I heard cars passing and conversations in German, but no sign of Shimon. I went back to Guttmacher's office and asked Yuval to radio the sentinel outside whether he could see Shimon.

"He can," came the answer, "but he can't approach the door. There's too much activity in the street. He's hiding behind a parked van waiting for the commotion to let up."

I rushed back down to the door and waited. I heard the door lock being worked on, and a moment later it opened. "Quick," said Shimon, "go out. Andy is waiting for you in a black Mercedes taxi one hundred yards up the street."

I removed my shoe rubbers, gloves, and cap, and gave them to Shimon. "Your stuff is here as well," I said, pointing to the floor, and slipped out the door while Shimon entered the bank, closing the door behind him. I started walking slowly up the street. The street was dark with few cars passing, many of them taxicabs and police. I saw Andy waiting for me in the Mercedes. He drove me back to the safe house.

As I entered the room I could hear the report: "Team two is outside the target and is on its way to the safe house."

I could hear a slight sigh of relief in the room.

"Team three reports increased police activity in the area. They think it's connected to the blackout. The utility company workers broke the control-box lock, but the power is still not on. They're still checking the box."

Benny looked at Eric. "Let's wait," said Eric.

"Team three reports power restored in the block. Utility company workers leaving but the police cars are still in the area."

"Call team number one. Report if any of the bank's alarm systems were triggered after power was restored."

"Negative," came the answer. "They took care of it before the power went on again; they have the keys, remember?"

"Ask team three if their car has been detected."

"No, their scanner just picked up the police radio; they believe that the police patrol is routine. Anyway, they're still in the rented office."

"Good," said Eric.

"Team two reports arrival at safe house and radio reporting is off."

Eric wiped perspiration from his forehead. I was surprised, considering he was such a cold-blooded eel; I figured he probably sent his wife a written memo if he wanted to have sex with her.

Hours went by. I stretched out on the couch. Only the intermittent sounds of incoming reports broke the silence. Just before 5:00 A.M. Eric asked, "How are they doing there?"

"Twelve files copied; there are at least four more."

"OK, tell them to wrap it up. Remove the cash and the relevant files together with four additional files that are clearly, I repeat clearly, uncon-nected to the Iranians, and leave."

So Eric was extending Benny's idea. They would look even more like random burglars by taking unrelated files. "Wait," I said to Eric. "Tell them to search Guttmacher's desk drawers."

"Why?" asked a surprised Eric. "There couldn't be anything important to us in the desk."

"True," I said, "but we want to create the impression that burglars broke into the bank, and that's what a burglar would do." My training kicked in again.

"OK," said Eric, and gave the order.

The man with the headset said to Eric, "They found a personal diary and a checkbook and ask what to do with it."

"I suggest you tell them to photocopy all entries in the diary during the past month, but take the checkbook," I said. Eric agreed. "Tell team three to scour the area before they're picked up," he added.

Fifteen minutes later the word came. "Team one outside the target."

"All clear," came the response a few minutes later. "Teams one and three are on their way to their safe houses."

I shook Eric's hand; it was wet with perspiration. "Congratulations," I said.

"Thanks for your help," said the visibly drained Eric. "Now we need to see what we got." Eric's technical staff started dismantling the equipment. Minutes later Tom and Jeff of team three walked in. They were unshaven and looked tired. "Mission accomplished," said Tom.

"Good work," said Eric. "Did you clean the rented office?"

"Yes, I made sure nothing was left behind aside from the documents intended to be left there, those collected from the garbage cans of a big Hollywood studio." He chuckled. "The landlord will be surprised that his tenants disappeared, although the rent was paid until the end of the month."

"That has been taken care of," said Eric. "A letter will be delivered to him on Monday giving him notice, a check for another month's rent, and an apology that the film-making project was delayed for several months."

Benny smiled.

"Now," continued Eric, "go home and get some sleep. I mean all of you, excluding the technical staff here. Our men will wrap up all the equipment and make sure nothing is left behind. As of now, this place is abandoned. Benny and Dan, I'll see you at the other safe house today at four in the afternoon. My men will pick you up from your hotels at 3:35 P.M. Each of you should leave here in opposite directions, even if you need to go to the same area. U-turn later. Leave at five-minute intervals. Remember, although it's early Sunday morning, there could be people outside. Don't arouse any suspicion; none of us look as if we belong here. Female members of our team, please leave together with a man to make it look like you are returning from a party."

I got back to my hotel but couldn't sleep. The whole day had been intense; the adrenaline rush still hadn't subsided. Then I thought of Ariel. More calming than a pill. I fell asleep.

Tom picked me up on time, as usual, and took me to another safe house. The apartment was located in a high-rise building that looked out of place in this suburban neighborhood. But multistory buildings are a good location for a safe apartment because they give you a certain degree of anonymity. In a building with only six units every one may know everyone else, and a strange face can breed curiosity.

Benny and Eric were already there with the two men I'd seen earlier in the operation center. "These are my supervisors from Langley," said Eric. "Phil Richards," he pointed at a tall, slim man in his early fifties. I shook his hand. "And this is Arthur Brown, my direct supervisor." Brown was a stocky African American with a firm handshake.

"Dan, nice to meet you. I've heard a lot about you."

"Please, I can explain," I said grinning.

He smiled. "Not right now, we've got work to do."

"We've had only an initial review of the material from the bank," said Eric. "Most of it relates to the transactions Guttmacher was making with Broncotrade and the Iranians. It looks promising but we'll have to analyze it thoroughly."

"What about me?" I asked. "Anything about DeLouise?"

"We don't know yet. There's still a lot to check out. If it's here, you'll get it, don't worry."

We continued in a cordial exchange of conversation, but there was really nothing more to be said. We'd have to go through the files before any conclusions could be drawn.

"OK," I said as I got up. "I guess my tour of duty for you has ended. Just let me know when I can come and work on these papers. I've still got my own job to do."

"Sit down," said Brown politely, "you're not done yet."

I sat back down on the couch waiting for somebody to say something. Nobody did, so I ventured a question.

"What about the break-in into Armajani's apartment? Anything interesting there?" I asked.

"That yielded only one file," said Brown. "Eric, let him see it." He sounded content.

The first document had ten pages. It bore an official Iranian flag in green, white, and red and a green seal. I looked over Eric's shoulder as he went through the pages. It was typed in Arabic script on thin airmail paper.

"It's written in Farsi," I said, after giving it a first glance behind Eric's shoulder, "because there are few extra letters to Arabic."

"Can you read Farsi?" asked Eric.

"No. The letters are Arabic, which I can read, but I'd have no clue what they say except for a few words that entered Farsi from Arabic."

"Never mind," said Eric, "we made a quick translation," and handed me a stapled document.

I took the document and started in. The header read "Top Secret" and then came the words "With God Almighty's Blessing." The letter was dated 13 farvadin 1369 and was addressed to Cyrus Armajani and Farbod Kutchemeshgi.

"What is that date?" asked Brown.

"The Iranian solar calendar," I volunteered. "Years are numbered by the years since Mohammad's Hegira in 621 A.D., so the Iranian year will be 621 years less than the Gregorian year that began on January 1. That makes the year 1369. Farvadin is April. And since they say in the letter that this is the Islamic Republic Day, I presume the correct date to be April 2, 1990."

The document was titled "Iran's Pride."

"Before you continue," Eric said, "I should mention that 'Iran's Pride' is a code name assigned to their nuclear weaponization program, which is closely connected to their delivery system, a ballistic missile."

"OK," I said, and continued reading from the translation. "Today is Islamic Republic Day. The Great Iranian Islamic nation is about to demonstrate to the world its scientific ability by building an atomic bomb to safeguard our nation's leading position in the region.

"This entire program is subject to the most stringent confidentiality.

Under orders of Ali Akbar Hashemi Rafsanjani, our president, all activities in this program must be under the guise of 'intended for civil or peaceful use.' If asked, we offer the explanation that the purchases of the materials are for 'civil use such as oil refining, food and dairy production, car and truck manufacture, pharmaceutical research, and drug production.'"

Brown moved to the couch. "We know that Iran is building two uranium-enrichment facilities, which will operate in concert with the larger facility planned at Natanz."

"Dan was already briefed on that," said Eric.

"OK," said Brown.

I scanned through some more pages in the document.

"I see an updated list of materials and equipment the Iranians need. It indicates that quantities and delivery dates would be advised as soon as possible. It includes the potential vendors for the supply." I paused for a minute and quickly read on. "Here's an interesting part. They write that 'there have been several sabotage attacks by the Israelis on factories the Iraqis used in Europe and we expect that to happen to our facilities if agents of the Zionist entity or the American infidels discover our nuclear activities. You should engage special means to protect yourselves and be extra careful with respect to your suppliers and vendors. You are not allowed to befriend anyone without our prior approval. Any new approach to you, as benign and as random as it may seem, must be regarded as an attempted contact by the CIA or the Israelis."

"There's no need to read out the entire document," said Brown after patiently listening to my reading. "All I want you to do is to quickly compare it with DeLouise's list, the one you saw during the meeting with the Iranians at Guttmacher's office."

It took me about ten minutes to go through the pages of machinery and chemical compounds, carefully itemized.

"It looks very similar to the list I gave you earlier," I said. "DeLouise did a good job by keeping these lists. What I see here partially matches DeLouise's list."

"It seems that they didn't give him the whole list, just the bits they wanted him to get," said Eric.

"But DeLouise had two lists, a short one and a longer one. I guess the short one was given to him by the Iranians, and then he probably stole a complete copy from Guttmacher," I suggested.

"Anything here to confirm the authenticity of this document?" asked Brown.

"The fact that the list checks with DeLouise's adds to its credibility, but a fake document could be copied and that wouldn't convert it to a genuine document. Our analysts will verify authenticity," chipped in Benny.

"If it's genuine, it's a gold mine," said Richards, cautiously. "This could save us months of work. Some of the machinery and materials are dual purpose, so I wouldn't be surprised if those vendors don't even know the true intended use of their equipment or materials."

"I don't think any of them are that naïve," I said. "The smell of money just clouded their judgment more than a little."

"I'm not giving anyone a clean bill of health," said Benny. "However, some of the manufacturers of the dual-purpose materials could have been duped by the Iranians."

"We need to do a lot more research before we jump to conclusions, and this is a perfect time to do it," added Brown. "After that it's a political decision."

"We already know some of the names," said Benny, "but this is the first time our information has been supported by an official Iranian document boasting about their campaign of disinformation."

"Let's squeeze the juice out of it first," said Eric, "and then see what to do with the pulp."

I thought that the next document in the file would shock everyone. It appeared to be a copy of a CIA report on the Iranian nuclear program.

If the document were genuine, then the Iranians had a mole. How else could they have gotten it? At first glance it looked genuine. It had the CIA letterhead and was dated August 1, 1990. Eric narrowed his eyes and read it briefly. Then he handed it over to Benny and said, "Please read it out loud, then tell us what you think." He seemed to be in a testing mode.

Benny put on his small rimless glasses and read. "This is an updated report concerning Iranian nuclear activity.

"The 1981 Israeli Air Force's bombing of the Iraqi Osiraq reactor and subsequent developments highlighted fairly early on that Iraq was fostering a nuclear weapon interest. Dr. Jafar dhia Jafar, head of Iraq's nuclear weapons effort, has indicated that the Israeli bombing of Osiraq prompted his government to proceed with a secret enrichment program. Although the Israeli attack cost Iraq almost one billion dollars, the world did not punish Israel for its aggression. That caused Iran to resort to subterfuge concerning its own nuclear program."

Benny put down the document, removed his eyeglasses, and looked at Eric. "What's this bullshit? Is it for real?"

Eric smiled. "Please continue," he asked.

Benny let out a sigh and said, "Let me read it first." Five minutes later, Benny came up with an answer: "This is garbage. Somebody was trying to create a document purportedly written by the CIA, while in fact it is a compilation of several different news reports appearing in the media in recent years."

"The problem is that although Iranian sources claim their scientists have the necessary skills and technology to master the construction of an atom bomb, we don't think they do," said Eric in a decisive tone. "Therefore, they're also working in other directions: purchasing gas centrifuges and developing gaseous diffusion, chemical enrichment, and laser isotope separation to produce highly enriched uranium and plutonium to build a bomb. Substantial resources and effort are going into gaseous diffusion."

Benny looked at Eric with a puzzled look. "Is there a purpose for this fake document? Where are the secrets?"

"There aren't any," said Eric. "Although Iranian agents were having trouble trying to buy essential equipment on the open market, which is now embargoed, we think the Iranians may nevertheless have been successful in their purchasing missions."

My heart started beating faster. Iranian A-bombs and the trigger in the hands of the ayatollahs?

Eric continued. "Iran is capitalizing on the strong desire of Western technology companies to make sales wherever they can. They look the other way when questions come up about the true end-use of the technology or equipment they supplied. The Iranians are toying with business-hungry companies, and they are able to obtain a considerable amount of proprietary information from these firms for free."

Benny didn't comment, but nodded his head and obediently continued reading the document: "The atomic bomb design 'weaponization' is the responsibility of the Iranian scientists and technicians. At this time Iran has detailed plans for building an implosion nuclear device containing a mass of highly enriched uranium at its core. They are also purchasing conventional explosives to be put around the central mass to detonate simultaneously. They implode and compress the fissile material into a supercritical mass. At that instant, neutrons are injected into the material to initiate a chain reaction and explosion."

Eric suddenly moved in. "Benny, no point in reading any more. This is a fake document. The Iranians doctored one of our official publications to make it look like a secret document. They inserted some accurate information, a lot of bullshit, and some half-truths. I wouldn't be surprised if they intended to leak it to a newspaper that would then publish it as a genuine CIA document."

"As psychological warfare," I said, "that document could still serve a purpose. By appearing in the media it would achieve two goals. The first would be to embarrass the United States at a crucial point when President Bush is trying to complete his coalition of countries to fight Saddam's invasion of Kuwait. I guess exposing the United States as a leaking sieve would not be too popular with the coalition countries. And if the Iranians could manage to hint that they have a mole within the CIA, then they'd score double. The second goal would be to spread fear among Iran's oil-rich neighbors concerning Iran's nuclear might. That may have a domino effect on the Gulf States and even Saudi Arabia. They could fall into the Iranian's hands like ripe fruit off the tree."

"Precisely," said Eric, in one of the very few instances in which he completely agreed with me. Well, after all, I was supporting his line of thinking.

There was a moment of silence in the room. Benny was the first one to break it. "The Iranian document is excellent for us. I could think of some interesting operations following these leads. Israel can't allow the Iranian fanatics to become the new Nazis of the Middle East. We have to believe him when they say they want the Jews thrown into the sea."

"Would Israel consider preventive measures against the suppliers to Iran?" asked Phil.

"I wouldn't rule anything out," said Benny candidly. "We could do it ourselves or let the public do a preparatory job."

"What do you mean?" asked Phil.

"Well, if we leak some of this stuff to the media, or just the identity of the European suppliers, Israel would again be justified in its effort to bury the Iranian nuclear program."

"I see," said Phil.

"Let me share with you recent intelligence," said Benny. "We have indications that the Iranians are negotiating with the Soviets to purchase an advanced AVRII uranium enrichment processor system to be installed at Natanz and at Moallen Kalayeh sites. They plan a 'close-looped fuel cycle.' That means that Iran will be able to produce fuel for its nuclear bombs."

Benny paused, drank a sip of water, and continued. "We know that Iran is also getting technical cooperation from Syria, which in 1989 deployed its Scud-C missiles along its southern border with Israel and equipped the Iranians with sarin nerve gas. Iran may try to use the Scud-C missiles for the delivery of their bomb to Israel."

"They would have to reduce the bomb's weight first," said Phil, "otherwise the missiles wouldn't get to Israel from Iran."

"But from Syria they could," snapped Benny. "Syrian-Iranian cooperation is not limited to exchange of technical information."

Phil Richards and Arthur Brown nodded in agreement.

"I'm sure you know," added Benny in a serious tone, "that Iran has sent several thousand students to Western universities to study physics and chemistry, to acquire the necessary expertise. The Iranians refrain from sending too many students at the same time to the same university or region, to make it difficult for the Western intelligence services to appreciate the number of Iranian students abroad and the technical skills they acquire."

"Yes, we know that," said Phil. "We are closely monitoring this activity."

Benny paused, while we patiently waited for him to continue. I saw how Benny was arming the bomb he was about to drop. Here it came.

"We also know that until 1988 the United States had been providing classified satellite intelligence to the Iraqi government during their war with Iran. Iranian agents in Iraq stole that information. Now the Iranians know what the U.S. can see, and therefore, how to deceive you."

Phil Richards, Arthur Brown, and Eric Henderson didn't blink. "That was a strategic decision that was appropriate at the time," said Eric.

"Some decision," said Benny, with a hint of mockery. "Take this as an example: knowing the limitations of the U.S. satellites, the Iranians are building large disguised and dispersed bombproof facilities. They are fooling you."

Eric was not deterred. "Let's work with what we have," he said, completely undistracted by Benny's criticism. "We know that Iran's uranium-enrichment program is being pushed ahead. They are preparing to convert uranium to enriched uranium metal, a must for an A-bomb. Iran is also working on laser technology to enrich uranium. They are planning a highly advanced laboratory, the Jabr Ibn Hayan at the Tehran Nuclear Research Center."

"Why uranium and not plutonium?" asked Benny.

"Because plutonium requires reprocessing spent nuclear fuel, which in turn requires a reprocessing plant."

"How do we know that these planned facilities are not for energy-production purposes?"

Eric waved his hand. "Because if they were meant as an alternate fuel supply, why are they planning a heavy-water installation? The Bushehr plant will be operated by light-water reactor. But if they plan on using heavy water, with its extra hydrogen atom, that's an indication that they are making weapons-grade plutonium."

"I've always believed our own reports that Iran's nuclear weapons program is substantial," said Benny. "They're not doing it as a public relations stunt. The Iranian clerics really want to export their Islamic revolution by force. With an A-bomb in their arsenal, more people would listen."

Nobody responded. The room went silent. Brown and Eric were collecting their papers; it seemed that the meeting was ending.

Now it was my chance to turn up the heat. All this political and scientific detail was in my way.

"Eric, I have a question. How long did DeLouise work for you?"

Eric smiled in embarrassed surprise. "What makes you think he ever did?" he asked, while avoiding my eyes and arranging his papers.

"I guess it's true, then," I said. I had known the answer already.

"Tell me about it," countered Eric.

"DeLouise received a tourist visa to the United States on an expired Romanian passport. It's impossible today, and it was definitely impossible in 1957, when Romania was a part of the Communist Bloc. So I gathered the restrictions were deliberately ignored. Given DeLouise's identity, it's obvious who was interested in him. One plus one is two."

"Not so fast," said Eric. "It was a one-time deal. In 1957 I was still in elementary school, but I recently looked this thing up. DeLouise wanted to emigrate to the United States but he didn't qualify for an immigrant visa because he lacked a sponsor. So he offered us information about recent French nuclear developments in exchange for permanent residence in the United States. The price was right and we agreed. That's the whole story."

"But why did he receive the visa on his expired Romanian passport rather than on his valid Israeli passport?"

"He didn't qualify for a regular immigrant visa, so the only way to grant him a green card was through the asylum program. Under that program, it would look better to grant the status on a Romanian passport even though it was expired. In fact it even helped, because if ever questioned on that he could claim that his persecution by the government included a denial of a valid passport. Romania was a country with a dictatorial regime, which could explain to any probing eyes why he received asylum. We couldn't offer the same explanation with respect to a democracy like Israel."

I took a step forward and ventured, "Was DeLouise doubled?" Meaning, was he recruited by the CIA to be a double agent.

"Definitely not," said Eric. "It all happened after DeLouise had already left the Mossad, and he specifically conditioned the deal on the insistence that no questions concerning Israel or the Mossad be asked during his debriefing. For us, DeLouise was a 'walk-in,' a one-time informer."

I didn't say anything, but Eric's explanation seemed to answer the question I'd been asking myself since September, when I'd received David Stone's memo assigning me to DeLouise's case: why had DeLouise received a U.S. passport on an expired visa? — a circumstance so unusual that it had immediately set off alarm bells in my head. DeLouise's deal with the CIA may have been only a one-time deal but he'd left enough of a trail to help me make a breakthrough in my own case.

"That was why the Justice Department and the FBI couldn't locate him thirty-three years later," I said. "There was no indication in his file that he had lived in Israel for a few years as Dov Peled." Eric didn't respond. I knew why. CIA could not share the information with other U.S. government agencies.

We had to get back to the present. I was about to get up and leave but Eric stopped me.

"Here's what I want you to do. Call Guttmacher and ask to see him together with Armajani and Kutchemeshgi as soon as possible."

"Why?" I asked, "I thought this thing was over."

"Not yet. We asked you here and showed you the documents for a purpose. We need postoperation reconnaissance. We need to know their next move after the break-in. You're the only one who can do that. Tell them you want to report on your Moscow trip."

"But you still have the transmitting pen on his desk. That should tell you what's going on," I said.

"No. It stopped working the day after the break-in. Either they found it or the battery is dead."

"So they'll be looking for anyone who had access to Guttmacher's office and could have put the pen there. Is that a wise idea, to return to the lion's den now?"

"There is some risk," conceded Eric, "but you'll be wired again, and our men will be outside if the meeting gets ugly."

"OK," I said, not particularly liking the idea but nevertheless willing.

"Duty calls," said Benny, who'd picked up my tone.

On Monday afternoon I called Guttmacher from a street pay phone. "I've just returned from Moscow and I need to see you and the Iranian gentlemen," I said matter-of-factly.

"I'm glad you called," said Guttmacher hastily. "There have been some developments and we're meeting tomorrow morning at ten o'clock in my office. Please be there."

That was easy. I called Eric to report.

"Good, we'll come to your hotel at eight-thirty to dress you up."

On Tuesday at 10:00 A.M., wired for sound, I walked into Guttmacher's office. Kutchemeshgi, Armajani, Guttmacher, and a somber-looking Iranian man in his early forties were waiting in the adjacent conference room. DiMarco, Broncotrade's president, wasn't there, as I'd expected.

"Good morning gentlemen," I said, and sat down next to Guttmacher. I looked at the newcomer sitting across the table next to Kutchemeshgi and Armajani, waiting to be introduced. When that didn't happen, I said, "I'm Peter Wooten."

The grim-faced man nodded, while Kutchemeshgi said briefly, "That's Colonel Kambiz Khabar; he's a member of our counterintelligence team."

My heart skipped a beat. Iranian counterintelligence was infamous for its ruthless treatment of their targets; if prisoners survived their interrogation, they never needed a manicure. He looked like a soldier, definitely out of place in a tailored three-piece suit. The desert sun had given his face a harsh, implacable look. His presence here could mean only one thing: they thought that the Saturday break-ins were not simple burglaries, but intelligence operations. He said nothing.

"Where is Mr. DiMarco? Isn't he coming too?" I asked Guttmacher, in an obvious effort to show that Khabar's presence left me indifferent.

"Unfortunately there was an accident over the weekend," said Guttmacher, "Mr. DiMarco was killed in a car accident in Milan."

"I'm sorry to hear that," I said. "What happened? Was he driving?"

"No, he crossed the street and a passing car killed him. It is so unfortunate."

I tried to digest the news. DiMarco's death sure didn't sound like an 'accident.' Was it the Iranians, the Mossad, or the CIA? There were too many deaths in this industry. I resolved to move to the antique books trade.

The atmosphere in the conference room, which wasn't cheerful to begin with, changed abruptly when Armajani said, "There's a traitor." I felt my stomach tightening. Nobody said anything. "Colonel Khabar is in Munich to investigate certain events. I demand that all of you cooperate with him."

Apart from the Iranians in the room, only Guttmacher and I came under the definition of "all of you."

"Of course," I said, "although I don't know to what events you're referring, because I've just returned from Moscow. What happened? You mean DiMarco's death was caused by a traitor?"

Col. Kambiz Khabar had no patience for my humor. "Strange things have happened since you first appeared on the scene."

I didn't like his attitude or his piercing eyes, particularly when he had a point.

"Why don't you tell me what you mean?" I asked, although I already knew.

"I mean that you're an American agent, an Israeli agent, or both!"

My heart was pounding hard. I was sure Eric could hear it.

"Is that a joke?" I demanded. "What is this person talking about?" I asked, turning to Guttmacher.

For the first time Guttmacher looked really frightened. "It's no joke," he finally said. "My Iranian friends are missing documents, and they think that insiders were involved in removing the documents."

"What documents?" I asked, hoping to gain time.

"Those concerning the Iranian purchases."

"I didn't take any documents," I said defiantly. "I left the file on your conference table when I left your office."

"Don't play dumb," shouted Khabar, "I know you're behind the break-ins. Tell me who sent you."

"Look," I said, getting up from my chair at the conference table. I wasn't in the mood to be interrogated by this hard-nosed Iranian. "I didn't come here to be yelled at. I'm not anyone's agent, and your accusations are preposterous. I have no idea what you're talking about. Call the police if something was stolen from you. This has been nothing but trouble. I'm the one who's inconvenienced, and I think this meeting is now over."

"You're not going anywhere," he said, getting up. He drew a .38 caliber pistol with a silencer, pointed it at me, and yelled "Sit down!"

Quickly assessing my options, I jumped to my right behind Guttmacher and lifted him from his chair by his shirt collar. He was heavy as a horse and sweating like one. Guttmacher became my human shield. I was taller, but at least he was wide enough. Khabar was standing across the conference table — to grab me alive he'd need help. Armajani and Kutchemeshgi were paper pushers, so I didn't think they'd constitute any serious opposition. I guessed he wouldn't shoot before he squeezed me for some answers. I had to concede, though, that my value for Khabar as a potential source of information was temporary.

"Move back," shouted Khabar, "or I'll shoot you both."

"No, please," cried Guttmacher.

I had no gun and I cursed Eric and myself at the same time for that oversight.

Kutchemeshgi and Armajani moved back next to Khabar. I moved the other way, toward the sliding double doors of the conference room, dragging Guttmacher with me.

"Don't shoot him," said Armajani. "We need him alive."

But it was too late. Khabar fired in my direction. The pistol blasted as the doors opened and Guttmacher's secretary walked in with a tray of hot drinks. "*Mein Gott!*" she exclaimed as the bullet whizzed past her.

In one swift motion I grabbed the coffeepot off her tray with my free hand and threw it at Khabar. I'd aimed for the head but hit the crotch. Spilled hot coffee and hard china did the trick. Khabar bellowed in pain and surprise and as he bent over and cradled his groin. I released Guttmacher, slid the length of the conference table and jumped on Khabar. We went to the floor, with me on top. Normally, that'd be punishment enough, but not in this case. I made an effort to grab his gun, missed, took the coffeepot from the carpet, and smashed his head with it.

He managed to fire another shot that hit the ceiling. Khabar's face was streaked with blood, but the blow was not strong enough to knock him unconscious. He was still struggling with me. I had Khabar's wrist. I slowly bent it backward until he dropped the gun on the carpet. Suddenly I heard voices shouting in German. Not Eric's men, for sure. None other than Polizeidirektor Karlheinz Blecher walked in, escorted by six policemen, their weapons at the ready.

One of the cops approached us quickly and took Khabar's gun from the carpet. I got up slowly. Khabar was still down, blood covering his face. He looked around and realized that the scuffle was over. He wasn't stupid. The cop handcuffed him and pulled him over to a chair.

"Who are you?" demanded Blecher.

"I'm Colonel Khabar, an Iranian military officer."

"What a pleasant surprise," said Blecher, and for a moment I thought something was wrong. No, it was just Blecher's sense of humor. "We've been looking for you," he said. "You're under arrest. INTERPOL has just notified us that they've been searching for you. They'll be impressed at how efficient we are," he concluded in irony.

"Who is looking for me?" asked Khabar. "And on what charges?"

"Italy, for question number one, and the charge is murder of one Signor DiMarco," answered Blecher dryly.

"Sir," said Guttmacher, trembling, "Colonel Khabar has just tried to kill me. He's totally crazy."

"That'll be another add-on to the long list of good deeds Colonel Khabar is being accused of."

Khabar said nothing as he was led away and betrayed little concern. This wasn't surprising. Iranian agents abroad rarely feared arrest. If they were apprehended for whatever reason, you could be fairly sure that citizens of the arresting government would soon be kidnapped somewhere in the Middle East, and that an exchange would quickly be arranged through Iranian intermediaries offering their help for "humanitarian reasons."

"Herr Hans Guttmacher," said Blecher as he approached Guttmacher.

"Yes?"

"You are under arrest for the murder of Raymond DeLouise. You are also under arrest for the kidnapping of Ariel Peled in Germany, grand larceny, and the attempted kidnapping of Ariel Peled in Moscow. Other charges including conspiracy and violation of Germany's export laws shall also be brought against you. Anything you say will be used against you."

Guttmacher had gone pale. I was sure he was going to faint. Two policemen approached to handcuff and search him.

Blecher turned to me. "And who are you, sir?"

I wanted to say, "Are you kidding, Blecher?" but kept my mouth shut, realizing that Blecher was protecting me. I put on my best frightened look.

"I'm Peter Wooten, an American attorney."

"Take his passport and his local address as well; we'll need his testimony," he said to another officer.

That was fine with me. I owed Blecher a lot of testimony, and I was glad to have waited as long as I had. Now I could do it all in one session.

Guttmacher didn't look at me when the cops led him out. Armajani and Kutchemeshgi were still standing next to the conference table. Blecher approached them. "You are under arrest for violation of Germany's export laws, and for an attempt to smuggle nuclear materials in violation of German federal laws."

"We have diplomatic immunity! You can't arrest us. I protest!" said Armajani, enraged.

"Why do you think you have immunity?" asked Blecher almost cordially.

"Because I'm an Iranian diplomat accredited to the government of Italy, and so is this gentleman," Armajani pointed at Kutchemeshgi.

"This is Germany," said Blecher wryly. "Your immunity is good only in Italy." Turning to the policemen, he snapped, "Take them away!"

XI

A couple of weeks later I arrived at the Munich police station with Benny. Snow was starting to fall, not enough to accumulate on the ground but enough to paint the silver-lined branches of the ever-green trees in white.

"Do you know what Blecher wants?" I asked Benny as we cleaned the mud from our shoes at the entrance.

"No, he just called and asked that we come to the station for a short meeting. Ron and I met him yesterday," he added, in a voice that told me that something was wrong.

"What happened?" I asked, although I'd already guessed.

"Blecher raised hell."

"Is my ass in a sling?"

"Was," replied Benny.

"Past tense?"

"Yes. We got you out of it somehow. We promised that in the future the German police would not be the last to know when representatives of foreign countries play cops and robbers on their soil."

"Thanks," I said in relief. "Who else will be at the meeting today?"

"Blecher didn't say, but Eric told me today that he and Ron Lovejoy will be there too."

Benny shot a pointed look in my direction. "Aren't you going to ask if Ariel will be there?"

"Will she?" I admitted in defeat, realizing that my interest in her had become public knowledge.

"I think so."

It had been two long weeks since I'd last seen her; two long and aching weeks somewhat eased by a seven-day vacation in Vermont with my children. Eric and his staff had been very busy analyzing the material found at the bank and in Armajani's apartment while I'd been feeding on the trail that led to DeLouise's money.

Surprisingly, there wasn't a lot concerning DeLouise's assets. I suspected that most of it had been left behind in Guttmacher's vault, and I wondered why. The documents that had been retrieved from the vault were nevertheless valuable, since they gave me a good many leads to Swiss bank accounts. But there was a missing link: the proof that these bank accounts and various trusts were in fact DeLouise's. It could still be done, I thought, but I expected a long legal battle. However, the days weren't as tense as before the operation. A carnivore dissecting and devouring his prey is somewhat calmer than when he is stalking.

I wanted to finish it all and move on, and this sudden meeting could be the last phase of the entire operation.

When I entered the briefing room with Benny, I saw Ron Lovejoy, Eric Henderson, Mina Bernstein — and Ariel.

A minute later Blecher came in. Without much ado, he said, "It's all over. Guttmacher has confessed."

Sitting or standing, we all leaned closer, waiting for Blecher to continue.

"I have a written statement from Hans Guttmacher in which he confesses to all charges. Therefore, I don't think we'll need the testimony of any of you at a trial."

"Tell us what Guttmacher said," said Ariel. "I want to know how he thought he could get away with everything he's done."

"I think you have a right to know," agreed Blecher. "According to Guttmacher's confession, approximately three or four months ago DeLouise sought his advice about how to move his money from Switzerland to Germany without revealing his whereabouts. At the beginning of their relationship, DeLouise told him that the amount was only one million dollars. But when Guttmacher was able to transfer it without letting the Swiss bank know where the money finally landed, he gained DeLouise's confidence. Guttmacher said that DeLouise wanted to move his substantial assets from Switzerland to another location but didn't know how to do it without leaving any trace. He feared the movement would reveal his new location to his pursuers: two divisions of the U.S. Department of Justice, one of which he was sure had called in INTERPOL, and the Colombians.

"So after the first million was successfully transferred, DeLouise became convinced that Guttmacher could help him; Guttmacher started moving DeLouise's money in relatively small amounts through third parties until it ended up in Germany. Although Guttmacher's bank commissions for the transfers were hefty, DeLouise was pleased.

"Then Guttmacher suggested that DeLouise participate in the financial package of the Iranian purchase of nuclear equipment and materials. It was more a matter of disguising the true identity of the buyer and the final destination of the goods than financing the transaction. The Iranians had the money available, but they wanted the transactions to look like commercial contracts between individuals and companies for peacetime use rather than purchases by a government already on the U.S. list of pariah countries."

"Did Guttmacher know about my father's Israeli Mossad background?" asked Ariel.

"I don't think so; he never said anything," said Blecher. "I don't believe your father would have told him that, knowing how deeply Guttmacher was involved with the Iranians."

"Guttmacher said that when DeLouise agreed to participate, DeLouise even suggested bringing in his own contacts in the Soviet Union and elsewhere, and the Iranians agreed. So instead of being simply a 'front name' for the Iranian nuclear purchasing mission, DeLouise had become a recruited agent as well."

"What the Iranians didn't know, though, was that my father had his own agenda, and had never intended to deliver what he had promised," said Ariel.

Blecher nodded and continued. "DeLouise brought a sample of trace nuclear material and the Iranians became enthusiastic. They gave him two million through Guttmacher's bank as an advance payment and the bank guaranteed their advance. As collateral DeLouise gave the bank an assignment of a $2.05 million deposit his company kept in a Swiss bank.

Guttmacher said that the whole advance matter was nothing but an elaborate money-laundering scheme to free up some of DeLouise's money that was still stuck in Switzerland. So Guttmacher received two million from the Iranians and gave it to DeLouise, but DeLouise never returned the advance or delivered the goods. Then Guttmacher withdrew the $2.05 million collateral deposit from the Swiss bank, returned two million to the Iranians, and kept his fifty-thousand-dollar commission. Everybody was happy."

"Why was my father happy?" asked Ariel.

"Well, for one thing, he'd laundered two million dollars at a cost of fifty thousand dollars. That's cheap in this trade," volunteered Eric. "However, Guttmacher's bank collected the collateral DeLouise gave Credit Suisse only after DeLouise was murdered. In short, the operation was successful, but the patient died."

"So DeLouise was planning to work for free if he ended up with his own money less the commission Guttmacher collected?" asked Ron.

"No. The plan was that the Iranians would pay him five million dollars, half when they'd receive proof that the materials were ready for shipment and the other half when the goods arrived. But that time never came. And DeLouise never ordered U.S. computers for the Iranians or nuclear materials from the Soviet Union. The whole thing was a hoax he perpetrated."

Blecher continued, "But let's go back again. DeLouise's confidence in Guttmacher grew. He was lonely in a strange city and felt that he had painted himself into a corner. Guttmacher became his friend and listened to his gripes and stories. He entrusted him with his important documents. Herr Guttmacher understood that this man DeLouise had a huge fortune; this only fueled his greed. He realized that DeLouise was also disillusioned with his American wife and son because they never came to visit him in Europe. He felt they had given up on him. Guttmacher heard about Ariel, the daughter DeLouise deeply loved and said he was going to take care of."

I looked at Ariel. Tears had come to her eyes.

"Then one day DeLouise told Guttmacher he was being followed. He was sure the Colombians had found him again. Guttmacher calmed him down and sent an ex-policeman to check it out. The ex-cop discovered that the people trailing DeLouise were Iranian agents who probably wanted to make sure DeLouise wasn't an agent of a foreign-intelligence service. They posed no imminent danger, but Guttmacher never told this to DeLouise."

"Why didn't he tell him?" asked Mina.

"Because the fear made DeLouise even more dependent on Guttmacher. Remember, this businessman couldn't go to the police, and with his fortune, he was isolated and fearful in a foreign city. His only stable channel to the outside world was Guttmacher.

"The incident gave Guttmacher an idea, though. Since he kept all of DeLouise's banking documents and knew about the extortion attempt from the Colombians, he called Ignacio Perez, the Colombian, and offered an exchange: in return for DeLouise's head, Guttmacher would hand over the documents incriminating Perez for money laundering and bribery of judges and politicians in the U.S."

"What was Guttmacher's plan?" asked Benny.

"Guttmacher thought that if all the documents and the keys to the money were under his custody, his new friend would be expendable, and he could keep millions of dollars of DeLouise's money. Because only DeLouise and Guttmacher knew where the money they secretly transferred from Switzerland was hidden.

"Perez agreed and sent three of his men to Munich. Two of them followed DeLouise and killed him in the street in broad daylight.

"Guttmacher delivered the incriminating documents, but when Perez received them he saw that a crucial document was missing, the one showing contributions to politicians and judges. He called Guttmacher to complain, but Guttmacher couldn't give him that document — he'd simply never had it. Perez threatened Guttmacher, who didn't know what to do, and there was no one he could ask about that document. DeLouise was already dead. Guttmacher knew what Perez was capable of.

"Next, Ariel entered the picture. Unbeknownst to Guttmacher, DeLouise, who felt threatened by the fact that he was being followed, had asked Ariel to come from Israel. Fearing that he would be hurt or killed before Ariel arrived, he did two things. First he reserved Ariel a room at a small pension; he didn't want her to be seen at the hotel with him. Ariel is an Israeli carrying an Israeli passport, so her presence next to DeLouise posed a danger to them both. Then he left letters for her with the pension's manager. By that time, DeLouise probably distrusted Guttmacher. Then Ariel arrived and called Guttmacher."

"Yes," said Ariel, "when I realized that I couldn't find my father, I called the one person whose name was mentioned in the letter my father had left me at the pension: Guttmacher. He said he didn't know where my father was, but asked me to leave the name of my hotel in case he heard from him."

Blecher continued. "By then Guttmacher understood that by bringing his daughter to Munich, DeLouise had also brought her into the conspiracy. He had to get rid of her. He told Perez that DeLouise had given the missing document to his daughter. Therefore, the only way to get it back would be to kidnap her, and after she surrendered the document, to kill her. Perez's men followed Ariel from her pension and kidnapped her."

Ariel picked up the story from there. "I didn't know what they wanted. I had no such document. But I had to gain time, so I told them it was in a safe-deposit box and that only my mother and I had access to. So they made me call my mother, and I asked her to come. I tried to hint that I was in danger and that she shouldn't come, but she misinterpreted what I said to mean that because I was in trouble I needed her. Then I was able to escape and told the guys at the consulate to call my mother to stop her from coming. But she'd already been here. They said they'd taken her back to Israel, and I decided to go to Moscow on my own."

"You were either very brave or very reckless," said Eric. "These people are ruthless. You were a target for a bullet in the back of your neck."

Ariel smiled in embarrassment. I looked at her. She was more beautiful than ever. Her copper hair was braided the way I was growing to like, and very light eye makeup highlighted her deep blue eyes. She was again wearing a stunning business suit and looked beyond my reach.

"The kidnappers were afraid to tell their boss in Colombia that Ariel had escaped, so they frantically started to look for her. They contacted

Guttmacher and squeezed him, wanting to know who DeLouise's contacts were in Munich. They hoped to trace Ariel through them. Guttmacher was frightened enough to give them Dan Gordon's name. Actually, he also gave them Peter Wooten's name."

"Guttmacher gave them my name? The son of a bitch. He would sell his own father if he only knew who he was. Problem is, even Guttmacher's mother doesn't know his identity," I said in contempt.

"Yes. He did, and they got hot on your trail."

"Wait," I said. "I'm confused. I thought you said the Iranians followed me."

"Correct," said Blecher. "But at any given time you were being followed by both the Colombians and the Iranians. The Colombians saw you enter the Mielke Bank. Guttmacher told them you were DeLouise's partner, so they assumed you may have retrieved something from the bank that was connected to DeLouise, perhaps the missing document. Therefore, when you left the bank, one of them attacked you."

"Why didn't he take the envelope I had in my pocket? I was unconscious."

"The elevator door opened and people came out, so he ran away. But you got even," said Blecher, "because Rodriguez, the man you caught and beat up in your hotel room, is the one who attacked you outside the bank. We have his confession as well."

"Then how did they know I was in Moscow?" asked Ariel.

"Guttmacher told them," said Blecher. "I think you called him to say you were going to Moscow and gave him the name of your hotel."

"How stupid of me. I should have known that because Guttmacher was the Iranians' banker, I should be careful with him," said Ariel.

"Two of them traveled to Moscow," Blecher continued. "One of them searched Ariel's Moscow hotel room while the other guarded the entrance. The person who went to Ariel's room was still searching when Ariel surprised him and he tried to drug and kidnap her."

"That's when Dan came and kicked the hell out of him," said Ariel. I thought I heard a slight ring of appreciation in her voice, but I could simply have been hoping for it.

"That man and his partner are now in police custody in Moscow. We are asking for their extradition to Germany for the murder of DeLouise. The good news is that lately Soviet authorities have started getting rid of perpetrators they don't want by simply putting them on planes to places that do want them, with appropriate advance notification to the receiving authorities. We could have them sooner than we usually do."

"How did the man watching the entrance to the hotel miss my arrival with Dan?" asked Ariel.

"I don't know. He should have seen you and recognized you; after all, you'd been his prisoner. I'll ask him after he's extradited."

I had a question. "The Munich hotel registration of DeLouise was under the name of Peled, but Guttmacher knew him as DeLouise. Had Guttmacher discovered the double identity?"

"Not immediately," answered Blecher. "Guttmacher knew only DeLouise, not Peled. The suite that DeLouise had rented at the Excelsior consisted of two adjoining rooms with different numbers. He simply registered one room under the name of Peled and the other room under the name of DeLouise. He paid the manager to keep it a secret. DeLouise kept the door between the rooms locked when he was out. When a call was made to Peled, it was forwarded to one room, and calls to DeLouise were forwarded to the adjoining room. However, the reception guest roster listed only Peled, not DeLouise. He simply gave Guttmacher his room number so that he wouldn't ask for Mr. DeLouise when calling him at the hotel. Anyway, Guttmacher was the only person calling DeLouise in Munich. It was simple and ingenious."

"Why did my father keep the door between the rooms locked?" asked Ariel.

"Your father was a cautious person. Since he was maintaining a double identity in the hotel, he wanted to make sure that if anyone broke into DeLouise's room he'd find only stuff connected to DeLouise and while in Peled's room there were only things connected to Peled."

"Did it work?" I asked.

"Apparently," said Blecher, "Guttmacher was really surprised when I told him about the two rooms."

"So he had two rooms," I interrupted. "That explains the hefty hotel bill. What was in the room?" I asked, concealing the fact that I already knew this from the list I had "engineered" from the city morgue.

"Copies of airline tickets and a trip itinerary to Kenya, South Africa, and Hong Kong," smiled Blecher. "DeLouise wanted to create the impression that he had left Germany. But that was to no avail. All these precautions didn't help him much, because he was living in the hotel, and it was when he went out to get a newspaper that he was shot. DeLouise and Peled were both killed by the same bullet."

"How did you come to suspect Guttmacher?" asked Eric.

"He had been under our watch for some time because of his suspected money-laundering activities," said Blecher. "The Bundesnachrichtendienst — the federal intelligence service — was also interested in him because of his dealings with the Iranians. But from my perspective as a police officer, the criminal activity in this case was first discovered by following the lead Mr. Dan Gordon gave us." He smiled, looking at me.

"Oh?"

"Yes, do you remember the telephone number you deciphered from the call the kidnappers made after they received the call from a female Israeli agent to the pay phone impersonating Mina Bernstein?"

"Yes, now I remember," I said. "It seems like ages ago."

"The good lady returned unexpectedly to Israel with the ransom note. Since Ariel was free, she didn't realize we needed the note with the pay phone's number for our investigation. Consequently, we didn't have the number the kidnapper dialed from that phone until Dan gave it to us. We tried to get the number from Mrs. Bernstein through the Israeli Consulate, but that took time, and Mr. Gordon gave us the number first. That number led us to an apartment in central Munich rented by a man who told the landlord that his name was Manfred Holst. But the physical description given by the landlord matched Guttmacher's. We showed the landlord several pictures and he immediately identified Guttmacher as the person who had rented the apartment. From that point on everything was fairly easy."

"Why did Guttmacher confess?" asked Ron.

"He had no choice. I showed him Rodriguez's testimony, which directly incriminated Guttmacher as the man who, together with Ignacio Perez, instructed him to kill DeLouise and kidnap Ariel. We have proof connecting Guttmacher to Perez and to the rented apartment where Ariel was kept, as well as other evidence. But I think, most of all, Guttmacher believes that only a German prison can protect his life. The Colombians are sure he cheated them. In fact, I suspect that the revelation that DeLouise was in fact a former Israeli with a daughter living in Israel helped Guttmacher confess."

"How did Guttmacher find out?" asked Ariel.

"When you arrived in Munich and called him, you told him that you had just come from Israel."

"That's right," confirmed Ariel. "I didn't know that I had to conceal my nationality from my father's banker. Only later did I discover that he was also the Iranians' banker."

Blecher continued, "Guttmacher was surprised and alarmed by this news. Ariel became an immediate danger for him — yet another reason to get rid of her and steal her father's fortune. However, the risk posed to Guttmacher if the Iranians discovered Ariel's nationality was minimal in comparison to his horror when we told him that DeLouise was a former Mossad agent."

"Why?" asked Ariel. "Wasn't my father's Israeli background enough of a risk?"

"Maybe," said Blecher, "but after Guttmacher heard about DeLouise and his Mossad connection, he confessed immediately. Can you imagine what the Iranians would do to Guttmacher if they discovered that the man to whom he introduced them to work on their secret nuclear program was an Israeli spy? A German prison is Guttmacher's best shelter from the Iranians for the next hundred years."

Ariel nodded and smiled.

"The Iranians are certain that Guttmacher conspired with DeLouise and DiMarco to betray them; they are also convinced that certain recent nocturnal events at the bank and in Armajani's apartment were directly connected to Guttmacher's betrayal."

Blecher paused, looked at Benny, Ron, and Eric with half a smile, and said with exaggerated formality, "But of course we have no proof or any suspects in these two recent events, so the investigations of them are now closed." Benny and Eric nodded lightly; they were professionals, so they didn't smile in return.

"Any questions?"

"Mr. Blecher," I said, "your timing in arresting Guttmacher and the Iranians was perfect, almost too perfect. Was it a coincidence?"

"No. We received a phone call. Ask Mr. Henderson here, he'll tell you."

I looked at Eric. So he was the one who sent the police after hearing the direction my meeting with the Iranians was taking. Would it be the one good deed that would open the gates of heaven to him? St. Peter would probably tell him that one isn't enough. Eric turned his head to me, smiling.

"Thanks," I said.

"Mr. Blecher," said Ron, "did you ever recover the missing document that incriminates Perez?"

"No. I don't even know if it ever existed. It could have been a ploy by DeLouise; we'll never know. He took that secret to his grave."

I had another question that had been tormenting me for a while. "Mr. Blecher, there is one open question. If Guttmacher arranged DeLouise's murder, why did he let me continue with my impersonation as DeLouise's partner and let me in on the Iranian documents?"

"Because he couldn't read you. On the one hand he was sure that the 'partner' story you told him was a bluff, but he didn't know who you worked for. Guttmacher told me that at the beginning he suspected you were hired by the Iranians to look over his shoulder, so he didn't mind you getting the information. In fact, he used your appearance to show the Iranians that he tried to undo the damage created by DeLouise's disappearance. Then he was sure you were a CIA agent, then a Mossad agent. He hired a local detective who discovered that your hotel reservation was made by the American Consulate for Dan Gordon. On the other hand you introduced yourself as Peter Wooten. Guttmacher was certain that both names were fake. From Guttmacher's perspective, as long as the Iranian operation remained unfinished, he couldn't touch you. When Guttmacher got a whiff of DeLouise's fortune he began looking for ways to get rid of the Iranians, but he didn't know how. Therefore, his plan was to blame you for any failure, hoping they'd direct their wrath at you, leaving him unscathed. He also thought of exposing you as a CIA agent so that the Iranians would take care of you and include you in one of their special early retirement programs."

I didn't smile.

"He finally told them that he suspected you of killing DeLouise. So to an extent it was convenient for him to have you around."

"So what stopped him?"

"The fear that you were working for the Iranians after all. But as far as Guttmacher was concerned, you were living on borrowed time. Once he had complete control over DeLouise's money, you were next on his purge list."

"And why was that?"

"Because obviously you had some connection to DeLouise, and because you knew about the documents that he was keeping for Ariel. Anyone who was connected to DeLouise compromised Guttmacher's plan to take over the DeLouise money and therefore had to be eliminated.

I wasn't elated by the news that I had appeared on someone's hit list. Guttmacher was so devious, I was sure that even his shadow was crooked.

Blecher looked around and said, "If there are no further questions, then we're done. Thank you very much for your help." Blecher and his aide shook hands with us and left.

Benny, still on the sidelines, then asked me a key question. "Did you solve your problem?" he asked.

"Which one do you mean?" I asked.

"Where is the DeLouise money?"

"I don't know yet," I answered, suspecting Benny might be ahead of me.

"So, it won't be long," he added, only fueling my suspicion.

"One problem I did solve," I said.

"Which one?"

"How my good friend led me in the direction intended all along by the Mossad. I was blind, maybe because I believed him."

Benny's expression got serious, and he gave me that amused quizzical look. "What did I do?"

"Manipulation," I said, not knowing if I was mad at him or not. "From the first minute I called you, you knew that DeLouise had been murdered. You also knew that he was connected to the Iranian military-purchasing frenzy, and yet you told me nothing. Of course, I have no problem with the fact that you forgot to mention that DeLouise was working for the Mossad again. I suspect a sweetheart deal: information on the Iranian transactions in return for a safe haven anywhere on the globe, if he failed to reach an agreement with the U.S. government for a safe return to the U.S. without being prosecuted. I guess the shelter would be anywhere *but* the U.S. or Israel."

"Why did I have to tell you? You were chasing DeLouise's fortune. That was on your mind, and I helped you out. Not that I confirm your theory, but how did you figure it out?"

"It was clear that both DeLouise and Ariel were working for you. Ariel only recently, probably when she escaped from her captors in Munich into the Israeli Consulate. But I believe DeLouise was enlisted as a one-time unremunerated recruit when he started his contact with the Iranians. My suspicion was confirmed when I realized that Ariel gave me the original Iranian file her father had left her. I concluded that you already had a complete copy and that you allowed Ariel to give me the file, to achieve two goals: to lead me away from the suspicion that Ariel worked for you, and to make the delivery of the Iranian file through me to the CIA look authentic, without any sign of collusion between DeLouise and the Mossad. Obviously Israel could do without the scandal the U.S. could make if it were discovered that Israel was helping an absconding suspected felon."

Benny gave me another of those cat-that-ate-the-canary looks. "You were interested in DeLouise's money, Dan, and we had other interests, so what's so bad about a few maneuvers that could help an old friend in a way that helped you and the U.S. as well?"

"You could have told me."

"I couldn't; that would have put you in a mess," countered Benny pointedly. "I don't forget that you work for the U.S. Department of Justice, and if I had revealed our interests you would have had to report it to your superiors. That would have made things far more complicated."

I had to admit that Benny's sophistication was impressive. I'd asked for routine help, and that enabled him to help me walk in the right direction. At the same time, he put himself in the loop and kept his options open; he could participate in break-ins to steal documents essential for Israel's security but also be covered under the American umbrella if the operation went sour. And the biggest achievement of all: recruit an old operative who could maneuver the Iranians and report on their activities. So many birds and only one stone.

"OK, you got what you wanted," I said, "while I'm stuck with an endless pile of paper. And while I sort things out, DeLouise's money could vanish."

"Patience," Benny assured me. "I'm sure the solution is not too far off."

"Benny, you mentioned earlier that DeLouise had told you that he knew that my office was looking not just for his money but for him as well. Did he tell you how he'd found out?"

"Yes. Early in the game, his California lawyer heard from the clerk's office of the Federal District Court that the U.S. intended to serve DeLouise in Switzerland with the summons and complaint in the civil proceedings. The lawyer was a veteran of the Civil Division of the Justice Department and was familiar with its policy to locate debtors of significant amounts even if they are overseas."

So there was no security leak in my office after all.

As we got up to leave, I looked at Ariel. I wanted to talk to her but I felt a cold wind blowing from her direction. She left the briefing room and walked into the corridor. I joined her uninvited.

"So Blecher says that you were the one who exposed me to Guttmacher," Ariel accused. Her voice was icy.

"How did I do that?" I asked, hurt and disappointed that she would choose those as her first words since parting from me weeks before. I didn't know how to bridge the rift between us. From the tone of her voice, it sounded as if Ariel was also going to blame me for a whole list of man-made or natural disasters.

"When you told Guttmacher that you knew that he was holding the envelope my father gave him for me. Since he knew that my father was dead, he presumed that I was the only person who could tell you that, and that showed him we were working together. Since he suspected you, I was contaminated as well."

"That's not quite right, Ariel," I said apologetically. "There is a simple explanation. It was my only way of convincing him that I was in the loop; I hoped that, by demonstrating that I had read your father's letter, Guttmacher would be convinced that I was in fact your father's partner in the deal with the Iranians. Obviously I didn't know he was the villain. I'm sorry I caused you trouble." I didn't add that given Blecher's account, Guttmacher planned to kill Ariel regardless. There was no point in kindling more friction between us.

Ariel looked amused. She was toying with me. But when she saw my grim face she added, "Don't worry, I don't blame you. You didn't know. You see, when my father was killed, Guttmacher was sure he was home free with the money. He didn't realize that my father was too smart to trust him. My dad wrote me that he was suspicious of Guttmacher and therefore prepared new documents for me that replaced all the stuff Guttmacher was holding. But Guttmacher didn't know that my father was bypassing him and leaving new instructions for me. The letter you saw telling me to contact Guttmacher was written before my father started to suspect him."

"Your dad was a clever man," I put in. "He left a back door open."

Ariel nodded. "So from the moment you gave that detail to Guttmacher, to gain his trust, I became dangerous for him. He realized that I knew that he'd kept the money. He was convinced that I was the final roadblock between him and more than many millions of dollars, so he had to have me put out of the way."

I decided not to argue with her. There was no point in reminding Ariel of her own contribution to Guttmacher's decision to eliminate her.

"I'm surprised you even agree to speak to me, if that's really your opinion of me," I said, trying to think how difficult it would be to erase all the dreams I had about Ariel. There seemed to be no chance for any of them to materialize.

"I was angry at you. I trusted you, and I was disappointed to realize that you betrayed my trust, until I saw the whole picture."

"I don't think I've ever betrayed your trust," I protested. "I may have kept some facts from you, but please understand, I was doing my job. You were the daughter of my target. You were the clue to the resolution of the mystery."

"It was difficult to understand," said Ariel, "because I thought you were working for the Mossad. But then when I found out that you weren't, at least not any longer, I started my own little investigation to find out who you were really working for."

I was too surprised to say anything.

"When the Mossad agents took my mother from the pension, she asked them about you and discovered you weren't one of them."

"So how did you find out who I was working for?"

"Rather easily, actually. Benny told me."

"The collaborator," I said, realizing that not only had Benny manipulated me throughout to achieve the Mossad's goals in the DeLouise-Iranian matter, he had also meddled in my private life.

"No," she said, "not at all. He really loves you. He's the one who cooled me down. He helped me understand exactly what was happening."

My tongue was dry. I'd blown it, at least with Ariel. The success we'd had with the Iranian files didn't mean much when I realized that Ariel was now out of reach.

"There is something else," she said quietly, sensing my feelings.

I looked directly at her, suddenly at a loss for words. I felt bitter and defeated.

"What? You forgot to tell me the name of the plague I've just contaminated the world with?"

"There's no need to be sarcastic," said Ariel. "I just want you to know that I wasn't completely truthful with you either. So now we're even, aren't we?"

"But did I step into a new trap?" I asked, "What else did I miss?"

"Moscow. I mean, when I went to Moscow, I had a mission."

"I know that," I said, "you've already told me. You wanted to expose the suppliers of nuclear materials to the Iranians."

"That's the part I told you," she confirmed, "but there was something else." She hesitated.

She got my attention. She saw a question mark blinking in my eyes. "Go on, tell me."

"The Moscow idea was not mine."

I saw where she was heading. "It was Benny's ploy," I said matter of factly.

Now it was Ariel's turn to be surprised. "How did you find out? I don't believe he told you."

"No, he hasn't. I suspected you were working for someone in Moscow; your story just didn't make sense to me. So I called Benny from Moscow and asked him if you worked for him."

"And what did he say?"

"He denied it," I said. "I can't always tell when Benny is not telling the truth, but I know when he's outright lying."

Ariel narrowed her eyes again. "You couldn't have figured it out by yourself? Or did you?"

I had to decide quickly whether to look smart or be truthful. I chose the latter.

"Remember when you were attacked and I ran to your room to pack your things?"

Ariel nodded.

"Well, I took a quick look and found your phone book."

"And?"

"There was a small piece of paper in it with just a five-digit number. I recognized the number; it's the code you need to punch in after you've dialed a Belgian telephone number. Once the correct code is recognized, the call is automatically transferred to Benny's private line at his office in Tel Aviv."

Ariel was stunned. "So you did figure it out after all!"

"Yes, it was really simple. He'd given me the code for the month. The only logical conclusion was that your contact with Benny had to have been very recent. But since you denied knowing who he was, you were lying to me on that, too."

Ariel lowered her eyes.

"So you've been working for him all along?"

"No, just for the trip to Moscow. When I ran from the kidnappers in

Munich to the Israeli Consulate and told them how angry I was about my father's murderers, Benny's guys suggested that I get even."

"How?"

"They wanted me to go to Moscow to get some more samples of materials from my father's contacts."

"Why? What was the purpose?" I asked, although I already knew the answer.

"I don't know, they just wanted me to meet with them, get another sample, give them some money, and tell them that we'd like to do more business in the future."

"I guess you met them before I came to Moscow, because you were under my radar as soon I arrived. Besides, who's 'we'?" I asked.

"Me and my dad," she said,

"But he's dead," I responded. "I saw him dead."

"The Russians didn't know that."

"Aha," I said, "so Benny pulled off another brilliant one, keeping the flame burning for future reference."

Ariel's eyes shone. "Flame?"

"Yes, by sending you to follow up on your father's initial contacts while they were still hot, the Mossad was letting the Russians think that the Iranians were genuinely interested in their merchandise. Now the Mossad could infiltrate their rogue operation, manipulate it, maybe get to the bottom and the top at the same time. So now are we even in the truth department?" I asked.

"Well, not exactly. My father had left his will with Mr. Bart to be delivered to me." This got my attention yet again.

"You never mentioned it when we talked in Moscow. You mean there was a third envelope?"

"Yes," she said. "I didn't know about it until I read my father's letter again, the one you retrieved from the safe-deposit box. Do you remember the last sentence in that letter?"

"Not exactly. What did it say?"

"I was to tell Mr. Bart the nickname my father called me when I was just five years old, and that Mr. Bart would laugh."

"Yes," I remembered now, "I didn't understand what it all meant."

"I couldn't either," said Ariel, "but when I reread it, I decided to see Mr. Bart again. I had the chance ten days ago when Blecher asked me to return from Israel as a potential witness. Otherwise, I'd have gone on my own."

"Did he laugh?" I asked, realizing, of course, that there was a code in the instruction.

"No. He didn't laugh, but he gave me the third big envelope. The nickname was a code word my father gave him to release the envelope only to me. My father paid him nicely for the service."

"What was your nickname?"

"Ponchick," she said, smiling in embarrassment. "As you know, the word means 'jelly donut.'"

I laughed too. "And what was in the third envelope?"

"The final truth, the resolution, and the rewards," she said enigmatically. "My father wrote me in the accompanying letter that his second wife and her son, who is my half-brother, had been taken care of financially through a maze of family trusts he had established while they were still living in California. Therefore, he wrote, his entire estate should be mine. To guarantee that only I would get the money, he prepared notarized assignment instruments, surviving his death, which transferred title of all his assets to my name. He even wrote checks made out to me on all his cash accounts."

"Good for you," I said, fearing that now I'd find myself fighting Ariel over the money her father left her. What else could go wrong? "Are you a rich woman now?" I asked bitterly, seeing where the conversation was going.

"What would you like me to be?" she asked teasingly.

I didn't like this conversation, and I wasn't about to continue with it.

"Look, Ariel," I said. "Please, you're tormenting me. I admit I made mistakes. I apologized once, I'm apologizing again, but please don't rub my nose in them. Since you are your father's sole heir, I guess you understand that the U.S. government has a civil judgment against your father that can be satisfied from his estate. You're up for a long battle with them over that."

"No," she smiled, "there will be no battle."

"What do you mean? The judgment is valid and can be enforced against your father's assets, even if they are outside the United States and have already been transferred to you."

"Oh, I know that," said Ariel, "but still, there'll be no battle over the money."

From my lowest point, which was my exact location at that moment, I didn't see what she meant.

"How much is the judgment for? Do you know?" she asked.

"Yes, I have a copy somewhere."

"Let me help you. The amount is $91,211,435.09, according to the clerk of the United States Court for the Central District of California."

"You mean you called there to find out?"

"Yes," she said, "I needed to know."

"Why?"

"How else could I write this check?" she asked, and pulled out a check and gave it to me.

It was a Credit Suisse bank check made out to "United States Treasury" in the amount of $91,211,435.09.

I couldn't help it, my hand shook a bit as I held the check.

"Take it to your boss. This is at least some reward for everything you did for me. I know I could have battled the government for years in courts to reduce this amount, but I decided against it. Judgment is satisfied in full."

"Why" I asked, "are you giving up all these millions if you think you could keep some of it?"

"Because there's plenty more where it came from. After making this payment to the government, I'm still left with more than sixty-five million dollars in cash and securities and a lot of real estate throughout Europe and Japan. That's a lot of money for a single woman who's lived until now on an annual salary of eighteen thousand dollars and occasional gifts from her dad. Life is too short to spend it on litigation over more money. I have enough. And that money, or the majority of it, belongs to the U.S. government. I don't believe my father stole it, but the bottom line is that his bank collapsed and the government had to make good on its promise to the depositors to guarantee their deposits. So under either theory, the government has some right to receive back what it paid to the depositors."

I folded the check and put it in my pocket. I wasn't in the mood to tell her that her legal theory was suspect, if her father was indeed innocent.

"I'll deliver the check to the U.S. Treasury through the consulate." I realized that although I'd be a hero in Washington, I would never see Ariel again. Wealth and anger in a woman are a lethal combination in any relationship.

I managed politeness, as unhappy as I was. "Thank you, Ariel. It's very considerate of you to let me deliver the check and get the credit."

"You deserve it, Dan. After all, you saved my life."

This whole hallway conversation was ridiculously formal and artificial. I'd gone through it, but I hated every moment of it.

I put out my hand, and Ariel shook it in return. I left without another word. My eyes were damp. I tried to pretend that it was because of the cold Munich wind, or dust. But it wasn't cold inside the room, and there was no dust. I'd lied to myself. Again.

I went to the American Consulate, walked directly into Ron's office, and handed him the check. "Please send this in the diplomatic pouch to Washington, for transmission to the Treasury. Ariel Peled gave me the money. The case is closed. The estate of Raymond DeLouise has satisfied the judgment in full."

"She did *what*?"

I told him about the conversation I'd just had.

"You must have done something to that woman," Ron said, shaking his head in disbelief.

I didn't comment, trying not to think what she'd done to me.

Ron made a copy of the check, wrote on the copy "Received from Dan Gordon for delivery to the U.S. Treasury," dated and signed it, and gave it to me.

"Congratulations," he said. I didn't feel like celebrating.

I called Stone and reported the collection I had just made. He was elated, and after congratulating me he said, "I don't hear any joy there, Dan."

"No. There's no joy. I'm a little unhappy at how this matter came to an end."

"Dan," said David, "do you hear what you're saying? I don't recall many cases when we've had such complete success. You're the one who's going to get the credit for it, but you sound as if you lost the whole case."

"I know. Stupid, isn't it?"

"It's the woman," said David, without putting a question mark at the end of his sentence. He knew.

"Yes," I admitted.

"Come home," said David, "and spend more time with your kids."

"I guess that's what I'll do," I said. "I'm sending the check through the legat." That was it. Short, and not so sweet for me.

I went out to the street and decided to walk to my hotel. I had earned the right to be a worry-free tourist. Both my assignments were over, and yet I still felt a weight on my shoulders.

As I walked I began to notice something odd out of the corner of my eye. Each time I passed a store window I could see a black BMW just slightly behind me, driving slowly. The hair stood up on the back of my neck. Here we go again. Someone was clearly following me. I continued walking as my mind clicked through the possibilities. Who would be following me now? DeLouise was dead. The Colombians, the Iranians, and Guttmacher were all in prison in one place or another. Was a reserve force sent out? Was it the check? I'd already given it to Ron.

I had two choices — to dry clean it by entering a narrow street against traffic where the BMW couldn't enter or to turn back and confront the driver.

I suddenly felt as if I'd had enough of all this. I was not in the mood for games. I stopped, turned around, and walked directly to the car. The windows were tinted so I couldn't see who was inside. As I got closer, the car stopped and the passenger door opened. I stepped up carefully, ready for anything — gun, fist, or foot.

"Please get in," I heard Ariel's voice from behind the wheel.

My jaw dropped as well as my defenses. She was the last person on earth I'd expected to follow me, and yet the first I could have hoped to see on my lonely walk. But I wasn't ready for more berating, not even from Ariel.

I hesitated. "Come on. I promise I won't bite," Ariel said.

Why was I holding back? Who was I kidding? I got in and Ariel drove off. "I just rented this car yesterday and I still haven't figured out all the buttons."

I said nothing.

Ariel drove onto the autobahn. I was still quiet. She didn't speak either. I remembered how nice it had been when we were together without the need to talk. Though there were some questions on my mind, I began to relax, and smiled at how easily that wonderful feeling came back between us.

Ten minutes later Ariel took the first exit on the outskirts of Munich and, after driving for several minutes through a beautiful neighborhood, entered the courtyard of a villa. I had no idea where we were.

She parked the car and got out. I didn't follow, maybe in something of a daze. Ariel walked around to my door and opened it. "Come," she said softly.

I followed her as she entered the house. The place was gorgeous. The foyer was huge with a high ceiling, crystal chandelier, and soft Persian carpets. Some very good oil paintings hung on the walls; gleaming mahogany and glass cabinets displayed pre-Columbian artifacts and antique English silver hollowware.

"What is this place? Why did you bring me here?"

Ariel came closer to me. I smelled her light perfume, the one I had missed so much.

"Don't make me beg," she said.

I was surprised, "Beg for what?"

"For you to notice me," she said.

"Notice you?" I asked in utter disbelief. "Ariel, I can't get you out of my mind. You haven't left me since the day we met."

Ariel held my arm. "Come, let's go into the living room." I followed her.

A fire blazed in the fireplace; Rubinstein's recording of Rachmaninoff's Piano Concerto No. 2 played softly in the background.

"What is this place?"

"It's mine," said Ariel. "It's one of the assets my father left me. Until recently, the ambassador of a South American country used it as his residence. I wanted you to be the first to see it, before I helped the staff find other jobs and put it up for sale."

Was she flashing her riches at me? That didn't fit the Ariel I thought I knew.

"Why me?"

"Because."

"Because what?"

Ariel didn't answer. She went to a table and poured red wine from a carafe into two crystal goblets. She handed me one and raised hers. "This is to the future, for the good things that are about to happen."

Ariel was clearly toying with me again. I felt sucked into her game, not knowing what would come next.

"I'll drink to that," I said and sipped.

She came to me, took the glass from my hand, put it on the table, and kissed me. First lightly as if she were testing the waters, then passionately.

We moved to the sofa. "Hold me," she whispered in my ear, "just hold me. I need to get used to you again. I saw you every night in my dreams, and now you're here."

Ariel curled up in my arms. I looked at the fireplace, touched her soft hair, her face, her body, while the music conjured vistas of natural landscapes and a vast expanse of surging waves. Ariel closed her eyes. I bent to kiss her again, but she was already asleep.

"Nice beginning," I said to myself.

ACKNOWLEDGMENTS

This novel was written because one night jet lag won. In a small hotel in a remote country, after rolling from side to side for two hours, I finally gave up trying for slumber, went to the small desk, and turned on my laptop. The words that poured out had been lodged in my mind for some time. Obviously, in my years working for the U.S. Department of Justice I could not share the spine-tingling aspects of my work with anyone but my supervisors, and some adventures not even with them. Sadly, these events, which are sometimes more intriguing and thrilling than the best fiction I have ever read, are buried in reports submitted throughout the years. The story of Dan Gordon and his battle against the invisibles is my idea of the next-best thing. Many of my friends and family members read the first drafts and encouraged me to continue, particularly Dr. Jacob Dagan and Prof. Yehuda Shoenfeld. I would like also to thank Bob and Gloria Blumenthal; Alexandra Margalit, for helping me with the minute details of Munich that had escaped me; and Ed Watts. Sarah McKee proved to be not only an astute lawyer but an excellent reviewer who helped me describe the red-taped insides of the Justice Department, from which, as an outside consultant, I'd largely been spared. Many thanks to David Epstein, once my supervisor and mentor, now a very dear friend, who knew with immense wisdom and experience when to let me rush forward and when to shorten my leash. He called me a pit bull — I never knew if he meant it as a compliment, because a pit bull finally lets go. A friend from the Mossad who wishes to remain anonymous helped me put things into perspective. Marc Jaffe helped me turn a manuscript into a novel, and Nicola Smith was my patient but relentless editor. Alan Lelchuk and Chip Fleischer are old and new friends who made this book a reality.

My in-laws have always been concerned with my safety, my sister shares that fear, and my wife, daughters, and sons are my best and worst critics. My daughters spent many hours reading drafts and making corrections, and I know how difficult it was for them to be introduced to the far and dark side of my work. My wife also endured the nonfictional tension of my long absences. Many of the hours I spent writing this book were taken away from my family, and my gratitude for their sacrifice is eternal.

Read on for a sneak preview of

THE RED
SYNDROME

The second Dan Gordon
Intelligence Thriller
by
HAGGAI
CARMON

Steerforth Press
Hanover, New Hampshire
IN STORES JULY 2006

FOREWORD

Terrorism has no borders, no authority, no laws, no territory, and no moral considerations. Nothing stands in its perpetrators' ways. Terrorists regard disastrous and devastating consequences as achievements, not failures. They turn their own military weaknesses into strategic might. What good are tanks, missiles, submarines, or nuclear weapons when a determined handful gets access to substances that can kill millions? Many leaders and scientists believe that it is only a matter of time before bioterrorism strikes, causing thousands of casualties.

Bioterrorism uses pathogens, bacterial and viral agents, or biologically derived toxins against people, livestock, or crops. Through the spread of these agents, terrorists seek to inflict massive fatalities. Unlike nuclear weapons, bioterror weapons are relatively easy to make, and unlike chemical weapons, only small amounts of biomaterials are sufficient to wreak havoc.

Is the world ready? I have had the privilege of preparing Israel for the task: As Israel's deputy minister of defense, I took the initiative to make bioterrorism issues a priority in Israel's strategic defense. My communications with other governments led to the realization that many were ill prepared for the prospect of bioterrorism. It is essential for the governments of the free world to develop, test, and implement public policies and operating procedures regarding bioterrorism. The scientific community also needs to be vigilant on this key matter by actively engaging in research to develop countermeasures.

Haggai Carmon has crafted a fictional but all too real tale. It takes place in the clandestine world of bioterrorism, where sinister plots are intertwined with money-laundering schemes. In the book, cooperation between the Mossad and the CIA is all that stands in the way of bioterrorism. By combining keen knowledge of the real-world situation, gained through his personal experience, with a vivid imagination, Haggai Carmon manages to draw the reader's attention to the real risks our modern society faces. This book provides a public service by raising awareness of terror financing and bioterror. What is remarkable is that it does so while telling a damn good story I couldn't stop reading.

— EFRAIM SNEH, M.D.

Dr. Sneh is a member of the Knesset, Israel's parliament. During his military service as a medical doctor, he commanded the medical team of Israel's forces that rescued the hostages from their terrorist captors in Entebbe, Uganda. In 1981–82, as brigadier general, he was the commander of the Israeli armed forces in southern Lebanon; in 1985–87 he served as the head of the West Bank's civil administration. Dr. Sneh was elected to the Knesset and served as member of the Knesset's Defense and Foreign Relations Committee, as deputy minister of defense under Yitzhak Rabin, as minister of transportation, and as minister of health. He is currently serving in several Knesset committees, and chairs the subcommittee for Israel's defense strategy.

1

January 2003, Stuttgart, Germany

The prisoner in the red jumpsuit was visibly nervous. He couldn't hide the subtle tremor in his left hand, which gripped a cigarette. He was very thin. Stammheim, the maximum-security prison in Stuttgart, Germany, where Andreas Baader and Ulrike Meinhof had been found dead in their cells in the 1970s, didn't exactly serve gourmet food. Even so, Igor Razov was too thin, as if consumed from the inside. His mustache had nicotine stains, as did his uneven teeth.

"Good morning," I said, entering the visitor's cell and setting down my briefcase, which contained only a yellow pad. The less you carry into the prison, the faster the security check goes. I decided to be as polite as I could, to distinguish myself from this man's interrogators. "I'm Dan Gordon from the U.S. Department of Justice. I'm here with the consent of your lawyer, Dr. Bermann." I looked at his lawyer, then at the court-approved interpreter, a heavyset, thirty-something woman who sat quietly in a corner opposite the German prison guard. Dr. Bermann nodded. No wonder he'd approved; I'd paid him five hundred dollars for the honor and promised an additional thousand if his client would give me the information I needed. It was Bermann's only way to get some real money for representing Razov, having helped him avoid extradition from Germany to Belarus, his homeland. There, Razov would have had to face the hangman, following a conviction in absentia for murder. I'd paid, and now the floor was mine.

"I'm sure your lawyer has already told you, but to avoid any misunderstanding I must reiterate that I am not in a position to make any promises concerning your extradition to Belarus or the death penalty you're facing there if you are indeed extradited. The United States is not a party to the legal proceeding against you; your case is entirely in the hands of the German and Belarus courts and governments."

I spoke in English. Bermann had assured me earlier that Igor had learned rudimentary English in Minsk, and had then improved it while living in New York these past few years. Bermann and Igor communicated in English, because Igor didn't speak German and Bermann didn't speak Russian or Belarusian. Bermann had brought in the interpreter, Oksana, as insurance, in case of a failure of communication.

As I spoke, I realized that this statement sounded very formal, full of legal jargon, and was too complex and long. But I had to say it. I had to make sure that both he and — more particularly — his lawyer understood the rules of our meeting. The last thing I needed to hear later was that his lawyer had argued for special consideration because Razov had talked to me. The Belarus government would file a complaint, and I'd find myself having to explain. Again.

"Do you understand that?"

Igor was motionless. He didn't even look at me. I knew he understood by the gaunt, haunted look he cast at the opposite wall. I was betting that his desperate situation would help me crack my case — one of the several international fraud and money-laundering cases I was investigating for the Department of Justice. Igor had to have answers for me because I could no longer ask his two comrades. I'd arrived in Minsk, Igor's hometown in the republic of Belarus, too late to talk to them. They had already been executed. But Igor still had a pulse. At least there was that.

Caveats aside, I had to give Igor a glimmer of hope, something to cling to. Otherwise this interview would be like trying to get a parrot in a pet shop to speak on command. "Helping me would make your life easier, more comfortable," I went on. "It would mean money to buy things at the prison's commissary. I could also ask the warden to let you watch television longer than the other inmates. It could mean a lot of other things that would ease your stay here, but you must help me first."

Igor said nothing. His head stayed down.

The German prison guard shifted in his chair, bored. It crossed my mind that his presence was inhibiting Igor, so I asked him to wait outside. The guard gave me a disapproving look and said, "I'm here to protect you, but I can leave if you want."

"Yes," I said immediately. "Please wait outside, I'll be fine."

Igor, handcuffed and frail, didn't pose much of a threat. I was twice his size, and besides, my favorite class during my training at the Israeli Mossad Academy had been martial arts. Sure, a few decades had passed since then and there hadn't been much use for those particular talents in my current position at the DoJ, but I wasn't too worried.

I asked Igor another question. Still no response.

"Dr. Bermann, would you please come outside with me for a moment?"

We stepped outside the cell, leaving Igor and the interpreter behind.

"I thought you said he spoke English," I said, wondering if my earlier speech had been wasted on Razov.

"He does, he does," Bermann assured me, although I suspected he wasn't that sure.

"Unless he gives me some answers," I said, "our deal is off. I hope you realize that."

"Yes. I don't understand Igor. He promised me he'd cooperate with you. Let's try again."

We went back to the cell, and I continued.

"Are you familiar with Boris Zhukov?

"Have you been working for him?

"You left Minsk and moved to New York in 1994. Why did you return to Minsk? Was it only to whack Petrov, or was it also something to do with Zhukov's money?

"How is Zhukov connected to the wire transfers you were making?"

Not a word.

"We know about your ties to Zhukov, but just knowing him doesn't mean you did anything wrong. I'm not here for your criminal case. I'm interested only in the money side of your relationship with Zhukov. Do you understand that?"

I kept going for another ten minutes. Igor was silent as a grave on a winter's night.

Seeing his thousand dollars slipping away, Dr. Berman made a last effort. "Igor, you promised me you would help Herr Gordon. Nobody is going to find out that you said anything. That's impossible, right?" He turned to me for confirmation.

"Absolutely," I agreed quickly. "I guarantee that everything you say stays in this room. All I need from you is guidance concerning the source of some money transfers that we think are connected to Zhukov."

Igor didn't even look at me. Bermann continued feebly, but to me the effort seemed futile. Bermann inspired no more confidence than a nurse trying to convince a crying boy that the doctor approaching with a syringe big enough to inoculate horses isn't going to hurt him.

I had read Igor's FBI file before coming. I realized that he knew better than to cooperate. He feared his colleagues in the Belarusian mob, on both sides of the ocean, more than anything; certainly more than the wrath of his own lawyer, a pompous scalawag lucky enough to be appointed by the court in this open-and-shut case. What could Bermann do to him if he refused to talk — stop bringing him week-old Russian newspapers? Complain to the prison warden? Write a letter to the editor of the prison's bulletin?

But Misha, Boris, and Yuri — to name just a few of the guys still on the loose — could find a thousand ways to make him wish he'd never been born, to make him pray that his thirty-seven years on this planet would end quickly. He knew that, because he was one of them; he was the one who'd pulled the trigger that led to this mess. Who would have thought that eliminating the president of a trading company in Minsk could cause so much commotion?

This Petrov had refused to pay his dues to Boris Zhukov. So under orders from Zhukov, a thug named Misha had told Igor to go to Stuttgart to await instructions. Misha was a huge person who inspired fear in everyone; his burly resemblance to a raging bear gave his gang the nickname *Mishka*, or "bear" in Russian. The Mishkas were a notorious crime group that had operated in the chaotic streets of Minsk before branching out to New York. Misha took orders from nobody but Zhukov.

Less than a month later, word arrived: Go to Minsk and waste Petrov.

So Igor did. He'd always obeyed orders, first in the Soviet army fighting in the final years of its war in Afghanistan, then as part of the Mishkas. Igor was proud to be considered a member. Indeed, his achievements in Minsk had drawn the attention of Zhukov, who needed more muscle in New York. A quick fictitious marriage to an American woman was arranged; she got a thousand dollars, and Igor got a green card and moved to America. Three years later, Igor had become Zhukov's confidant, and was occasionally sent to foreign countries to carry out "sensitive" jobs. Including this one.

What Igor and friends did not know was that Petrov was married to the daughter of a police chief, who apparently didn't like seeing his daughter widowed. Special orders were immediately sent: Get them! A week later someone ratted to the police that Igor had escaped to Germany. The three other gang members were still at large. An international arrest warrant was issued through INTERPOL. From there it was easy. The German police made inquiries through informers within the local Russian community. Igor was identified and arrested while sitting in a local bar.

As for me, I had traveled from New York in the dead of winter to a German maximum-security prison. I'd had to endure the terrible noise of slammed metal doors and the ominous spectacle of German prison guards clad in long winter coats and leather boots. I'd had to sidestep the vicious-looking German shepherds on short leashes. I'd had to endure sitting in a small room with a guy who reeked of cigarettes — and other odors beyond description. And what did I get in return? Nothing. Igor wouldn't even talk. How inconsiderate could he be?

There wasn't much I could do. Despite all Bermann's pleading, Igor remained silent. He had had his say once, and now it was time to be quiet. Igor wasn't thinking about being reincarnated in this world as a better person. He had far lesser dreams.

When it was clear the situation was hopeless, I left. The security checks exiting the facility were as stringent as those I'd had to clear entering. Given their clientele, and the kind of lowlifes in their business, the German prison system wasn't taking any chances. They simply wanted to make sure that the Dan Gordon leaving at 11:52 A.M. was the same Dan Gordon who'd entered the prison at 11:04 A.M. — not an inmate assuming my identity to reach the better food, better company, and freedom in the outside world.

Even empty-handed, I was relieved to be out of that place.

It was raining — freezing rain atop the snow already on the ground — and the streets were muddy. Snow might be romantic when you're curled up near a fireplace with a lover, a blanket, or both. Less so when you're in a foreign city with no taxis in sight.

I entered a coffee shop in Aspergerstrasse just outside the prison and ordered hot chocolate. I warmed my hands against the mug. It instantly brought back memories of my childhood in Tel Aviv, when my mother used to make me cocoa in my favorite mug while telling me how she'd escaped the Nazi Holocaust by emigrating from Belarus to Israel seven years before the war broke out. She made it out before every gate was shut to the Jews. My uncles and aunts stayed behind and perished. My uncle Shaya was a student in Stuttgart at the time and thought nothing would happen to him. More than half a century later, I was in the same city where an uncle I had never met was murdered just because he was Jewish.

Snapping out of my reverie, I tried to figure out how to break the news about Igor's silence to my boss, David Stone, the director of the Office of International Asset Recovery and Money Laundering in Washington, DC.

"It's a waste of time trying to make him talk," I'd said to David last week when he'd authorized my trip. "I know these guys. They'd rather die. Any death by execution you'd threaten them with would still be a summer holiday in comparison with the death by slow torture their friends offer."

David had nodded. "Still, we shouldn't let this opportunity slip away."

Igor probably knew that Germany wouldn't extradite him to Belarus until it was sure he wouldn't be executed like his buddies. The extradition treaty between Germany and Belarus provided that anybody extradited to Belarus from Germany must be spared capital punishment because of Germany's opposition to it.

"After Igor is finally extradited to serve a life term in Belarus," David had continued, "he won't even open his mouth to yawn. Our only chance to verify our lead is while he's still in Germany, isolated from fellow gang members and informers. Just the fact that Igor has agreed to meet you could be a good sign — it means he's already taken a huge risk. That might indicate that he'd be willing to take even more chances and give us some info."

"There could be another explanation," I said. "First, I spoke only with his lawyer, Bermann. The smell of money could have clouded his judgment, making him forget to check with Igor; Bermann's consent seemed a little too fast. Second, even if Igor *had* agreed to talk to me, it could still mean that he needed the meeting to signal his friends outside prison that he was sending me back empty-handed. That would serve as proof that he wasn't betraying them."

"I understand," David replied. "Zhukov is in the United States, and unless we have probable cause, we can't arrest him. He will most likely refuse a voluntary interview. He's done that before. But Igor is outside U.S. jurisdiction, so if the German prison authority and his lawyer agree to the interview, what do we have to lose?"

"Okay, you're the boss. You tell me to go, and I will." I could hardly have sounded more reluctant.

"*After* the travel authorizations. You know the rules," added David.

I did. First the Federal Republic of Germany had to authorize my visit; anyone traveling on official U.S. government business must have the prior approval of the host government. Second, under the Federal Chief of Mission Statute, federal employees can operate in a foreign country only with the U.S. ambassador's consent. Although rarely done, the embassy could even assign a representative officer to be present during all of my activities.

As far as I was concerned, all of this was unnecessary red tape. The same music was always being played and replayed: David demanded that I comply with the rules; I tried, but if I couldn't, I left evidence showing I tried. David knew of my tendency to cut corners. He didn't mind pretending that things never happened — as long as I understood that if the

9

shit ever hit the fan I'd be the only one showered. On a good day I might have time to duck.

A few days later the paperwork was complete and I was on my way.

I stirred the hot chocolate, wiping my eyes, which had become teary from the cigarette-smoke-filled café air, and thought that now David would have to concede that I'd been right.

Still, I wasn't the kind of person to rub someone's nose in his mistakes, particularly when that someone was my direct supervisor. Moreover, I knew he'd had a point: Igor Razov could eventually help solve part of my puzzle, even if he was only a pawn. It was just a temporary hurdle; I needed to find a way to jump it.

I ventured back into the relentless rain and returned to my hotel. I changed my business clothes and wrote my report. No accusations, just the tale of a wasted visit to prison. I went outside and called David from a pay phone in a dome that failed to shield me from the wind and rain. When I call people, I observe certain rules, one of which is not to call from my hotel room. It's an old habit left over from my Mossad days: Hotels keep a record of your calls. For the same reason, I rarely use my cell phone when on assignment. I don't think I should be that transparent to foreign governments who think I'm just a tourist.

"Did he talk?" asked David.

"Silent as a husband."

"So the trip was a waste?"

"Well, not yet. While I'm here I want to dig deeper. I have a few ideas, and I'll need INTERPOL assistance."

"What for?"

"I need to see the German arrest file and ask them to issue a search warrant for this guy's local residence. He must have lived somewhere here before his arrest. It might contain some interesting stuff."

David hesitated. Even though I was investigating money laundering, a crime, INTERPOL might not be much help. A U.S. request via INTERPOL could almost certainly get me Razov's German police file. To get it fast, though, I'd have to offer to translate it myself and hope that the Germans would go along. "We might have better luck going through the police attaché at the German embassy in Washington. Still, a search would require a judicial order, so we'll have to send an MLAT request, and that might take more time than we have."

I couldn't help but think about my son, Tom. Before he'd grown to a towering six foot three, sporting a ridiculous goatee and out-of-fashion sideburns, he used to ask me what the meaning of *money laundering* was. He'd grown up hearing the term bandied frequently around the house. "No, it's not a big washing machine that cleans the dirty bills," I used to explain to him. "It's when thieves want to hide their stolen money from the police, so they transfer it from place to place hoping it will become 'clean' in the process and can't be traced back to their criminal activity. Money that criminals made by breaking the law is always dirty, so they want to make it seem like it came from someplace legal."

I told David now, "I think I'll push this forward on my own." Until he decided to request a search pursuant from the Mutual Legal Assistance Treaty in Criminal Matters (MLAT), I could use the time to find out where Razov had lived and with whom he had associated.

"Okay, where can you be reached?" David asked.

"I'm at the Grand Astron Hotel in Stuttgart." I gave him my numbers.

I had little hope that the German police file would contain anything meaningful. After all, Razov wasn't in their prison as a result of a crime he had committed in Germany; they were simply keeping him in escrow until he could be extradited to Belarus. The intelligence on Igor's German activities would be as thin as he was. And of course U.S. investigative agents and police could not conduct criminal investigations outside the United States without the approval of the host country, which is rarely given. But, I reasoned, I was also after the money. That was civil law, not criminal — at least not usually. I only hoped that my so-so legal analysis wouldn't be tested in reality.

At last the rain was letting up. I walked to the nearby city square and asked a local policeman in a black uniform where I could find a café or social club frequented by Russian immigrants.

He gave me an unfriendly look and said, "Try Café Moscow, right off Schlossplatz in downtown Stuttgart."

I finally found a cab, which dropped me off at the café. It was lunchtime. As I entered, heavy cigarette smoke and the smell of vodka assaulted my nose. Posters of old Soviet-era movies adorned the walls, and Russian music was playing.

The café was filled with burly men and a few women with push-up bras and too much makeup. I sat at the bar, squinting through the stinging smoke. I ordered a vodka martini and scrutinized the crowd. Five minutes later I had company. Compared with similar institutions, the response time here was relatively slow.

"How are you, big man?" said a young woman who pulled up a chair to be closer. "American?" She had a pronounced Russian accent.

I nodded. I didn't feel too welcome in Germany as an American. At the time President George W. Bush was trying, without any success, to persuade France and Germany to join the coalition to topple Saddam Hussein. Several street demonstrations against the United States had taken place. In Berlin a remembrance of the World War I antiwar communist leaders Rosa Luxemburg and Karl Liebknecht had turned into a march of ten thousand demonstrators protesting U.S. plans to invade Iraq.

"Buy me a drink?"

Well, despite my nationality, I could apparently still attract the bar broads. I consciously let myself be drawn in. Her agenda might have been the bulge in my pants — my wallet. But I also had an agenda, as she would soon find out.

"What would you like?" I said.

"Buy me champagne?" came the expected response. Next, she'd be served with colored water and I'd be charged for the best French champagne.

"No, dear," I said sternly, "vodka should be just fine." In a softer tone I added, "Isn't it too early for champagne?"

She smiled and asked the bartender for vodka.

I watched him pour from the same bottle he'd used for my drink earlier. As long as I was paying for vodka, let it be that, and not tap water.

"Tourist?" She leaned toward me to give me a better view of her generous breasts. A mixed smell of cheap perfume, bad alcohol, and cigarettes was sufficient deterrent to any thought of taking a two-hour leave from my duty. Two hours? Make that ten minutes.

"Yes, on business just for a few days."

"What kind of business?"

"I'm in microelectronics sales for the computer industry."

"Is business good?" No subtlety there: She was aiming directly at the size of my wallet.

"Business is okay. You sound like you're Russian, am I right?"

She nodded and sipped her drink.

"Do you speak Belarusian? I need somebody who could do some translations for me. Know anyone?"

"I'm from Russia. In Belarus, they speak a different dialect, actually a different language."

"I know, but I was thinking anyone who speaks Ukrainian or Belarusian would have very little trouble understanding the other language. Isn't it the same with Russian?"

She shook her head. "Russian speakers would have difficulty understanding either language. But I could ask here for you."

"Thanks. That would get you another drink from me."

"Nothing else?" There was a tone of seductive disappointment in her voice.

"We'll see about that later," I said, calculatingly ogling her generous cleavage. I hoped I was leading her to expect a financially rewarding transaction, albeit one that had to be postponed. For a millennium, as far as I was concerned.

She got up from the bar stool and walked to a table where four men were playing cards. A minute or two later she returned. "There's a woman in town who came from Minsk, that's in Belarus. I'm sure she could help you."

"Does she speak any English?"

"I don't know."

"What's her name?"

"Oksana Vasilev."

That first name sounded familiar. Could it be the same heavyset woman I had just met in prison? It would be good if I could get her to talk to me.

"And what is yours?"

"Kiska."

I smiled. It meant "pure" in Russian. "Where would I find her?"

"I don't know where she lives, but try the courthouse, across the *platz*. The people here said she was looking for a job as an interpreter and that the court keeps a registry of interpreters. Maybe she's listed."

"Smart girl," I said, and she looked at me to see if there would be any reward other than the drinks.

"I need to go, but I promise I'll be back," I added, slipping a twenty into her cleavage. I never dreamed of coming back for her. My mother's warning rang in my ears: *Don't pick that up; you don't know where it's been!*

I walked to the courthouse a block and a half away and found Oksana's address. Back outside, I hailed a cab and asked the driver to take me on a short tour. Although I didn't think anyone would be interested in what I was doing, old Mossad habits died hard — I needed to be sure.

Stuttgart itself is beautifully located in the Swabian Mountains, at the edge of the Black Forest. Both Porsche and Mercedes have plants there, so the city is home to predominantly working-class neighborhoods.

"Do you want to see the Daimler-Benz Automobile Museum? Perhaps the Mercedes-Benz factory? It is in Sindelfingen, very close to us," asked my cabbie. He was dark with a huge mustache, but his German sounded perfect. A green crescent on the dashboard gave away his country of origin: Turkey.

"No, thanks." I looked at my guidebook. "Why don't you pass through the Black Forest. I'd like to take a short walk."

A few minutes later he drove me to a wide-open picnic area in the forest. It was empty of people. I looked at the sign in German and below it, its English translation, and burst into laughter.

IT IS STRICTLY FORBIDDEN ON OUR BLACK FOREST CAMPING
SITE THAT PEOPLE OF DIFFERENT SEX, FOR INSTANCE, MEN
AND WOMEN, LIVE TOGETHER IN ONE TENT UNLESS THEY
ARE MARRIED WITH EACH OTHER FOR THIS PURPOSE.

I wished I had a camera. I took a short walk, getting some fresh air —
and making sure I had no company.

Next, the cabdriver drove me to the glockenspiel at the Rathaus so I
could listen to Swabian music. We continued past the Alte Staatsgalerie,
then Killesberg Park, the Schlossgarten, the Ludwigsburg Palace, and the
botanical gardens. An hour later, according to what I could make out in
the passenger's-side mirror, I was convinced that my paranoia was
unfounded.

Finally we arrived at Oksana's address. It was a shabby-looking two-
story apartment building in a side street of a working-class neighborhood. Although it was only 4:10 P.M., it was already getting dark; other
than passing cars, the street was quiet. It was getting colder and soon
snow would cover the broken pavement, giving this place a well-deserved,
albeit temporary, face-lift.

There were three mailboxes attached to the wall next to the building's
main entrance. Oksana's name was clearly marked on the bottom box. A
closer look gave me heart palpitations. Below her name was written IGOR
RAZOV, although an effort to scratch it off the nameplate was visible.

So she wasn't just an interpreter. Was she a roommate, a partner, a
supervisor, or all these penalties combined? I rang her doorbell and
waited a few minutes, but there was no answer. I looked inside the let-
terbox. Empty. It was time for some action. I went to the back of the
house. A small concrete structure housed the garbage cans. I looked
around. Nobody was there. It was already pitch dark. Snow started to fall,
muffling even the street noises. I opened one trash can, and two cats
jumped from the other, petrifying me for five long seconds. I put my right
hand deep into the can. I couldn't see much, and the smell wasn't helping.
The can contained just two dripping plastic bags with household trash. I
dropped them and wiped off my hands with a piece of newspaper. I
couldn't tell if they were Oksana's trash bags, but given the freezing temperature and the dripping liquids, the bags had only recently been
deposited.

I lifted the lid off the other can. Inside were two plastic trash bags of
frozen garbage and one bag of papers for recycling. I untied the latter bag.

Russian newspapers were on top. I was getting close, unless there were other Russian speakers in the building. Below these lay a few envelopes, but all with windows — no addressee name. I stuck my hand in again, this time fishing out invoices and handwritten letters in Russian. I emptied the newspapers into the trash can and took the bag with the remaining papers. I hoped that the city of Stuttgart would forgive me for mixing garbage. I hid the trash bag under my coat and hastily walked to the street. I walked up a block, but saw nothing unusual or suspicious. I got on a city bus, getting off a few stops later next to a cab station, where I hailed a cab to my hotel. I must have smelled, because the receptionist gave me a funny look. In my narrow room, I opened the bag and spread its contents on the carpet. I realized I'd hit the jackpot as soon as I started rummaging through.

I meticulously went through every piece of paper, setting aside both empty envelopes without the sender's address and Oksana's utility bills. If I needed proof that I was digging in Oksana's trash and not that of a neighbor, I need go no farther. I dumped the useless junk back into the trash bag — let it rest in peace. Next, I picked up six handwritten letters in Russian script in their original envelopes. They carried a Belarusian stamp and the sender's address. I couldn't tell who the senders were, given my limited knowledge of Cyrillic script, especially handwritten. But the addressee's name appeared Latin letters, probably to help the German letter carrier identify the addressee: Igor Razov.

From my prior Department of Justice cases, I knew that Belarus had a long tradition of using Lacinka, the Belarusian Latin script writing. Until the 1920s Lacinka had been more popular than the Cyrillic alphabet. As the Soviets moved in with their Russification policies, however, Lacinka almost entirely disappeared.

Next were thin, carbon-copy receipts. My heart started racing again. There were banking receipts from Germany, Panama, Venezuela, Saint Kitts and Nevis, and one from a bank in the Seychelles. Most of the papers were second or third carbon copies. Some were slightly torn; others had coffee and other unidentifiable stains. All smelled bad. I opened my room's window. Cool fresh air entered. I breathed in deeply, hoping the smell would go away. Then a sudden wind burst sent the papers on the carpet flying, and I immediately shut the window. Reviewing these documents had to take precedence over recoiling from the stench. I reorganized the papers and continued.

Next came deposit slips — some of them blank — used-up check-books, a three-page handwritten document covered with numbers and Cyrillic script, and two black-and-white family photos. I had no idea whose family.

I sat next to the desk and tried to read the bank receipts. The Justice Department's lab would need to take a better look at them, but from what I could already make out, the numbers were big: At least sixty million dollars was reflected in these documents. On four deposit slips I could clearly identify Igor Razov's name. The other receipts were smudged. My suspicious mind kicked in again. The fact that Razov left behind such compromising evidence looked amateurish. Maybe he'd never thought the German police would arrest him. But once in prison, wouldn't Oksana at least shred the documents? Why did she wait until now to dump these papers? Or maybe Oksana was smarter than that, and was deliberately constructing a false trail for me to follow? I had no answer. Not yet.

I worked for three hours, until my eyes grew sore. I took another look at all the documents I had found, made a list, and put them in a big manila envelope. I returned the trash I had no use for to the original plastic trash bag.

I thought of Alex, my Mossad Academy principal instructor. *We teach you to see in everyday events things that others don't. Underneath anything you hear or see, there are hidden undercurrents. These undercurrents, the minutiae, the details, can direct a careful observer toward evidence or conclusions that the average, unobservant observer would miss. A trail could begin with something mundane and unpleasant. Remember, every finding is only a lead to the next discovery.*

Obviously, today's findings bore out this wisdom.

I leaned back. Was today cleanup day for Oksana? The used envelopes carried postal stamps dated two and three months ago. Of all days, she'd decided to throw out Igor's stuff *today*? Hardly a coincidence. Given the fact that I'd left the prison five or six hours ago, the only possible explanation was that she'd returned to her apartment not long before my arrival and had removed all papers connecting her to Razov. But why? Igor had been in prison for over a month now, and the German police had never bothered to search his home. Had Oksana guessed that my next move would be a request to the German authorities for a warrant to search Igor's apartment? How could she know?

I'd never mentioned getting a search warrant to anyone but David, and that had been from a pay phone in the street. Had it been bugged? Unlikely. I'd chosen it at random. The only remaining conclusion was that *I* was bugged, or that whatever enemies I'd just discovered had planted a mole in David's office.

The latter option was simply not possible. I was up against a criminal organization, not a superpower. The phrase *Never say never* didn't seem relevant here.

I decided to go with the more logical explanation. I turned on the TV and closed the curtains. I completely undressed and went through all my pockets, the jacket lapels, my shirt and tie. Nothing but fabric. I inspected my shoes and socks. Nothing. I sent my fingers through my hair. Just hair and some dandruff.

I unscrewed the telephone handset to see if it had a harmonica bug — those transistorized transmitters that are inserted into the mouthpiece, making it a hot mike. Nothing. I opened my briefcase and emptied its contents on the bed. It all looked benign. I pulled out my radio frequency detector. Today's wireless transmitters are so small that they can be hidden in many common objects, including neckties, eyeglasses, and pens. Thus visual inspection of objects can be insufficient. My detector scanned radio frequency ranges from 30 megahertz to 2.4 gigahertz, which are the ones used by most wireless video and audio devices.

I spread my clothes and shoes on the carpet and scanned them slowly. An amber light on the detector went on, telling me that a device emitting a radio signal was close. I scanned again, but the amber color remained steady. I turned to my briefcase: nothing. So where was it? I threw my coat over the chair and scanned it. The light changed to red. I had a bug in my coat. I kept scanning, carefully — and then I saw it. A pinhead-sized device had been inserted behind the lapel. Oksana had stuck it into my coat when I'd left the prison cell to talk to Dr. Bermann. She'd known who I was and that I was coming to interview Igor.

I washed my hands thoroughly and got dressed. I pulled the tiny transmitter out of my coat and placed it next to the television, blaring at full volume.

Enjoy the music, comrades, I thought, and walked out to have dinner. The smell of garbage was still in the air, but the sweet scent of success was already taking over. I took the elevator to the hotel basement and dropped the trash bag into a giant trash receptacle. I went to the reception desk and deposited my newfound treasures in the hotel's safe. The fact that somebody had gone to the trouble of hiding a microphone on my coat lapel indicated I wasn't alone; someone was watching me. As a precaution, I thought about changing my plans to go out and instead have dinner at the hotel restaurant. But then I reconsidered. It was in my nature to be defiant, to ignore doubts, to dispense with routine safety measures. This rebellious streak sometimes got me into trouble but also led me to victories. My ratio of trouble to success wasn't bad.

I walked into the nearly empty snow-covered street, looking for a good German restaurant. As I crossed the road to a corner restaurant, I felt the first blow to my head. Because I'd just turned, the slug lost some impact, although it was still too strong to ignore. I completed the turn and saw two guys built like linebackers, intent on finishing the job. The first guy aimed at my solar plexus. My Mossad martial arts instructor had told us drily: *A blow to the gut could kill. This is one of the best ways to knock out your enemy. And if you doubt me, think of the great magician Harry Houdini. He died from an unexpected blow to his gut.* I instinctively shifted to the side, redirecting the blow to my obliques — the muscles around my ribs. It was painful, but I could tell I'd avoid damage to internal organs. The second guy punched my head directly, hitting my right ear. Against my instincts, but in keeping with my Mossad training, I moved forward. Recoiling backward would actually have resulted in my head taking the punch at full force.

It was time to go on the offensive.

I made a full-body swing and kicked the shorter guy hard in his groin; as he bent forward I kicked him again. My shoe hit his lower abdomen and my knee smashed into his face. That did it. He fell on the sidewalk vomiting. He'd be quiet for a while until his dinner completed its journey onto his clothes and the sidewalk. The other guy shot a quick look at his friend on the ground and realized that fists weren't enough. He pulled out a knife. I had no weapons other than my hands and my experience. Because I was much taller than he, and had longer arms, I jabbed the fingernails of my right hand directly into his eyes; with my left I punched his kidneys so hard I was afraid I'd broken my wrist. He groaned in pain, dropped the knife to the pavement, and tried to push my hand out of his eyes. I let him cover his eyes with his hands as I swiftly picked up the knife and hurried back to my hotel.

The entire episode had taken only a minute or two, and we didn't seem to have attracted any attention. There were no pedestrians around, and the few cars that were passing hadn't bothered to stop. I took inventory: Other than breathing heavily, a ringing in one ear, and my disheveled clothes, there'd been no serious physical consequences. I went up to my room, leaving the front door open so as not to lock myself in with an intruder. When I was certain I had no uninvited company, I bolted the door.

Who were these guys? Was the attack random, a failed robbery of a tourist, or was I was the intended target? It had to be the latter. They hadn't tried to rob or kill me; one bullet would have done that. Their purpose had been to intimidate, to send me a message to back off. First the bug in my coat, now the attack. I got the point: Their next move could be less friendly. But I had no intention of taking these hints seriously.

Since I had no further business in Stuttgart, my first instinct was to check out of the hotel and leave Germany. But reason overtook anxiety, and I changed my mind. In any case I would have to find another hotel for the night, or go to the airport immediately. I did not want to meet up again with Igor and Oksana's associates.

I waited in the room until the early morning, then checked out; two porters carried my luggage. I walked between them, making them an improvised protective phalanx, and ignoring their surprised expressions. I took a cab to the Echterdingen airport, checking occasionally to make sure I had no escorts behind my cab. We were alone on the road.

From the airport gate, just before boarding, I called Dr. Bermann. "I'm writing my report and I need your help."

"I am very sorry, Herr Gordon" he said candidly. Well, of course he was; the nincompoop had dragged me all the way to Germany only to realize that his smelly client wouldn't talk. He could have done it over the phone and spared me the trouble.

"I spoke to Igor again. He is not responding to my request to reconsider talking to you. In fact, he won't even discuss it."

"Too bad about that. Anyway, I need to describe our meeting to my boss. Could you please give me the interpreter's full name?"

"It is —" He paused for a minute. "— let me see here . . . *ja,* her name is Oksana Vasilev."

"Got it. And she is an official interpreter?"

"Yes, authorized by the court."

"You were lucky to find a Belarusian interpreter; I don't suppose too many people in Stuttgart speak that language."

"You are correct, Herr Gordon. In fact I think this is her first job. After our first telephone conversation, I asked Igor if he knew of any Belarusian interpreters because we would need one for his court hearing. A few days later, Frau Vasilev called me and said she spoke both German and Belarusian and even some English, so she could be an interpreter in Igor's case. I assumed Igor had sent her. I told her that she had to register with the court first. It took her one week to prepare the application, and now she is an official interpreter with the court. Otherwise she would not have been permitted to enter the prison. If Igor or Oksana were to have any difficulty with English, then I could translate from English to German and Oksana from German to Belarusian."

"Nice of you to think of it, and at the same time to help her," I said, thinking of the chaos a twice-removed translation could cause.

"I think so, too. She told me that she was new in town and needed a job. I paid her fifty dollars just to be in the prison for one hour. I don't think she made that much in Belarus in a month." I could almost see him grinning in self-satisfaction.

I called David from a different airport pay phone; my cell phone could easily have been picked up by a sophisticated listening device. After my encounter with the state-of-the-art bug, I didn't want to take any further chances.

"There have been some positive developments," I said.

"Igor changed his mind?"

"No, something else. I'll send in my report and we can discuss it after you read it. I'm on my way back." I decided not to mention the attack. There were too many people around me waiting to find an available pay phone, or maybe to eavesdrop on me. I couldn't be sure.

Back in my New York office, I forwarded to David in DC my summary of the facts I had gathered from Oksana's trash.

On December 1, 2002, Igor Razov opened a bank account at the Global Kredit Privatbankiers in Frankfurt am Mein. On the same day, he deposited into that account sixteen cashier's checks totaling approximately $60 million. Four days later, that money was wire-transferred to Barclays Bank in Nevis, the federation of Saint Kitts and Nevis in the Caribbean, into an account owned by Bright Metalwork, Ltd., a Nevis company. A week later, the money continued its route through Panama City to Caracas until it resurfaced as a deposit made by Sling & Dewey Goods and Services, PLC, registered in Australia. Then the money was sent, probably by mail or by courier, to Eagle Bank of New York. Additionally, several checks were drawn on a bank in the Seychelles Islands. The source of the money is still unknown.

I called David two hours later waiting for his litany of praise. Nothing. It had taken a full week of my life to unravel the whirlwind tour of the laundered money around the world. I'd rummaged through garbage, taken a beating, and endured a ringing ear, and this was the thanks I got? Granted, it took me only twenty minutes to actually write my report.

"Good progress," he finally said. "But we need to know why the money traveled as it did. Usually money launderers take one or two interim steps, not five or six. Why so many? And where did Igor get this kind of money, anyway? It's way out of his league."

"No clue. I have no doubt that the money isn't his. Maybe it's Zhukov's."

"We looked into that possibility, too. The whirlwind is also very much unlike Zhukov."

"Maybe this one is different; Zhukov's or not, somebody worked very hard to obscure this money's source. But there could be any number of other possibilities," I said.

"Keep going, then. Sort them out," said David.